The Little Café in Copenhagen

Julie Caplin

A division of HarperCollins*Publishers*
www.harpercollins.co.uk

Harper*Impulse* an imprint of
HarperCollins*Publishers*
The News Building
1 London Bridge Street
London SE1 9GF

www.harpercollins.co.uk

This paperback edition 2018

2

First published in Great Britain in ebook format by
HarperCollins*Publishers* 2018

A catalogue record for this book
is available from the British Library

ISBN: 9780008259747

Printed and bound by CPI Group (UK) Ltd, Croydon, CR0 4YY

For the Copenhagen Crew, Alison Cyster-White & Jan Lee-Kelly, my dearest friends, partners in crime and thoroughly wonderful travel elves. #highlyrecommendedtravellingcompanions

PART ONE

London

Chapter 1

'See you later.' I dropped a quick kiss on Josh's lips and we exchanged a knowing smile. He pulled me towards him and went back for a second lingering kiss, his hands finding their way inside my coat to slide down my bottom and then start inching up my dress.

'Sure you don't want to stay a bit longer?' His voice held a note of husky suggestion.

'No. I can't. You're going to be late, and,' I glanced over my shoulder, 'Dan might walk in at any second.' His flatmate had the unerring ability of a Labrador sniffing a crotch to interrupt at precisely the wrong moment. My flatmate, Connie, had much greater diplomacy; in fact she had social skills.

He let go of me and picked up his cereal bowl, leaning against the kitchen counter, lazily eating as if he had all the time in the world.

'See you later.' He winked.

I picked up my laptop case and closed the front door of his, far nicer than mine, flat, and hurried down the road to the tube station mentally reviewing all that I needed to get done that day.

After two years of seamless travel to work, albeit sweaty, stuffy and crowded with the regular frustration of delays and hold ups, I missed my stop. The first time ever. This travel hiccough should have registered. In London, you have to be on the ball all the time. Checking your emails, phone messages, social media threads, it was endless. I missed my stop, simply because I was too absorbed in thinking *what a load of bollocks* as I read an article on some latest lifestyle fad over someone's shoulder. *Hygge*. My flatmate Connie had been muttering about it the other night, waving some book about and lighting candles left right and centre in a woeful attempt to make our dismal flat homelier. As far I was concerned a couple of candles were never going to compensate for our landlord's hideous taste and before I knew it the doors had closed on Oxford Circus.

Having to get off at the next stop and go back down the line didn't make me late, only later than usual. I'm always at work super-early. Showing my commitment. How serious I am about my job. Not that I mind or I'm trying to score brownie-points, well maybe just a few. I just can't wait to get there. Oh, God that sounds real eager, arse-licker, beaver. It's not like that at all. I love my job, as a public relations Account Director. I work for one of the top PR agencies in London. I say I love my job, I do most of the time. The office politics and promotion manoeuvring I could do without and the pay could be an awful lot better. But hopefully that was about to change, I was overdue a long-promised promotion. Then I'd be earning a bit more and I could afford to move to some-where where there isn't a ten-inch Mohican fringe of blue mould growing down the living room wall.

Tube stop fiasco aside, there was time to treat myself to a Butterscotch Brulée Latte and it was only when I was in the queue that I saw a text from my boss, Megan, asking if I could pop in and see her first thing.

With a quick smile, I shoved my mobile back in my bag. There wasn't going to be time to see her before heading up to the boardroom where every other Friday all fifty-five people in the agency met for our bi-monthly staff internal comms briefing, where new business wins and general big news – like promotions – were announced. I had a pretty good idea why she wanted to speak to me. I'd been waiting long enough for this day. Two weeks ago, following my shining, yes you are the dog's bollocks appraisal, I'd made my case for the vacant position of Senior Account Director, which I was reasonably, no very, confident had been well-received. Megan had been hinting there might be some good news soon.

Despite wanting to bounce with anticipation as I took the stairs up to the third floor, I tapped up on my heels, decorous and professional, taking small neat steps as dictated by the tailored, fitted black dress which Connie insisted on describing as my Hillary Clinton funeral look.

I took a seat in one of the ergonomic chairs which my posture flatly refused to co-operate with. The lime green, moulded plastic wave shapes were supposed to make you sit properly but my back had made it quite clear that it was more than happy to sit improperly.

Trying to sit comfortably, I checked out the room as people slowly filed in. Recently re-decorated, the boardroom now sported a Mother Earth look, complete with one green wall of plants about three metres square. I wasn't convinced that it didn't harbour a huge variety of bugs and beasties. Supposedly it was inspiring as well as practical; apparently it produced fresh oxygen (was there such a thing as stale oxygen?) to help stimulate creativity. At the same time a little Zen indoor waterfall had also been installed to promote calm, mindful thoughts, although I found if I needed to go to the loo, it stopped me thinking about anything else.

Despite the pretentiousness of the boardroom, every time I looked around, I relished the sight of it. I'd made it. I worked for The Machin Agency – one of the top London public relations companies. Well on the way to the next step of my five-year plan. Not bad for a girl from Hemel Hempstead, allegedly the UK's ugliest town. And today, I'd take another step.

The Managing Director took the floor and two seconds later Josh sidled through the door. Just in the nick of time he slipped into a seat on the front row, catching my eye very briefly as he passed me. I hadn't saved him a seat and he wouldn't have expected me to. We'd agreed that no one at work needed to know that Josh Delaney and Kate Sinclair were seeing each other, especially when we worked in the same team in the consumer department of the agency.

Ed, the MD, had a string of announcements to make and I sat waiting in anticipation.

'And I'd like to make an announcement regarding our most recent promotion.'

I sat up a little straighter and uncrossed my legs, trying to muster up a humble but deserving expression. This was it.

'I'd like you all to join me in congratulating Josh Delaney on his promotion to Senior Account Director.'

'Kate.' I looked up at the brusque tone of my boss. As usual she looked perfect, her thick auburn hair slightly waved, feminine but not too girly, wearing a tailored dress, figure hugging but not too revealing and standing tall and lean in heels, kick-ass and mean. 'Can I have a word?'

I nodded, suddenly not trusting my voice. I'd seen the hint of sympathy in her eyes.

I followed her into her office and closed the door at her nod, sitting down gingerly on the retro dark grey sofa which always looked more inviting than it was.

'I wanted to speak to you before the meeting this morning. You're usually here by then.'

I shrugged. 'Tube malfunction.' There was no way I was admitting to her that I'd missed my stop. That wasn't the sort of thing I did.

She folded her arms and paced. 'I'm sorry you had to hear like that. I know you were keen to get that promotion but ... on balance the board felt you needed a little bit more experience. A little more gravitas.'

I nodded. Agreeing. Miss keen-to-please, my boss is always right, crap. Gravitas? What the ... was that?

'And,' her painted mouth turned down in a moue of disgust, 'you're still young.'

I was exactly the same age as Josh. I knew what she was getting at.

'They wanted a man.'

She didn't respond immediately. I took her silence as acknowledgement.

'They were very impressed with Josh's ideas for the skincare brand. I think that was what swung it in his favour. He's got creativity and that ... gravitas.'

I nodded again, feeling like a bloody woodpecker. Creativity my arse. Just bloody good at palming off my ideas as his.

Inside I was still steaming. Lead balloon gutted. During the meeting I'd managed to sip unconcernedly at my ridiculously poncy, expensive drink while regretting buying the bloody thing. Most of all I regretted not practising the Oscar nominated, gracious loser and I'm only the teeniest tiny bit disappointed look. Two things really stuck in my craw, one he'd never so much as mentioned he was going for promotion and two 'the ingenious ideas for a mobile app for a new skincare campaign,' which just so happened to be mine.

'Kate, we do value you very highly and I'm sure in another couple of months we can review things.'

I lifted my chin and nodded but even she could see the slight wobble of my lip. Although she probably had no idea that as I looked back down at the spiky heels of the killer black I'm-about-to-be-promoted court shoes, I was busy imagining them making contact with a certain person's soft and tender bits.

She sighed and shuffled some papers on her desk. 'There is something ... it's just come in. I suppose you could have a look at it. We weren't going to bother but ... well you've got nothing to lose if you fancied having a go.'

It wasn't exactly the most encouraging crumb but it was something.

I tilted my head, pretending to look interested while trying to hide the seething disappointment.

'Lars Wilder's been in touch.'

'Really?' I frowned. Three months ago Danish entrepreneur Lars Wilder had the London agency scene twittering like love-struck groupies desperate to secure his business.

'Having appointed,' she named our biggest rivals, 'he's fallen out with them and he's still looking for the right publicity campaign to open his new Danish department store. He didn't like any of their ideas. He's looking for a fresh approach. This could be a great opportunity for you to prove yourself.'

'But?' I asked sensing her diffidence.

'He wants a presentation the day after tomorrow.'

'Two days?' She was having a laugh. Except she wasn't, she was deadly serious. Normally we spent weeks preparing for these presentations, which involved all singing and dancing PowerPoint slides, glossy artwork and lots of research about the market.

'He's flying to Denmark at lunchtime and wants to come in before his flight. I was about to call him and say we couldn't do anything but ...'

'I'll do it.' I'd bloody show Josh Delaney and the agency bosses.

'Are you sure?'

'Yes,' I said. OK I was stark staring mad but no one was going to say I didn't try.

'No one will expect you to win the business, of course, but

it will look good that we didn't say no to him. You'll earn major brownie points by having a go. It's a long shot but we have to be seen to try.'

'What's the brief?' I said putting my shoulders back. Nothing to lose and everything to gain.

She held out a single white sheet of paper. I did a double take. Where was the document we usually received with pages and pages of stats and fancy fonts, headings and sub headings about ethos, values, market background and the MD's inside leg measurement?

Hjem
Bringing the heart of Hygge
to the UK on Marylebone High Street

'That's it?' I stared disbelieving at the simple typeface tracking across the pure white paper like footprints in snow. This was my *great opportunity*. She had to be kidding. It was like being given a pair of nail scissors and asked to make the pitch at Wembley match ready for the FA Cup final. My career and the chance to show Josh Delaney that I was back in business came down to this?

Chapter 2

'Connie,' I called racing into the flat, shedding my bag and shoes as I darted into the kitchen. 'I need your help. And we might as well have this.'

She jumped up from the table and her spot behind the ever-present pile of exercise books, eyeing up the bottle of Prosecco I had in my hand.

Our flat had been a lucky find, purely on the basis that it was affordable. The open plan lounge had one of those thin industrial textured carpets that you can feel every nail in the floorboards through and a few sparsely dotted items of furniture which stopped the place looking completely barren but it was a close-run thing. The key feature of the room was the flat screen TV hooked up to a DVD player which provided our main source of entertainment as we were permanently broke and spent plenty of nights in with a bottle of wine in front of a rom-com, wrapped up in a duvet to keep warm because it was always freezing.

The heating was dependent on a boiler with a decidedly work-shy temperament. Our landlord didn't seem terribly worried about getting it fixed, and we'd hit complaint fatigue.

'Oooh Prosecco. Good vintage too. Co-op six ninety-five I believe.' Connie's eyes lit up as they did whenever alcohol was involved.

'No, Marks and Sparks, Victoria Station. Nine ninety-nine. I bought it yesterday when I *thought* I was going to get promoted.'

'Oh shit. You didn't then? What happened?'

'Bastard Josh Delaney happened.'

'What did he do?' Connie hadn't actually met Josh, as he preferred me to go to his place.

'What didn't he do? Stole my promotion. And do you know what else he did?' my voice reached a pitch boy choristers would envy, 'stole my idea and made out it was his.'

'Couldn't you tell anyone?'

'Not really. Bit hard to explain to the MD about that post-coital chat in which I shared a brand strategy and an idea for a new app.'

Connie held up her hand. 'Babe you're blinding me with science and seriously, if that's your pillow talk, you do need to get out more.'

'You had to be there.'

'I'm glad I wasn't.' She put her glass to her cheek. 'What did he say?'

I closed my eyes and shook my head.

His persistent texts had only ended when I'd agreed to meet him in the stairwell. No one in our company ever took the stairs.

He did at least have the grace to apologise.

'Look, Kate. I get that you're disappointed. But I have to put it into context. I mentioned the app idea in passing. I didn't lay claim to it at all and never at any time said it was mine. I was going to say it was yours but they'd already picked the idea up and run with it.'

'But you could have said you were going for the promotion. Why keep it quiet?'

'I wasn't that fussed at first. But then ... well you turn thirty and you start thinking about the future. It's alright for you. I'm going to be a breadwinner one day. I need the promotions.'

'Pardon.' I repeated his words in as scathing a tone as I could muster against utter incredulity. 'You're going to be a breadwinner one day?'

I put both hands up to my cheeks in disbelief. He couldn't be for real.

'Kate, one day you're going to get married, have kids. You don't need the income.'

'I-I ...' Spluttering was about the only activity I could manage.

'Come on, Daddy's going to bail you out when you've finished playing career girl.'

'Seriously!' I stared at his handsome face, suddenly seeing the weak chin, with the faint beginnings of a jowl, floppy public schoolboy hair that hid a receding hairline and the well-cut suit concealing a slightly soft belly. 'Whoever said Neanderthal man died out forty-thousand years ago, lucked out big time.'

Finishing my story, I bitterly took a slug of Prosecco and raised my glass towards Connie in a toast.

She snorted Prosecco out of both nostrils, sniggering and sniffing which set me off.

'You are kidding me.'

Connie was virtually family having lived two doors down from me all my life. Our mums met in ante-natal and when we both moved to London, there was no one else either of us even considered living with. We'd been through a lot together. Her mum ran off with the milkman, no lie, and mine had a run in with an aneurysm that wiped her life out in an instant. One minute she was there, the next gone, leaving a huge hole in our family, that to be honest had never really been patched.

I shook my head, biting my lips and sniggering along.

'You'd better tell your dad to start polishing his Rolls.'

I shook my head and our laughter quieted.

'Sorry Kate, what an arse.' Connie knew that I helped Dad out with the mortgage payments.

'Top me up,' she held out her glass. 'So, did you dump his sorry ass?'

'Too right I did.'

'Excellent girl. And then did you chop off his gonads?'

'Damn, I knew there was something I'd forgotten.'

We chinked our glasses together again. Connie propped her chin on her hand and we lapsed into thoughtful silence. I'd made light of Josh's betrayal but it hurt. We'd not been going out that long but I'd enjoyed being one of two for a change. London could be a lonely place for one. It was nice having someone to do things with. We both worked hard, which is why it had worked well. We had so much in common.

'Katie, is it worth it?' Her voice had softened.

I swallowed. Connie and I didn't do serious.

'Is what worth it?' I asked chucking back the last of my Prosecco, feeling the tension take hold of my shoulders.

'You know. Your job. That's all you seem to do these days. Work. Even Josh, he was to do with work. You need to have some fun?'

'I have loads of fun.' I winced. 'In fact, I've got a do coming up. Although I was supposed to be going with Josh. Any chance I can borrow the blue dress?'

'Of course, you can. Where are you going?'

'Erm ... it's um ... black tie thing.'

Connie groaned. 'It's work, isn't it?'

'It's an industry awards thing. Newspaper Circulation Awards. But it will be fun and I love my job.'

'Riveting. Not.' She put her glass down and pushed the exercise books to one side. 'Seriously Katie, I worry. You're like a little hamster on its wheel. Running, running, running and occasionally you dive off for a sunflower, but you ram it in your cheeks for later. I know I work hard but at least I have the school holidays to unwind. When do you take time for you? When I go home for the weekend, Dad makes an effort. When you go home, you clean your dad's house, tidy up after him and your brothers. And restock their kitchen cupboards. You can't fill in for your mum for ever, you know. They have to do it for themselves eventually.'

'I worry about them. I worry about Dad not eating properly.'

'And you think that's going to help?'

It certainly helped assuage the guilt that I'd abandoned the three of them.

'They're family, I have to help them. I earn a lot more than them.'

'I know, but let's face it. John could bloody pull his weight. How many jobs has he had? He always has to leave before he's sacked because he's a lazy git. Brandon, well,' her mouth lifted in the slightest of smiles when she mentioned my younger brother, 'he's something else. But he's not stupid. That replica Tardis was incredible. Daft sod.'

My brother was a sci-fi fan and in his spare time liked to knock up life size replica models of things from his favourite films and TV series.

Connie tapped her glass against her fingernails and straightened up. 'If he stopped bloody playing effing *Fifa*, he could get a much better job. He ought to be doing more than having a pissing part-time job in that car breakers yard. And your dad is not as useless as he likes to make out.' Her mouth firmed in a zipped shut line as if she'd said as much as she was going to on the matter.

An uncomfortable silence threatened to descend. I loved her dearly and she certainly understood me better than the menfolk in my family but they were mine to criticise, not hers.

'You said you needed my help, so if it isn't setting out to track down bastard Delaney with a very sharp knife, which probably wouldn't go down with my Head if we got caught, what did you want?'

'That book of yours. The one about candles.'

'The Art of *Hygge*.'

'Pardon?' I laughed. 'You're not going to be sick, are you?'

'No, you numpty.' She grinned at me and just like that, we were back to normal. 'It's a Danish word,' she said the word again, which sounded like Who-ga and still sounded like she was praying to the big white toilet god. 'Spelt h-y-g-g-e.'

'That's how you say it, is it? I did wonder. So what's it all about? Danish interior design?'

She turned horrified eyes my way. 'Nooo, it's much more than that. It's an attitude. An approach to life.' She rummaged in the big shopping trolley that always seemed to be at her feet. Being a teacher seemed to involve carting around an awful lot of stuff. 'It's by some hot Danish guy, second cousin to Viggo Mortensen, who runs the Institute of Happiness or something.'

I perked up at the mention of Viggo. Both of us had had a serious crush on him ever since we'd seen *Lord of the Rings*.

'I've been reading all about it. Did you know Denmark is the happiest country in the world?'

'I was reading an article about it on the tube this morning, but I'm not convinced. They seem to have a very high death count, obsessive female detectives and never-ending rain according to all those Scandi thrillers I've seen. Not looking that happy to me.'

'No, seriously. It's all about making your life better through the little things.' Her earnest expression stopped me from taking the piss. 'Hence the candles.' She pointed to three candles on the mantelpiece and pulled a face. 'They're supposed to help make it cosy.'

'They're not working.'

'I know. The mould on the wall doesn't help.'

'We should get onto the landlord again. Although after Dad's house, my expectations are pretty low these days.' I rubbed at the shadows under my eyes. She was right about the hamster wheel. There just weren't enough hours in the day. 'I need a crash course in hy ... however you say it. I've got a pitch the day after tomorrow. Can I borrow your book?'

Chapter 3

I was having second thoughts. It was the day of the pitch. The biggest pitch of my career and my one chance to show Josh and the board exactly what I was capable of. So why was I placing a hell of a lot of faith in a few candles, some birch twigs, an expensive lamp and the combined efforts of the studio team's furniture removal talents? When Megan promised to sign off my expenses, I'm not sure a two-hundred-pound lamp was quite what she had in mind, but the effect of its gentle pool of golden light was exactly like the picture in Connie's book.

I couldn't afford to think about how tired I was. Last night I hadn't got home until gone ten, after trawling Oxford Street, then staying up until the small hours perfecting my traditional Danish oat biscuits that Connie had sworn were so *hygge*.

Yesterday's preparation for my big pitch involved reading Connie's book from cover to cover, studying images on the internet of socks, candles, cashmere blankets draped around loved up couples and mitten covered hands clutching steaming cups of chocolate, followed by a shopping marathon.

Apparently, the Danish love affair with candles extended to the work place which was the principal starting point for my campaign to win Lars' business. I'd arrived at the office at seven this morning with the sole goal of hyggifying, a new verb in my vocabulary, the smallest meeting room in the building. Making it cosy was going to be a tall order, but I had every faith in candles and expensive lamps.

There was also tea, two brightly coloured mugs bought from Anthropologie, with an L and K on them, and the plate of my home-made cookies. Even though they looked very wonky and that was the third attempt, I'd had quite a job keeping the rest of the office in check around them.

The scene was set or as much as I could hope for. I'd arranged two chairs, which didn't match but they were the most comfortable I could find, after a Goldilocks' style tour of every room in the building, around a rather lovely birch table, a forgotten sample from Ercol which had been used for a photo shoot. On a bookshelf that I'd commandeered from another floor, I'd removed all the books and then scouted round to find ones with colourful spines that looked pretty together.

I'd not gone overboard with the candles, sticking to five; a tasteful group of three on the table and two on top of the bookshelf where I'd also put the kettle, a coffee pot, tea pot and milk and sugar etc. Apparently, it's a Danish thing. Making a thing of making the tea and the coffee.

I fiddled with the birch twigs which I'd arranged in a cheerful sunshine yellow pot until the call came from reception that he'd arrived. They didn't look the least bit homey, no matter what I did they looked like some twigs with a ribbon tied round them shoved in a pot.

Blonde, of course, and charming, Lars Wilder, CEO of Danish department store Hjem, was tall and exuded that outdoor healthy look that you associate with northern Europeans. Or at least I did after all the reading and researching I'd done yesterday. At over six foot, he had a definite Viking look about him.

'Good morning, I'm Kate Sinclair.' I held out my hand, reading his body language which oozed relaxed and at ease, unlike me who had a box of frogs leaping about in my stomach.

'Good morning, Kate. I'm Lars. Thank you so much for agreeing to see me this morning.' I examined his face for any irony. Clients who paid our kind of fees usually expected you to jump through hoops for them.

The subtle lighting contrasted with the bright lights of the corridors outside and I noticed Lars shoot an approving glance around the room.

'Please take a seat.' I ushered him towards a cracked leather tub chair, with a throw tucked over one arm, opposite a trendy 80s leather slung on metal contraption which was far more comfortable than it looked.

I busied myself making tea. Strangely the task of making the tea made the small talk somewhat easier as I asked him how he'd found the journey.

Eventually we sat down, although it felt as if I'd wasted a good ten minutes of the meeting waiting for the kettle to boil.

'Great biscuits,' said Lars reaching for a second one from the plate, his head still nodding approval.

'Thank you.'

'You made them?'

I lifted my hands palm upwards as if to say it was no big deal, while thinking of the state of the kitchen this morning and the plastic Tupperware of reject cookies stacked up on the side. Connie and I would be eating them for weeks.

He took a bite. 'Very good.'

'Family recipe,' I lied. My mother made a mean Victoria Sponge but she'd never made an oat cookie in her life.

'Ah, family,' he gave me a broad smile, stretching his hands expansively out to the side to emphasize his words. 'It is so important ... and family recipes. My mother is famous for her *kanelsnegle*.'

I tilted my head and smiled back as if I had the first clue what a *kanelsnegle* was when it was at home.

'She thinks every problem can be solved with a pastry.'

She sounded a bit odd to me but I held his gaze as if it were quite normal, he was clearly very fond of her. 'She runs a café, Varme, it means warmth in Danish. It's a very special place. My mother loves to look after people.'

I almost sighed out loud. But wouldn't it be nice to have someone to look after you? For the last few years I felt like I'd been completely on my own, swimming hard against the tide.

'It's that warmth and homeliness I want to bring to the UK.'

Lars cleared his throat and I realised with a start, I'd drifted away. 'My mother would approve of this, it's,' he looked around the room, 'very *hygglich*. You've done well. Very imaginative and perceptive. It's very Danish. I can see you have an understanding of *hygge* already. I like the mugs.'

'Thank you. And thank you for coming today and for giving me the chance to talk to you.' My formal words dried on my tongue when Lars let out a bark of laughter.

'No, you're not. You're cursing me for the short notice and the sparsity of information.' The clipped Danish accent sounded charming and robbed the words of their bluntness.

Diplomacy warred with honesty for a moment.

I smiled at him. 'Well, it isn't the most orthodox approach but we were intrigued.'

'So intrigued that your company wheeled out the big guns.'

Maybe that accent didn't quite disguise the bluntness. I might not be a big gun but I was an up and coming sharp shooting pistol. Then he added with a charming smile, 'And the home-baking.'

'I was intrigued and I'm not afraid of a challenge. As you said this meeting was arranged at very short notice, however I work in the lifestyle department, my clients include a soft furnishing company, a coffee company, a chain of cheese shops and a boutique hotel group. I'm more than qualified to manage your account. My boss, who is out at meetings all day today (I mentally crossed my fingers) felt I would be the best person to talk to you.' And not the most promotion hungry.

'I didn't give you much time to prepare, but you seem to have coped well. And you didn't bombard me with emails with lots of questions.' He looked around the room. I knew he was looking for the projector and laptop.

I put my hand up as if to halt his flow. 'I'll be honest. I haven't prepared anything. Not because there wasn't time but because I felt you're the expert and you would know what you want. I know you've seen several different agencies, all top ones in their field. And all will have come up with brilliant ideas, but you clearly didn't like any of them.

'I figured it was easier to talk to you to find out what you're looking for. The orthodox response didn't sound as if it was going to help.'

Lars grinned and stood up to pace the room, his hands behind his back. 'I like you, Kate Sinclair and I like the way you think. We Danes prefer a gentle approach. And already I can see you have a grasp of the mindset of *hygge*.' When he said it, *hygge* sounded much less threatening New Zealand Hakka and a lot more appealing.

'That's kind of you to say, but I think I've got a long way to go. You should see where I live.'

'Exactly,' interjected Lars. 'Every agency wanted to tell us what it was. It's indefinable and means different things to different people. When it's right it's right. I've sat through so many presentations. If I hear about one more give-away promotion of instant *hygge*, *hygge* make-overs and *hygge* holiday breaks, I'm going to melt down every last candle in the UK.

'The agencies we've seen have been too ... It's difficult to put into words. They were too,' he shrugged again. He looked around at the room, smiling with a nod towards the candles. 'Clinical and business-like. This. This, you've got it exactly right.'

I nodded and let him carry on.

'Our store, Hjem, will be about much, much more than candles and blankets and products to buy, which is what everyone seems to think *hygge* is about. I want people to feel it throughout every department of the store, to spend time in the store, in the book department, in the cookery department. There'll be displays, corners to sit in, demonstrations in flower arranging, cookery, card making, knitting classes, making Christmas decorations. It's going to be a vibrant community as well as a department store.'

'It sounds interesting,' I said, wondering how the hell that was going to translate into a public relations campaign.

'But it is important that people understand about *hygge*.'

I nodded. It sounded a tad ephemeral to me.

'So I would like to take some people to Copenhagen and show them a flavour of how the Danes live and how our society works, so that they can really appreciate *hygge*.'

'That's a great idea,' I said, blithely thinking that a trip to Denmark would be rather nice and how charming and warm Lars was.

'You see Kate, that's why I knew you were the right person for the job. Every other agency has said it would be too difficult, that people wouldn't want to go to Denmark for more than a night. I think we're going to work well together.'

'We are?' Was he offering me his business?

'Yes, I've looked at all these agencies and what I was searching for was the right fit. You are the right fit. I like the way you think.'

'So, I'd like to get started straight away. Do you think you could draw up a list of six journalists?'

'Six journalists?' I asked.

'Yes, for taking the trip to Denmark. I think five days would be just the right length.'

When he said people, he hadn't mentioned that those people had to be journalists. 'Six journalists. Five days,' I echoed.

He nodded approvingly. 'Perfect. In five days we can show them the finest things Copenhagen has to offer and teach them all about *hygge* and I know just the person to help.'

Oh hell. No wonder the other agencies had fallen out with him. I knew from past experience that it was hard enough persuading journalists to turn up to things in London for one evening, let alone commit to a five-day trip abroad. If I managed this, it'd be a miracle. What had I done?

Chapter 4

You lucky cow. Connie's message popped up as I was putting the finishing touches to a press list, a week later. I scribbled a few more notes before picking up my phone to text back.

I'll bring you back some Lego.

Or you could take me too. I could pretend to be the Gazette's travel correspondent. Who'd know?

If I get really desperate I'll let you know.

I was still buzzing from exceeding everyone's expectations and winning the pitch. Now all I had to do was find six journalists to go on the trip. Easier said than done. I got full honours mentions in the despatches at the Friday meeting and this time I did practise my modest, shucks-it-was-no-big-thing, Oscar winner's acceptance look – with an additional helping of *take that* Josh Delaney.

The bastard gave me a mocking salute of well done. It

might even have been touched with reluctant admiration. Although he got his own back in our very first meeting with Lars after I'd won the business. When I'd run through the proposed list of journalists for the trip, he just had to say something. He couldn't resist showing off his knowledge. 'Have you thought about approaching the *Sunday Inquirer*, Kate? They have double circulation of the *Courier*. Benedict Johnson is the new lifestyle editor there.'

Normally correspondents move from paper to paper, magazine to magazine and I would have come across them before. This guy's name didn't ring any bells. Trust bloody Josh to be one step ahead.

'I'll speak to him and see what he says,' I said with a gracious smile at Josh. Still up to his rat-weasel tricks then.

'Can I speak to Benedict Johnson, please?' I'd put on my best friendly, perky voice.

'Speaking.' He sounded a little terse but it was difficult to tell in one word.

'Hi, I'm Kate Sinclair from The Machin Agency. I'm—'

'You've got five seconds.' No mistaking the cynical hostility in those words.

'Pardon.' Shocked, I couldn't quite believe that he'd said that.

'Four.'

What I should have done was tell him to go do something anatomically impossible, but I was so taken aback and flustered, I went for the four second pitch.

'I'm calling to find out if you'd be interested in coming

on a press trip to Copenhagen to find out why the Danish have been cited as the happiest nation in the world. It would be a week-long trip that would take in a variety of destinations as well as a visit to the Danish Institute of Happiness.'

'No.' And then he put the phone down on me. I took the hand-piece away from my ear and looked at it disbelievingly. Rude sod.

I slammed the phone down. What an arrogant prick. Who the hell did he think he was? Where did he get off being so rude to people?

I redialled his number.

'Are you always this rude?' I asked.

'No only to PR people, people offering to reclaim my PPI and timewasters. You're all inter-changeable.'

'And you're not even prepared to think about it. You don't know who I'm working for.'

'No. And I couldn't give a toss, even if it's the Crown Prince of Denmark himself.'

When someone is so rude to you, it's actually wonderfully liberating because you can be rude back to them.

'Are you always this narrow-minded?'

'How can I be narrow-minded? I'm a journalist.'

'You seem it to me.'

'What – because I don't write PR puff articles or promotional pieces?'

'I'm not asking you to write a puff or a promotional piece. I'm offering you an opportunity to find out more about the Danish way of life and what we could learn from it.'

'Which would of course just so happen to include writing about your client's product.'

'Yes, a lot of the time, but this is different.'

'If I had a pound for every PR that told me that.'

'Excuse me, I'm not a PR. It's not even a thing. A public relation. My name is Kate and I'm doing a job the same as you are. If you'd give me the chance to explain instead of barking at me like a mad fox, you'd see my clients want to promote a concept rather than their specific store.'

'Mad fox?'

I heard a strangled laugh.

'I've not been called that before. Plenty of other things but definitely not mad fox.'

'If you're this direct I'm not surprised. Perhaps I should offer you a week at charm school,' I said, starting to enjoy myself.

'Do such things still exist? Now that might be an idea for a feature.'

'Are you typing that into Google?' I asked hearing the tell-tale click of keys.

'Might be. Or I might be doing some work, which is what I'd planned to do until you interrupted me.'

'Look, I've phoned you because I thought you'd be interested.'

'You don't even know me.'

'I know the paper, the kind of features the lifestyle section has run before. This isn't a product placement sell.'

'Ah, so there is a product.'

I paused.

'Ha! I knew it.'

'It's a new department store but it's a concept.'

'A concept, that sounds a bit wanky to me.'

I winced. When you put it into words, it did. When Lars spoke about it, it all made perfect sense.

'It's called Hjem. It will be opening later in the year, but the owners want to take a small select group to Copenhagen to explore the idea of *hygge* in more depth.'

'Candles and blankets. Been done to death.'

'That's exactly it. You see you've dismissed it without understanding what it entails.'

'I don't need to understand anything. I'm not interested. Not now. Not ever.'

'And you don't think that attitude isn't perhaps a tad narrow-minded.'

'No, it's called knowing your own mind and not being influenced.'

'Could I at least email you some more information and a copy of the itinerary?'

'Nope.'

'You won't even look at one little email?'

'Do you know how many emails I get every day from PR people?' He spat the P out and groaned the R.

'You're really grumpy aren't you?'

'Yes, because I get bloody people like you pestering me constantly.'

'I think you could do with a trip to Denmark; you might learn a thing or two.'

There was a pause and I waited, bracing myself for him to

slam the phone down on me again. Instead I heard grudging amusement in his voice as he said, 'Do you ever give up?'

'Not if it's something I believe in,' I said playing semantics with the truth. I believed in Lars' vision and what he wanted to achieve. But if I were being totally honest I'd probably side with him in the 'when did a blanket and candle combo solve a problem' camp.

'Sorry, I'm still not biting, but nice to talk to you, Kate, whatever your name is. You've enlivened an otherwise dull afternoon.'

'Glad to be of service,' I said crisply, looking down at the stop watch app on my phone. 'And this time you gave me two minutes and four seconds of your time. You might want to rethink the five second strategy.'

He began to laugh. 'For a PR, Kate Sinclair, you've grown on me.'

'Shame it's not mutual,' I said sweetly, putting down the phone.

I crossed him off the list and decided to try the other journalists on our list, hoping they'd be more receptive to a trip to Copenhagen than Benedict 'Mad Fox' Johnson. 'Sounds lovely darling,' said the lifestyle editor on the *Courier*, 'but I've been offered a press trip to Doncaster. Who'd have thought Doncaster or Denmark?'

'Surely I can persuade you to come to Copenhagen.'

'Sadly sweetie, you could persuade me all too easily. Problem is the person you have to persuade is She Who Must Be Obeyed, the old harridan in charge of advertising revenue. A man with lots of cash and a whopping advertising budget is paying for the press trip up north. Unless you can promise her that your client has an ad spend, I'm destined for the frozen north.'

Luckily after many, many emails, back and forth, Fiona Hanning a lifestyle blogger, Avril Baines-Hamilton from *This Morning* and David Ruddings of the *Evening Standard* all said yes, much to my relief. Conrad Fletcher somewhat to my surprise, being a cynical old devil, and a very old school glossy interiors magazine journalist said, 'Why not? Haven't been to Copenhagen in an age and the old expense budget could do with an outing. Christ, you wouldn't believe how tight they are these days.'

'That's probably because you keep ordering three hundred pound bottles of wine at lunch on expenses,' I teased. He referred to the rather fabulously over the top restaurant very near to the magazine offices where he worked, as his HQ. I'd enjoyed several lunches there with him. He wasn't everyone's cup of tea but I found him good company and his knowledge of the interiors industry was encyclopaedic as was his endless fund of gossipy stories about many of the people in the field.

'You know me so well, Kate dear.'

I saved Sophie from *CityZen* for last, confident she'd be an easy nut to crack. She was a friend of Connie's from university and I'd met her a couple of times and liked her a lot. I gave my watch a quick glance as I picked up the phone. Just enough time before I had to dash home and get ready for the awards do this evening. Now I was going on my own it was imperative Josh knew what he was missing.

'Hi Sophie, its Kate Sinclair, I'm looking for a journalist who might be interested in coming along on a press trip to Copenhagen.'

'Ooooh, pick me, pick me.'

'Oh, alright then.'

There was a stunned silence.

'Really? You're inviting me?'

'Yup. A week in wonderful, wonderful Copenhagen.'

Sophie made a funny sort of noise, an office friendly suppressed squeal before saying, 'Hmm, I'll have to think about that ... for about a nano second.' There was another funny squeak. 'Eek. Yes. Yes. I'm in! How lovely. It will be so great.' Her words bubbled out.

'I haven't even sent you an itinerary yet.' I laughed. 'What if it's a tour of the local coal mine, steel works and plastics factory?'

'Who cares? There'll be food. That's all I need. Oh, how exciting.'

'I'll email you some more details.'

'I can't wait. I've never been to Scandinavia. I'm going to have to buy one of those duvet padded coats, like they all wear. With white fur round the hood. And some thermal gloves.'

'Er Sophie, the trip's at the end of April, it's going to be a bit warmer then. I think you can put Barbie's arctic exploration outfit back in the wardrobe.

'Talking of which, I need to go and nick a dress out of Connie's wardrobe.'

'How is she and where are you off to?'

'She's fine. Still knee deep in children at work. And I'm off to the National Newspaper Circulation Awards.'

'That sounds deadly, apart from free booze.'

'It's at Grosvenor House and dinner is included.'

'Get you.'

'Only because the company has sponsored an award. We've got a table. Unfortunately my ex will be there.'

'Oh, bad luck.'

'Yes, although Connie did offer to fix me up with one of her teacher colleagues.'

'That was nice of her.'

'His name was Crispin,' I said indignantly.

'Oh, is that a problem?'

'I'm not sure I could take anyone called Crispin that seriously. It sounds like a small horse to me.'

Sophie giggled. 'You can't dislike someone just because of their name.'

'True, although I spoke to a Benedict today and I'd have thought a Benedict would be a hottie.'

'Not Cumberbatch?'

'No, this one wasn't nice at all. But thankfully he doesn't want to come on the trip, so I won't ever have to find out.'

Chapter 5

Pulling up outside the hotel where the awards were taking place, and having the top-hatted concierge open the door I felt a bit of a fraud in my borrowed dress. One of the poshest hotels in London, it was a long way from the budget hotel in Hemel where I'd been a chambermaid in the student holidays. Men in smart dinner suits with elegantly attired women were milling around the entrance to the ballroom.

Thanks to Connie's make-up, my eyes were now a smoky grey, with a lot more eyeliner and shading than I'd have dared and her dress was fabulous.

Only she could pick up a Vera Wang bridesmaid's dress in a charity shop when she was looking for costumes for the school. The simple stylish unembellished design was one of those that looked nothing on the hanger, sleeveless with a stark boat neck but when you put it on the heavy satin slithered into place wrapping itself around your upper body down over your hips while the skirt swished sinuously like waves frothing around your feet. Dead simple except for one killer feature, the low back which dropped in sinuous folds to just below the waist. It required a very careful choice of underwear.

I smoothed my fingers down the silky fabric with a smile as I stepped out of the cab, marvelling at how close it had come to being cut up for the three kings' cloaks for the Ashton Lynne Primary School nativity last year.

As I tripped down the steps holding Connie's silver beaded clutch, a couple of heads turned which was rather nice.

Thankfully our party was already gathered in one corner of the bar around a table with a champagne bucket and several glasses, one of which had my name on it. As I approached, the first person I saw was Josh, handsome in his dinner suit, reminding me very briefly of what I'd seen in him.

He gave me a slow smile and I saw the spark of interest in his eye. 'Wow, you look–'

'Thank you,' I said primly cutting him off quickly. 'Have you seen Megan? Is she here yet?'

'Yes,' he gave a rueful smile. 'You're not going to forgive me, are you?'

'Nothing to forgive.' I smiled and turned to walk away to check the table plan to his right.

He caught my arm. 'Kate, you're being pig-headed about this. We can still be friends.'

I shook him off. 'I don't think so. Work is the most important thing in my life right now. I'm not letting you or anything else get in the way again.' I spotted Megan with a couple of other people from work and edged my way through the crowd towards her.

'Kate, hello. Would you like a glass of fizz? And this is Andrew.' She introduced the short bald man at her side.

Before I could say hello, she'd thrust a full glass into my hand. 'He's on our table.'

Which was short-hand for *play nice*, he's one of the agency guests on the table the company had paid a lot of money to sponsor.

'He works for the *Inquirer*,' she said a tad too enthusiastically. 'Sorry I forgot, what is it you do?'

Andrew turned and thrust a small sweaty paw my way. 'Pleased to meet you,' he brayed, his tone so rich and plummy he was almost a caricature. 'Andrew Dawkins. Sales Manager. *The Sunday Inquirer*. And you are?'

'Kate. I work with Megan at the Machin Agency.'

'Another PR?' He literally shouted the words, his mouth wrinkling in a subtle, 'well you're no bloody use to me' expression, but he bore his disappointment well, with consummate good manners. 'And how long have you worked there?'

'Five years.'

'Time to move on then,' advised Andrew, waving his glass at me. 'Keep moving. That's my motto. Never stay anywhere for longer than two years.' With a burst of laughter, he added, 'Otherwise you get found out. That's how I got to be Sales Manager.

'All about networking, y'know. Getting to know the right people. I could introduce you to a few people. Agency bosses.' He slipped his arm through mine, terribly chummy and enthusiastic, so that it was hard to decide whether the graze of his hand on the far edge of my breast was inadvertent or not.

I took a good slug of champagne and moved out of range so there'd been no room for doubt again.

'You work at the *Inquirer*, do you know Benedict Johnson?'

Disgust wreathed his shiny forehead. 'I meant proper contacts, not hacks. I could give your career a serious boost,' he boasted and gestured with his glass towards a series of men picking them off like target practice. 'CEO, Magna Group, Finance Officer, Workwell Industries. Name someone you want to meet.'

'I'm fine thanks.'

'So why do you want to meet Johnson?'

'I don't want to meet him, I'm curious about him.'

'Fancy him, do you?'

'No,' I gave him a disdainful look his comment deserved. 'I've never met him.' I frowned remembering our conversation. 'I had words with him earlier today. He's quite hostile to PR people.'

'That's because he thinks himself a serious journalist. Or at least he was.' Andrew's smile was malicious. 'Got booted off the business desk. Too good for lifestyle or so he thinks.' His eyes sparkled with malevolent glee.

'I er ...' I felt almost sorry for Benedict Johnson.

Andrew smiled. 'How the mighty are fallen. He's one of them. Your typical serious journalist. They all think they're God's gift and about to uncover the next Watergate. What they don't realise is without,' he rubbed his fingers and thumbs together, 'advertising revenue they wouldn't have a job. So what do you want with him?'

'I invited him on a press trip. He didn't fancy it.'

'I'd go on a press trip with you.'

'That's kind but I'm not sure the client would buy it.'

'Who's the client?'

'A new Danish department store opening in London. We're taking a small group of press to Copenhagen.'

'Nice work if you can get it. And he turned it down?'

I shrugged. 'I'm sure he had his reasons.'

I might not like Benedict Johnson, but I didn't like Andrew Dawkins any better.

Andrew lapsed into thought, his small grey eyes screwed up in concentration. 'Lot of potential advertisers might be interested in that. I'll see what I can do.'

I wrestled with my conscience for less than a nano-second and refrained from saying, *that would be great* but neither did I say, *don't worry I've invited someone else now*. This was my career we were talking about.

A very formal toast master, in full red-trimmed regalia, called the event to order but there was no reprieve for me. I found myself sitting next to Andrew and his wandering hands. There was nothing for it but to get stuck into the champagne and arm myself with a fork.

The awards, it sounds ungrateful to say, were no different from the other awards I'd worked on. The same anthemic music. The same slick script from a well-known stand-up comedian, on his very best behaviour, and lots of excessively dull and grateful middle-aged men, coming up to collect their glass engraved trophies.

The wine was plentiful and the food not bad considering how many people they had to serve and please. Chicken is always the common denominator on any corporate menu.

An army of well-drilled waiting staff edged the wall nearby

and then began to serve the first course during which I noticed Andrew's foot brushing my calf a few times too many.

By the time the main course plates were being cleared, my patience had run out. When his hand brushed my thigh again, I struck, ramming my fork into it.

'I'm so sorry I didn't realise that was you. I thought a tarantula was crawling over my leg. I have a phobia.'

Andrew gave me a tight smile, while wringing his hand to his chest.

A waitress appeared sidling between us with a pretty pink and white desert.

'Not for me, thank you,' I said shaking my head. 'I must go to the loo,' I excused myself to Andrew, who rose at the same time like a perfect gentleman, except he put a steadying hand on my hip that was a tad too familiar.

I gave him a cool smile and fled, taking my glass of champagne with me, skirting the white linen covered tables, my skin crawling as I knew he watched me go. I regretted that his last view of me was the dramatic drop of my dress curved in smooth folds to below my waist. The dress might have been very demure at the front but it wasn't at all at the back.

Climbing the stairs, I moved along the balcony to a quiet spot where I stopped to look out over the impressive sight of the Great Room, with its ranked rows of white clothed tables, in uniform lines, perfectly laid with linen and floral arrangements. I couldn't look directly downwards as it would have made me dizzy and I stayed an arm's-length from the brass rail but it was quite safe looking across the room. I crept a little closer to the barrier and took a sip of my champagne, sorry to realise the glass was almost empty and raised it in a small silent toast to the huge chandeliers glittering like extravagant clusters of diamonds. My mum would have been so proud of this. Of me being here. I could hear her voice in my head.

You make something of yourself love. Work hard. Do well. That's all she wanted for us, to do better than the previous generation. She'd had three jobs, working at a nursery in the mornings, then going on to be a dinner lady at a local school where she was also a cleaner in the evenings. None of them had been particularly well paid and money had been tight.

With one hand safely clinging to the brass rail aware of the hum of voices rising up, I gazed at the tide of well-dressed people and swallowed a lump as I smiled mistily. This was a world away from where I'd grown up. She'd definitely think this was doing well.

'I'd like to say penny for them, but I think they're worth a lot more.' The husky deep timbre of the voice, with a decidedly seductive undertone, held a definite edge of flirtation.

I stiffened for a second wanting to preserve the moment. Of not being disappointed when I turned and not disappointing. My common sense, blurred around the edges by champagne, went AWOL and instead of turning, I answered.

'I think they probably are.'

There was a brief silence as I carried on looking across the huge room, over the sea of people at the tulip shaped chandeliers.

'Did you know there are over five hundred thousand crystals in each of the chandeliers?' I rather liked his opening gambit and the slight lilt in the chatty tone of his voice as if he'd taken up the challenge of trying to impress me enough to get me to turn around.

'No.' I smiled to myself and took a tiny sip of champagne, lifting my head so that my hair fell lower down my back, feeling aloof, regal and mysterious, wanting to spin the game out.

'Or that they weigh a ton each and were designed in the 1960s.' He stepped closer so that I was aware of him lowering his voice so that only I could hear him.

'Impressive,' I purred because the moment seemed to demand it. I was so not a purrer in real life but this was a Cinderella moment with its fabulous setting, complete anonymity and the false confidence of an expensive dress.

'Did you know ... this used to be an ice rink. Queen Elizabeth learned to skate here.' My skin tingled in silent invitation and almost unaware of it I subtly arched my back.

'Really,' I said, smiling even more.

'Three times Olympic champion, Sonja Henje skated here in the 1930s.' The cadence of his voice whispered past my ear.

'Never.' Silent laughter bubbled in my voice.

'And they used to play international ice hockey matches here.'

'Who knew?'

'A lot of the machinery is still there, under the floor.'

'Useful to know.'

'And final fact, The Beatles played here once.'

I leaned away over the balcony imagining the scene.

'And that is my last fact.' He said the words rather like a magician with a flourish at the end of his act.

I hesitated, loath to break the interlude. Instead of turning to face him, I twisted slightly, my chin not quite touching my shoulder so that he could just see my profile but I still couldn't see him.

'And very interesting facts they were too. Are you a tour guide? A historian?'

'No, I spoke to a chatty barman. Talking of which, can I get you another glass of champagne? That one appears to have run out.'

'Observant too. I'd love another one, thank you.'

'And will you still be here when I come back? Or will I find a solitary shoe?'

I looked at the slim gold watch on my wrist, an inexpensive Lorus that had once belonged to my mother. With a sudden laugh, I said, 'It's a while until midnight. I'll still be here.'

With careful grace, he plucked the glass from my hand without touching any other part of me. The gesture made my insides quiver.

I smiled. I had no idea what he looked like but he smelled delicious, a combination of subtle expensive aftershave and good clean washing powder.

Despite my best intentions, I couldn't resist taking a quick peek over my shoulder after a good few seconds. He ploughed confidently through the small crowd around the bar, a man who knew what he wanted and where he was going. I think that purposeful movement won me over as well as perhaps the reassurance of a tall, slim build, a full head of hair and an extremely well cut suit.

I turned back to the view of the room and waited for his

return, smiling to myself, trying to imagine what he looked like.

'Still here then?'

I nodded, a sudden leap in my chest, as I realised I was going to have to turn to face him.

I felt the cold touch of the tip of the glass at my back. The unexpected intimacy thrilling and challenging. Did I turn around and face him? Or did I keep making him work for it?

The cool glass traced its way down my spine. Suggestive and subtle at once, it set every nerve ending alight.

Neither of us said a word.

The glass continued its way down my spine, and was then replaced by the teasing touch of a finger, delicately tracing the same path. I arched into the touch, heat flushing along my cheekbones. The glass came to rest just above the folds of the dress. Tiny flares of electricity raced across my skin.

He took the glass away, a cold imprint tingling on my back, cold and then almost hot.

I took in a breath, holding it for a good few seconds before slowly, slowly turning to take the champagne glass from his outstretched hand.

Our fingers brushed and he held the glass until I lifted my head to smile shyly at him, feeling feminine and womanly for once.

A smile curved his lips, a faint, barely-there dimple appearing in his stubbled left cheek which glinted in the light with a touch of dark golden and amber bristle that matched the dark auburn of his hair. This was the point where reality was supposed to kick in. He wasn't supposed to be drop dead gorgeous, with amazing planed cheeks or those full lips, that I should stop looking at right now! I waited for the fuzzy champagne buzz to vanish and for him to wink at me and say goodbye. He certainly wasn't supposed to have the sort of shoulders that had been honed either on a rugby field or in a swimming pool or be so tall that he topped me by a good few inches in my heels. Despite the good looks, it was the quiet calm self-confidence that he exuded that sent my stomach into a tail spin, along with the sharp intelligence shining in the grey blue eyes.

'Hi.' His low tone imbued with much more than a simple hi, sent a dart of awareness straight between my legs.

'Hi,' I said a tad breathlessly. This was so not me, all girly and awash with sexual attraction to a complete stranger. I didn't do things like this but I couldn't seem to help myself. It was so hard meeting people in London, let alone gorgeous, drop-dead handsome men who seemed as interested as you were.

'I'm Ben.'

'Kat ... tie,' I said not wanting to have the brusque business-like syllables of my name at work. Katie was my name at home. When mum was alive. I wanted to be that Katie, the one who was in touch with her feminine side. The one who didn't have to battle all the time to be someone.

'Cheers,' he lifted his glass and tapped mine. 'To chance meetings.'

'Cheers.'

We smiled at each other again and sipped at our drinks.

He moved next to me to lean over the rail clutching the glass in one hand.

'I wonder how many people know it used to be an ice rink,' I said peering down. 'It must have been huge.' It was hard to imagine the swish of skates on ice or the cold air hanging in the art deco room.

'There's a picture somewhere in the hotel.'

'We'll have to look for it sometime.' The words slipped out far too easily but something about him and the out of time situation made me fearless.

'Are you asking me on a date?' His words held a teasing lilt.

I raised a haughty eyebrow. 'No.'

'Shame, I might have said yes.'

'How do you know I haven't got a boyfriend tucked away?'

His eyes narrowed with possessive perusal. 'Because no man in his right mind would let you out in that dress on your own.'

'What's wrong with it?' I asked, suddenly worried he thought it was slutty and too inviting.

The quick smile held reassurance along with amusement and a hint of something else that had my heart picking up an extra beat. 'There's nothing wrong with it. I'd say it's perfect. It hints at far more than it reveals. Tasteful, stylish and sophisticated.' His mouth dipped on one side, in cynical self-deprecation. 'All of which is in short supply this evening ... and that's just the men.'

'I can concur with that,' I said thinking of Andrew's sweaty paws.

'Want me to protect your honour and call the cad out?'

'No, I can wield a fork with the best of them.'

'You didn't stab someone?' His eyes widened with mock horror and a touch of admiration.

I shrugged, let a smile play around my lips. 'I didn't draw blood, or at least not the first time.'

'Ouch. Remind me not to mess with you.'

'I thought we'd agreed that we weren't going to go out on a date, so that would seem unlikely.'

'In the spirit of not going on a date, I am wondering what sort of date we wouldn't go on.'

I leaned on the balustrade. 'We wouldn't go wandering through the hotel, looking for historic pictures. Or leave this glittering occasion in full swing and go wandering down to the Serpentine.'

He considered for a moment and turned to reveal a bottle sticking out of his pocket. 'And we wouldn't take a bottle of champagne with us.'

The unspoken invitation sizzled between us. I smiled and stood up from the balustrade.

'Why don't you show me this picture?'

Just as he took my hand, lacing his fingers between mine, the familiar sound of a mobile phone jangled, bringing us both to an abrupt halt. Like cowboys reaching for their guns, we both went for our phones, him shoving a hand in his inside pocket and me taking my clutch bag from under my arm.

He frowned as he looked at his screen and then back at me with apology as he answered the call.

Saved by the bell. The familiar sound and both of us going for it, reminded me of real life. What on earth was I doing? Lulled by the moment and being a big girl in a posh frock. I wasn't the sort that picked up complete strangers, particularly not handsome Prince Charming types who were way out of my league. Moreover, there was no time in my life for a relationship; I had goals, things to do. Gut instinct told me that this mysterious stranger posed far too big a risk. I'd been hurt by Josh and I hadn't felt one tenth of the spark elicited by this man. He was a man you could really lose your heart to.

I mouthed that I was off to the ladies and slipped away, doubling back down the stairs to my table, confident that among 2,000 people I'd lose myself easily.

Chapter 6

'Hello, Kate Sinclair.' I absently picked up the phone as I stared at my computer screen, trying to be sensible and write a press release instead of replaying my Cinderella scene over and over in my head. Unfortunately I'd dashed off without leaving a glass slipper or a mobile phone number, so it would never come to anything and I couldn't decide if that were a good or a bad thing.

'Pleased with yourself, are you?' snarled a voice down the phone.

Sitting up smartly I turned my chair away from the screen.

'Sorry?' I frowned immediately, thinking he must have the wrong person.

'You are Kate Sinclair, aren't you?'

OK, so not the wrong person.

'Yes,' I said slowly trying to place the angry voice. 'Do I know you?'

'Unfortunately, you're about to. Benedict Johnson, lap dog,' he spat.

Ah, the angry journalist. Why the hell was he ringing me? I had no idea but given his initial rudeness yesterday the opportunity to mess with him was too good to miss.

'How the mighty are fallen, the other day you were Mad Fox,' I observed, picking up a pen and doodling on my lined pad.

'Then, I wasn't dancing to your tune.'

'Clues would be good at this point.'

'Playing innocent, are we?'

'It would be difficult to play otherwise because I have absolutely no idea why you're calling me.'

'Didn't you hear the good news?' Sarcasm curdled the words.

'Hans Solo didn't die in *The Force Awakens*? Douglas Adams got it wrong and the meaning of life is forty-three? Take That are back up to five members?'

'I'm too bloody furious with you to even find you funny.'

'Sharing's good. Psychologists recommend it.'

'Copenhagen. Press trip.' He bit the words out with enunciated precision.

'Journalist. Said no.'

'Journalist forced to say yes.'

'I'm all out of arm twists, so I'm not sure how you figure that. I've not forced anyone.'

'Not directly. I don't like sneaky, underhand people. You should watch out who you make deals with in future.'

'I've got five perfectly reasonable people who have agreed to come to Copenhagen and are delighted. I'm not sure I want you along anyway.'

'Too bad. Because now thanks to your conniving you're stuck with me.'

'Do you always talk in riddles?' We were getting nowhere with this conversation and while I was enjoying it on one level, I had other things to do. 'Seriously. You carry on but I have absolutely no idea what you're talking about. I've asked another journalist to go on the trip.' They'd turned it down too but he didn't need to know that.

'The Advertising Manager said that you'd suggested it would make a great feature and that he could sell a lot of advertising off the back of it. He went to his boss, who went to my boss and suddenly ... it's a very good idea if I go on a junket to Copenhagen.'

'Sorry still no idea what you're talking about. I haven't suggested any such thing. You've got the wrong person,' I said confidently.

'Not according to Andrew Dawkins.'

'Andr...' my voice trailed away guiltily.

'All coming back to you, now is it?'

'I ... er I, didn't say that to him. I don't ...' I sputtered as I desperately racked my brains as to what I'd said to him two nights previously.

'No, of course not. Because he couldn't possibly know that I'd been invited on a trip unless he'd spoken to you.'

'Look, I'm sorry–'

'Too bloody late now. You'd better send the itinerary over. I'll see you in Copenhagen.' With that he slammed the phone down before I'd had a chance to tell him that I certainly hadn't put Andrew up to it, or that we were meeting at Heathrow.

Chapter 7

Through bleary eyes, I clocked that Heathrow, even at the insane time of five o'clock in the morning, was surprisingly busy. Cleaners trailing huge carts with mops sticking out at odd angles roved the open expanse of the terminal, while half-asleep shop assistants battled with metal grilles opening up with weary determination, oblivious to travellers around them pulling the ubiquitous black luggage along.

As I waited by the check-in desk, I looked at all the paperwork for the fifth time. Passport. Contact numbers. Laptop. Luggage. My hands were shaking. Ridiculous. Yesterday's last minute pep talk from Megan had put the fear of God into me.

'Are you sure you'll be able to cope with six of them?' she'd asked me. 'Press trips are hard work.'

'I know,' I'd replied, thinking how hard could it be? What could go wrong? We had an itinerary. A guide.

'People think it's a cushy little junket, but journalists have a habit of wandering off piste and doing their own bloody thing. You need to make sure they toe the line. No ducking out of this trip or that visit. You lose one, you lose them all.'

'OK,' I'd nodded again, trying to look serious and attentive.

'There's a lot resting on this.'

I'd got that with bells on.

'And don't let them take the piss with expenses. There's a budget for this trip.' She'd paused and given me a searching look.

'I'm just wondering if you ought to have some back up.'

'Back up?' I'd echoed. It was a press trip not a flipping drugs raid.

'I'm wondering if we ought to send Josh Delaney with you.'

Firmly I'd reiterated how confident and sure I felt about the trip. Megan had no idea that this was the big time compared to my previous travelling experiences; a couple of trips to Ayia Napa with Connie and school friends and a long weekend in Barcelona, which had been mainly about sun, sea, shopping and sangria.

It would all be fine though; there would be someone meeting us at the airport, although he had the less than confidence instilling name of Mads.

That was yesterday, now this morning the cold reality of being responsible for six adults, some of whom were older than me, more sophisticated and a lot more travel savvy, had sucked all the confidence out of me like a dementor. What if someone lost their passport? Got ill on the trip? Didn't like the hotel? The more I worried, the more things I thought of to worry about.

Across the terminal building I watched a girl wearing a rather fascinating long hairy coat, which made me think of an orangutan. She shifted her huge duffel style bag from one shoulder to another before standing, rubbing the back of one very long leg with the foot of the other. The awkward gawky motion reminded me of a stork wondering whether to take flight or not.

Was she Fiona or a one man zoo? I squinted at her again. The copies of everyone's passports made them look like a bunch of convicts and bandits. When I tried to catch her eye, she was busy with her phone, so I decided she wasn't my blogger at all. I took another look at the photocopies and when I glanced up, a bit like the weeping angels in *Doctor Who*, the girl had moved closer.

I looked at my watch even though no more than three minutes could have possibly elapsed since the last time I checked it.

The girl had moved a touch nearer.

'Kate, my darling. What on earth do you call this godawful time?' I turned to see sixty year old Conrad Fletcher, from *Interiors of the World* magazine. What he didn't know about interior design and who was who in the industry wasn't worth knowing.

'Morning Conrad, how are you?'

'Knackered. It's a good job I like you otherwise I'd have turned my alarm off and gone back to sleep. And then the taxi driver was a surly sod. Oh, here's the receipt by the way. You can give me cash, saves on all the bother of both of us having to do paperwork.' Conrad patted the cab receipt into my hand. 'And a coffee wouldn't go amiss, I'm parched.'

'We'll go for a coffee as soon as I've got everyone rounded up.' The girl now lurking to our left just in front of the check-in desk bobbed up and down on her toes like a small girl trying to get attention from a teacher without being too obtrusive. I suspected she might be my lifestyle blogger, Fiona Hanning.

'Hi, are you Fiona?'

She blushed scarlet and nodded with very quick short sharp jerks before making eye contact as warily as a deer stepping from the edge of a forest glade.

'Hi, I'm Kate. Nice to meet you.' I held out my hand. Her hand shot out from the sleeve of the hairy monkey coat, grabbed mine, squeezed and then retracted before I could even blink.

'This is Conrad Fletcher, he's an interiors writer. Conrad, Fiona Hanning, she writes the blog *Hanning's Half Hour.*'

Mild panic stretched across Fiona's face as I introduced them but thankfully Conrad didn't have a shy bone in his body.

'I love your blog darling. Such a clever idea.' You never knew with Conrad whether he was bluffing, he liked to make out he knew everything and everyone, and although I'd never caught him out, I did occasionally wonder if it was all a front. To my surprise, he started talking about a recent article on the blog about upholstery of all things and then making suggestions for a follow up piece, with names and contacts she might try.

Fiona didn't say much and seemed much better able to cope with this type of human interaction, being talked at rather than required to join in.

'Conrad, well if you're here, I must be in the right place.' Avril Baines-Hamilton, a regular *This Morning* presenter, had arrived wearing a huge fur hat, outsize sunglasses and a full length down coat, belted in the middle. Making her grand entrance, she drew to a halt and dropped the handles of two pull along cases, a Gucci carry on case, which I recognised as the Bengal tiger edition, much featured in magazines, a snip at eighteen hundred pounds, and a second much larger bog standard Gucci case.

'Hi Avril, we've met before. I'm Kate.' She made no sign of recognition and she didn't take her sunglasses off which I always think is rather impolite.

'Have we?' I couldn't see the expression on her face for obvious reasons but her slightly indifferent bored tone bugged me. We were going to be spending the next five days together and a small fortune was about to be spent showing her the finest that Copenhagen had to offer. She could at least summon up a bit of enthusiasm.

Refusing to let my irritation show, I plastered a PR cum air hostess smile on my face. 'Yes, several times but I suspect you meet lots of people. It's hard to keep track. Now, I know it's obvious but can I check you've all got your passports with you?'

Fiona immediately started patting her pocket and pulled out her passport straight away.

Conrad rolled his eyes good naturedly and dipped his hand inside his slightly shabby camel cashmere coat. He started to frown in consternation.

'Don't even think about it, Conrad,' I said. 'I know you and it would not be funny.'

'You're no fun.' He grinned, devilment dancing in his eyes.

'Not on this trip, no,' I said in a suitably schoolmarm tone, hoping that he'd be sympathetic to me. When I'd invited Conrad, it had been a bit of a surprise that he'd not already been booked. Now when it was too late, I remembered that if he chose, he could be a liability. He was known for being a little bit rebellious and taking the mick with his expense account. I needed to be firm with him because if he decided to lead the other journalists astray, I'd be sunk. Avril would follow his lead without a doubt. Fiona, I couldn't predict.

'Morning,' a quiet voice said in my ear. I whirled round to find David Ruddings who freelanced for the *Evening Standard* standing behind me, his usual gentle smile on his face.

'Hello David, how are you?'

'Excited.' His face wreathed into a smile. Shame he was gay, he would have been perfect for Sophie, they both had that sunshine approach to life, although where she was bubbly and bright, he was quiet and beaming.

With an internal sigh, I calmed. Sophie and David would be a good influence and I could count on both to be on my side. Of course, the completely unknown quantity was Benedict Johnson, who probably would lead the charge if Conrad decided to be mischievous. And where the hell was he? I looked at my watch.

Five minutes to go before the official meeting time.

'Good morning,' Sophie's voice trilled and there she was exuding brightness and cheer, like a blackbird fresh from the dawn chorus. I knew Sophie through Connie and as we'd met a few times it was rather nice to see a friendly face.

I introduced her to the rest of the group, letting them chat among themselves. There was plenty of time before the flight but I was conscious that everyone would probably expect a coffee. I for one could murder one.

'Everything alright, Kate?' Sophie's low voice interrupted my thoughts.

'Yes, fine. One more to come.' I looked around the airport hoping that Benedict Johnson might materialise at any second. Surely he wouldn't stand me up. That would just be rude, although I wouldn't put it past him to deliberately miss the flight. Rude was his default.

'Well he'd better get a move on, I'm dying for a coffee,' muttered Avril.

'Another five minutes. I'm sure he'll be here soon.'

'I want to go to duty free. So we have to have coffee after security.'

Five minutes ticked by slowly and I forced myself to make light chit-chat and look completely unconcerned. Should I let them go through passport control and get settled or should I wait here for Benedict? The queue for check-in was starting to build up.

'Kate, look I desperately need to get some essentials in duty free. I can't hang around here any longer. It really isn't on.'

'And I'm in dire need of coffee, darling. Actually, breakfast wouldn't come amiss.'

See – exactly as I predicted, Avril and Conrad had teamed up already, the high maintenance twins. They looked at me expectantly.

From behind them, Sophie flashed a sympathetic smile.

I was reluctant to let everyone out of my sight. This was worse than being a teacher on a school trip. Connie had told me enough horror stories. If I let them all disperse I might not round them up again.

Avril sighed heavily and pouted. Even behind the celebrity hat and sunglasses combo, I could tell she was sliding into petulance.

'Tell you what,' I said making a quick decision. 'Let's get our bags checked in and join the queue. Hopefully by the time we get to the front, he'll have arrived.'

Everyone grabbed their bags and as we moved to join the queue, a helpful young man opened up a new check-in desk and summoned us over.

One by one everyone checked in their bags, as I scanned the area. Where the hell was he?

Now all the bags had gone and everyone looked at me waiting for me to decide what to do next. With a sigh, I knew I had to make a decision. Letting them go through passport control without me felt like an irresponsible mother hen waving goodbye to her babies, but there'd be severe dissension in the ranks if I didn't.

'You all go through passport control. And I'll meet you ...' at the gate felt too late.

'There's a Café Nero there,' offered Sophie.

'I'll meet you at Café Nero.'

'Thank God for that,' said Avril. 'And you'd better give us our boarding passes. We'll need them for duty free and if you don't turn up.'

'I'm sure Benedict will be here very soon,' I said, wishing I could be sure of that.

I sifted through the printed boarding passes and handed them out to everyone.

Avril grabbed the handles of her bags and wheeled around like a racehorse under starters orders. 'If I don't get my Clarins stuff, this trip will have been a complete waste of time.'

Conrad looked at me and made no move. I suddenly realised that I was expected to pay for breakfast. Of course, I was. I looked around at the party realising that was what everyone was waiting for and Sophie caught my eye and nodded almost imperceptibly. The perfect ally. I pulled out my purse which bulged with English cash and Danish Kroner.

'Sophie, would you mind doing the honours for me?' I pushed a couple of notes into her hands. 'Can you pay for the coffees and give me the receipt?'

'No problem.' She winked and took the money. 'Come on then troops.' She turned and led the way falling into step with Fiona and David while Conrad and Avril followed up the rear. As they walked away down the airport concourse, I felt a sense of premonition; I had a horrible feeling that was how the group split was going to be for the whole trip.

I looked at my watch again. At least my case had gone on the plane, they wouldn't leave without me. Not to start with anyway. There was another fifteen minutes before the check-in desk closed. Should I call Benedict?

As part of my preparation, I'd asked for everyone's mobile number and being super-efficient, I'd pre-programmed everyone's numbers into my contacts the other evening.

I paced up and down in a small circle around the check-in desk. When I called Benedict's number, my heart sank as I listened to, 'This mobile is currently switched off.' Did that mean he was on the tube, on his way? Still asleep with his phone switched off for the night?

Impatiently I called again in case he'd been in a bad signal area, or he'd just got off the tube and was on his way up, as I kept an eye out for a vaguely quiff haired bandit, which was all I could glean from Benedict's fuzzy photocopy of his passport picture. Every time I looked up at the overhead digital clock another two minutes had elapsed. It was like some horrible magical trick where time sped up in direct proportion to my increasing stress level.

I looked at the check-in desk. Still seven minutes to go. Only three people left in the queue. One desk had already closed up. I looked at my mobile. No messages. Fifty-three minutes until the flight left. I looked down the concourse. Was he coming? The familiar burning sensation low in my stomach made me stop pacing. I took a deep breath. I needed a coffee and something to eat.

At what point did I give up? Once the check-in desks closed? What would I do if he turned up after then? Book another flight? My stomach knotted itself tighter.

Two minutes and counting. I looked at my phone. Still no word. This was ridiculous. I should be with the rest of the group; they were my responsibility. Benedict Johnson was now over three quarters of an hour late. I'd more than given him the benefit of the doubt.

With one last look at the check-in desk, catching the eye of the supervisor there, who looked suitably pitying at my dejected appearance, I turned to walk down towards passport control.

Out of the corner of my eye, I spotted something like a tornado in the distance, a man running pell mell down the concourse, dragging a case.

The man behind the desk had stood up.

'Wait,' I called rushing over to him. 'I think my colleague's here.'

The man pursed his lips.

'Here you can start with this, can't you?' I pushed over the paperwork and the copy of Benedict's passport.

The man in a leather jacket and jeans came flying to the front of the queue and slammed up against the desk, passport in hand.

'Benedict Johnson, I presume,' I snarled less than charitably given the poor chap was bent double trying to catch his breath, almost prostrate at my feet, and hiding the fact I was bloody relieved to see him.

His passport picture didn't do him justice, not that I could see much but the back of his head. His dull fuzzy passport picture suggested stoned serial killer, not this man whirling in, leather jacket flying and zinging with energy.

'I've just ... made it ... from ... the tube in ninety ... seven seconds,' he puffed as the man on the desk tried to peer sideways to look at his face.

I had an impression of thick hair, well cut and an unusual shade ... oh shit ... of dark auburn hair.

I had a moment of flight or fight panic as he slowly straightened. At least I had the tiniest advantage of realising before he did as I schooled my face into polite indifference, while inside my heart banged with all the merry inappropriate joy of a big bass drum.

'Cinders!' he said, 'What are you doing here?' He hauled his case onto the conveyor belt as the man snapped on a label and handed back his passport. 'Benedict Johnson. Ben.'

My eyes met his and for a second we stared at each other until his sharpened with sudden quizzical intelligence.

'Oh shit, you're her. PR woman.' His groaned words were all I needed to calm the silliness inside.

'Oh shit, yes I am.' Suddenly it was much easier to remember Mad Fox and not the brief connection at the awards do. Clearly, I had drunk far too much champagne that night. 'And you're late. We need to go now.' I turned, hauling my laptop bag onto my shoulder.

His face tightened. 'Bossy much? You should be grateful I'm here at all because quite frankly there are other places I'd rather be right now.'

'You're doing that barking mad fox thing again.' Now I'd seen the colour of his hair, I was delighted with the original quip.

'I reserve it especially for bossy manipulative PRs.'

I pushed my tongue against my cheek and sighed. 'The flight's in fifty minutes. We need to get through security and meet up with the other five people who got here on time.'

This was his moment for effusive apology and excuses. Instead he shrugged and picked up his canvas satchel and slung it over his shoulder. 'Come on then.' We marched along keeping a good couple of metres between us like an invisible wall of enmity, although I had a hard time keeping up with his long-legged lope which I was fairly sure was deliberate on his part. Inside I was absolutely gutted. My fairytale moment with the most delicious Prince Charming had been well and truly stomped on. How could he and Benedict Johnson possibly be the same person?

Chapter 8

By the time we fought our way through passport control and made our way to Café Nero, our flight had been called and it was time to go straight to the gate. At our arrival everyone started gathering their bags. I quickly introduced Benedict. I couldn't bring myself to call him Ben.

'Hi everyone, sorry I'm late. Slight domestic emergency.'

Funny he could manage an apology to them.

'Where's Avril?' I asked, noticing a lone coffee cup on the table and realising I was missing one. God it was like trying to herd cats. Was it going to be like this all week? No sooner had I got one journalist I lost another.

Sophie frowned and looked at her watch. 'She must be still in duty free. Do you want me to go and look for her? Oh, here's your receipt, by the way.'

'Thanks.' I took it from her with a distracted smile. I'd have to go and look for Avril myself. I was supposedly in charge; I couldn't keep asking Sophie to help. 'Why don't you all go down to the gate and I'll go and find Avril.' I wanted to add, *and please for the love of God can you stay together?*

Thankfully Avril was in the queue at duty free. I looked

at my watch. We had ten minutes before they officially started boarding, although she had more in her basket than my entire make-up stock. I hoped the check-out girl was on it today.

'Just letting you know the others have gone down to the gate.'

'Oh, really.' Her mouth turned down. 'I don't suppose anyone got me a coffee.'

'I don't think so, no.'

'I'll have to grab one on the way to the gate.'

'I'm not sure there's going to be time.' I did wonder whether I ought to offer. I wasn't quite sure how far the duties of a host extended.

Her lips pursed in a tight smile of self-satisfaction. 'Of course there is. Our bags are on board, they can't go without us.'

I stared at her unable to find anything to say in response to her outrageous self-absorption.

I finally steered her to the gate having given in and bought her coffee while she was paying for nearly two hundred pounds worth of face creams and perfume. As we arrived a voice over the tannoy announced that seat numbers one to thirty could board.

'That's us,' I said brightly to the other ... What! There were only four journalists waiting.

Having to go and find Fiona in the loos made the two of us the last to board.

'Let me take care of that for you, madam. You need to take your seat. Now.'

The stewardess's voice had a veiled hiss to it, as she added,

'We need to leave. We're already late.' The unsaid, *thanks to you* hung in the air.

'Can I just …' I quickly pulled out my purse and a guide book, scattering tissues and receipts on the floor.

Like a chastened schoolgirl, I finally slid into my seat which of course was next to Benedict. He and Conrad must have swapped seats, as I'd put him in the window seat, away from me.

'I'm so glad I didn't rush,' he observed, not even looking up from his newspaper. I glared at the top of his head as I settled into my seat sorting out the seat-belt. In the seat behind I could hear Avril complaining about the amount of legroom and wondering rather loudly why we weren't flying business class. Thankfully across the aisle I could see Sophie smiling and talking to Fiona in a reassuring way.

Last-minute checks were done and then the air crew disappeared to their seats as the plane taxied down to the runway. All the usual excitement of going somewhere on a plane had been replaced by an overwhelming sense of responsibility. Suddenly I felt very small and inadequate, so I closed my eyes and pretended to go to sleep. How on earth was I going to manage the six journalists? Just getting them all on the plane had proved a Herculean task and I felt stressed out already. What was it going to be like when I had a whole city to lose them in? It didn't bear thinking about.

That stress must have taken more out of me than I'd realised because I fell into a doze and woke with a start, which made Benedict turn and give me an unfriendly stare. I hoped I hadn't been drooling or anything. My scarf was draped across his knees and surreptitiously I pulled it back conscious of him ignoring me.

All his attention was focused on the crossword he held up, although a small part of me was pleased to see that he didn't seem to be making much headway.

'Sorry chaps, I need to pop to the loo,' announced Conrad, bobbing up from his seat. I moved out into the aisle and Benedict followed me. As I stood behind him, I could smell the same clean smell combo that I'd smelled before and it brought a vivid reminder of the details of that night and the shimmering tentative flirtation between us.

Unable to help myself I studied the short hair at the back of his neck, trimmed neatly to the nape, fighting the sudden crazy urge to stroke down the golden hairs tracing down the column of his neck. Thank goodness I hadn't given in to crazy compulsion and done anything stupid that night. At least I had the sense to run out before things had gone any further. And the jury was most definitely out on what might have happened if his mobile hadn't rung.

It had been a silly transient moment that meant nothing. Too much champagne, two strangers and a touch of bravado. Totally meaningless. A possible hook-up that thankfully we hadn't pursued.

And now I was going to pretend that that evening had faded so far into insignificance that it hadn't even registered.

Unfortunately, certain parts of my brain hadn't got that memo and when he turned around to face me, something inside me went a little haywire. I think my mouth dropped open a little bit, and I might have let out a stuttery breath as his cool blue-grey eyes met mine. I didn't even like the guy for crying out loud, so why was my heart tripping the light fandango, like it had never laid eyes on a handsome man before. Seriously, he was rude, arrogant, horrible. He wasn't even that good looking. Not really. Passable. Nice shoulders. Nice eyes. Nice face. Interesting face, one of those all put together nicely sort of faces. Just nice, mind you, not drop-dead gorgeous or anything. OK, he was drop-dead gorgeous but that didn't mean anything.

He blinked and for a second we were back on the balcony of the Great Room, awareness buzzed through me and I was horribly conscious of him. A flash of sensation as my memory unhelpfully reminded me of the charged moment when he'd touched my back.

I stiffened and took in a sharp breath.

'Everything alright?' I asked, being ultra-professional.

He pursed his lips. 'No.' With a flick of his wrist, he looked at his watch. 'I should be sitting at my desk, typing up the notes from an interview I did last night. Instead I'm here, at twenty thousand feet, stuck with a group of people I have nothing in common with,' at this point he glared pointedly at me, 'away from home, for a whole week.'

Any lingering butterflies upped and died right there. I studied him for a second seeing the tension sitting in the taut lines around his mouth.

'Look Benedict—'

'Ben,' he corrected.

No, Ben was the tempting, teasing guy in the tuxedo. Benedict was Captain Grumpy, and him I could handle.

'We can go over and over this. How much you don't want to be here. Blah, blah, blah. The fact of the matter is, you are. You can choose to be miserable and resentful and not get anything out of it or you can suck it up and enjoy yourself.'

The woman to my right raised her head listening eagerly, enjoying the show.

'Or,' he smiled grimly, 'I can enjoy myself at your expense and find my own stories.'

'There is that,' I said, 'but it would be a little unethical, don't you think?'

'Unethical. Me? After you set Dawkins on me. I think your own ethics need a little polishing.'

I ducked my head; he might have a very slight point.

'I'm off to the loo, while I can,' he said indicating over his shoulder with a nod before he turned his back and stalked off down the aisle.

Two air hostesses, a good ten seats away working their way down the aisle, doing battle with a trolley both gave him appreciative second glances.

With him gone I sat back down out of the way and pulled out a guide book to Copenhagen that I'd ordered and not got around to reading, but it didn't hold my interest. The huge range of choices belied the slim volume, and although I tried to dip in, the more I read the more daunting it felt or maybe there was something else on my mind. Idly I picked up Ben, no Benedict's, crossword, with a quick look over my shoulder.

He'd got a couple of clues. As I read some more, one caught

my eye *Foxy lady's top, after sound measurement before long* (7).

Some of the letters had been filled in, including a V which gave me the biggest hint. I smiled, no I smirked. Vulpine. Another word for foxy. The *l* from the top of lady, *vu* was volume unit and another word for long was pine.

Six across was definitely vulpine. Grabbing the pen tucked into the seat pocket, I filled in the answer in small neat capitals, grinning from ear to ear as I did it and then casually replaced the pen and crossword as if I'd never touched them.

'Alright Kate, dear,' asked Conrad suddenly appearing at my shoulder. I jumped and moved to let him back into his seat.

'Yes fine.'

'Intense young fellow, our Ben,' he observed with a knowing glint as he settled back into his seat. 'Not sure he's over fond of you.'

'He doesn't like PR people. His editor insisted he came on the trip.' I shrugged.

'Ah. So, nothing personal then,' he winked, 'I'm sure you'll win him over.'

'Hmm,' I said with a forced smile. It was personal with a capital P and there was sod all chance of winning him over.

I glanced at the crossword with the ghost of a smile. It wasn't as if I was planning on trying that hard.

It was a relief when the air hostess appeared to take tea and coffee orders, although ordering for the whole party across several seats took a while and it was only when the hot cups were safely installed on the seat back trays, that Benedict picked up his newspaper again.

Holding my coffee cup with great care, I pulled the itinerary out of my bag. It would be just my luck to spill boiling hot coffee over Ben's leg. I scanned the list of activities of the latest version, which now had much more detail added to it, when he took in a short sharp breath.

I reread the same sentence again, keeping my eyes peeled to the words on the page and didn't say a word.

'You filled my crossword in!' He sounded horrified and disconcerted.

I didn't say a word, simply looked at him, dispassionate and cool.

He rustled the paper and slapped it down onto his lap, glaring at me.

With a gentle smile I looked down at the crossword. 'And I think nine down is environment.'

With a casual shrug I turned back to my book which was pretty difficult because I wanted to laugh at how mad he was. You could almost feel the kettle about to blow. Understated fury steamed from him, almost evaporating from his skin. Copenhagen was going to be hard work, but perhaps I could have a little fun too at his expense ...

PART TWO

Copenhagen

Chapter 9

Slick and modern, Copenhagen Airport looked very much like every other airport I'd been to, except that the signs were indisputably Danish with their funny slashed Os and As with tiny round circles and there was a replica statue of the Little Mermaid.

With all bags reclaimed, I led my unruly group out through nothing to declare. I could have quite happily kissed the man holding up a white board which read Hjem Party/Kate Sinclair. He stood directly opposite our exit and there was no missing him.

Suddenly feeling much more confident and sure of myself, I strode over to him. Once he'd introduced himself as Mads, thankfully appearing quite sane, he quickly led us out of the terminal to a waiting mini bus.

'So, this is the beautiful city of Copenhagen, capital of Denmark, the happiest country in the world.' He grinned. 'You're going to hear that a lot over the next few days, but it really is true. We have our own institute of happiness. And you'll hear a lot about our social care, our taxes and our liberal approach. My job is going to be to show you a little taste of the real Denmark, but there's gonna be lots of down-time for you to go out and do a bit of exploring for yourself.

'Tomorrow, we will see the city from the water, which gives you the best views.' He pulled out a rolled scroll of tatty paper, unfurled it with a flourish and waved it like a flag. 'And you'll also get your first taste of proper Danish pastries. You have to try one of our famous *kanelsnegle*. But for today we will stop for lunch, followed by a tour of the royal palace at Amalieburg followed by dinner in the hotel this evening.'

He finished every sentence with a triumphant uplift in his tone that was charming and endearing at once.

Benedict was absorbed in his phone, looking utterly disin-terested. I wanted to kick him in the shin and tell him to stop being so rude, but Mads, who shared a few genes with the Duracell bunny, seemed totally oblivious and continued pointing things out from the windows.

'What's *kanelsnegle* when it's at home?' asked Avril, wrin-kling her nose.

'Cinnamon Snail,' piped up Sophie, gesturing the shape with her hands. 'A cinnamon flavoured roll. Proper Danish pastry. I can't wait for that. I've been trying to get the recipe right for the magazine.'

So that's what they were, I'd never got around to looking them up ... or Eva Wilder's café Varme. Lars had included his mother's café on the extensive itinerary as a regular pit stop. For a big successful business man he'd been surprisingly soft and rather sweet about his family.

Fiona had perked up since we'd got off the plane and was busy taking photos of absolutely everything. I could sense suppressed excitement as she sat on the edge of the seat gripping the door, although she didn't make eye contact with anyone. Next to her Sophie and David seemed amused by her snap happy attack on the view through the glass and chatted between themselves including her in their comments, although she didn't respond. Conrad and Avril were laughing together at the very back and already getting on like the proverbial house on fire, I just didn't want to get burned.

Although I did note that Avril had posted on Twitter, *Arrived in Denmark, home to popular royal family, cinnamon snails and happiness #WonderfulCopenhagen #presstripantics*

If this was work I could take it. My chin almost hit the floor when we pulled up outside the hotel. It was abs-o-lutely bloody gorgeous, none of your three-star rubbish I was used to. This was five-star all the way, from the top hatted and grey wool coated doormen with their brass railed luggage trolleys to the quiet stately elegance of the vast reception area.

'Now this is more like it,' said Conrad, a broad grin wrinkling his face, making his moustache twitch with pleasure as he looked around. I tried to look as if it were all part and parcel of another day at the office but failed miserably when Sophie sidled up to me and whispered, 'Wow. Seriously.'

'I know,' I whispered back, almost giggling with a mixture of giddiness and terror. 'I wasn't expecting this.'

Shit. I wasn't expecting this. Putting six people up in a hotel like this was going to cost a fortune. My stomach turned over. This was serious business. And I was in charge.

There was a slight rushing in my ears as I stood there. How

quickly were they all going to realise that I was a complete fraud. I knew about as much about *hygge* as could be written on the back of a fag packet and believed in it about it as much as I believed in fairies.

Avril, the first to hand her cases over to the doormen, didn't bat an eyelid as she sauntered over to one of the sumptuous grey velvet sofas and sank down gracefully crossing her slender legs, the epitome of elegance. David was a lot less sangfroid, if the little jerky movements and grins at the sight of everything was anything to go by and lord love him, he didn't mind who knew it. He followed Avril and sat down in a pale lemon upholstered chair with the same furniture arrangement but not too close. The scene reminded me of our old dog, Toaster, whose distance from the gas fire was measured by the mood of Maud the cat who ruled the house with an iron whisker.

Fiona slowed right down, and turned on the spot, head tilted upwards as if trying to take in every last detail of the décor. The walls held the sheen of expensive wallpaper, a subtle stylish grey against the white wooden trim around the floors and ceilings. Exquisite flowers, their colours harmonising perfectly, decorated the room; purple cala lilies arranged in a tall simple glass vase on a mantelpiece reflected two-fold in a gilt-edged mirror, large tied posies of blousy ranunculas in a gorgeous warm pink filled the centre of occasional tables and tiny pots of white cyclamen tastefully dotted the dark mahogany reception desk.

I sent a dozen pictures of my swanky hotel room via WhatsApp to Connie, a tad mean, perhaps, as no doubt she'd be knee deep in reception children at this time of day. It was a delaying tactic as I almost didn't dare touch anything. The bed with its crisp pure white sheets and designer accessories was so huge you could get lost in there. Like a thief in the night, I opened drawers and cupboards, checking out the sewing kit and shoe cleaning cloth before moving into the bathroom and hesitantly picking up the posh smellies, Sage and Seaspray. I took a quick sniff of the opulent scent which made me feel even more like a fish out of water.

I perched on the very edge of the bed, bouncing slightly on the soft mattress, wondering what to do, unable to dispel the sense of being an intruder casing someone else's life. Unpacking seemed presumptuous; it almost didn't feel right to put my clothes in the wardrobe. Unsettled and lost, I took in a deep breath, wishing I wasn't on my own.

My mother loves looking after people. Lars' words floated in my head. Suddenly I longed for a touch of down to earth normality. A café with coffee and warm pastry sounded perfect.

In my newly purchased feather down coat, which from looking at everyone at the airport was going to make me fit right in, I felt awfully brave stepping out from the hotel, even though according to my map, Varme was only a few streets away. It felt like an awfully big adventure. This was my first trip abroad on my own and the poshest hotel I'd ever stayed in. With a quick look heavenwards, I beamed to myself. Mum would definitely approve. With a brief pang, I imagined what it might have been like, if I could have told all her all about it.

It took me less than five minutes to navigate the cobbled

streets to find Varme and five seconds to fall head over heels in love with it. Cute, quaint, there was also something I couldn't quite put my finger on, which made it so appealing. It certainly wasn't fancy, not like the hotel. The name was written in copper metal letters about twenty centimetres high in a sensible reassuring courier font, Varme, like flames licking the bordering grey painted wood. Which made sense as the translation of Varme in English was warmth. The floor to ceiling windows painted in the same grey trim were sandwiched between huge thick sandy colour stone walls, more like the walls of a fortress. A tiny flight of steps led down into the café to glazed doors and when I pushed them open I was immediately assaulted by the smell of cinnamon and coffee and almost wilted with pleasure on the spot. One cup of rather dire coffee on the plane did not cut it as far as my body was concerned.

A small, slight woman with a perky blonde ponytail was clearing tables with quick neat economy. Dressed in black jeans and a black jumper, she looked up and said, 'God morgen,' with an easy smile, giving the table a last wipe and turning to face me.

'Hello, I'm looking for Eva Wilder.' My sensible ballet pumps squeaked slightly on the herringbone pattern arrangement of the tiles on the floor as I took a step towards her, trying not to look around the room in wonderment. There was so much to see, drawing your eye here, there and everywhere. Long and narrow, either end of the room had white walls painted with flowers, blurry, watercolour style that looked contemporary and smart rather than twee and cottagey.

'And then you've found her.' Her eyes sparkled with genuine delight. 'You must be Kate. Lars has told me all about you.' She threw down her cloth and came over putting both hands on my arms and studying me with smiley assessment which slightly unnerved me as if somehow, I'd unknowingly graduated to long lost member of the family. 'How lovely to meet you. I just know we're going to get along. Welcome to Varme.' Without pausing to draw breath she pulled me over to a chalky white painted table and pushed me into a seat.

'Let's have a coffee and you can tell me all about yourself.'

'Coffee would be lovely,' I said with prim English politeness, hoping she'd forget about the latter.

'And *weinerbrod*?'

I was about to decline but my stomach let a howl of resistance, so audible Eva didn't wait for an answer. I knew from some pre-trip research that bizarrely what the rest of the world called Danish pastries were, in fact, called Viennese bread in Denmark. Go figure.

'Yes please, I've only had one coffee today and that was on the plane.' I pulled a face, to illustrate its woeful quality.

'Then, we must fix that.' Like her son, she had a slight American intonation to her accent. Unlike his bright blue eyes, hers were a merry brown that danced in a small petite face like a mischievous sprite. It was difficult to imagine that she was mother to the strapping Lars, he must be nearly twice her height and she certainly didn't look old enough.

I sat down and took advantage of her busy industry to take a good look around. There was a central counter in the middle of the long back wall, with rows and rows of copper coloured coffee canisters on the back wall along with grey painted racks of plates, cups and mugs. From here I could pick out the famous Royal Copenhagen Blue floral pattern on the white china. On the front of the counter were glass domes, under which a wonderful selection of cakes, pastries and desserts sheltered. In between them were glass cabinets filled with colourful open sandwiches which looked too well-decorated and ornate to eat.

Behind was a serving hatch through which you could see a small, very compact kitchen, which was clearly where the delicious smells were coming from.

'Columbian coffee today, I think,' she said giving me another one of her appraising looks.

I nodded. 'Sounds lovely.' Something about her impish smile made me add, 'Although to be honest, I worked as a barista when I was a student and I'm not sure I'd know Columbian coffee if it bit me.'

'A useful talent. If you can make coffee you'll never be out of a job. I'll have to set you to work if we get busy.' Despite her wink, I was pretty sure she meant it.

'Do you run this by yourself?'

'Most of the time although I have some part time help from friends and students.'

'It's a lovely place.'

On the walls around the café, pale mint green glass shelves housed little vignettes, perfectly formed displays. Five delicate wine goblets made from deep purple glass. Seven silver eggs in different sizes. A single antique cup and saucer with a whole shelf to itself. The eclectic mix worked well and fascinated me. I'd never seen anything quite like it but it didn't feel designery or that someone was trying too hard.

'I love the glasses,' I said pointing to them. 'You have some beautiful things.'

'It's the Danish way. It's been psychologically proven that looking at something beautiful makes people happier. That's why as a nation we are so keen on our design. I picked the glasses up in a flea market years ago, but I've got so many now and I couldn't bear to part with them. They look rather nice there, don't they?'

Which matched my impression that each item had been put out simply because they were liked.

'Gosh your English is amazing.'

She laughed. 'I lived in London for many years. Here.' She came to the table and unloaded a tray passing a tall china cup and saucer my way with a little jug of milk. 'Nice and strong. And *spandauer*.'

Spandauer turned out to be a square pastry with turned up corners and a jammy red middle, the glistening buttery edges as delicious as they looked when I took the first crumbly mouthful and the strawberry jam bursting with sweetness.

'Mmm,' I groaned unable to help myself. 'That is delicious. Everything's been a bit of a rush this morning.'

'Well now you can relax.'

'I don't know about that.' I gave my watch a quick check. 'I need to be back at the hotel to round everyone up in half an hour.'

'Plenty of time.'

'Don't forget I'm the one working. The others are the guests. I'm on duty.'

'Does that worry you?' she asked rather too astutely to my mind.

I nodded.

'Here put my number into your phone. You can always call me if you need anything, but I know you will be fine. And while you're here, you're not on duty. My son wanted you to experience the real Denmark, to relax and enjoy our Danish hospitality. For you and your journalists to see for yourselves why we keep being voted the happiest country in the world. I need to finish a few things but we can chat.'

She wandered over to check on the only other customers in the café, a middle-aged couple in one corner and a teenage boy plugged into his iPhone at the bar by the window.

I sipped at my coffee as she delivered pewter mini buckets of flowers to each table along with handwritten menus displayed in little A5 photo frames.

'Those are cute,' I touched the delicate glass photo frame on my table.

'Flea markets again in England. People there throw so many things away.' She held out another pretty etched silver photo frame. 'In Denmark, we don't buy as many things but we keep them for a very long time. And we like to buy very good design and high quality.' She pointed upwards.

'Lights are a big thing in Denmark.' Above us were three large waterfalls of glass but around the edges of the room were lamps of varying height. 'You will find that a student might buy a very expensive Paul Henningsen lamp for thousands of Kroner because it is important to have nice things in our homes but not lots of nice things.'

The couple beckoned her over, asking to pay their bill and I took advantage of Eva's absence to pull out my phone to check my emails which were still flooding in as usual. Despite being out of the office for a full week, there was no chance of putting an out of office message on my email. I was still expected to be on call for my other clients and any press enquiries as usual. So much for relaxing.

I answered a few before Eva came back. 'Tell me a little about yourself.'

My mind went blank. What did you tell a complete stranger? I had no idea where to start.

'Well, I live in London. I work for a PR agency and Lars has asked us to help launch his department store.' I ground to a halt and shrugged as she waited expectantly, gentle eyes watching me.

'Not married. No children?'

'No.'

'A boyfriend, perhaps.'

I shuddered, thinking of Josh. 'No. Not at the moment.'

'Ah, there was one.'

'Yes but ... well I don't really have time for one.' And the most recent had been a gobshite. I didn't think that would translate. 'Work is ... well my main focus at the moment.'

She stroked the petals on the flowers on the table. 'Yes, but there is more to life than work. For a pretty young woman like you. Friends, family.' Her eyes twinkled as she pulled at a few dead leaves, her head cocked like a cheeky robin.

'My family live just outside London. I see them, of course. I have two brothers.' And what would they make of Copenhagen? John went on lads' holidays, the gruesome details of which seemed to involve copious quantities of cheap lager, clubbing until dawn and sleeping indiscriminately with available women. Brandon had been saving forever to go to a *Star Wars* convention in California, although him ever getting there was about as likely as a trip to the moon and Dad, well, he hadn't been on holiday since Mum had died.

'My mum died when I was fourteen,' I blurted out. I rarely told people that and surprised myself by telling Eva. There was just something about her though. She was so warm and friendly.

'That's very sad.'

'Yes, well it was a long time ago,' I said reaching for my phone but when I picked it up I was reluctant to look at the screen under Eva's careful scrutiny.

'That's hard for a young girl.'

I chased down a few flakes of pastry with the tip of my finger and nibbled at them to avoid looking at her.

'The café is lovely. How long have you been running it?'

Eva smiled. 'For six years. I started it not long after I split up from Lars' father.'

'Oh, I'm sorry … I didn't know.'

'Like you say it was a long time ago and *I'm* much happier.' Her mouth twisted ruefully. 'Anders is not Danish, well, he is but he spent too long in the US and London. He's a workaholic.'

I frowned not quite understanding.

'That's not the Danish way. We do not live to work. I hoped when the children left that he would want to stop working so hard. We lived in London for many years and then when we came back to Copenhagen, I thought that he would slow down. That we would do more things together but he couldn't let go. We had everything. A lovely house. Our children had grown up. It was time for us to be a couple but he is still in his office working and working and working. Life is short. Now I spend time with my friends.' She rested her chin in her hands, exuding serenity and a confident sense of calm. She didn't sound unhappy or regretful. 'I have made a life here. Many of my customers have become friends. I have made something of my own but that I can share.' Her face brightened. 'I love to cook. Feed people. Look after them. I am very privileged to do this for the people of Copenhagen.'

I nodded. Each to their own. As far as I was concerned cooking was one massive chore, a necessary evil that entailed washing up and cleaning up and far too much of a waste of time. Thank God for the express supermarkets which made it much easier to do smash and grab style grocery shopping and buy ready-meals.

'What sort of things do you like to cook?' she asked.

Oops she'd taken the nodding as agreement. I froze and picked up my coffee gazing into it for inspiration.

'Erm, well you know ...'

She pinned me with a 'gotcha' grin which left me nowhere to go but fess up.

'There's never enough time. I work late and me and my

flatmate are in at different times. There's not much point in cooking for one.'

It was difficult to take offence at the amused disapproval in the quick shake of her head.

'I think this trip to Copenhagen is just what you need, Katie.'

'It's Ka ...' I paused and changed my mind. The warmth in her voice softened my name reminding me of my mum. Suddenly there seemed a world of difference between a Kate and Katie.

Chapter 10

Being on a guided tour with everything organised for you was, I decided, a rare luxury. Our first walk took us to the Little Mermaid, considerably smaller than I was expecting – despite the clue in the name! Then on to the royal palace at Amalieburg, actually four palaces arranged around a square, with soldiers who looked remarkably like our own Queen's guard in their traditional bearskins with dark navy tunics instead of our red ones. Mads got very excited when he spotted the Danish flag flying over one of the palaces, a sign that Margrethe, as if she were a neighbour rather than the Queen, was in residence.

He grinned. 'Our royal family is very popular and Margrethe is famous for being an unrepentant die-hard smoker, even in public.'

Clearly with no sign of the queen popping out for a quick fag round the back of the recycling shed (the Danes are big on recycling), we gave up queen spotting and headed for lunch at Ida Davidsen, a family run restaurant concern 'crazy for' the typical Danish open sandwiches, smorrobrod.

Sophie made Mads say the word five times before she was

89

happy with her own attempt. He explained that Danish pronunciation was very difficult for foreigners as the Danish alphabet has 29 letters, the ø, å, æ all being separate letters with a distinct and very subtle vowel sound that was very difficult for people to reproduce.

I fell into step next to her as we headed for lunch.

'I'm so looking forward to this. Open sandwiches here are amazing. I can't wait to try them.' She paused and gave my arm squeeze. 'Thank you so much Kate for inviting me. This is going to be such an amazing trip.' She beamed at me so warmly I smiled back.

'My pleasure. I'm so glad you could come. And you genuinely wanted to come.' I glanced over my shoulder. 'I had a devil of a job persuading some people.'

Everyone but Ben had been asking lots of questions. He'd spent more time on his phone and several times I'd caught him yawning as if bored. He could at least make some effort.

'Really? I can't believe that,' said Sophie looking round at the others. 'Who wouldn't want to spend five days in Copenhagen instead of being at work? Although, it is a pretty mixed bunch you've ended up with. David's lovely. I've been on a trip with him before. Easy going. You'll have no trouble with him. Avril and Conrad, I'm not so sure. And Ben, I don't know at all, but he's a bit of a hottie, isn't he?' She waggled her fair eyebrows in a woeful attempt at lechery.

I shrugged as if far too professional to comment. If only she knew. I was ready to strangle him. He'd made sod all effort to join in, constantly tapping away on his phone like a recalcitrant teenager and yawning when he thought no one was looking. Unfortunately, I couldn't help watching him, constantly trying to gauge his reactions, which so far hadn't seemed that positive.

'Good job I'm all loved up with James.'

'Your boyfriend?' I seized on the change of subject. I didn't want to think about or discuss Ben, especially not regarding the subject of hotness.

'Yes,' she sighed. 'He's pretty lovely.'

'How long have you been together?'

'Nearly two years.' She hugged herself and glanced at me. 'I'm hoping he might pop the question soon.'

'Are you living together?' I asked.

'Sort of, that's the only difficulty. His mother is quite ill, so he works in London four days a week and then goes back to Cornwall on a Thursday to look after her. Honestly the care system is crap. You can't get carers over the weekend. It makes things a bit trickier but I keep thinking that if I can freelance one day we could both move down there. I don't want to live in London for ever. What about you? You with anyone?'

I was about to tell her about Josh but caught Ben giving me one of his usual glacial glares, in sharp contrast to the warm looks the first time I met him.

My lip curled. 'No, I was. But I'm off men for the foreseeable future.'

The restaurant looked unassuming from the outside, almost like the front of someone's home but inside had that stylish Danish design look that was quickly becoming apparent was part of the Danish psyche. Dark wood tables and chairs were arranged in neat order while the white painted walls were full of photos of famous patrons, cartoons and several of a very smiley Ida Davidsen, who was very much a real person.

Who knew that the humble sandwich could be such a work of art? The menu featured over 250 and we were urged to go and check out the rainbow display in the cabinet. It was so utterly mouth-watering, I wanted one of everything.

Piled on the dark rye bread were rows of thick juicy pink prawns, the deep amber of smoked salmon in rolls with black fish roe and wedges of sunshine yellow lemon sprinkled with dill, ripples of rare roast beef decorated with delicate shavings of pale cucumber and rolled herring encircled by quartered eggs, chopped chives and long slivers of spring onion.

Sophie was in seventh, eighth and ninth heaven. 'I think I might have to stay here forever. How on earth do you choose?'

'My stomach thinks it's died and gone to heaven,' said Conrad, pulling out a pair of glasses and studying the display.

'I'm not even sure what half of this is?' said Ben.

'That's slices of pork,' said Sophie pointing. 'That's ...'

She was very knowledgeable as you would expect from a food writer.

'Gosh, they look pretty calorie heavy,' said Avril, rubbing at her none-existent stomach. 'I don't want to go home the size of a house.'

Looking at her skeletal tiny frame, going home the size of a normal person would be quite a feat.

'Can we order some extra?' asked Sophie as everyone mused out loud about what they might choose when we sat down at our table, which had been reserved. The place was almost full, it was very popular. 'Everyone needs to try something new.'

'Hmm, I'm not sure that I fancy pickled herring, thank you very much,' said Avril turning up her patrician nose as she read the menu.

'Ah, but you must for your food education. What if you discovered you loved it?' said Sophie waving her hands towards the displays.

Avril winced and went back to her menu.

'There are some amazing ideas here. I think I can do a whole recipe feature on open sandwiches for the magazine.'

'That would be good,' I said, my brain clicking into action. 'Maybe you could do a cookery demonstration, a reader event for the magazine at the store.'

'Won't it have a café or restaurant?'

'No, apparently that's a very English thing.'

'Shame, but I'm sure we could definitely do a cookery demo,' said Sophie, bubbling with immediate enthusiasm. 'My editor would love that. We're always looking for subscriber events. I could talk about the types of bread. Rye bread. The toppings, traditional and modern twists. Pickled herring and somersalat, smoked cheese and radish, corned beef and Danish pickles.'

'Sounds great. And we could tweet about it. Take lots of pictures and run them on Instagram.'

'And Facebook,' Sophie chipped in.

I whipped out my notebook.

'God, do you ever switch off?' asked Ben from across the table. For most of the morning he'd had little to say and seemed far more interested in his phone. As soon as we'd sat down he'd asked the waitress for the WiFi code.

'It's my job,' I said pointedly. Since we'd arrived he'd barely joined in, focussing on his own emails.

'Some job,' he muttered, going back to his phone again.

The group dynamic splintered into two main conversations, Sophie, David and I chatting with Mads, while Conrad and Avril had discovered a rich vein of gossip about an editor they both knew on a celebrity gossip magazine. Fiona scuttled around the table when we'd arrived, selecting the furthermost chair, tucked back in the shadows as if hoping to fade into them. She sat fiddling with her camera and I wasn't sure how to involve her without blatantly pointing out her isolation.

Ben seemed equally reticent but at that moment, looked up and caught me surreptitiously studying him.

He straightened and leaned across the table and spoke to Fiona.

'Any good shots?'

Her head lifted with her usual startled fawn look of alarm and she froze for a second.

But the others were busy talking, so she handed her camera over to Ben. Head bent he pored over the images, holding the camera between careful fingers, nodding every now and then.

'These are great, Fiona,' he said quietly about to hand the camera back but unfortunately Avril heard him.

'Oooh let's have a look.'

I saw the pained expression on Fiona's face and the apologetic one on Ben's as everyone crowded around behind his chair for a closer look.

'Wow, these are really quite good,' said Avril. 'Great shot of the Little Mermaid. I love that picture of the palace in the foreground and the sea in the background. I took one and posted it on Twitter but it's nowhere near as good as that one.'

Ben scrolled through them. 'I'm not sure about that one,' he teased pausing at a blurry shot of David and Conrad in front of one of the soldiers outside the palace.

'For the love of Jesus, Mary and Joseph, please delete that shocker. I look like a geriatric drag queen after a nine-day bender,' drawled Conrad with dramatic weariness. Instead of ducking her head and blushing, Fiona let out a small giggle.

'I'll delete that one for you.'

'I should bloody well hope so,' said Conrad. 'Any chance of a glass of wine with lunch? I've built up a rare thirst.'

Ben passed the camera down to Sophie and I who were on the opposite side of the table and we flipped through the digital shots. Fiona was a very talented photographer. She'd captured a few of the group and I was struck by the pictures of Avril. No wonder she thought they were so good; she looked like some Hollywood starlet, although clearly conscious of the camera as there was a posed quality to a lot of the shots. There was one exception. It had been taken while we were at the Little Mermaid statue and Avril was gazing out beyond the statue to sea, lost in thought. Fiona had captured Avril bathed in a sunbeam, totally unaware of being photographed, her beautiful face filled with haunting sadness and her hunched shoulders bowed as if they carried the weight of the world. It was so different to the face she normally let the world see, it made me wonder what was on her mind.

When I handed back the camera to Fiona, she tucked it away, her face pink with pleasure.

'I think you might just have got yourself a job as official photographer,' I said. 'I wonder if we might buy some of them for the campaign.'

'No, I'll send them to you.'

'No,' interjected Ben, shooting me an unfriendly scowl, 'You charge for them. They're bloody good and it's business. You own the copyright. Don't let anyone take advantage of you.'

Everyone was diverted by the arrival of the coffee and I gave into temptation and kicked him under the table, not quite as hard as I would have liked to.

I glared at him and said in a low voice 'I offered to buy them.'

'Touchy, aren't we?' His superior smile wound me up even more.

'I didn't like the insinuation that I might take advantage.'

'Wouldn't be the first time, would it?'

I rolled my eyes at him. 'God, you're like a dog with a bone. Bear a grudge much? When are you going to let it go?'

He grinned like a small boy in the playground, which is exactly how he was bloody behaving.

'Never?'

'Guys, what's everyone having?' asked Sophie in an overloud voice as the very pretty Danish waitress finally came to take our order.

Sophie waved her fork at me. 'Kate, this herring is delicious. Do you want to try some? Come on everyone, you've got to try something. It's good for your food education.'

I had a feeling we were going to become well acquainted with that phrase over the next few days.

In the end, spoilt for choice, we'd ordered a selection to share, although Sophie insisted that everyone try the four types of herring despite their reservations.

Like everyone else, I didn't fancy herring, not being a big fish lover but the expression of eager expectation on Sophie's face, made me lead the charge and grab a fork to poke at the nearest thing on the plate, a piece of rye and caraway bread with a herring, carrot and ginger mix on top.

'Wow,' I said as the flavours hit my tastebuds with a satisfying zing, 'That's gorgeous.' I went back for a second bite, eyeing the concoction with far more enthusiasm. 'Really,' I looked around at the others, 'you should try it.'

Sophie beamed like a proud mama as everyone else, even Avril, took forkfuls from the dishes she'd pushed into the middle of the table.

'Really rather good,' said Conrad, reaching out for a second larger portion and wolfing it down as if he hadn't had a good meal in days. 'Who knew herring could be so versatile?'

We all burst out laughing and soon everyone was sharing tasters with each other, as Sophie with Mads' help explained what everything was.

'So what's next on the agenda?' asked Ben looking at his watch as Mads paid the bill and everyone rose to their feet, their chairs scraping and elbows bumping with convivial cheer engendered by good food, satisfied stomachs and a two hour lunch. 'I need to make a few phone calls. Get an article finished off.'

Ignoring the weary tone, or maybe he was oblivious to the nuances, Mads beamed. 'The rest of the afternoon is yours to relax and enjoy. Tonight, we will eat at the hotel restaurant and then everyone can have an early night ready for a busy day. Tomorrow morning, we will start the day with a trip to Varme to meet Eva Wilder and she will demonstrate how to make Danish pastries for you.'

Ben pulled a face. 'Great.'

Sophie rubbed her hands with glee. 'It is great, you miserable oaf.'

I could have kissed her even though she said it in a teasing, cheery manner that robbed the words of any offence and I think he almost smiled at her.

Even though I knew it was absolutely the wrong thing to do, I couldn't resist adding, 'Just think, you can impress your girlfriend with your baking skills, Benedict.'

He shot me a sour look as he pulled on his coat. 'It's Ben and I don't have a girlfriend. I don't need to impress anyone.'

'How about your family then?' I persisted, pushed on by some little demon. 'I bet they'd love you to cook for them.'

A grim line touched his mouth and like a shutter coming down all animation left his face, leaving a cool blank expression and he gazed past me through the window. 'Perhaps.'

Maybe if I hadn't been studying him surreptitiously throughout the trip, I might not have noticed it, but I blurted out, 'I'm sorry,' realising that I'd touched something raw.

Surprise echoed in the startled flick of his glance back my

way, a second of distrust as his eyes narrowed and then an inscrutable expression descended as he held my gaze before nodding in silent acknowledgement and then turning away. For a moment, he looked so isolated and solitary. Recognition tugged in my chest. Everyone else was oblivious to the barely-there exchange as they busied themselves gathering up bags and buttoning up coats. I stared at his broad back, feeling as if I'd intruded on something when I should have known better. Families were complicated. For a minute, I fought against the urge to go and lay a hand on his sleeve. I wasn't sure he would thank me but some part of me just wanted to let him know I understood and he wasn't alone.

Chapter 11

'I'm knackered,' said Avril looking at her watch as we walked into the hotel foyer.

'And my feet are bloody killing me.' She slipped off her leather Russell and Bromley tasselled loafers and stood in her dainty stockinged feet, before whipping out her phone and photographing them.

'I'm going to post on Twitter ... Weary feet, hashtag Wonderful Copenhagen, Smorebrod, Amelieberg. All ace. Hashtag press trip antics.'

I knew exactly how she felt; I'd been on the go since five that morning.

A hot bath in the gorgeously decadent hotel bathroom and a nice cup of tea would go down a storm.

'A drink will sort you out,' said Conrad. 'It's well past the yard arm. How about the hotel bar, Kate, my love?'

'I think people are probably a bit tired.' And some of us still had work to do. Last time I checked my email there were a stack of messages demanding my attention.

'I don't mind,' said David, who seemed quite keen on the idea. 'Sounds like a good idea.'

'Will that leave us enough time to get ready?' asked Avril, tucking her shoes under her arm, pulling a mirror from her bag and checking her make-up.

'Bags of time. Besides you're gorgeous as you are,' said Conrad with his old-school charm, before adding, with a mock lascivious leer that had everyone laughing, 'No one's going to kick you out of bed, darling.'

Avril, standing next to me, responded with a tight smile and I think only I heard her quiet words hidden under the burst of laughter, 'Not sure my husband would agree.'

Unfortunately, after a quick confab everyone but Avril and Ben decided to go to the hotel bar and they both headed to the lifts. I watched them go, rather enviously.

This was exactly what I'd feared. Not being able to control everyone.

'What's everyone having?' asked Conrad gaily. 'Shall we put it on your room tab, Kate?'

I gave him a tight smile. Oh God, the bill could be huge. Megan would kill me.

'Just a water, thanks Conrad,' I said hoping that everyone would follow my abstemious suit. No such luck. Three beers, and a large red wine later, an astronomic bar bill was presented to me.

Despite craving a break from being on duty and having to be 'on it', when I finally retreated from the bar, I found the quiet luxury of the room a little bit disconcerting. The silence had a deadness to it that wasn't so comforting. I'd already unpacked and wasn't quite ready to tackle my emails yet. I wasn't sure what to do with myself. Flicking through the channels on the TV, everything was in Danish apart from BBC News.

I put it on for some background noise.

It was so rare for me to have time to do nothing. I wasn't sure what to do with myself.

Picking up my phone I WhatsApped Connie a picture of the open sandwiches at lunch, with the caption *Smorrebrod.*

Tough life, babe, but someone's got to do it. While some of us are up to our arses in frigging frogspawn – Springwatch time again in reception class.

She sent me a selfie of her lower trouser leg with a jelly sweet stuck to it and the caption, *Harribrod*, which made me laugh out loud. She always managed to make me feel better, although she'd be furious with me if she thought I wasn't making the most of this plush hotel room, the fabulous bathroom and the chance to luxuriate in a lovely deep bath for a change.

I plugged in my Bluetooth speaker, selecting my favourite playlist on my phone, a selection of indie rock tracks and ran a bath.

After wallowing in the hotel's Sage and Seaspray foaming bath wash, singing along to the Kings of Leon, I felt a whole lot better. A lot of which had to do with the rare exercising of my vocal chords. As a kid I used to sing all the time, school productions, university reviews and amateur productions – as I got older I'd got out of the habit. I'd forgotten how uplifting it could be.

Gathering together make-up and tonight's outfit, I remembered I needed to recharge my phone. I could pop it on quickly before I went down. Rooting around in my suitcase, I hunted for the cable. There was no sign of it.

Mentally I retraced my steps yesterday as I packed picturing it on the side in the kitchen where I'd left it. Damn I'd have to ask if I could borrow one.

The hotel's dining room, the last word in elegance and luxury, was situated on the top floor with a misty grey view of the sea and sky in the distance. Heavy damask cloths covered each table and more flowers decorated the room, with vases of grape hyacinths on each table.

Only Ben and Avril were missing when I arrived and I slipped into the chair beside David. Conrad had already ordered a bottle of red wine and held court waving his wine glass about. I winced as I picked up the menu. There were about eight kroner to a pound which made the expensive prices look even more eye-watering. The cheapest bottle was a scary four hundred and fifty kroner, thankfully, I calculated that was a mere fifty quid.

'Evening Kate,' he called. 'To our hostess.'

'Did he leave the bar?' I asked David under my breath.

'No, I popped back to my room and when I came back down, he was still in the bar, I had to drag him in here to dinner.' We both studied Conrad's wiry frame.

'I don't know where he puts it.' I shook my head. 'He never seems to get drunk.'

David tilted his head. 'He doesn't drink quite as much as

you think. He never empties a glass before he tops it up. Although the amount he does put away would still fell a couple of rugby players.'

Avril arrived looking stunning in a figure hugging red dress which turned several heads as she sauntered into the restaurant. She made a big fuss of not wanting to sit at the end of the table, so I swapped with her so that she could be in the middle next to Sophie and Conrad and opposite Mads and David. Fiona quite happily settled into the seat next to David.

I looked at my watch. Still no sign of Ben.

The waitress came to take our order.

I went around the table and whispered to Mads, 'Should we wait for Ben?'

Mads shook his head. 'No, I've learned on these trips, you carry on otherwise your whole schedule goes out the window. It's ten minutes after we arranged to meet. When he comes, he can order then.'

'Maybe I'll give him a call.' Personally, I'd quite happily let him starve, ungrateful sod.

I slipped out of the dining room and the barman caught my eye and beckoned me over.

'Could you sign your bar bill? Room three-two-one?'

I gulped at the cost of Conrad's additional drinks after I'd left.

Signing the slip, I turned and called Ben's phone. There was only one bar left on my battery. It clicked straight through to answerphone. I waited for a minute, checking my emails quickly and then called again. Still no answer. I sent a quick text as polite as I could manage.

We're waiting for you to order. What time do you think you'll be here? Kind regards Kate.

By the time our second course had arrived, Ben still hadn't turned up and there'd been no response to my text. My fists clenched underneath the table. He was determined to follow through and be a pain in the arse.

There was still no sign of him when the waitress gathered up our plates.

'What about you, Kate?'

'Sorry?'

'Do you want some cheese? Or a dessert?'

'Er ... what's everyone else having?'

I'd glanced down at my phone and seen a text from Megan.

How's it going? Everyone behaving themselves?

Oh shit, what would she say if she knew Ben was already doing his own thing?

'I don't know anything about Danish cheese, apart from Danish Blue,' said Sophie. 'I'd like to see what else they have.' Conrad agreed to join her although I'm not sure that he knew anything about cheese. He seemed incapable of turning down anything that was going free. It wouldn't have surprised me if he'd produced a couple of sandwich bags and loaded them up with the left-over bread at the table.

I checked my phone again and then saw that it had now died. It forced my hand.

'I'm going to check on Benedict.'

Before anyone could say anything, I stalked out of the dining room.

I might have guessed as I stormed down the corridor that his room was the one with the empty dinner tray sitting right outside it.

He'd had room service! That was just rude.

Thankfully there was a doorbell because otherwise I might have looked like a lunatic woman hammering on the door. I held my finger down on the bell.

After a good minute, I heard cursing and mumbling through the door, not that I cared, I kept my finger firmly pressed on that button.

The door flew open and a tousled, sleepy Ben stood in front of me, blinking dopily, in black jersey boxers and nothing else. Something tugged in my chest at the sight of him as my mouth went dry.

'What the ...?' he asked frowning, looking confused and ... gorgeous.

He had no right looking like that, all cute, sleepy and adorable. He wasn't adorable. He was rude, surly and horrible.

'Sorry, I was worried about you.' My shrewish tone made it clear that I was anything but. 'Forget the time?' I gave the tray on the floor a pointed look.

Instead of answering or even bloody apologising, he turned his back and walked back into the room leaving the door wide open.

I was so taken aback I opened my mouth but nothing came out. So I followed him.

Almost oblivious to me, he stumbled back towards the bed and flopped backwards, pulling the sheet over him. His eyes closing instantly.

What. The. Hell.

My eyes widened as my hands curled into fists. The ... the ...

He lay there oblivious to me and I stood there too gobsmacked to say or do anything.

I took a step closer, puzzled now. Was he ill?

Was that why he'd not come down? Had he got some medical condition? Had he been ill? I sniffed as if that might give me a clue but the room smelled perfectly normal.

My heart picked up a beat or two as I stood in the semi-dark room. He'd left one bedside lamp on which emitted a golden glow.

I took an uncertain step towards the bed. My first aid training from Girl Guides was long out of date. About the only thing I could remember was check the patient is still breathing, and that wasn't in doubt. I watched the slow rise and fall of his broad chest. Heck no, he was definitely breathing, even so I couldn't seem to peel my gaze away from his chest. My hormones were leading the charge, squealing yum, yum. A light dusting of tiny freckles dappled his skin, which had that slight gold cast of a redhead who's acclimatised to the sun. Fine dark copper hair dusted the smooth skin of the centre of his chest between well-defined pecs before arrowing down his stomach and disappearing beneath his boxers.

His eyes were closed and his face had slackened, one arm thrown above his head, the other stretched away. I picked up musky male scent and my own breathing hitched as I stood over him. I barely knew him and watching him in bed felt so personal and wrong but what if he were really ill? I had no idea what I'd do. I could get Mads to call a doctor. What if he was hospitalised? What if he were seriously ill?

With a tentative hand, I leaned over towards the centre of the bed, my knees bracing the edge to keep my balance and reached out to touch his forehead to check his temperature, the only other sign of illness I could think of.

'For fuck's sake go away,' he growled and like some horror film, his eyes flicked open staring up at me.

'Eeek,' I squeaked and toppled over right on top of his chest. Of course, I pushed against him, trying to scramble off as quickly as possible, my hands all over his chest. My fingers tingled at the touch and my heart raced like a startled deer.

'What the fuck are you doing?'

'I-I could ask you the same,' I said, trying to appear unmoved, as I pushed myself back on my feet beside the bed, brushing myself down as if each stroke would help me regain my dignity which was hanging in tatters around my ankles.

'I'm sleeping. Or at least I was until some weirdo tried to get into bed with me.'

'I wasn't trying to get into bed with you,' I squeaked indignantly and then remembering the dignity thing, added. 'No one's that desperate.'

'Who said anything about being desperate?' His voice had dropped, deliberately smoky, and he gave me a piercing look.

Oh hell. My hormones danced into life, sending a rush of

... of ... something spiralling through my system leaving me a touch weak-kneed.

Hiding the sudden breathlessness, I snapped, 'I thought you might be ill. Obviously I was wrong. Just inconsiderate and rude.'

'And how do you figure that?'

'It would have been courteous to let me know you weren't joining us for dinner. Now that you're on this trip, the least you could do is make an effort to join in. I see you availed yourself of room service.'

'Or perhaps I was so darned tired, I wasn't thinking straight on account of not having slept for two days. In fact, the thought didn't come into it. I was running on empty. I needed food and sleep. There was nothing beyond that.'

'Why haven't you slept? Deadline? Great party?'

'My sister's husband upped and left her with a baby and a toddler. Arrived on my doorstep in the middle of the night. Between a wailing heartbroken sister, crying baby and toddler tantrum of the highest order, it was a tad difficult catching any shut-eye.'

'You don't look the sort to babysit.' Not that I knew him that well, but with the stylish clothes, manbag and well-groomed appearance he had that non-dependent, unencumbered look about him, a bit like my brother John. Although it was hardly a good rule of thumb, Brandon's unkempt appearance suggested he could have half a dozen offspring crawling all over him.

'I'm not,' he growled. 'I like my sleep. It was supposed to be a one off. Except now I'm not there, I'm here where I didn't want to be, she's taken up residence and my neighbours are sending complaining texts every five minutes and she's asking frightening questions like "where's the stopcock?". What the fuck does that mean?'

'It means she wants to switch off the water,' I said practicably.

'I know that, but why?'

'Probably flooding the place out,' I said helpfully.

'Thanks, you're not helping.'

'I wasn't trying to.'

We lapsed into silence and then I realised how awkward it was standing there with him in bed.

'Right well, I'd better go.'

'And now I'm wide awake.' The huge yawn that accompanied these words suggested otherwise and I could see his eyes drooping again.

'Sorry,' I said feeling a tad guilty. 'I don't suppose I could borrow your phone charger?'

'Why? You left yours at home?'

'Funnily enough, yes. That would be why I'm asking.'

'Snarky much?'

'Clearly the mad fox in you brings out the snark in me. I'm normally very polite and kind to dogs and small children.'

'Somehow, I find that difficult to believe,' he muttered and closed his eyes.

I stood there for a minute studying the sweep of his dark lashes against the pale skin, his eyes were shadowed purple. Despite looking washed out, the planes of his face and the tousled hair still packed a punch. He was a handsome bugger.

I swallowed, feeling a bit like a peeping Tom. I'd been trying to tell myself that I'd built up the moment at the Great Room and my Prince Charming couldn't possibly be as good looking as I'd thought and that I'd misremembered in the light of the next morning, but no it appeared my memory was spot on where the physical aspect was concerned, it just short-circuited when it came to his personality, which was completely charmless. Unfortunately, I had to overlook that as I still wanted something from him.

'Ben?' I whispered. He couldn't have fallen asleep again.

He grunted and turned over muttering, 'Shut the door on the way out.'

Chapter 12

Eva pressed a cup of coffee into my hand the minute I walked into Varme the next morning, like some wonderful magician.

'You're up very bright and early,' she said, unhurriedly stripping off her apron and guiding me to a table, bringing her own cup of steaming coffee with her.

I inhaled the coffee. 'Thank you, that smells lovely. Just what I needed.' And I hadn't even realised. 'I thought I'd pop in while the journalists are having breakfast, make sure everything's ready.' And have a bit of time to myself. The thought of being with them all day was a touch daunting.

Eva raised an amused eyebrow as if she could see straight through me.

'Sit down and have a pastry. It's a big responsibility looking after other people.'

'Oh gosh this coffee is wonderful. Thank you.'

'You're very welcome. How was your first day?'

'Fine. Busy. Tiring. But OK. I needed to ... you know get out this morning. I had no idea it would be so ... well, being with them all the time. They're adults so they shouldn't need looking after.'

Eva smiled. Despite my worry about the language barrier, she had no problem following my incoherent answer. 'I wonder if that is worse. They don't do as they're told, which makes your job doubly hard I would imagine.'

I laughed at her instant understanding. 'At least tomorrow will be easier; we're going on a boat trip. I can't lose anyone on a boat.'

Eva laughed. 'Unless someone falls overboard.'

'Don't even suggest it,' I said laughing with her. 'That would be a disaster.'

'And it's not going to happen. Are they a nice group? I'm looking forward to meeting them all. I thought during the cookery demonstration I'd get everyone involved. They can all make pastry today.'

'Sophie will love that. David and Fiona will join in but I'm not so sure about the others.'

'Don't you worry. Leave them to me.'

'Yes, you'll be OK with them,' I paused not wanting to look weak in front of her, but she had a way about her that elicited confidences. 'Some of them are older and more experienced than me.' I thought of Conrad. 'I don't feel that confident bossing them about or laying down the law.' I thought about the wine bill from dinner. 'If I'm not more authoritative they'll walk all over me.' Conrad could run through the allotted expense budget in one day.

'And would that be the end of the world?' asked Eva, with a merry twinkle in her eye.

'It probably won't go down terribly well with my bosses. It won't look as if I'm very organised or in charge.'

'And that's important to you? Sorry,' she looked at her watch, 'Would you mind helping me re-arrange the tables?'

'No.' I followed her as she cleared a few chairs away and together we moved tables to form a central bank of them.

'It matters to you, being organised and in charge?' Eva cocked her head to one side, her eyes studying me carefully, giving the impression she listened to every word and the subtext beyond.

'I'm trying to get a promotion. This trip is an important step in that direction.'

'Ah and what does promotion get you?' She directed me to another table and I took the opposite end and helped her shift it into place. Her calm, matter of fact question held no judgement or inflection, as if she genuinely didn't know the answer.

'Well, more money – always nice. And more ... prestige. You know, it's a measure of success. Other people can see you're rising up the ranks. They can see you're doing well.'

'And do you enjoy your work?'

'Every day is different. I get to do lots of interesting things and I look forward to going in every day.' Except that the last bit hadn't been true for a while and especially not since I had been denied the promotion. It had left me resentful and grudging of the hours I spent in the office when everyone else had left. Being left to do my own thing on the Hjem account had been the most creative and enjoyable thing I'd done in ages. The strict division of labour in the agency meant you usually did one element of a job. Working on Hjem had been like the good old days when I'd first started in PR and worked for a tiny agency where everyone pitched in to do everything. With a sudden pang, I missed those chaotic and less organised days which was crazy, the Machin Agency was a top five agency. Who wouldn't want to work there?

Finishing my coffee, I stood to leave, butterflies of anxiety starting to stir in my stomach.

'See you in a minute,' said Eva. She laid a reassuring hand on my arm. 'Don't worry, everything's going to be fine. You're in Denmark now. Why not enjoy it?'

All the warm, cosy feelings I'd acquired in the last half hour went up in a puff of smoke the minute I saw Benedict pacing up and down outside the front of the hotel, his mobile jammed to his ear. He broke off as soon as he saw me and said something rapidly to finish the call.

'You stole my charger,' he said accusingly.

'I borrowed it,' I said. 'You did say I could.'

He raised an eyebrow. 'Hmm that's not quite how I recall the direction of the conversation.'

'You didn't say no,' I said, winding him up was such fun, even though I now remembered just how tired he'd looked and felt the teensiest bit guilty.

'You caught me at a weak moment. Do you think I could have it back?'

'Of course,' I said, with a deliberately sunny smile as if he were the one being unreasonable. I dipped into my tote bag and pulled it out. 'Here you go.'

'Thanks,' he said still grumpy, with purple shadows like bruises under his eyes.

Guilt pricked me and my voice softened, 'Are you OK?'

He looked up, his blue-grey eyes narrowing sharply. I held his gaze. 'You still look ...'

With a slow sigh, he nodded, not quite smiling but coming close, 'Tell me about it, I look like shit ... but I feel a hell of a lot better than I did.'

Our gaze held a while longer, and then for want of anything else to say, I nodded and said, 'Good.'

'Morning Kate, Ben,' said Sophie, appearing behind him, bouncing on her toes. 'I am so excited about this. Baking! My favourite thing. I'm so glad Lars arranged this for us as part of the press trip.'

'Glad it's yours,' muttered Ben.

'Go on,' she gave him a dig in the ribs with her elbows. 'You know you'll love it when you try it.'

'I wouldn't count on it.'

Sophie and I exchanged a grin.

'Hello and good morning,' called Eva gaily, welcoming everyone as if they were old friends.

She ushered everyone around one of the tables, inviting us all to sit down. As they all gazed around the lovely café, I felt a sense of quick, invested pride and I had no idea why. I'd only been here once before. Perhaps it was because I already felt at home here.

'This morning, you're all going to get your hands dirty and we're going to have lots of fun talking about life in Denmark.'

From anyone else the words could have sounded a bit too

cute but with Eva, it was impossible to feel cynical. She began handing out striped aprons. 'Now, here. There is one for everyone. Katie, this is for you.' To my surprise the apron had my name embroidered on it.

'Sophie. David. Ben. Fiona. Conrad. Avril. Excellent. Everyone is here. First we're going to have coffee and then we're going to do some baking.' She made it sound as if it were the most exciting thing possible and Sophie clapped her hands. 'Goodie.'

I caught Ben roll his eyes and Avril give him a conspiratorial nudge, as if to say we're all in this together.

Once coffee had been served, Eva started to organise us all.

'Now cooking and looking after people makes me happy. And I think it shows in the food.'

I paused and hung back checking my emails on my phone quickly. Damn, I'd received ten already from work since breakfast that all needed responses.

Ben also whipped his phone out and cursed under his breath. He excused himself and stepped outside the café and I saw him walk to the other side of the road, his phone jammed to his ear, where he stood, head bowed, shoulders hunched and kicking at one of the cobbles with his heel. I wondered if his sister had located the stopcock yet.

I dealt with a couple of emails and then realised Eva was standing over me. She gently took the phone from my hand and tucked it in my pocket.

'You and Ben will work here.' She led me over to the table. 'David, you will work with me. Sophie, you and Fiona can be together, and Avril and Conrad together,' she looked reprovingly at them over her rimless glasses, 'but you have to behave.'

'Who us?' quipped Conrad, mischief written all over his face.

'Don't know what you mean,' smiled Avril, for once looking positively light-hearted.

'In Denmark we're famous for our pastries, which we call *Weinerbrod*, which translates ironically as Vienna Bread because the recipes were brought here by Austrian bakers. Today I'm going to show you how to make the typical *spandauer*.' She shot me a conspiratorial look and smiled. 'Food needs to be made with love. Everything tastes better when it's made with love. Leave your worries and cares at the door.'

'Ooo, that's fab,' said Sophie, grabbing her bag. 'Let me write that down. I'm going to quote you on that in the magazine.'

'Baking makes me very happy and here in Denmark we celebrate the little things that make us happy. Perhaps that's why we're such a happy nation? Have you heard of *hygge*?'

'Yes,' everyone chorused dutifully, except Ben who held up a hand like a child in class.

'What exactly is it? Apart from lighting candles and buying expensive cashmere shawls.'

Eva beamed at him. 'It's taking pleasure from the simple things in life, like taking a pastry home from work, making a cup of coffee and sitting to enjoy every last mouthful,' she paused and then added with a twinkle, 'and not feeling at all guilty about a single calorie.'

'Having pastry with no calories would make me very happy,' said Sophie as we all laughed.

'What makes you happy?' Eva's eyes danced around the group. 'Conrad?'

'I guess eating and drinking,' he answered before adding flippantly, 'it's always good to know where the next meal's coming from.'

'I don't think I am happy,' said Avril suddenly and then as if surprised by her unexpected admission, stared self-consciously out of the window avoiding catching anyone's eye.

'Food, making it and sharing it. Oh and my boyfriend,' said Sophie quickly filling the awkward gap.

'Singing,' I blurted out. It wasn't exactly true, but I felt I needed to say something to back Sophie up and draw attention away from Avril who looked close to tears. Besides, I wasn't sure I could say what made me happy. I'd enjoyed hyggifying the office when Lars came in. I'd been happy when everyone had liked the cookies I'd made. It didn't amount to an awful lot. Did my job make me happy? Once it had, now I wasn't quite so sure.

'Company,' said David. 'Being part of something.'

Eva clapped her hands as if delighted by her pupils. 'Togetherness is very important. This is very much *hygge*.'

Ben gave a low snort and I glared at him. Luckily Eva didn't seem to have heard or if she did she ignored him and carried on. 'Creating that feeling of togetherness involves connecting with others without fear of judgement. In Denmark people don't try to take the centre of attention. No one is more important than anyone else.' She shot Ben a blithe smile and I hid my own. Maybe she had heard him after all.

'Ok, now, it's time to bake.'

Fiona sighed. 'I should have brought a GoPro, so I could film us while we all make pastry.' She frowned, tilting her head as if she might figure out another solution.

'Do what I do,' suggested David. 'Stick your phone in your pocket and film from there.'

'That's brilliant.' Fiona switched on her phone and stuffed it into the top of her apron, swinging her chest around to capture us all.

'You look a bit like a Dalek,' said Ben, watching her jerky movements as the rest of us started to laugh.

'I will film you. I will film you.' Fiona lurched around the table.

It took a while for us all to calm down and start following Eva's instructions although she didn't seem to mind. In the meantime, Ben had slipped outside again with his phone.

'Tip the butter, sugar, yeast and milk into the bowl and mix. Yes, Avril you do need to get your hands dirty.' Eva's final instruction was given with a gentle reproving smile which brought a very delicate pink blush to Avril's face.

I looked out of the window. Ben was still out there on his phone but he looked up and caught my eye.

I nodded my head towards the table in a not so subtle 'you need to get in here' gesture. The cheeky sod simply smiled and then turned his back on me.

What would he do if I marched out, grabbed his phone

and rammed it down his throat, apart from choke of course? He really brought the worst out in me.

He finally deigned to return by which time everyone else was already kneading their dough.

'I'll watch,' he said coming to stand next to me. He peered at the bowls arranged in front of us from a safe distance, like a commuter standing behind the lines on the platform.

'For goodness sake, stop being a big girl's blouse and get stuck in,' I said and grabbed the bowls of pre-weighed ingredients and tipped them into the main bowl, handing him a whisk.

With a sniff, he rolled up his shirt sleeves and took the whisk from me.

'Ben, what does *hygge* mean to you?' Eva asked.

Ben stopped stirring his mix and looked at her, his pose on the defensive side.

Ooh, I liked her. Straight for the jugular.

He met her gaze head on. 'No disrespect, but I think it's a fad, if I'm honest. Clever marketing. I get the cosy stuff, styling your house, making it look nice with candles and stuff. But it's just an interior design trend.'

Eva nodded, smiling but non-committal, like one of the cool teachers in school. 'Anyone else? Here like this,' she paused to help Fiona, whose dough was making a bid to escape over the edge of the table. 'Don't be scared of the dough. It needs a good work out.' She held up her biceps. 'Pastry making keeps you fit.

'It's very difficult to explain *hygge* to someone who hasn't experienced the long dark winter months of Scandinavia and it has a lot to do with our national psyche. As a nation, we love our design and it's not limited to certain sections of the population, class, education or wealth. Every Dane knows the names of Arne Jacobsen, Paul Henningsen, Hans Wegner.'

Conrad nodded. 'Chairs, lights, architecture. Some of their designs date from the sixties and still look fresh today.'

'Exactly and that is reflected in our homes. In England, you say an Englishman's home is his castle, here the home is a haven of *hygge*. We spend a lot of time inside in the winter months and so over the years, our homes have become a place to create special times, look after yourself and others. To entertain people you care about. Your friends and family. An evening can start at six and go on until at least one o'clock in the morning.'

Sophie said something to Fiona and David about cooking, so missed Avril's plaintive comment, 'That would be no good for me. I have to be up for breakfast TV. That would play havoc with my schedule. My husband is always complaining about the state of our house. I'm the messiest person on the planet. He never used to mind.'

'Perhaps you need to give it and I'm thinking, him, a bit more attention.'

The others were busy chatting and missed Eva's gently spoken observation. Avril looked slightly taken aback but it was impossible for her to take offence as Eva's words held no hint of judgement.

Eva scooted around everyone supervising their technique. It was hard work as I discovered when I took over from Ben.

'This is very good exercise and I often think it's a good way to get rid of any bad feelings you might have.'

Sophie laughed. As a veteran baker, she'd immediately got into the proper rhythm and wasn't rubbing pitifully at her arms like the rest of us. 'I quite often imagine my boss, she's an absolute dragon. Oops I shouldn't have said that.'

Everyone laughed.

After everyone had kneaded to Eva's stringent satisfaction, we were allowed to sit down while the dough proved for a well-earned coffee.

'So Eva, why is Denmark the happiest place?' asked Ben, his journalist hat well and truly in place.

'Work here in Denmark is very different to the UK. On average Danes work thirty-five hours a week and finish in time to pick up the children from school.'

'Sounds cushy,' said Avril. 'I can't imagine that going down terribly well in my office and we're all women.' She paused before adding, 'Having children might as well be career suicide.'

'Here there is no badge of honour to be gained for working long hours.' She looked at me. 'Or for constantly checking your emails after hours or when you are away from work.'

It was all very well for her to say that. Running a café didn't bring with it the same sorts of stresses and strains of an office based job but then again it didn't have the same prestige or career opportunities.

As if she read my mind, she added, 'In Denmark everyone is very equal. What you do as a job isn't so important.'

'But you have very high taxes,' said Ben.

'Yes, but everyone does, whether you are the man who works in a shop or the boss of a big company. And people are well paid for the work they do. Everyone has the same chances because there is a good support system for all. Health and education are free. We have the lowest divide between rich and poor in Europe.'

After twenty minutes of lively debate, comparing the utopian Denmark, Eva turned her attention back to the cooking and we put our aprons back on and went back to work.

'Now I will show the secret of light airy crisp pastries. Come.'

She rolled the proven dough out and then took a large piece of butter and dipped it into flour and then with her quick precise economic movements, showed us how to roll butter between sheets of greaseproof paper.

'Now, it is your turn.'

'I think I'll duck out, if you don't mind,' said Conrad. 'I'm worn out already. Food's not my thing.'

'Oh, but you've got to give it a go, now you're here,' said Sophie.

'Never too late to learn,' David chipped in. 'And home-cooking can save you a fortune. Much cheaper to make things from scratch.'

Conrad's face sharpened with sudden interest and he gave a reluctant smile.

'Go on, then, I'll give it a whirl.'

I looked at Ben. 'You can go first.' I handed over the rolling pin. He took it dubiously, which made me say, 'You have used one before, I take it.'

'Not since food tech,' he muttered. 'And that was a while ago.'

He wasn't the only one but I certainly wasn't about to admit it to him.

Across the way, Sophie was already expertly wielding her rolling pin, explaining to Fiona the best technique.

Greaseproof paper rustled and the wooden rolling bins banged on the table, as Eva wandered around tweaking people's hold on their utensils, with quiet words of encouragement.

Ben's brow furrowed in concentration and his tongue glued itself to his upper lip, which made him seem a lot more human, as he set to trying to master the rolling technique.

'David that's excellent,' said Eva, pointing out his even and well-shaped butter pat.

'Thank you. I do quite a bit of baking at home,' he admitted shyly. 'It's a good way to pass a few hours and you have something at the end of it. Although,' he paused, 'it would be nice to have someone to share it with.'

'I used to be quite a baker. My sponges were as light as anything. Before me and my husband were married,' said Avril crisply cutting over his words, brushing flour from her apron, and surveying her neat results. I realised she was fiercely competitive. 'He loves cakes.' She looked wistful. 'Coffee and walnut's his favourite. I haven't made that in ages.'

After five minutes Eva stopped us all and everyone showed their progress. Sophie and Fiona's butter was perfectly shaped in a long flat oval, along with David's who looked rather pleased with himself. For someone who professed not to be interested in food, Conrad's like Avril's, was also surprisingly neat.

'Oh dear,' laughed Eva when she came around to our side of the table. Ben's floured butter looked rather like a map of Denmark, jagged edges with various islands adrift from each other and rather sticky and squashed.

He winced. 'Hmm, not sure what I've done wrong.'

'Not feeling the love, perhaps,' I quipped and received a glare from him.

'You've over rolled it,' explained Eva, pushing the butter smeared greaseproof paper aside. 'Made it too warm, so the butter is melting too much. Your mind wasn't quite on it. With cooking you need to focus on the job in hand. Leave the work behind and stop worrying about those emails. Let's start again. You can join in this time, Katie.'

'Oh, it's OK. I don't need to.'

'Yes, you do,' said Eva firmly, pushing her rolling pin into my hand and explaining again what we needed to do.

Ben shot me a triumphant grin and I glared at him.

'Both of you, off you go.'

'Yes, Miss,' teased Ben as she walked off to supervise the others.

Damn. I grabbed my pat of butter feeling stupidly self-conscious; everyone else had made it look easy. Grabbing the butter and sprinkling flour half-heartedly over it, I set to work quickly. It wasn't as if I was ever going to make this again. Bugger, it was harder than it looked. The butter massed up into one lump and then when I tried to roll it, it squished away.

'I think you need more flour,' observed Ben gleefully.

I pursed my lips and ignored him. What did he know?

I set to again but my butter was beyond help.

'Not feeling the love either,' said Ben with a sly grin when he saw my mangled butter.

'It's harder than it looks,' I muttered, flushing. I hated not getting it right.

'Don't worry,' sympathised Ben, 'I'm sure your talents lie elsewhere.'

I gave him a sharp look but he seemed genuine and I softened, saying with uncharacteristic weakness, 'Hmm, I'm not so sure about that.' I stared down at the table, suddenly conscious of his nearness and a sense of disorientation. What was I good at? Work? That didn't say much about me. Fiona had her photography. Avril had a husband, who clearly doted on her, as well as an amazing career. Sophie had a passion for food. Conrad had his reputation and knowledge.

Eva showed us how to roll the layers of butter between the dough and shape the finished pastries and by the end of the demonstration, there were several trays of *spandauer*, dotted with strawberry jam, ready to bake.

We sat down at the tables with coffee as she whisked about tidying up, Sophie assisting her. Sophie didn't seem to be able to sit down for any length of time.

'It's been a wonderful morning,' said David looking round at the group. 'I spend so much time on my own.' I saw his Adam's apple dip. 'I-It's nice to be ... with everyone. I have to admit, I do get very lonely.'

'Oh, David.' Sophie laid a hand on his arm. 'I know what

it's like. Before I met James, I felt like that. You can be surrounded by people but invisible, especially in London.'

'Well, you know how it is with freelancing. With the Internet and email, you don't need to go out as much and meet people. You can get everything online. My editor communicates by email.'

'What about family?' asked Sophie.

'I moved away from Cumbria years ago. My sister and dad live up there. I see them at Christmas but I put everything into my career. Came to London. Worked. Moved around.'

'But what about friends?' Sophie persisted. 'You seem a pretty personable bloke to me. No halitosis, dodgy geography teacher clothes or obvious unseemly habits.'

David crossed his legs. 'Yeah, I've got friends. Plenty of them but it's not the same. Most of them have families. Other priorities. Busy at weekends with their own things. You wake up one morning and everyone else has moved on.' He took his glasses off and turned them over in his hands. 'God, I didn't mean to say any of this stuff. I think you've given us truth serum, Eva.' He shot her a grateful look which she returned with a sympathetic smile. 'There are only so many art galleries and museums you can visit on your own. You go out for the sake of it. Just to get out. I shouldn't complain I've got my own house, a big one, but I rattle around on my own in it. It was my mother's but she died several years ago. I have to force myself to go out for a walk otherwise I might not leave for days.'

'Lucky you, old chap,' said Conrad in his gravelly smoke-roughened voice. 'After three wives, I've been taken to the cleaners. I'm renting a bedsit in Clapham, the arse end of Clapham at that. Through the keyhole, it ain't. You can take me out to lunch any time you like,' he said. 'I always thought I'd be glad of the peace and quiet, but I can't stand being on my own and my place is a bit cramped, so not that conducive to having visitors.'

'I'm in Clapham too,' said David.

'Well plenty of fine watering holes in the area and we don't even need to get a cab home,' said Conrad. 'Talking of which, what time is lunch? And is it time for a drink yet?'

'Why don't you take a lodger, David?' suggested Eva.

'I've never thought of that. I don't need the money, so it didn't occur to me.'

'Don't need the money!' muttered Conrad into his coffee.

I ducked my head and smiled, feeling just a little bit pleased; this session in the café, that in truth I'd been a little bit sceptical about, had really brought everyone closer together. Even Ben had joined in properly for once.

The morning was rounded off when the *spandauer* came out of the oven and there was much hilarity at the results, with some very misshapen pastries. Ben and I shared a chagrined smile, ours were the worst, Sophie's were perfect and Avril's very good. She smiled and took lots of pictures, immediately posting one on Twitter.

Look what we made. #WonderfulCopenhagen #presstripantics

'I'm going to WhatsApp these to my husband. Prove to him I can still cook and that I'm not so high maintenance after all.' Her words held a poignant mix of defiance and petulance.

'I'm going to use this recipe in the magazine,' said Sophie.

'I'm going to put the pictures up on my blog,' said Fiona and with a sudden grin she added, 'And I'll be naming names.'

'Good God, dear girl. Do you want to ruin my reputation?' teased Conrad, although he looked rather pleased with his results and picked up his tray of pastries posing for her as she snapped off a couple of shots. 'I guess it might add to my debonair man about town image. Impress a few ladies.'

'I'm sure they will be, they look great,' said Fiona, showing him the pictures she'd taken. 'David, you next.'

She seemed to be revelling in her new role as official photographer.

Conrad peered at them. 'Excellent work. Thank you, young lady.' Fiona nodded with quiet pleasure. It was rather like watching a bud unfurling in the sun.

'Take one of me,' said Avril, with a perfect Instagram pout.

'Brilliant as your pictures are,' said Ben dryly, 'I'd rather not be seen posing with pastries, I'll never live it down in the office. I got enough stick as it was abandoning my post for a week's jolly.' For once the look he shot me was much less hostile, you could almost imagine he was enjoying himself.

Mads appeared bang on the dot of twelve-thirty, after we'd all eaten some of Eva's home-made fish soup and whole-grain rolls, scooping us up in readiness for our next trip.

'Right everyone it's a short walk to our very fine Kopvahn Station, where we will take a train to Helsingor. Or as you may know it Elsinore. Kronberg Castle, the home of Hamlet.'

'I've been so looking forward to this,' said Fiona and then

stopped, as if she'd startled herself by volunteering this piece of information. With her customary blush, she ducked her head mumbling. 'I love Shakespeare. And *Hamlet*.'

'No disrespect to the bard and all that but I'm going to duck out,' announced Ben. 'Work has called; I need to get an article finished.'

'Is it far?' asked Avril, now looking uncertain. 'What time will we be back? I don't want to have to rush this evening when we go out again.'

'It's forty-five minutes on the train,' said Eva firmly. 'And you'll be back by five-thirty.'

I was grateful to Eva and while she was extoling the virtues of the visit to the others, I took Ben to one side.

'I appreciate you have work to do, but ...' I could relate as I had a ton of stuff building up too.

'This is pure tourist stuff. It'll be background material at most.'

'Yes, but if you don't come, how's it going to look to everyone else?' The brief glimpse of a slightly different Ben the previous night, made me think I might appeal to his better nature.

'That's not my problem.'

'If they all start playing hooky, it will make my life very difficult.'

His grin was without any hint of malice but no apology either. 'You should have thought about that before you coerced me into the trip. Presumably they were all willing victims.'

I smiled back, 'You mean they saw the opportunities this trip offered.'

Suddenly stern, his eyebrows drawn together like two angry

slashes, he looked down his nose at me, 'They don't write serious pieces.'

I stepped back, feeling his annoyance, our brief accord dashed away.

'Oh, come on, your article is as likely as anyone else's to end up wrapped around a portion of chips.'

'So says the PR girl desperate for coverage.'

'I'm not desperate,' I hissed. I didn't like the way he made me sound.

With a brief twist of his lips he made his scepticism clear. 'Whatever I write, it's what I've chosen to write. Not told to do. Fish and chip wrapper or not, I aim to inform and enlighten.'

'And your information is better than anyone else's?' I asked sarcastically.

Anger flashed on his face. 'You and Dawkins are quite a pair, aren't you?' His eyes narrowed with dislike.

A flicker of shame twisted my stomach. I wasn't that bad. Just getting the job done. 'I don't know why you keep on about him. I only met him briefly.'

'I'm sure there was enough time for him to tell you all about my fall from grace.' His words echoed with bitterness and his jaw clamped with sharp edged defiance.

Before I could respond, Mads tapped my elbow, indicating we needed to leave.

Luckily no one else had decided to follow Ben's lead, as he peeled off from the group towards the hotel to an echo of cheery goodbyes, and the rest of us walked the short distance to the central station.

Chapter 13

The next morning we met in the hotel lobby, waiting ten minutes for Avril before she finally arrived, clicking across the tiled floor in stylish suede high-heeled ankle boots. With her long dark glossy hair and immaculate make-up, she was rocking the super model about to jet off somewhere exotic look as opposed to a canal boat trip.

'Excellent, everyone is here,' said Mads, seemingly not the least bit bothered about Avril's late arrival. 'Now we have a guided boat trip from Nyhaven, the famous harbour area, a two-minute walk from here.'

'A boat trip?' Avril sounded horrified. Hadn't she read the itinerary? 'Will we be warm enough? It'll be cold on the water.'

'The boats have very good heating on them,' said Mads with his usual reassuring smile.

'I can't bear being cold. I need a scarf. I have a cashmere one in my room.' With that she tripped across the reception back to the lift. I pointedly looked at my watch, which was completely wasted as she was long gone.

By the time Avril had returned, swathed in the most beautiful Cashmere wrap, David and Conrad had wandered to the other end of the street and Fiona was nowhere to be seen. I was wondering how many days into the trip it would be before I succumbed to a nervous breakdown or bought leads for everyone. It took another ten minutes to round everyone up before we finally set off.

Even Avril who stumbled and tripped on the cobbles along the route, complaining frequently, asking how much further it was with the petulance of a teenager being dragged out for a country walk, was silenced by the picturesque scene of Nyhaven.

The waterfront teemed with colour and life, the facades of the buildings painted in blues, reds, oranges and yellows while the pavement cafés were full of people sitting outside under outdoor heaters sipping at coffees. Tall-masted fishing boats edged the canal, the smell of fish and tar permeating the air, while the lines on the masts of the boats clinked rhythmically in the brisk sea breeze along with the plentiful Danish flags which fluttered and flapped furiously.

Of course, we'd missed the boat we'd intended to catch, what with Avril and her heels, and dreamy, head in the clouds Fiona, who with her ever-present camera was in her element, snapping away at everything. It was difficult to get cross with her when you could see the shy smile of delight on her face at every turn.

The weak spring sunshine lit up the buildings and the tall green topped towers of churches giving everything a warm fairy-tale glow but didn't dispel the chill of a brisk wind coming from the water. I was grateful for my new down jacket which was much warmer than its flimsy weight first suggested. I snuggled into it, wrapping my scarf tighter and burrowing my nose into it. With Mads in charge, I was free to bring up the rear and enjoy the scenery.

We went down a flight of steps to the ticket kiosk and the short queue was despatched with quick Danish efficiency, leaving us plenty of time to walk around to the boat bobbing in the water waiting for us. There were already a few people on board sitting underneath the curved glass roof.

'Right,' said Mads, handing out the tickets. 'I shall meet you here in one hour. There is a guide on the boat.'

'Right,' I said doubtfully.

I waited as the others filed onto the boat.

'Don't worry, Kate. You will be fine on your own. You don't need me. I will be back in one hour. I have some things to arrange for tomorrow.'

He was right of course. It didn't need two of us. On board the boat, everyone would be together with no chance to wander off and, unless someone fell overboard, which in these boats was highly unlikely, nothing could go wrong and I could relax for the next hour and enjoy the scenery.

Sophie led the way, striding across the small gap between the jetty and the boat and nimbly skipping down the stairs into the boat, followed by David and Conrad. Avril paused at the top, like a horse baulking at a jump, tossing her hair over her shoulder.

'Here,' Ben went down the stairs, waiting at the bottom for her, holding out his hands to guide her down.

'My hero,' she said, flashing him one of her zillion kilowatt smiles, which could have brought an army to its knees. Ben was no exception, his eyes widened and his hands slipped to her waist to lift her down from the last step. She whispered something to him with a low husky laugh and then sauntered off, hips swinging, down the gangway.

As I took the top of the steps, he looked up at me, raising his eyebrows.

'I don't suppose you need a hand, do you?'

'No, of course not,' I said sharply ignoring the unfavourable comparison with Avril. She was the sort of woman men looked after. He waited at the bottom as I passed by and offered the same courtesy to Fiona lurking at the back as usual.

The others had all opted for the seats at the rear of the boat, out in the open.

'This is perfect,' said Fiona and then put her hand across her mouth at the uncharacteristic outburst, coloured bright red and plumped down into the nearest seat. Ben came down the gangway, looked at me and then Fiona, and with a twist of his mouth he stopped, surveyed the two spare seats and with an abrupt turn took a step back and sat down next to Fiona.

The boat sat low in the water and high above us on the wooden canal sides, people sat with their legs dangling over the edge, chatting to each other, taking pictures and generally watching the world go by. With the colourful buildings as a backdrop behind them and everyone so relaxed, some waving down at the canal boats, drinks in hand, there was a festive air as if everyone were on holiday today.

For some reason, it made me smile and I tilted my face up to the sun, I was going to ignore Benedict Johnson and be grateful that today he'd turned up. For the next hour, I could pretend I was on holiday and with everyone confined to the boat, I couldn't lose anyone. It was a relief to have them all in one place.

Avril leaned down and rubbed at her feet before saying, 'Honestly someone could have warned us there'd be walking.'

Sophie, next to me, rolled her eyes and smiled without any sign of malice. 'Avril, those boots are fab but seriously what were you thinking?'

'Well how was I to know the place was full of bloody cobbles? It's the twenty-first century for goodness sake; you'd have thought they'd have proper roads by now. There's quaint and there's bloody uncivilised. Denmark is supposed to be a haven of design style. How do Danish women cope? Thank goodness I went back for this.' She tossed the stylish, gossamer weight cashmere scarf over her shoulder, where it flowed in loose, soft undulating folds down her back.

The boat dipped and bobbed as the engine revved and pulled away from the harbour side, doing a many pointed turn in the canal before chugging along the picturesque water-front. At the front a tall gangly teenager with a chin full of scruffy blonde bum-fluff stood up and took the microphone. He didn't look old enough to buy a pint, let alone take a tour out, but his introductory spiel, in English, Danish, Italian and German, soon had me changing my initial impression, this wasn't the Saturday boy that had been drafted in.

'Please remember to stay inside the boat. The bridges are

very low. Now here we start our journey. In the eighteenth century these buildings were brothels and pubs and merchant houses.'

Obediently we all turned to look at the jewel bright buildings above us, the classic image of Copenhagen, which made everyone get their phones and cameras out to take pictures. Although the green, blue, yellow and ochre painted buildings were of different heights and widths, there was neat uniformity about them giving them the spit and polish of soldiers on parade.

At the end of the canal, the boar swung out past the Royal Danish Playhouse, an imposing contemporary structure, into a much wider channel crossing the open water with a long slow lazy turn. Out here the water was choppier, but the boat glided smoothly through as the guide pointed out Paper Island, with its art centre and shipping container street food. The old industrial newspaper buildings weren't the prettiest but in typical Danish recycling fashion, it had been transformed with an open area at the front full of modern deck chairs and people soaking up the spring sunshine. Even at this distance across the water you could sense a buzz and exciting vibe about the place.

'That's where you get the best street food in Copenhagen,' said Sophie. 'I'm trying to work out when I can go there.'

'The hotel has free bicycles,' I suggested. 'You could cycle here from the hotel.'

'Oh Lordy, you're not getting me on a bike,' drawled Avril.

'Nor me,' said Conrad. 'Don't worry lovie, you can prop a bar up with me instead.'

'Now that sounds like a plan.'

'I think cycling would be fun,' said Sophie, smiling as usual at them. 'Hmm, I wonder when I can do that.'

In my head, I gave the itinerary a quick assessment, it had been deliberately planned with plenty of free time so that the journalists had some time to themselves to explore the city and to get a feel for the Danish way of life.

There was a rustle on board, as everyone turned to look at the striking Royal Opera House. Dominating the bank, it stood like some modern-day juggernaut in stark contrast to the pretty buildings of Nyhaven. A huge steel cantilevered roof reached out towards the water defying gravity, with majestic arrogance which was softened by the beehive curve of glass below. Through the vast glass frontage, the guide pointed out the three light sculpture created by some famous sculptor. Even at this distance their artistry shone. As the young man described the gold leaf ceiling and the details of the interior materials, it was clear that this was a country with a deep and resonating pride in all its art and design.

'Have you been to Copenhagen before?' Benedict asked Fiona, who'd been busy taking lots of pictures of the Opera House.

'No.'

Her prickly response, effectively shutting down his attempt at conversation made me smile in sympathy but I'd underestimated him.

'What gave you the idea for your blog, *Hanning's Half Hour?*' He'd turned to Fiona again. I admired his fortitude. 'It's a neat title,' he added, as gently as a vet dealing with a nervous kitten.

His touch could be equally gentle, I remembered with a discreet shiver.

'T-thank you.' She ducked her head, stroking the edge of the lens of her camera as the boat slowed, the tick of the engine dropping to a dull throb as it bobbed on the water near the bank offering a sea view of the Little Mermaid statue.

Fiona stood to take a picture of the back of the Little Mermaid, swaying precariously, tutting and muttering as she viewed the image. Angling the camera again, she tried another shot falling back against Ben's legs before swaying forward again. He lifted a hand and steadied her.

'We don't want you falling in.'

She blushed furiously. 'Thank you.'

'That's OK.' A sudden attractive smile lit up his face, one I remembered well. 'Tell you what, can you take a couple of pictures for me as we go back? The Opera House is a good story. Big business being altruistic or a massive tax dodge. The funding to build it was quite controversial. I could do with a couple of decent pics. Would you mind?'

'No.' Fiona gave him, what I think was her best shot at a smile, 'that's fine.' She fired off another couple of quick photos and seemed pleased with the results when she sat down to review the images.

'That's a pretty fearsome looking camera. You look like you know what you're doing with it,' said Ben, his voice had gentled when he spoke to her and I noticed he kept an unthreatening distance.

'It's a Nikon D500. Ten frames per second.' She ran on for a couple of minutes spouting technical information that meant absolutely nothing to me or I suspected to him, but he nodded the whole time. It was the most I'd heard her say and it was fascinating to see her blossom, talking so authoritatively about photography.

Bloody Ben Johnson intrigued me. Despite his protests that he didn't want to be here, I'd been watching him out of the corner of my eye for the last ten minutes and he seemed to be fascinated with everything the guide said. Where was the mad fox who barked down the phone at me? This man, listening carefully to the guide, those sharp intelligent eyes taking in the sights, his face animated and thoughtful by turn, reminded me far too much of the Ben at the awards night and that brief unnerving connection between us. The one I'd turned tail and run from.

The boat turned from the open water, where the sea air, tangy with salt, buffeted us into the shelter of a canal which ran down the centre of a quiet residential street lined with gabled houses. It felt rather like Amsterdam, which the guide told us was the inspiration behind the architecture.

'Now we are coming to St Saviour's Church, this is one of the most beautiful churches in Copenhagen with its famous spire and external staircase. You can see it through here.'

Everyone craned forward to catch a glimpse of the church and its black and gold spiral staircase winding up the outside of the tower.

'Please sit down at the back.' The guide's voice over the microphone held a touch of weary repetition, making me wonder if any tourists had ever been decapitated en-route. 'There's a low bridge coming up.'

A few daring souls desperate to capture the elusive glimpses of the church through the buildings hung on til the last minute, including one Italian gentleman who'd been reprimanded several times for not sitting down as instructed. You could tell the guide was getting quite fed up with him, as was his daughter, who was now nudging him with embarrassment.

Despite the shelter of the street, a sudden fierce gust of wind funnelled down the canal, snatching at Avril's scarf tossing it upwards, billowing into the air like a spinnaker and enveloping her head. The gossamer light fabric moulded to her face like an ancient death mask. In sudden blind panic, she stood with flailing hands, to try and grasp it but the wind mischievously took hold tossing it higher in the air like a spiral of smoke whipping the ends further from her grasp.

'Avril, sit down. Sit down,' yelled Ben as the shadow of the bridge loomed over us, a slow inevitable foreshadowing of incipient menace.

'My scarf. My scarf,' shrilled Avril, her back to the danger as she reached again to rescue the fabric flapping and rippling like a flag. As the wind gave one last playful gust and tore it away, she lunged to her feet, her hands reaching vacantly into the air.

'*Sid ned. Sid ned. Sit down. Sit down. Hinsetzen. Siediti.*' The urgent voice of the guide was doubly amplified by the microphone and a chorus of support from the other passengers. Cries of alarm echoed, bouncing back from the walls of the bridge.

With that awful slow-motion, horror-film inevitability the

stone arch of the bridge loomed behind her. Around me I heard horrified gasps and I tried to move my frozen feet.

There was a sudden blur of movement. Avril screamed and dropped to the floor.

Ben's lightning reaction, hurling himself across two seats, felling her with a rugby tackle just as the boat slid out of the sunlight, had brought her down. Somehow at the same time David had managed to catch the scarf and held it gingerly like a trophy he didn't know what to do with.

The tour guide yelled and the engine cut out leaving the boat bobbing under the bridge and a shocked silence.

Avril lay motionless, face down on the floor, a vivid red pool already crowning her dark glossy hair, the bright scarlet stark in contrast.

I knelt down next to her, almost too scared to touch her, gulping in a breath as a hot flush followed by ice cold swept over me. Shit. The weight of responsibility almost floored me.

I needed to do something. Take action, instead of standing there helplessly looking useless.

I reached out a shaky hand towards her shoulder. I could see from the gentle movement of her back that she was breathing. 'Avril.'

Ben came to kneel next to me and to my surprise put his hand over mine, giving it a quick squeeze as he whispered, 'I thought I reached her in time.' He bit his lip, his eyes full of worry.

I squeezed his hand back. He'd been amazing. 'You did. She bumped her head on the seat on the way down.'

143

With a gentle hand, I touched her shoulder. 'Avril. Can you hear me?' I felt her body tremor beneath my fingers.

She gave a muffled faint groan while the guide stood over us looking terrified and equally useless under the nakedly curious gaze of the other passengers.

'She's conscious,' I muttered to Ben, our heads so close together I could see a couple of beads of sweat on his forehead. 'That's a good sign ... I think.'

'Yes,' he whispered back. 'What do we do now?'

We exchanged a wry oh-shit-we're-left-holding-the-baby-now look.

'Stop the bleeding, I think,' I said aware of the sticky seep of blood through the knee of my jeans. 'And find out where she's bleeding and how bad it is.'

'Good plan.' His approving nod gave me a much-needed confidence boost.

Ben shielded me from the watchful gaze of the others as with tentative fingers I pushed through Avril's hair. No lumps or bumps.

With a groan she rolled onto her side, blinking up at us, confusion clouding her eyes.

'Stay still, Avril,' I said, immediately spotting the gash to the left of her forehead running into her hairline, bleeding profusely.

I dug into my bag and grabbed a travel pack of tissues, wadding them and pressing them against the wound.

She winced and closed her eyes. 'It hurts like hell.'

I took her hand. 'You're OK. Everything's going to be fine.'

Somehow the words reassured her which was just as well

because I hadn't a bloody clue. And then a slice of knowledge popped helpfully into my head.

'Head wounds bleed a lot. They always look a lot worse than they are,' I said it loudly hoping that it would reassure everyone including Avril.

'However, we do need to stop the,' I nodded to the gash, speaking to Ben in a low voice sounding like an extra in *Casualty* stating the bleeding obvious. Thankfully he nodded. The tissue wad had soaked through, the deep red darkening quickly.

Sophie was already on the case rounding up clean tissues from everyone and Conrad came up trumps, handing over two clean and pressed handkerchiefs.

I put them together, removed the tissues and pressed the clean hankies to her head.

We'd drawn quite a crowd by now, as the captain and the tour guide and a couple of other tourists stood watching. I asked Sophie to take over and went to speak to him.

Ben and I watched from the canal-side as the boat pulled away, Sophie giving us a little wave and a grimace of support as the rest of the passengers eyed us and whispered to each other. Avril sat on a bench sandwiched between us, Ben's arm around her holding her up. Sophie's wool scarf was wrapped around her head, holding my wadded-up scarf in place, Conrad's blood-soaked handkerchiefs having long since been cast aside.

I would have faced torture before admitting it, but I'd never been so relieved in my life at Ben's suggestion that he wait with me for Eva, who was on her way in a taxi.

Once we'd realised that Avril needed proper medical attention, I'd phoned Eva from the boat and she'd spoken to the boat's pilot who had agreed that the best solution was to get us off the boat. The plan was to take Avril to Eva's local doctor where they would be able to assess the damage.

'Do you want me to call anyone for you?' I asked Avril after looking at my watch for the ninety-fifth time. Eva had said ten minutes but it was turning into the longest ten minutes of my life.

Avril, understandably subdued, had barely spoken since the accident but I was so worried she might have concussion; I needed her to keep responding as much to reassure myself as to keep her conscious. With a dismissive pout, she lifted her chin and shook her head, immediately wincing.

'No, there's no point.' Her lips thinned. 'Christopher will be at work. There's no point bothering him.'

'But wouldn't he want to know?' I asked. Wasn't that the point of being married? Having someone else to worry about you, care about you.

'No,' she said pulling up her handbag, pathetically poking into it, until she found a mirror.

'I'm not sure you want to do that,' I said, trying to ease it from her fingers. 'Seriously.'

She clung on with limpet fingers, flicking it open. 'My God, what do I look like?' She opened another zipped compartment, revealing a slim leather bag from which she pulled out a lip pencil and two gold cased lipsticks, some expensive make I couldn't begin to hazard a guess at, before checking the colours and deciding which one would light up her ghostly pallor. With careful, expert strokes, she took her time outlining her lips, wincing with every movement of her head, but kept going before applying a bold red, glossy finish, much to the horrified fascination of Ben.

He caught my eye and raised one eyebrow as if to say *seriously?*

With a frown, he got up and pushed his hands in his pockets standing awkwardly.

My heart went out to her. I knew what her painstaking make-up routine hid. It wasn't about the lipstick or gloss – it was psychological armour, designed to help her deal with a situation that made her feel alone and vulnerable.

When I put my arm around her, to my surprise she leaned in putting her head on my shoulder. I gave her a squeeze and prayed the cavalry would get here soon.

Chapter 14

Thanks to Eva phoning her doctor in advance, she and Avril were whisked straight in as soon as we arrived, leaving Ben and I in the empty waiting room. We sank into seats looking around at the clean white modern room. Even the chairs were stylish and comfortable. A far cry from the functional, bottom numbing ones of the surgery at home which was always full and you had to wait hours to see anyone.

'She seems nice,' said Ben, filling the sudden awkward silence.

'Mmm,' I said.

'Yes, very motherly.'

'Thank God I had her number.' I slumped in my seat, exhaustion seeping into every muscle, the adrenaline hangover leaving me wrung out.

'Hmm, not quite what you were expecting.'

'You can say that again.' I sighed thinking how close to disaster we'd come. 'It doesn't bear thinking about.' I put my head in my hands. 'Shit. Can you imagine? Journalist decapitated in Copenhagen.'

'Yeah imagine the headlines. Not quite what you were after.'

I looked up at him sharply.

'Sorry,' he grimaced and put out a hand to touch my forearm, 'I honestly didn't mean it like that.'

I wilted back into my seat, closing my eyes, feeling sick all over again. It could all have been so much worse. 'Oh God.'

'Hey, are you OK?' He leaned over me, his eyes narrowed with concern and for a moment I was transfixed by the unusual colouring of dark brown copper tipped lashes framing those blue grey eyes. I ducked away from his gaze feeling a pony kick to my ribs slam of attraction. I sucked in a quick silent breath as his hand slid down my forearm, the hairs bristling to ticklish attention as his warm fingers skimmed inch by inch, before coming to rest on top of mine. I fought the urge to turn it palm up and lace my fingers into his, ignored the beguiling siren suggestion that I could let everything go and let someone else take care of me for a change.

'No. Yes. I don't know.' I looked up at him, into guileless eyes and bit my lip, all my fears suddenly crowding in. 'I don't think I'm cut out for this, after all.'

'What super PR girl?' His mouth quirked and he squeezed my hand. 'Of course you are. All in a day's work.'

'You've been talking to my friend Connie,' I said suddenly wishing she were here. 'She says things like that.'

'Do you organise her too?'

With a shaky half laugh, I said, 'God no, she's a primary school teacher. Organisation is printed all the way through her like a stick of rock. She wouldn't have let something like that happen on her watch.'

'I've come to realise that when dealing with children you have to have finely honed skills, octopus genetics and eyes in the back of your head. You couldn't possibly have predicted that would happen. Avril's an adult. Admittedly of the princess variety, so maybe the child thing should have applied, but you handled it.'

His soothing words carried a reassuring thread of quiet warm approval, like sunshine breaking through clouds on a grey day.

'We handled it. You were really helpful. Thank you for staying with me.'

'I didn't do much.' He shrugged, lifting broad shoulders in a dismissive gesture, but he'd done more than he realised.

'Moral support goes a long way, when you don't know what the hell you're doing.'

A gentle heart-tripping smile filled his face as he gave me a slow once over.

'Super PR girl admitting that.' He lifted a teasing eyebrow. 'No one would have guessed. You do cool, calm and collected well.'

'Really? Is that praise from the scary mad fox journalist?'

'Scary? Me?'

'Yes, when you bark a five second warning down the phone. At least with a nuclear threat you get a whole four minutes.'

He laughed out loud, a deep belly rumble of sheer amusement. 'You caught me at a bad moment.' His mouth quirked with wicked humour, 'And I don't like PR people.'

'I think you might have made that clear.'

'Sorry I should rephrase that. I don't like PR people ... in general.' He flashed me a quick intimate just-between-the-two-of-us smile which made my heart get all silly and do some strange miss a beat thing.

'Gosh. Should I get out the flags?'

'Bit soon for that,' he teased, mischief and amusement dancing in his eyes. 'But I know plenty of people who would have wailed and screamed and made a drama out of the situation and wait for someone else to come to the rescue and scoop up the pieces. You didn't.' He looked down at the blood-stained knees of my jeans.

'Mmmn,' I wrinkled my nose looking down at the dark patches turning rusty around the edges. There was no coming back from stains like that; they were destined for the big clothing bank in the sky.

He shook his head and pushed his hands through his hair before tucking them behind his head and stretching his legs out in front of him. 'Funny, I've had so much damn drama in the last forty-eight hours and this is the most relaxed I've felt.'

'Sister still not found the stopcock?'

He laughed. 'It's not funny. Now she's finished flooding the flat below, she's complaining that I didn't have the foresight before she turned up on my doorstep with baby, and demon spawn from hell five-year-old, to child-proof my one-bedroomed flat, which coincidentally,' he adopted a falsetto, '*isn't big enough*. Apparently, these *free* lodgings are too dangerous for the children. Little Teddy, aforementioned five-year-old *Hell Boy* got out into the corridor and took himself off in the lift.'

I couldn't help it but I giggled and he raised his eyebrows. 'I'm serious.'

'Sorry, I shouldn't laugh. I don't know your sister but,' I

lifted my shoulders, 'that sounds may I say it, a tad unreasonable.'

'You mean I'm not an insensitive bastard who never thinks of anyone but himself and his collection of football trophies.'

'Well,' I wrinkled my nose as if giving it serious thought, 'Trophies, collections, you say? Ooh, yeah. That's classic insensitive bastard territory.' I suddenly grinned at him and added, 'Bloody good job you got invited for an all-expenses paid trip to Copenhagen, then.'

He laughed.

'You tell my sister, Amy, that. She thinks I've buggered off deliberately to inconvenience her.'

'And won all those trophies, don't forget.' I wagged a jokey finger at him.

He laughed again. 'I wasn't bragging or anything.'

'I didn't think you were. Blimey, if my brothers had a trophy between them I'd be celebrating. We have a life size Sith Infiltrator in the garden, not to mention the replica Tardis dashboard with working reactor core in the shed.'

'Pardon?' He looked at me as if I'd gone completely mad.

'I'm serious. My brother Brandon likes building sci-fi models. Look.'

I showed him Brandon's website, a labour of love, scrolling through the gallery of pictures of his previous projects.

'Bloody hell, that's …' he enlarged the picture on the screen, 'mental.'

'Yeah, people have said that about him before.'

'No, seriously the detail is incredible. Is he a professional model builder?'

'Is there such a thing? No, he works at a breaker's yard, salvaging cars and bringing home stuff that catches his eye they can't sell. He created this website and he has a whole following of similar weirdos, except they're not. They all seem incredibly dedicated and supportive of each other.'

'And the reactor core really works?' Was that genuine interest on his face as he looked at the replica model, not quite life-size but near enough, of the inside of the Tardis.

For a moment, I wondered if he was one of them.

'Yes, along with *Star Wars*, *Stargate* and *Star Trek*, he has a minor obsession with *Doctor Who*.' I spluttered out a laugh. 'He's actually rather clever, the console of the Tardis works in the mechanical sense as in, it goes up and down and makes that weird wheezing train on acid sort of noise, but not in the real sense that the Sinclair family have been tripping backwards and forwards to Gallifrey on their summer holidays.'

'I meant, he can do all the hydraulics and electrical stuff as well?'

'Yeah, Brandon's a genius at all that stuff and a complete numpty with absolutely everything else.' I sobered. 'He's so smart in many ways but couldn't pass an exam to save his life.' I sighed.

'Are there just the two of you?'

'No, my other brother John, he's not so smart but thinks he is. He's got the gift of the gab and about as much work ethic as a sloth on go slow. His get up and go, got up and went the minute he started secondary school. He works in Debenhams and thinks he's doing them a favour.'

'So, you're the driven one. The high achiever.'

'Thanks. Hard-nosed bitch much?'

'I didn't mean that.'

'My mum wanted us to make something of ourselves. I was the eldest, I got the lion's share of the message.' I paused, before saying matter of factly, 'Before she died. And I've no idea why I said that. You're good at this journalist thing, aren't you? Making people talk.'

His face softened and he tilted his head, considering me.

'And I'd say you're good at this PR lark, listening to people, communicating.'

For some bizarre reason, I turned pink and had to look away.

Luckily Eva returned bringing with her a very pale Avril, who despite everything, managed to appear ethereal and glamorous. Her hair was damp where they'd obviously sponged away all the blood but somehow she'd escaped any bloody stains leaving only me looking like I'd been in a fight.

I jumped up.

'How are you feeling?'

Avril gave me a wan smile. 'Sore.' She touched her temple. 'Proper war wound. Five stitches.' Her eyes sparkled with some of the haughty princess I was used to. 'Dishy doctor though.'

'Avril!' I bit back a laugh.

'He was.' We exchanged a rare conspiratorial grin. 'All Viking and blonde with very gentle hands. Made me feel all woman.'

And then she burst into tears.

Chapter 15

Looking small and rather defenceless, Avril huddled in one of the leather chairs in Varme, clutching her cup of coffee. She'd only just stopped crying which seemed to frighten her as much as it surprised me. Super-princesses like Avril didn't cry proper tears or dissolve into heart-breaking sobs or so I'd assumed.

Ben beat a hasty retreat and had gone back to the hotel to update everyone else while Eva had once again swooped in and took us around the corner where to my horror she unlocked the door to the coffee shop. Bless her, she'd shut up shop to come and rescue us.

'I'm s-sorry.' Avril sniffed. Without her usual confident attitude, she seemed like an uncertain teenager.

'Don't worry,' said Eva, leaning over and patting her hand. 'You need a good cry, I think.'

'I-I never c-cry.' As soon as she said it, she dissolved into fresh sobs.

Eva and I exchanged quick frowns and then she moved her chair next to Avril's and pulled her close in a hug. I sat watching, feeling a little awkward at witnessing her vulnerability.

Eventually her sobs subsided and she wiped at her face now streaked with mascara.

'Oh God, what must I look like.' Eva jumped up and grabbed a handful of napkins which Avril took, wiping her eyes with sudden angry strokes. 'I'm a mess.'

'Avril, you could never look a mess,' I said gently, ignoring the gothic smears marbling her face. With her high-cheek bone structure and creamy skin she still managed to look beautiful if a little dishevelled. If I'd had a crying jag like that, I'd be piggy eyed and snotty.

'I meant inside.'

'You're away from home. You've had a nasty shock. Of course, you're all over the place.' Eva handed her another napkin.

'That's not it. It's not the accident. I'm a fraud, you know.'

'I'm sure you aren't. We all get upset.' Eva's soothing words made Avril screw up her face in protest.

'No, seriously. I am. My marriage is in a mess.' She ducked her head as if ashamed of her confession, picking at the strap on her handbag which she clutched to her chest like some kind of shield. 'Christopher, my husband, isn't interested any more. I know he isn't.' Her petulant declaration sounded as if she were daring us to contradict her.

'He avoids me as much as possible. I know he hates spending time with me.' Her face crumpled again as she balled the napkin in her hand.

Eva's lips pursed. 'Now. Is that what you know or what you think?'

With a shrug, Avril looked a little defiant as if she wasn't used to having her view of the world challenged. 'I'm a disappointment to him.'

'How? You're gorgeous, successful,' I offered immediately worried that she might think if that was all I had to say, I was suggesting she was shallow. I needn't have worried.

Avril lifted a disdainful eyebrow and looked directly at me. 'And high-maintenance.'

I blushed and opened my mouth to try to deny it.

'It's alright, you might not have said it but most people think it. They're right, I am.'

'Yes,' interrupted Eva, 'but surely your husband knew that before you were married. Didn't he love you as you were? Has that changed?'

With a self-deprecating half-laugh Avril's mouth turned down. 'It used to amuse him. Before we were married, he'd tease me about it but he said he loved that I knew what I wanted and didn't play games. But now he's bored with it. I know he is!' She snatched up her coffee.

'Has he said that?'

'No, but I can tell,' she mumbled from behind her cup.

'How?' persisted Eva, to Avril's irritation. I realised she was expecting us to take her word for it.

'Well ...' she wrinkled her face in thought, 'we ... we used to sit together after dinner and talk. Now it's as if he can't eat quickly enough so that he can get back to his study. He shuts the door. And then comes to bed when he thinks I'm asleep. Although I never am.'

'Have you told him how you feel?'

'I shouldn't have to,' Avril's pout was back. 'He should know.'

I bit back a smile quite happy to let Eva continue her careful probing. There was bugger all I could contribute.

'What? Like you know that he's bored with you?' Eva's voice held a sharp snap, tough love breaking through, which had both Avril and I straightening up in our seats.

'But he is bored with me.' There was a slight touch of the defensive in her mutinous words.

'What's he doing in the study? Instead of being with you?'

'He runs his own business. I don't quite understand what he does. Computer stuff. We're very different. He doesn't get the whole media thing or how important my job is.'

'And is his job not important?'

Avril looked as if this was a complete revelation.

'Well of course but ...'

'So you haven't asked him about his work?' Eva's voice held the barest touch of teasing.

'No.' Avril's voice was a touch sulky. 'Computing stuff is boring.'

'Not to him,' suggested Eva.

Avril tossed her hair over her shoulder. 'I guess not.'

'When was the last time you took an interest in him? What he does? You said you used to bake for him? Coffee and walnut cake.'

Avril's mouth tightened. 'I don't have time these days.'

'Maybe you need to make time. Maybe you need to show him that you still care.'

'I do still care.'

'Do you tell him?'

'It's rather difficult when he's tied to his computer.'

'So how does he know? What if he's thinking that you're bored with him? That you don't care because you don't bake for him, like you used to?'

'That's ridicu ...' her voice petered out, her face crumpling with confusion. 'Oh.'

'It doesn't sound as if the two of you are communicating very well. Sometimes someone has to take the first step to change things. Do you want your marriage to succeed?'

'Of course I do.'

'Why?' Eva's blunt cut to the chase question had Avril's eyes flashing.

'Because I love him.'

Eva leaned back in her chair with the merest hint of a smug smile on her face. 'More than your job?'

Avril nodded.

'Then perhaps you need to show him. Make him that coffee and walnut cake he used to love so much.'

Avril dropped her head in her hands. 'Oh God, you're right. I'm such an evil bitch. It's all about me. I am high-maintenance but I love him. I've been so obsessed with how important my job is, I've stopped listening to him. Stopped making time for him. When we first got together, we had a golden rule. No talking about work for the first hour I came in. But we kind of lost sight of that. Oh God, it's me. It's all my fault. I'm the one driving him away. I've neglected him.'

Eva held up her hand. 'Enough.'

Avril's lips twitched. 'I'm being a drama queen again, aren't I?'

With a smile, Eva lifted her shoulders neither denying nor agreeing.

'I'm going to call him. Tell him about the accident. Make him a cake when I get home.'

Chapter 16

'For fuck's sake, you're kidding me.'

'No, but it's fine,' I said, keeping my voice low even though I was on my own in my room. I'd left it as late as possible to phone Megan, knowing that I could use the excuse I had to meet the others for dinner in a minute. 'It was just a small accident; I thought you ought to know.'

With one hand, I unzipped my jeans and tried to peel them down my legs.

Unfortunately, Avril hadn't brought her EHIC card with her which would have ensured free treatment, so I'd had to settle the hefty medical bill on the company credit card, otherwise I might not have confessed.

'What were you doing? You were there, weren't you?'

'Of course I was there.' I wriggled the denim past my knees, both of which had a rusty coating of blood which had crept into the wrinkles in my skin. 'We were all on the boat together.' Where did she think I was? I explained about the scarf.

'Stupid cow,' Megan hissed. 'I knew she'd be trouble. I might have known it would be her.'

'Actually, she's not that bad.' I certainly wasn't going to tell

Megan about her breakdown at the café or the vulnerable woman I'd seen beneath the glossy veneer.

'Hmph,' dismissed Megan. 'Is she going to sue?'

I swapped the phone to my other ear as I disentangled my jeans from my ankles, almost falling over as I hopped out of them.

'Sue?' That hadn't even occurred to me.

'Yes, hold us responsible as the trip organisers. You'd better write up a report, document everything thoroughly and email it through tonight. You were supervising properly, weren't you?'

'Yes,' I snapped, eyeing my legs and walking into the bathroom. 'But they are all adults.'

'As a company we – you – are responsible for their wellbeing. You're representing the company. If this gets out or she decides to sue ... What's that noise?'

I'd just turned on the taps to the bath, keen to clean myself up.

'Water. I'm running a bath.'

'Make yourself at home.'

'Megan, I'm covered in blood.' As soon as I said it, I wished I hadn't.

'What! You didn't tell me it was that bad. Christ, she is going to sue!'

'Head wounds bleed a lot.' I winced. 'It wasn't as bad as it sounds.'

'But what if she's got concussion? A bleed on the brain. People die from bumps on the head. Oh jeez, it could cause major reputation damage. We could be done for corporate manslaughter.'

'She's not dead yet,' I snapped.

'This is not the time for jokes, Kate. Are you sure she's OK? I'm really not happy about this.'

'Megan, I didn't mean to joke but I promise you, she's fine. She was checked out by a trained doctor. And I was there.' Honestly, if I'd realised Megan would get in such a tizz about this, I would have waited until we got back and fessed up when the credit card bill was due. 'She's OK and I seriously don't think she's likely to sue. She was very apologetic about the trouble she'd caused.'

'Hmph.' Megan went quiet.

'She didn't bump her head properly she ... er ... ducked in time.' I decided against mentioning Ben's heroic rugby tackle or how much worse it could have been.

'And there's no way you could have prevented it. No comeback on the company.'

'Avril has had a couple of stitches and she's lying down, but she was feeling much better. I'm going to keep checking on her every hour and we'll see how she feels in the morning.'

'Oh great. Will we need to fly her back? That'll cost a fortune.'

'I'm hoping she'll feel better.' Because it would be awful to be in pain, miserable and away from home stuck in a hotel, none of which seemed to have occurred to Megan.

'You'd better keep me posted. Call me tomorrow morning. Maybe I should send someone else out. Damage limitation.'

'Do you know what, Megan? No. I don't need anyone else. I managed the situation.' *With a little help from my friends.* 'No one else could have done anything differently. It was an unfortunate accident but I dealt with it. I got her to the doctor, sorted everything out and it's all fine.'

'Oh. OK. Well it does sound as if you've got everything under control.'

Well done for managing in difficult circumstances, Kate. Just once it would be nice to get some credit.

'What did the other journalists do while you were with Avril?'

'Oh, they were fine.' I didn't tell her that they'd spent the afternoon in the hotel bar. I dreaded to think how much that had cost.

'And what's the plan for this evening? Another fabulous Michelin starred restaurant for dinner?'

Make up your mind. One minute this is hard work and I'm incapable, the next minute it's a piece of cake and all that's involved is swanning off for dinner every five minutes.

'I need to check on Avril and see how she feels and depending on that we'll change the plan. I popped out to the pharmacy and bought some paracetamol and ibuprofen.'

'Smart move. Hopefully you won't have to change the dinner plans. *Avast* does look fabulous.'

My boss was devoid of any empathy. I'd purchased the medication hoping it might help alleviate Avril's banging headache and make her feel a bit less pathetic.

Megan wittered on. 'I looked it up. I had no idea Copenhagen was so foodie. That place is bloody hard to get into and it would be a shame to cancel. I'm thinking about getting Giles to take me for a long weekend.'

'If Avril is well enough we'll stick to the original itinerary and have dinner at *Avast*, if not we'll eat at the hotel again, so that I can keep checking on her. Make sure she's alright.'

'Good thinking. I like that. Means you can keep everyone together, even if eating in the hotel isn't quite the same.'

I bit back a smile, in case she could tell over the phone. She clearly hadn't looked up the details of the hotel.

There was a gentle knock at the door.

'Hang on, Megan, someone's at my door.' I looked round to find something to pull on as I didn't fancy opening the door in my pants.

'Let's hope it's not another problem.'

I finished the call, reassuring Megan for what felt like the ninety-fifth time, that I was coping just fine as I wrapped a towel around my waist and opened the door.

There was no one there, but there was an H&M bag sitting in front of the metal threshold. I looked up and down the silent corridor and picked up the bag.

Inside there were four pairs of jeans with a note and a receipt.

Not sure what size you are or what style you might like, so bought several. B

Seriously Ben had done this? Grumpy Ben.

That wasn't standard man behaviour. And definitely not mad fox behaviour.

As soon as Avril answered my light knock on her door, it was clear that her phone call had gone well.

'Everything OK? How are you feeling?' It was a bit of a stupid question.

She looked a far cry from earlier. Skilful application of foundation, blusher and powder had hidden the purplish bruise blooming on her cheekbone like an ink stain and she'd arranged her hair in an artful, messy top knot with lots of loose tendrils that almost hid the row of livid black stitches in her temple.

'I feel a lot better.' Her smile was shy. 'Christopher was cross that I hadn't phoned him before.' Her eyes shone. 'He offered to fly out to be with me. Insisted on having a Skype call because he wanted to make sure I was OK.'

'That's lovely. You see he does care. Eva was right.'

'She is lovely isn't she? I wish my mother was like that. You think I'm high maintenance, God you should meet my mother. Other people throw a scene; she's more inclined to three act plays. It can be sooo embarrassing. No wonder my father left her. I guess that's why I keep thinking that Christopher will go off me.'

I didn't like to say that perhaps she could try to change if she was that worried, but as she said earlier, her husband had known what she was like when he married her.

'What would you like to do this evening? I'm happy to stay at the hotel with you if you'd like a quiet night in.' I gave her full make-up a second glance.

'No, I've taken enough ibuprofen to knock out an elephant and put on enough slap to coat said elephant. I'm good to go.'

'Are you sure?' I asked doubtfully. 'If you change your mind at any point we'll call a cab and we can come back.'

'It took me half an hour to achieve this,' Avril pointed to the slight swelling on her cheek, 'I'm not wasting all that effort.'

Avril the TV presenter was back, stylish and elegant in a black playsuit, with tiny diamante buttons down the front.

'I've heard a lot about this restaurant from Stacey Wakely, the weathergirl with pretensions to present,' Avril gave a shark-like smile. 'And there's no way I'm having her outdo me in the best restaurants I've ever eaten in stakes. Besides I've already put on Twitter we're going there.'

We met everyone else in the lobby and they fell upon her with sympathetic cries. It amused me to see her accepting everyone's observation of how brave she was, with a cool incline of her head. She caught my eye over the heads and she gave me a small serene smile with a tiny wink. Oh yes, she was back.

The white washed brick interior of the restaurant was under-stated but clearly a lot of thought had gone into the clean, simple design. Sturdy rustic wooden tables and unfussy wooden spindle backed chairs were arranged in neat rows with elegant place settings of stylish cutlery and classic long-stemmed glassware.

Much was made of the fact that all the food served was local, seasonal and where possible foraged, and as a result the menu was extremely limited, one choice of starter, hake with mustard and horseradish, followed by the main course, beef, celeriac and cep mushrooms, with the added option of a wine menu to accompany each course. I wasn't too sure about the birch bark ice cream dessert.

'Wow this place is amazing,' said Sophie.

'I'm going to call you Little Miss Sunshine from now on,' I teased her, 'You say that about everywhere we've been.'

'It's true,' Fiona nodded, a little dimple appearing in her cheek. 'You do.'

'Well, it has been a lovely trip so far,' said David with stout defence, 'despite the accident today, although Avril seems to have bounced back.' He looked down to the other end of the table where she was having a lively conversation with Ben and Mads. I gave her a good hour and a half before the effect of the Nurofen ran out. 'I've enjoyed it.' His wistful sigh had Sophie patting his hand. 'I'm going to miss everyone.'

'We'll have to have a Copenhagen Crowd reunion,' said Fiona.

Conrad shuddered with a touch of drama as he reached for the balloon red wine glass. He had opted for the wine tasting menu which I could have predicted. 'I'm not sure about that darling. Not really my thing.'

'You're an old fraud, Conrad.' David laughed at him. 'You've had a good time.'

'Actually,' Conrad conceded with a mischievous twinkle, 'the company has been of a far better calibre than I expected. And,' he toasted me with his wine, 'the victuals and beverages of an excellent standard. Well organised young Kate. The last trip I went on, Lord, I thought I was going to asphyxiate on cheap perfume and overdose on Prosecco. I mean you can have too much of a good thing but after a while only a decent glass of red wine will do. Talking of which ...' He looked expectantly at me reminding me I was back on duty.

When the waiter brought the bread and butter – the rye rolls presented on a thick bed of cracked wheat and the butter curls sat on a lattice of pea shoots floating in a tiny glass saucer of water – it was obvious we were in for a treat.

With great ceremony an unexpected appetiser arrived, accompanied by a highly tattooed and very enthusiastic young chef who explained that the honey cured smoked salmon was to be wrapped in the sour dough pancake with the foraged salad of tiny white enoki mushrooms (which I'd never heard of before, let alone seen), wild elderberries, lamb's lettuce and slivers of cucumber. If it hadn't been for the manic passion of the chef, I might have thought it all a bit pretentious.

'Wait,' said Fiona holding up a hand in a halting motion as Sophie grabbed her fork, taking several pictures of the fallen angel, chef and the beautifully presented dishes which did look like works of art in their own right.

She teased Sophie by saying. 'Hang on, a few more.'

'Hurry up Fi, I think my taste-buds are about to spontane-ously combust in anticipation. It's a forager version of Chinese duck pancakes.' She waved her fork like a formula one driver on the grid revving in readiness for the green flag. Fiona rolled her eyes and put down her camera and Sophie dived in, scooping up a little of everything. I thought she might just orgasm right there on the spot, she was making so many *When Harry met Sally* moans of delight.

'Guys you've got to try this. Those little elderberries add gorgeous spicy sweetness. Oh my word.'

Silence followed as everyone tucked in. I'm no foodie but there was something a little bit alchemical and magical about the combination of delicate flavours. It was to die for. The next two courses didn't disappoint and Sophie was struck dumb for at least five minutes when she tried the hake. Her face displayed a combination of tortured pain and pleasure as she savoured the fierce piquancy of the mustard and horse-radish sauce.

By the time we reached the main course, all eyes were on Sophie when she took the first mouthful, waiting to see her reaction. She closed her eyes in blissed out happiness waving her fork, speechless and when I tasted the beef, which fell apart in my mouth, I had to agree, it was the best beef I'd ever tasted.

The arrival of the third course with the unlikely birch ice cream, no longer fazed me, although the light dusting of what looked like ash across the top was mildly off-putting, but everything had been so damn delicious the final course wouldn't dare be anything but incredible too. There wasn't an awful lot of flavour to birch but the accompanying lemon verbena sauce and tiny yellow meringues more than made up for it.

When the waitress came to take our orders for tea and coffee, I realised Conrad, who had gone to the gents when the desserts arrived, still hadn't returned.

'Do you think Conrad's OK?' I asked David who'd been sitting next to him.

'I think so. He seemed to be on good form, tucking into the wine.'

'But he's been gone for quite a long time.'

'Would you like me to pop down to the gents and check on him?'

'Yes please. Although knowing Conrad, he's bumped into someone he knows downstairs and is holding court and sharing their wine.' It seemed far more likely than him being slumped insensible in the loos. He could put a prodigious amount of red wine away without any obvious effect.

David laughed and headed towards the glass and wood staircase which descended to the lower level where there were more tables.

'My, my, my that was a fabulous meal,' said Sophie. 'I'd love to know how they make that ice cream.'

The waitress overhearing her, offered to take her to chat to the chef and Fiona, keen to get some photographs of the kitchen, followed her.

There was still no sign of Conrad or David, so I got up and headed for the staircase. I met David coming up the stairs shaking his head in puzzlement.

'I can't find him. I checked the loos. I had a good look around all the tables.'

'He must have come back up and we missed him. Maybe he's in the kitchen or something.'

We walked back to the table and I peered into the kitchen where I could see Fiona and Sophie but there was no sign of Conrad.

I turned back to the table standing beside Mads, Avril and Ben who were all still seated. 'I don't suppose any of you spotted Conrad? He didn't come through the restaurant, did he?'

'No,' said Avril, her head drooping a little. I could see she was starting to flag. 'His coat's still hanging up.'

'There was a fire exit downstairs,' offered David. 'That was the only other way out.'

'I'll go down and have another look,' I said biting back a heavy sigh.

'I need the loo, I'll come down with you,' said Ben. 'Check the men's again, in case he's doubled back.'

'Thanks,' I said. 'And thanks, David.'

'No problem. The daft old sod must be somewhere.'

I tramped down the stairs with Ben behind me, unease building in the pit of my stomach.

The fire exit was tucked around the corner from the toilets but was closed. 'Maybe he popped out and the door closed behind and he couldn't get back in,' suggested Ben.

'It's the only thing I can think of.' With the exception of a couple of locked doors bearing large notices *kun personale* which I guessed meant staff only, there was nowhere else he could possibly have gone.

Ben grasped the bar and pushed open the door. Immediately an alarm started wailing. Ben slammed it closed again.

There was a horrible silence throughout the restaurant as the chink of china and glasses came to an abrupt halt and conversation petered out.

'That is no exit unless it is an emergency.'

Facing the manager, I apologised, mortified. 'Sorry, we've lost a member of our party. He came down to the toilet and he's disappeared. We were checking he hadn't popped out for some fresh air.'

'Maybe your friend has returned to the table now,' suggested the manager looking less than impressed with my explanation.

Ben and I trooped past him towards the stairs like a pair of naughty children.

'Well he didn't go out that door, we'd have heard the alarm,' said Ben confirming what I already knew.

'Perhaps we've just missed him,' I said crossing my fingers in a vain hope that he'd suddenly reappear.

But my wishful thinking failed to materialise and when we got back to the table everyone was now wondering where he was.

'Well he must be somewhere,' said Avril, her head on her forearms on the table. 'Has anyone phoned him?'

'Good call,' I said and whipped out my phone, grateful to have something to do while everyone stood there looking to me as if I had all the answers. I gripped my mobile hard so that none of them could see the slight tremor of my hand. Conrad was going to turn up any moment with one of his stories. He'd have started talking to someone. A grown man was not going to vanish, even if this was the home of Scandi noir series *The Killing*.

I heard ringing from Conrad's overcoat hanging up on a peg on the wall behind where he'd been sitting.

'Maybe he's gone back to the hotel,' suggested Fiona with an encouraging smile.

'Maybe,' I said, wishing I felt a bit more convinced. Everyone looked at me as if I knew what to do. Sweat patches blossomed under my arms and my breath was tight in my chest but I lifted my chin.

'Well as everyone's finished their coffee, there's no point you all waiting here.' Especially not Avril who looked done in. It was agreed they'd go back to the hotel.

'You can't stay here by yourself,' said Sophie.

'Don't worry I'll be fine,' I said blithely. 'It's not far back to the hotel and I'd rather wait here for a while in case Conrad comes back.'

'But what if he doesn't?' said Avril, widening her eyes in anticipated horror, voicing my worst fear. I had absolutely no idea what to do. Call the police?

How could a grown man disappear? Inside I could feel the hollow panic building in my stomach.

'I'll wait with you,' offered Ben quietly.

'T-that's kind of you.' I looked at him. 'Thank you.'

That was the sort of thing Ben did. The right thing.

With a rustle of coats, chairs scraping the floor and a flurry of goodbyes, within a minute everyone had gone leaving Ben and I alone.

'Shall we sit down?' said Ben.

'Yes. Yes. That's probably ... yes.' We sat down. I fiddled with the little bowl of salt, poking at the crystals with the tiny wooden spoon, biting my lip and looking at the door, hoping Conrad would walk through at any second.

'Do you want another drink?' Ben asked.

I closed my eyes. I ought to be sensible and professional and have a cup of coffee. What if Conrad had had an accident? Wandered off, fallen in the canal?

'Kate?'

'Sorry, I'm ...' My voice trembled. 'I'm ...'

Ben's face softened and he reached over and took my hand.

'I'm sure there's nothing wrong. You know Conrad, he's old school street wise. Cut his teeth in Soho in the sixties. Knowing him he could have hooked up with some rich widow and run away with her for the night.'

I forced out a laugh. 'I bloody hope so. I feel so … useless.'

'Well don't. There's nothing you can do. He's a grown man.'

He called over the waitress. 'Two glasses of red wine, please.' He looked at me. 'You need one.'

Every time the door to the restaurant opened I looked up.

The waitress brought over the wine and Ben picked his up and we toasted each other silently.

'I never thanked you for the jeans,' I suddenly blurted out, my words running away with me. I should have thanked him before. 'I must give you the money. It was very thoughtful.' I paused, 'And you get major brownie points for choice of size and a style. I must take the others back. That was pretty impressive.'

Bemusement turned to amusement. 'I have a sister remember. Jeans are complicated. I was passing H&M on the way back.'

'I need to return to the others … but do you need to be there, how did you pay?'

'I paid cash, but just give the others back to me and I'll return them.'

'I'll give them back to you tomorrow. Are you sure you don't me to …'

'No, it's fine, there's a bit of down-time on your extensive itinerary.'

'It's not my itinerary. The client, Lars came up with it.'

'So, what made you go into PR?' The sudden question made me look up at him sharply.

'What? The devil's work?'

He laughed. 'Innocent question, I promise.'

I shrugged and gave him an assessing gaze.

'I'm worried this will come back and bite me. Or give you new ammunition for next time you speak to "a PR".'

'Well obviously, I'll be giving them two seconds from now on.' He shot me an arch teasing smile.

I rolled my eyes.

'I'd just like to say, that was the only time I've ever done that.' He toyed with the base of his glass ducking the question before asking, 'So why PR?'

'You're going to be disappointed.'

'Am I?'

'No, probably not, my reasons are as shallow as *you'd* expect.'

The quirk of his eyebrow suggested my honesty had intrigued him.

I gave him a withering look which was as much aimed at him as me. 'My reasons were pretty basic. I left uni. Went home. There was a vacancy in the agency in my home town. I went for it and got it. The most important thing was it was the sort of job you looked *smart* at.'

I could see him querying the word.

'Smart as in well-dressed, not intelligent. It sounded successful. Sort of professional. An office job with prospects. It sounded good. To be honest,' I said sweeping at the crumbs on the table, 'I knew nothing about public relations.' I focused on one particular piece of bread, stabbing at it with my thumb. 'I was the first in my family to get A levels let alone go to university. Mum was desperate for me to do well. Anyone who worked in an office was doing well.'

I lifted my shoulders and looked up from my impromptu table tidy. 'I went for that first job because it would have made my mum so chuffed.'

His eyes softened with sympathy.

'Don't worry I loved it. I really enjoyed that first job.' Every day had been different, I was young and enthusiastic and keen to please.

'And now?' How had Ben picked up on that?

I stiffened. 'I work for one of the top five London agencies. It's hard work but I'm doing OK and hopefully after this trip, I'll get promoted.'

The sympathy in his face vanished.

'What?' I asked.

'I'd forgotten, we journalists are a means to an end. Your golden ticket to the next level.'

'I'd hardly call you a golden ticket. You've been ...' I stopped short of telling him he'd been a pain in the arse from day one. 'So why do you dislike PR people so much?'

'It's difficult to know where to start,' he said pompously looking into his wine glass as if the answer would swirl up and jump out like a performing dolphin.

'I had a bad experience,' his mouth wrinkled as if he could taste it. Then he looked at me. 'Sorry. You're not a bad person. You just happened to be the first to ring me up afterwards.' He took a sip of his red wine. 'This feels like a confessional.'

'It's not going to go any further.'

'Doesn't matter, it's not exactly a secret,' his top lip lifted with a touch of bitterness. 'I was senior business writer. Working on a story about the chief executive of a retail group. About how he'd turned the fortunes of the company around. About his management practices.'

As soon as he said the company name I winced. He caught me. 'Yeah, that company.'

'The head of corporate communications was a girl I'd had a couple of dates with. We mutually, or so I thought, decided not to pursue things. She thought differently. I was working on the story. The day before the news broke, I rang her to check a fact, she never said a word, even though she knew he was about to go down.'

'Maybe she wasn't allowed to say anything. Or maybe she didn't know.'

'She knew.' He pushed himself away from the table to cross his legs and fold his arms, hunching slightly. I don't think he was even aware of the defensive barriers he'd erected. 'The day my article came out, the company broke the news with a press conference held at 9.00 am. She was official spokesperson and our news desk had been invited the day before. She knew alright. All she needed to say was, perhaps you should hold fire on the story.'

'Ouch.'

'Yeah. My senior editor was livid.' His shoulders hunched again. 'Hence my sideways move to the lifestyles desk. I should consider myself lucky I still had a job.'

'It wasn't your fault though.'

'When the paper's left looking that stupid, I don't think anyone gives a toss about fault.'

'I can see why you're ... suspicious. But on the bright side,' I lifted my glass and toasted him. 'I did get you away from babysitting duty.'

He let out a reluctant half-laugh, unfolding his arms and resting his forearms on the table. 'True but—'

My phone beeped and I checked the incoming text.

'Damn. No sign of Conrad at the hotel. Shit.'

I slumped back in my chair.

'Now what?' I asked aloud. 'Do I call the police?'

'What about the British consulate?'

'That's a good idea.'

'Although ...' he shrugged.

'Yeah, a couple of hours is hardly missing persons.'

'He's probably going to turn up in the morning absolutely fine. Just wandered off to get some fresh air. Got lost. He'll find his way back to the hotel eventually.'

'Do you think so?'

Ben nodded. Despite his words, which made lots of sense, they didn't help the coil of tension tightening in my stomach.

'Excuse me,' I looked up to see the manager looming over our table. 'We have found your colleague.'

'You have,' I said, jumping up, my legs feeling a bit strange as if they didn't quite belong to me. 'Oh thank God for that.' I beamed at him only to be met with an expression of icy disgust.

'Where?' I asked only now registering the veiled anger in his original clipped delivery. 'Downstairs.'

Instinct was shouting, this wasn't good. Had he collapsed somewhere and disgraced himself?

'Is he alright?' I asked standing up.

'He is fine,' said the manager, his thin lips curling. 'I wish I could say the same for my wine stock. Would you like to come this way?'

The truthful answer would have been no, clearly whatever awaited us wasn't going to be pretty.

I gave Ben a nervous, resigned look feeling as if I was being led off to the headmaster's office and turned to follow the manager. Without a word Ben stood up, put a hand on my shoulder with a brief squeeze and fell into step beside me as I trailed after the manager down the stairs.

One of the locked doors was now open. A gloomy overhead plain light bulb lighting the room revealed it was a wine store filled with rack after rack of bottles.

Propped against one of the racks, legs spread wide, sat Conrad.

'Kate, my dear girl.'

I winced as he grinned owlishly up at me.

'You've got to try some of this wine. It's awfully good.' He nodded at the open bottles lined up in front of him. 'This one is very good indeed.' With a shaky hand, he picked up one of the bottles and held it towards me for inspection.

'Oh, Conrad!' I let out a heavy sigh and closed my eyes for a brief second. I turned to the manager, red hot shame burning across my face. 'I am so sorry.' I cast a glance at

Conrad and shook my head ever so slightly. 'I will pay for all the wine he's opened. I am sorry.'

The manager's lips were pursed as tightly as a turtle's bum, pinched so firmly he looked in pain. Rigid disapproval came from him in sharp waves. Not that I blamed him, my fingers were clenched into tight fists, itching to strangle bloody Conrad, who didn't even have the decency to look the tiniest bit contrite.

'Come on old man,' said Ben, crossing to crouch beside Conrad. He helped him to his feet, which was quite an undertaking as Conrad was plastered.

The manager leaned over and plucked two unopened bottles from Conrad's jacket pockets.

'Oops,' said Conrad with a snicker, leaning against Ben, his eyes blinking and widening as he tried to focus.

I could barely meet the manager's furious gaze as he examined the labels of the bottles. His mouth twisted in displeasure as he hastily shoved them back in the correct racks as if anxious to get them as far away from Conrad as possible.

'You go sort out the bill and I'll get him upstairs and outside,' said Ben, nudging Conrad.

I pulled my purse out from my handbag and followed the manager's angry strides to the cash desk.

Chapter 17

The café cast a golden glow onto the cobbled street, a welcoming beacon guiding me in and I relaxed immediately as I walked through the door of Varme. After the previous night's escapade I'd been too strung out to sleep properly. As if she knew, Eva magically appeared with a steaming mug of coffee and a hot *kanelsnegle*, putting them down at a table and ushering me into the seat.

'Rough night?'

'How did you guess?'

She simply smiled and nodded towards the coffee.

I'd barely taken a sip when the door opened and my mouth dropped open in surprise. The last person I'd expected to see at this time was Conrad and it was clear from the protective way that David sat next to him, that he'd come along as reinforcements. My heart sank; this had become my little haven, where I started the day with just Eva, my coffee and pastry, before I faced the group. I was Katie here.

Conrad gave me a nervous smile, picking and worrying at the edge of the sleeve of his jacket. 'Morning Kate,' he croaked.

Good, it sounded as if he'd got a champion hangover.

Suddenly I was aware of Eva slipping into the seat next to me like a UN peacekeeper.

I took refuge in sipping the coffee and grateful for the slow hit of caffeine, while I tried to frame the first words.

'Kate, I'm terribly sorry. I am an idiot.'

I stiffened at Conrad's cheery unrepentant apology. Idiot wasn't the word I'd have used but before I could say anything, David frowned and nudged him discreetly.

Conrad edged away as if trying to escape. 'I don't know what came over me.' He shrugged his shoulders, all innocence as if he'd been gripped by some mythical uncontrollable urge.

'Conrad,' David's gentle remonstrance made the four of us around the table pause.

I shot his jacket pockets a pointed look and was pleased to see he had the grace to look ashamed. Conrad had always been a potential liability but somehow, I'd assumed that he'd have enough respect for me to behave. The realisation that he didn't hurt.

'So, what happened?' I was rather proud that I managed to keep my voice level and even.

'I was wandering past. The door was open. I thought I'd have a little look.' His gaze flitted towards the window and he tugged at the sleeve of his jacket.

'And a couple of bottles hopped in your pocket?' Weariness crept into my voice and I caught my lip in my teeth feeling close to tears.

'Now, now Kate. It wasn't like that.' His eyes shied away again. 'I was taking a quick peek and then the next thing I know, the door closed. I was locked in. No way out. Well, what was a man to do?' He lifted his shoulders in sheepish encouragement as if I might agree that he'd done the only thing sensible and attempt to drink the place dry. 'There were some jolly nice wines,' he added this time including Eva in his naughty-little-me routine. I noticed that David clenched his lips and folded his arms, exuding disapproval.

'I know, I paid the bill.' I looked at him but he went silent seeming to find the grain of the wood on the table rather fascinating.

Irritated beyond belief, I blurted out, 'But why Conrad? That's what I don't understand. Every luxury has been laid on for this trip.'

He swallowed and David nudged him again, this time adding with a stern hiss, 'Tell them the truth.'

Conrad screwed up his face, looked at David and let out a long deep breath, his shoulders slumping and then as if someone had pulled the plug on his bonhomie, his face sagged, the lines deepening ploughing furrows across his forehead.

'I'm broke. Flat broke. The magazine made me redundant three months ago. I freelance for them. Trips like this are a godsend. I can eat, drink and not worry. I saw the wine and ... I guess like a squirrel, burying nuts, it just takes over, this panic. Sheer blind panic. I grabbed a couple of bottles. Not even thinking. Save them for later. And then someone shut the door.'

He dropped his head into his hands. 'I'm about to move into the shittiest bedsit in Acton. It's all I can afford.' His breath hitched. 'My last wife took me to the cleaners. Took the house. If everyone knew ... I'd be a laughing stock. Conrad

Fletcher, the interiors expert, arbiter of taste, design guru who can't even afford to shop in Ikea.' He winced. 'Freelance work is hard to come by at the moment. The only thing I'm going to have is my pension. Once I stop working I'll have nothing.'

His pain filled words were touched with panic. 'I've got nothing. I'm sorry Kate, I'll pay back the money.' He paused, his finger brushing the bill as if he could hardly bear to look at it let alone pick it up. 'Somehow.' The final added broken word made me feel terrible, like a bully in the playground picking on someone much weaker.

'Oh, Conrad,' I said, feeling desperately sorry for him. He looked like a deflated balloon, a far cry from the sophisticated man who held court over lunch in the smartest restaurants in town, who had for years struck terror into designers with a few well-placed cutting comments.

'It's a sham. A house of cards.'

'Don't go overboard with the dramatics,' said David, his calm gentle tone at odds with the words.

Conrad gave him a sheepish nod. 'You're quite right, again. David's been very kind. He called first thing to see if I was OK. I am genuinely sorry. I get a bit carried away. Have a drink and it's all too awful to contemplate so I pretend it's not happening and I do silly things to block out real life. I've been an old fool. I will pay that money back for the wine.'

'Don't worry about that, Conrad,' I said reaching over the table and patting his arm. He suddenly looked much older than his sixty-six years. It felt very uncomfortable seeing this vulnerability in him. 'I'm sure the company,' I bit my lip, shooting a quick glance at Eva, it was her son that was picking up the tab for this trip, 'will pay.'

'Of course, it will,' said Eva staunchly. 'But you need to sort yourself out.' She looked at me. 'Kate, would you mind going to make another cup of coffee.'

'Er, no.' I rose to my feet slowly but she didn't say a word until I was out of earshot.

By the time I'd made three fresh coffees, forgoing one for myself, the three of them were nodding as if they'd just signed some great peace treaty.

'Want to share?' I asked more than a little put out.

Eva beamed at me. 'I think we've found a solution to Conrad and David's problems. Conrad is going to rent the top floor of David's house.'

David grinned. 'I've got plenty of space.'

'And I'm jolly good company,' said Conrad. 'And its only now he tells me he lives in one of those darling Edwardian terraces in Chapham North, which is so up and coming it's about to top Shoreditch.'

Eva sat back, with the sort of benign smile that said her work was done as the two men talked about David's house, the benefits of its location, the size of the rooms, the layout of the kitchen.

David's confession of being lonely the other day had sparked several thoughts. Were those black moments when I wondered what I was doing with my life, me standing on the edge of loneliness?

I glanced at my phone which had beeped. My Twitter notifications were there. Oh damn, Avril had tweeted.

Another fab day #WonderfulCopenhagen, although we almost lost one. Turned up in the wine cellar attempting to drink it dry #presstripantics

It was too much to hope Megan wouldn't see or hear about the tweet. She'd texted me. 'Call me.'

Chapter 18

Megan's words still rang in my ears when I met up with the others. After a heated conversation, where I had to explain about Avril's tweet, I felt thoroughly demoralised. Luckily, she didn't ask how much Conrad's escapade had cost and I hoped the credit card bill wouldn't land in the office any time soon.

This morning we were going to the Carlsberg Brewery and then on to the famous Round Tower, with a few hours free and then a much-anticipated trip to Tivoli Gardens, of which we'd had tantalising glimpses of ever since we'd arrived.

I was going to be keeping a close eye on Conrad. Apparently, the brewery had the largest collection of bottled beer in the world which numbered over ten thousand bottles. Yes, I was going to be keeping a very close eye on Conrad indeed.

The brewery was a hit with everyone, even Ben seemed to enjoy it, Fiona, as usual, managed to snap plenty of photos and Avril amazed us all by being somewhat of an expert on beer, it turned out she came from a minor brewing dynasty.

After that we headed to the Round Tower, which I was dreading. I'm not great with heights and certainly didn't want to let anyone in the group know. Disasters to date withstanding, I felt I'd come through and had garnered a bit of respect from them all. It looked as if I knew what I was doing and the last thing I wanted was to look an idiot in front of them all.

Luckily the Rundetaarn wasn't what I was expecting at all. I'd seen plenty of pictures of a rather gloomy looking Rapunzel tower, with narrow gothic windows but the real thing was so much more picturesque and much bigger than it looked. It promised spectacular views over the city. All I had to do was focus on looking out over the horizon and not down and I'd be fine. No one would ever know that my insides were already quivering at the thought.

As soon as we stepped inside, I fell in love with the bright and roomy white-washed walls of the tower. Reassuringly it looked more like a contemporary art gallery than an ancient monument. There were no steps at this level, instead a wide gentle path coiled upwards, its cobbled stones bathed in the sunshine pouring through the regular window niches set deep in the walls. Stark and simple, there was no sensation of height at all and I could concentrate on the leisurely walk.

'It was designed so that a horse and carriage could drive up here,' explained Mads as we wound our way up. 'Cars have also been driven up here and every year there is a unicycle race to the top and down again.'

'They must be crazy,' said Sophie. 'And have very sore backsides after bouncing about on these cobbles.'

I managed to avoid looking out of the windows, even though the others stopped regularly to peer out at the view.

None of them seemed to have noticed my periodic interest in my phone or my strategic photos looking back down the way we'd come.

We were almost at the top when Mads stopped and gestured to a small opening, almost like an igloo, in the very centre of the tower.

'Go in. Take a look.' Mads grinned. 'If you're brave enough.'

We bunched together no one wanting to be the first to enter the small space. Everyone but me seemed to be intrigued by the challenging smile on his face.

Ben squeezed past and went into the tiny opening, ducking his head as he went.

'Step out,' yelled Mads.

'Seriously?' Ben called back.

'Yes.' Mads flashed us his usual cheery grin. 'It's quite safe.'

I heard him whistle and then he backed out to join us. 'That's a scary thing. A leap of faith.'

Of course, everyone wanted to see after that, so one by one they filed in. I hung back like a good host at a dinner table, waiting for all the guests to take their turn. Of course, that was the wrong thing to do because it meant that at the end all eyes focused on me.

'Go on, Kate, your turn,' said Sophie. 'It's brilliant.'

I dithered, my heart starting to pound a little. 'No, you're alright. I'm sure you all want to get to the top of the tower and we need to keep to our schedule. Don't forget I'm one of the guides. I'm working.'

'Nonsense,' said Sophie and Avril backed her up.

'No honestly. It's fine.' I gave them a stiff smile, hoping the sheer terror didn't show. I did not want to go to pieces in front of them all.

Unfortunately, with a row of enthusiastic faces urging you on, it's very difficult to listen to your inner voice telling you that this is a crazy, stupid idea because how could anything at the top of a very tall tower, down a very narrow aperture, possibly be brilliant.

'Come on, Kate, we've all done it. It's important you join in,' Ben's voice held a note of challenge and I shot him a dirty look, to which he raised one eyebrow and quirked his lip.

Damn him. They'd all stopped waiting patiently. How could I not do it?

Taking a deep breath, I took a few paces forward. Mind over matter. For the sake of my job, I could do this. I was a professional. Of course, I could do this. Mads had said it was quite safe.

The tiny tunnel was quite claustrophobic. Once inside you couldn't turn around. The tunnel opened into a circular space, with a circle in the centre of the floor. I looked down ... whoa! Hastily I stepped back except there was nowhere to step back. Heart pounding, I forced myself to look again. Bloody hell, the hairs on my forearms spiked. Scary. Scary. Scary. It was a very long way down. A very, very long way down. You could see right down through the core of the building.

'Step on it, Kate. It's glass,' urged Mads.

What the ... Clever lighting created an illusion and there was a piece of glass over the top, not that it made me feel any better.

Behind me I could tell they were all peering down the narrow opening. I pushed out a tentative toe. Oh thank God, I could feel the glass. It was there.

'Go on, Kate, step on it.'

I closed my eyes, fingers clenched tight in my palms, took a deep breath and stepped out. My heart leapt in fierce gratitude at the feel of the firm surface of the glass beneath my feet.

Phew, I'd done it. Now I could go back, head held high.

I should have left it at that, but no I had to go and look down.

Big mistake. Huge.

The glass had gone. Completely vanished. I was hanging in mid-air.

Everything inside me melted as if my bones had been removed. I swayed for a second, fighting against dizziness, locking my knees trying to stop the sensation of falling. Any second now. I was going to feel myself falling, falling, falling, going down and down. I braced myself, fearful of the pain of landing, except in another part of my mind, I knew I was stationary despite the rushing in my ears, the blurry vision and the whoosh of my lungs as I expelled every last breath in a panicked gasp.

'We'll see you at the top, Kate,' called Mads and dimly I was aware of the group receding.

Now I was stuck, my feet glued to the surface of the glass and at any second, the glass could give way. Logically there was a tiny part of me knew the glass had been here for a long time – they wouldn't let tourists do this – an awful lot more of me saying that it was a possibility. The glass could break, the building was old, the bricks holding it in could give way. I was in a state of paralysis where none of my limbs seemed to want to do what I was telling them, mocking me with their greater self-knowledge. *Don't be stupid. Don't move an inch. If you move now you're doomed. Doomed. You'll fall right to the bottom. Moving will displace the glass. One inch and it will collapse.*

'Kate.' Vaguely I registered Ben's voice. 'Kate!'

I didn't dare move a muscle. Suddenly I was Tom Cruise in *Mission Impossible*, one tiny drop of sweat, one wrong move, a single twitch could tip the balance, send the glass falling and me with it.

'Kate,' Ben's low voice resonating with urgency came from right behind me.

'Mmm,' I said, my throat constricted by the tension in my neck from holding my head so still.

'Are you OK?'

'Mmm.' I couldn't even turn my head towards his voice.

'Have you got a problem with heights?' His gentle words were matter of fact.

'Yup.'

I heard him exhale.

'Can you move?'

'Nope.'

All I could see was the yawning hole beneath my feet and then a pair of leather size nines joined mine and Ben put both hands on my rigid arms, urging me to look up at him.

'You're OK. Come on. Look at me.'

I took in a gasp of shaky stutter breath, I'd been holding it for so long, scared even to breathe.

The touch of his hands gave me something different to focus on and I lifted my head.

His blue-grey eyes were full of gentle concern and he gave me a coaxing smile, squeezing my arms. 'A kroner for your thoughts.'

I swallowed, my throat too dry to answer.

'Haven't we met some place before? And here was I thinking you were clinging to that brass rail, overcome by my good looks.'

Somehow a stifled sob-cum-laugh escaped me and my feet magically unglued themselves from the glass as he gave me a gentle push towards the exit.

'Come on you, time to get out of here.' Like a shepherd, with a wobbly-legged lamb he herded me out into the bright white light of the corridor and over to one of the window niches, an arm resting in the small of my back, with gentle reassuring pressure.

I sank onto the stone lintel, and dropped my head to my knees. He sat down next to me, his thighs next to mine, his arm around my back and bending forward so his head was level with mine. Now I was safe, I was sucking in air, panicked breaths I'd been too scared to take earlier.

'It's OK, Kate.' Ben's arm squeezed me, pulling me closer, his words low and soothing. 'You're OK now.'

I huddled down a bit more, grateful for my hair obscuring my face. What an idiot, I was. What must he think? I closed my eyes tightly, as if that might stop him seeing me.

'Kate?'

Gentle fingers slid across my face, as he pulled back the curtain of my hair and carefully tucked it behind my ear.

And I was a complete goner. The tender touch sent my stomach into freefall and I turned to face him, shooting a panicked look into concerned blue eyes.

And what did he do? He cupped my face and stroked my cheekbone with his thumb. Now I couldn't breathe. Couldn't move. All I could do was stare. At him. At his lips. No, not at his lips. Not there.

'OK?'

Slowly I nodded, sucking in a desperate breath, trying to get my equilibrium back. This was Ben. Ben. Mad Fox Ben. The same Ben I'd wanted so desperately to kiss the first time we met.

His thumb stilled and his eyes travelled across my face until they met mine, in a heart-stopping moment of connection. For a second we stared at each other. My ribs seemed too tight around my chest.

'Sorry,' I whispered, rubbing at my eyes with my hands to break the connection. We didn't even like each other. 'I ... I feel like a fool,' I whispered.

He laid a gentle finger on my mouth. 'No, you're not.' He dropped the softest of kisses on my forehead.

'You're no fool, Kate Sinclair.'

I lifted my head and pressed my forehead to his. We stayed there for a few minutes and I felt as if I'd absorbed some of his strength and steadiness, enough to bolster me.

'Are you sure you want to go up to the top? Or do you want to stay here?'

I hesitated, unable to look him in the eye.

'You don't have to be brave.'

'I do,' I said trying to pull away from him. I'd so rather be on ground level. 'This is work,' I said softly, 'I'm supposed to look after everyone. I'll be fine if I don't look down.'

'And, I'll be with you every step of the way.' His hand slipped into mine as we stood and followed the path upwards.

There were steps up to the very top of the tower which then led into a tiny stone spiral staircase before you emerged out onto the top of the tower. The view was a perfect juxtaposition of Copenhagen, historic green bronze-topped buildings with wedding cake tiered affairs against a back drop of the sea, wind turbines and modern industrial chimneys as long as you stayed well back and didn't look down.

'You OK?' asked Ben as we reached the outside giving my hand one last squeeze.

Forcing the tremulous smile, I nodded. 'Yes. Thank you.' I could have wept. 'I'll take it steady. Look out and not down.'

'I'm going to take some pictures.' He pulled out his phone and took a step towards the railing at the edge. 'Sure, you'll be OK?' he asked again, this time with a teasing smile.

'I'm just going to stay right here. Become a wall-hugger.'

He raised an eyebrow in amused query. 'Is there such a thing?'

'There is now.'

I stayed well back from the railings around the edge and

leaned against the wall tilting my face up to the sunshine, as if I was basking in the rays rather than trying to regain my equilibrium. I heard him join the others and Mads' voice floated my way.

'That's St Nicholas Church; it was the third oldest church in Denmark but burnt down in the eighteenth century. It was rebuilt in the early nineteen hundreds, and the dominant ninety metre neo baroque spire was paid for by the brewer Carl Jacobsen.'

'Over there is Christianbourg Palace, the Danish parliament.'

And then I heard Sophie ask, 'What happened to Kate? Where is she?'

I closed my eyes tight.

'Work emergency. She had to take a call but it's all under control.'

I really wished I'd kissed that man.

Chapter 19

'Here you go.' Mads handed out the tickets in front of the impressive arched entrance to Tivoli Gardens. There was a buzz of excitement around us, as people moved forward, their heads craning upwards to look at the flaming torches on top of the triumphant archway and the rainbow of lights sparkling around the park.

I'd assumed the Tivoli Gardens were urban green space like Hyde Park or Central Park. No, it's a full-on amusement park smack in the centre of the city. Over the last few days we'd skirted around it several times, hearing the screams from people on a terrifying looking roller coaster racing on a track high above the park walls, seen the golden tower where people dangled at a huge height before dropping with startling speed and caught glimpses of extravagant golden minaret-topped buildings.

Tonight, as we approached it felt like I could relax and enjoy the magical wonderland glittering with lanterns, ornate tiers of brightly coloured bulbs and fairy lights. And hopefully I could get away from Ben for a while. Not that he'd sought me out during the rest of the day. It was me. My eyes seemed to have developed magnetic tendencies and Ben was due north. I kept finding my gaze sliding his way. And it had to stop. He was a journalist. I didn't fancy him. It wasn't professional. He didn't like me. All of which stacked up perfectly, except my stupid heart had a bit of a wobble every time his blue eyes caught mine sneaking a peak at him.

Fiona fiddled with her camera, holding it up and taking lots of shots as usual.

'I love this. I had no idea.'

'It's a big favourite. Especially in the summer when there are lots of concerts and events here. And at Christmas.'

'It's like Disneyland ... except a little bit more charming,' said Avril. 'We went there on our honeymoon.' She grinned. 'And do you know what my husband's favourite ride was?' She gave a despairing sigh. 'It's A Small World. This dumb boat ride around lots of little islands with singing puppets.'

'Avril. Wash your mouth out. That's my favourite too,' said Sophie putting her hands on her hips in indignation, laughing when Avril rolled her eyes.

'Actually, it is the oldest amusement park in Europe. Walt Disney came here and was inspired to create Disneyland.' Mads bristled with pride.

'Really,' said Fiona, letting go of her camera which was hanging around her neck. 'I didn't know that.' She beamed at me. 'Another great story for my blog. And I do love rides, don't you?' It was a rhetorical question and she'd already picked up her camera taking a few more shots as we queued to gain entrance.

The evening had turned chilly and we were all well-wrapped

up. I was hit by the scent of the popcorn and it immediately reminded me of visits to the funfair and the circus on Boxmoor Common when I was younger.

Once in, Sophie darted off to the popcorn stall and we waited gazing around us.

'Are you going to be alright on the rides?' asked Ben appearing beside me, hands pushed into his jeans pockets.

I stiffened, a starburst sensation blooming in my chest as if someone had flung a handful of little stones that had exploded one after the other.

'Well you won't be getting me on that thing,' I said, through almost clenched teeth. Act normal. He doesn't know. I nodded towards the track on the other side of the park dominating the skyline.

'The Demon.' He jerked his head towards it and we both looked up as a chorus of screams echoed across the sky.

'It could be called the Angel of Happy Feelings for all I care. It looks horrific.'

'Some people think it's fun.' His eyes twinkled and my heart did another of those stupid little flips.

'I'm not one of them,' I retorted. 'If I wanted my brains scrambled, I can think of better ways of doing it.'

He laughed and then pulling his hands out of his pockets raked his hair with one hand, pausing for a quick beat. 'How are you on boats? They have some rides for the little kids, I think.'

'You're so funny,' I said, light-heartedly slapping him in the ribs, deliberately pretending I'd missed the invitation.

'You'd be safe on one of those.' His eyes danced. 'What do you say?'

Before I could answer, Sophie grabbed my arm and offered me some of the popcorn spilling from the top of a candy-striped carton.

'Bumper cars,' said Fiona decisively. 'I love those. Nothing like a bit of road rage to bring out the true side of people. I want to see if David has a dark side.'

'Who me?' He assumed an innocent face. 'Be careful what you wish for.'

'Yeah, right,' said Sophie and we all laughed. David and Sophie were the most good-natured, easy going people I'd ever met. While she was sunshine and positivity, he was quietly amenable, supportive and under-stated.

'Seriously. Bumper cars. Bit tame,' said Conrad.

'What you're a white-knuckle rider?' asked Avril tucking her arm through his tweed overcoat.

'I'll have you know in my day, I worked a whole season on the dodgems on the pier at Southend,' he announced.

'You,' said Avril with tactless surprise. 'But I thought you were from a stately home. Landed gentry at least.'

'Lord no. My mother insisted I speak properly. She was an amateur thesp. We lived in a council flat.'

'Really?' I looked at Conrad with fresh eyes. He'd always seemed so posh to me.

'Yes, darling. People make assumptions. The trick is not to correct them.' He gave me a naughty wink. 'It's not where you come from, it's where you're going that counts.'

'I second that,' said Sophie, 'although I was very lucky. I did grow up in a stately home.'

'Don't tell me, your mum was the housekeeper,' said Avril

teasing and then looked horrified when Sophie replied, 'Something like that. More popcorn.' She shook the carton. 'Did we decide?'

'Yes,' said Fiona forcefully with a determined glint in her eye. 'The bumper cars!'

Everyone turned to look at her in surprise.

'Little Miss Shy and Timid has taken a hike then,' drawled Conrad.

Fiona blushed. 'Sorry.'

'Don't you dare apologise,' said David taking her arm.

'Sorry. I mean ...' she giggled.

'Let's put Fiona in charge for the night,' suggested Ben. 'Now that she's become all assertive and bossy.'

'Oh you,' she punched him in the arm.

Laughing we all fell into step and headed towards the bright lights and happy cries of the dodgems.

It turned out even behind the wheel of a dodgem, David didn't possess a killer instinct, not that he got a chance as Avril took charge and drove surprisingly sedately unlike Fiona who seemed to have a personality transplant and leapt into a car with Mads, taking great delight in ramming everyone. Sophie insisted I drove and we spent most of our time trying to escape the dual efforts of Fiona and Conrad to shunt us at every opportunity.

Ben chose to watch from the rail and every time I took a casual glance his way, he seemed to be looking in my direction.

'Where next Fiona?' asked David when we all came off in high spirits.

She wrinkled her forehead and looked around at us, but in an unspoken agreement we seemed to have agreed that she should be gang leader for the night.

'OK, The Demon.'

'Yay,' cried Sophie.

'Yessss,' said David and Conrad in tandem, with Avril adding, 'Bring it on.'

'Let's do it people,' said Fiona with a broad grin punching the air in delight.

Ben gave me a questioning look. I winced and ignored him.

Everyone moved forward but he held back and waited for me.

'Are you sure about this?'

'No,' I swallowed, 'but I can't ... I can't spoil it for Fiona. She's really pumped.' I gave him a brave I-can-do-this look. 'It won't kill me ... I don't think.'

'It is perfectly safe,' he agreed evenly. I could see that he was trying to be reassuring but that wasn't helping the time bomb of fear already ticking away in my stomach.

'It's all very well you saying that. You're not scared.'

'But you're supposed to be scared,' he said with a gentle smile. 'That's the whole point. The adrenaline rush. That's why people come to these places. You'll be fine.'

'I know.' I bit my lip looking up at the car careering on the skyline along the tracks outlined in white lights. 'What's the worst that can happen?' His eyes lit up, the keen intelligence shining and I could almost see the journalist brain tipping into over-drive.

'No, forget I said that.' I was sure he could think of several disasters and with my current track record, it didn't even begin to bear thinking about.

'Don't worry. Close your eyes and think of ... *hygge*.'

'Very funny.'

'It'll be over in a flash and at least you can say you've done it.'

I nodded.

'And I'll be with you ... if you want.'

Judging by the length of the queue, it was the most popular ride and as we stood in line, everyone debated as to whether we should have opted for the virtual reality option, with masks which apparently gave the added element of flying dragons surrounding you. I kept quiet. They had to be joking; the ride looked plenty scary enough without enhancements.

All too quickly the queue moved up and we were on the steps, getting closer and closer to the station where the carriage came in. What the hell had I been thinking when I agreed to this? I think I let out a little involuntary whimper and with leaden legs mounted the next step on the staircase, my hand cramping on the handrail.

Ben turned my way. I raised my head with a determined who-me-scared lift of the chin and gave him an approximation of a smile, stretching my face in the right sort of direction and baring my teeth. It probably would have frightened small children and it didn't fool him. His hand fumbled to take mine, giving it a quick squeeze. I closed my eyes, and squeezed back, waiting for his fingers to fall away but he kept my hand firmly clasped in his, stepping closer so that we were side by side.

'You look terrified.'

'I was hoping it didn't show.' My attempt at dry and deadpan failed big-time.

'Only because I was looking for it. You don't have to do this.'

I didn't, but I felt as if I ought to. I was part of this ragbag team. All for one and one for all. In the last couple of days after sharing those personal insights and problems we were creeping towards a hesitant bond.

'I'm going to have to.' I looked at Avril and Conrad on the steps above me, chattering excitedly and pointing to the riders already installed. 'It's safe right? A carriage on a track fifty foot over the ground, careering along at sixty plus miles an hour defying the natural law of gravity without a single safety net in sight.'

'Atta girl.' He grinned at me, his fingers tightening between mine in silent teasing.

I closed my eyes and couldn't help the quick shudder that shook my body.

'Kate,' he tugged my hand so that I faced him, and with a serious face he said, 'It lasts one minute. That's sixty seconds. It will be over before you know it.'

I let out a long breath.

'Sixty seconds?'

'Yup. A whole minute.'

'OK. I can do that.'

The queue moved forward with a start and suddenly we were almost there on the final platform. A smiling blonde girl (of course she was blonde and smiling, this was Denmark) took the tickets, guiding everyone into their seats. I took a step forward. There was still time to back out like the young boy and his mum who got to the top of the steps and then changed their minds. His loud wailing probably had a lot to do with her decision. If only I were seven.

And then the girl halted me and Ben. For a minute, I thought I'd got a reprieve, some divine intervention deciding we weren't suitable but no it was as simple as the cart was full.

'See you at the bottom,' called Fiona waving both hands at us, her excitement making her bounce up and down in her seat when she should have been clinging on to the padded barrier in front of her for dear life. Was the girl mad?

I held my breath as the cart crept out watching as it slowly started the first climb.

Ben looked down at me, something sizzled between us.

'That night, at the Grosvenor. Why did you run away?'

It was absolutely the last thing I expected him to say and it made me panic far more than the thought of going on the ride, so I blurted out the truth.

'I was scared.'

It wasn't what he was expecting me to say.

'Scared?'

'Yes.' I looked over his shoulder, self-preservation kicking in. 'And now I'm bloody terrified.' I winced as a wave of screams came flooding back down the track.

Something shimmered in his eyes, a fleeting combination of tenderness, intent and sympathy which made my heart jump in my chest with a miss-a-beat bump.

Unable to peel my eyes from his I watched as his head dipped closer and closer, until his nose grazed mine and his mouth touched mine.

Little sparks of electricity pinpricked across my lips, the initial tingle of skin on skin sending a charge racing through every vein with delicious warmth. As he lips moulded mine, the kiss deepening, I relaxed into his body as if it were home. The slow heady rush gathered speed as his mouth moved with a firmer touch over mine. It was everything I'd known it would be and exactly why I'd run. Alarm bells rang in my head, urgent klaxons, alert, alert, stop, stop, but my body was telling it to get stuffed.

His arms slipped around my waist, pulling me towards him. I wound an arm around his neck, at which point with a rueful smile he pulled away, leaving my lips dazed and confused.

His breath fanned over my ear as he whispered, 'That was twenty seconds, give or take.'

I took in a deep breath, my senses reeling. Twenty seconds of mind-blowing bliss.

'So if you think about it in terms of kisses, the whole ride equates to three kisses.'

'Oh,' I said faintly, touching my lips. That had certainly changed my perspective.

There was restive movement behind us as people anticipated the return of the cart which had already disgorged the previous riders. I focused on the tingling of my lips, my erratic pulse and Ben's warm firm hand holding mine. Rows of empty black seats like slightly menacing teeth awaited us, framed by the raised barrier waiting to snap you into place. Behind me excited, enthusiastic people pushed gently inexorably taking us forward. Ben took my hand again and steered me to the back as a thousand butterflies started trying to beat their way out of my stomach. I took a couple of shallow breaths as we filed into the padded seats of the ride. The barrier clunked down into place. The audible click making it all horribly final.

Then the ride started to inch out. Slowly, slowly.

One second. Two seconds. Three seconds. The hydraulics click click clicked with ominous inevitability, like the crocodile chasing Captain Hook. I gripped the barrier, my hands almost like claws. They were going to need to be pried off with a crowbar at the end.

I hissed in an indrawn breath as we crept closer and closer to the top, rising up the first steep incline with agonising slowness. Below us the magical landscape of the park spread out, shadowy trees and the lake shimmering with reflections. Away to my left, the horizon with buildings and towers was lit up against the night sky. With a lift of my heart which had nothing to do with the rising fear, I felt the reassuring warmth of a solid hand placed on top of mine. I risked a quick peep at Ben's face. His encouraging smile turned my bones to jelly.

And then we teetered for a second at the very top, before plunging over the edge.

Shit. Shit. Shit. Lights flashed and sped by, a blur of neon colour. We rushed down, down, down, hair whipped my face and the air racing past stole my breath. My heart pounded, my stomach falling and falling and then seconds later we were flying upwards, to a chorus of screams as we whistled through the night.

'Oh my God. Oh my God. Oh my God.' And then we were upside down and this time I squeaked, too frightened to unclamp my jaws to scream.

Ben's hand tightened, his thumb rubbing soothingly over the back of my bone-white knuckles, his thigh nudging mine as he moved his body closer.

With a wrench right, we twisted, tilting on the track precariously as if at any moment we might come off the rails. I hung on for dear life aware of someone ahead of us screaming like a banshee and people on the front row waving their arms in the air. I closed my eyes, as my stomach went into freefall. This was sheer hell. No bloody wonder the ride was called The Demon.

I staggered from the ride, Bambi-legged, buffeted by the flow of people bubbling with enthusiasm for the ride. Ben looped an arm around me and dragged me out of the downward stream to the side by a railing.

'Oh my God. Oh my God. I did it. I did it.' Babbling, I turned to face him, clutching his forearms.

'You did.' His indulgent approving nod added to my sense of jubilation and something inside me flipped. Gratitude and euphoria guided me and all my earlier reservations jumped ship, I leaned in to kiss him.

The minute my lips met his, with a ragged exhalation he pulled me to him, slamming my body against his. I squirmed as a shiver of uncontained delight flashed at the touch of his hand sliding up my back to hold me firm as his mouth slanted over mine, roving with determined possession. Another hand cupped my head as I kissed him back, thrilling to his muffled moan, my arms sliding around his waist, hanging on for dear life. I stretched up on tip-toes pressing my lips harder against his, diving headlong into the kiss. Nerve endings fried. I sank deeper, opening my mouth, giving in to the heady rush of emotion as his tongue touched mine, fireworks exploding like shooting stars. A languid warmth burned low in my belly, heating every vein. I wanted more and pressed against him, my hips nudging at his. In silent, heartfelt response he pulled me even tighter to his long lean body.

Sensations built, passion firing as I met every move of his mouth with answered hunger. My fingers crept up into his short hair, relishing the tingling in my fingertips as I raked them mindlessly over the coarse bristles.

Arms twisted. Noses bumped. Breaths came, punchy and erratic.

It was as if we hadn't got off the roller-coaster, feelings and sensation, looping and dropping with no control. I clung harder to him, trying to anchor myself, fearing if I let go I might fall. I'd never kissed or been kissed like this and I couldn't bear to let go. I wanted to hang on for ever.

It was almost too much to take. Breathing heavily, we finally pulled apart our gazes locked as I stood in the circle of his arms.

'Wow,' he said dragging in a long breath.

I nodded, aware of the pounding of my heart thudding so hard I could feel it vibrating against my ribs.

'Wow, indeed,' I whispered, still unable to tear my gaze from his. Dazed he looked back at me, his pupils wide, his hair mussed. It made me smile.

'Don't look so smug,' he growled, stilling but I could feel his ribcage rising and falling and see the racing pulse in his neck.

I lifted my shoulders in a tiny gesture of feminine pride.

'We need to get out of here,' he whispered. 'Damn, the others will be waiting for us.'

I nodded, my lips well-used and tingling.

'Meet me later? When we get back to the hotel? There's a bar around the corner.'

Our cold faces glowed as we swept into the warmth of the foyer of the hotel, David teasing Fiona about how much she'd squealed on the Sky Flier, Avril laughing at Conrad and Ben who'd chickened out of the Golden Tower and Sophie and I teasing each other over whose jeans were the wettest after the boat rides.

Ben and I had kept a discreet distance after The Demon, exchanging frequent secretive glances and checking the time on our watches, waiting for when we could return to the hotel.

'Kate,' boomed a voice, carrying over the heads of everyone and silencing the group.

I turned in the direction of the voice, an automatic response to my name as recognition hit ten seconds later like a dodgem slamming to a reverberating halt.

I felt as if I'd run into a door. 'Josh,' I said weakly, as he stood up from one of the seats in the reception area. I stared at him, refusing to voice the question or give him the damn satisfaction of answering, *What are you doing here?*

Instead I left him there, with everyone staring curiously at him.

'Do you know this man?' asked Conrad, his moustache quivering with gentlemanly valour.

'Unfortunately, yes,' I muttered, my heart sinking like a suet pudding. I stole one last look at Ben.

'Megan thought you needed reinforcements.'

I wanted to ask where they were, but I stopped myself in time.

'Hello everyone, I'm Josh Delaney, from the Machin Agency.'

'How odd. We're going home the day after tomorrow,' I said trying to sound cool and unemotional.

'Belt and braces. You know. Make sure the last few days go without any more hitches.' He attempted a winning smile at the group. 'It's not been plain sailing so far, has it?'

I heard Avril's indrawn hiss and saw horrified guilt fill her face as she whispered something to Conrad.

Feeling the quick flash of fury heat my face, I gritted my teeth at his patronising tone. What had I ever seen in him?

There was an uncertain pause and then Avril, completely ignoring him, said with her best princess hauteur, 'Are we still heading for the bar? I could murder a G&T. Do you want to catch us up Kate?' She crossed in front of me and gave me a wink.

'Yes, I'll see you in there in a minute.' I schooled my face hiding my amusement as bless them, they all patted me, waved and nodded as they trooped off towards the bar, Ben walking the most slowly as if checking I didn't need any intervention.

I could have kissed them all for the unspoken show of solidarity.

'You all seem very pally,' said Josh, reverting to his usual snide self the minute they were out of earshot. 'No wonder there have been a few problems.'

'Nothing that hasn't been handled,' I said, glaring at him. 'How dare you try to suggest I'm incompetent in front of them?'

'If the cap fits.' He shrugged and gave a sharky smile as I wondered at the cost of punching his perfect white teeth down his throat.

'Not one of them has any complaints about the way the trip has been run.' Or not that they'd voiced.

'Which is why Ed and Megan decided to let you stay.'

'Let me stay,' I squeaked like an irate guinea pig, taking a second look at his expensive dentistry. Maybe it would be worth the satisfaction.

'I thought it would be helpful to have a second pair of hands.'

'Pardon!'

'Oh for God's sake, Kate. Stop being so defensive. Think of this as an opportunity. I can report back on your performance over the next two days.'

'Defensive! You think I should just ignore the fact that you've waltzed in, without any warning.'

'Come on, Kate. You've been making a right hash of things. Accidents. Losing journalists. Running up huge bills. It doesn't look terribly professional and …' he looked after the retreating group. 'If I may say, I think I can see the problem. It all looks a touch too convivial. You've gone native instead of remembering you're supposed to be working. It happens, when you're not very experienced.'

I wanted to growl at him. *No, you may not say a damn thing.* Instead, I said hotly, 'We've been to the Tivoli Gardens. Everyone let their hair down. Funnily enough no one got lost or had an accident and if there was a place for that to happen that would be it.'

'Was that wise? You should be keeping a professional distance. These people are journalists. Contacts. They're not friends.' He curled his lip obviously remembering how Sophie and I had marched in together laughing.

His words also stung. These people had become friends. Sophie and I had already arranged to have lunch when we got back.

'Seriously Kate, there is a question over your professionalism. Getting too close to press contacts is always courting disaster. Look how Conrad presumed on your good nature. Next thing we know you'll be sleeping with Benedict Johnson.'

I coloured and he gave me a sharp assessing look, raising an eyebrow.

'That would be an unpardonable professional transgression.'

Chapter 20

As I rolled out of bed, a sense of depression descended. It was tempting to stay in bed. Text Josh, tell him he could take over.

That damn promotion was floating away like a helium balloon, with me destined to run after it for ever more trying to grab at its string. I flopped back onto the mattress. I'd rather think about Ben and that kiss.

Last night Josh had insisted on sitting in the foyer, going over the next two day's itinerary in detail, assessing all the possible risks, while the others had decamped to the bar. If only he knew that the biggest risk at that moment in time was Conrad doing serious damage to the hotel tab back in the bar, with a round of brandies for everyone.

'So, you're sure the walk to the Design Museum will only take twenty minutes.'

'Yes,' said Mads.

'And we'll leave straight after breakfast?' asked Josh again.

'People like to go back to their rooms. So, we will meet in the foyer at nine a.m. Everyone comes to breakfast at different times.' Mads and I exchanged a smile. Fiona was allergic to mornings and always rushed into breakfast at the last possible minute, invariably forgetting something that she had to return to her room for.

'No wonder you've been having problems. You should have insisted at the outside. Stick together. Stop people wandering off and doing what they please. These people will take advantage as soon as look at you.'

'What people?' asked Mads looking confused as if he'd had a complete lapse in his understanding of English.

'The press. The journalists on the trip. They're … well not quite the enemy but they're not our friends.' He shot me a dark warning look.

Mads continued to look perplexed and Josh tutted.

'Don't worry.' He turned to me. 'It's mine and Kate's job to keep a tighter rein on everyone. We'll lay down the law at breakfast tomorrow. Make our expectations clear.'

'Josh they're adults … it's not a school trip.'

'No, Kate,' he said emphasising the t in my name with a snap, 'it's a business trip, with clear aims, objectives and goals. And it's our job to see that they are all met. I think you might have lost sight of that.' His eyes bored into me. 'Give journalists an inch and they take a mile wherever they can. They're on the opposite side of the fence.' With a humourless laugh, he added, 'They rarely do us any favours. We're here for the client. This isn't a jolly; they're here to work too.'

'I-I know that,' I said trying to sit up straighter.

'Now, tomorrow's itinerary. I don't want anything to go wrong. Let's go over it and identify potential threats to our plans.' He'd pulled out of his Paul Smith man-bag, an A4 foolscap pad.

Seriously? We were going to the Design Museum. What did he imagine might happen? A large sideboard falling on someone? One of the group swallowed by a particularly over stuffed sofa?

In the pool of morning sunshine, I lay in bed with my wrist over my eyes mulling over Josh's words. Had I been too lenient with everyone? Been a bit too laissez-faire? Megan had said I needed to have more gravitas. Maybe I hadn't been quite as professional as I should have been. Wanting too much to be part of the group?

Kissing Ben.

No, not professional. Not professional at all. What had I been thinking? Stupid question, I hadn't been thinking at all. A dull ache in my heart throbbed at the thought of Ben. Held to ransom by hormones and post roller-coaster euphoria. If Josh got so much as an inkling, my career would be dead and buried. I still had two days to prove I could do this. I needed to speak to Ben. Tell him last night had been a mistake and that we needed to talk press coverage. That was being professional. That was looking out for my career. That had to come first. I'd worked too hard to get here to give it all up for a couple of kisses, no matter how mind-numbing, heart-stopping and brain-scrambling they might have been.

I sighed again. God it was only six o'clock. There was no way I could get back to sleep.

The lights glowed in Varme and down the steps I could see Eva flitting about. She probably wasn't even open yet, but when I appeared at the door, she rushed over and let me in.

'Morgen Katie. You're very early. Do you need coffee or perhaps a hot chocolate today?'

Eva's question was loaded with more than polite enquiry.

'Is it that obvious?' I shrugged off my damp coat. The morning air held a touch of sea mist and the promise of rain.

'Something is bothering you.'

'Someone.'

'Ah, I did wonder.'

I gave her a sharp glance and couldn't help smiling. 'Are you a white witch or something?'

'No, just an observer of human nature. Come in the kitchen with me, while I make some hot chocolate. It will go perfectly with the chokolade snegle I'm making and I could do with some help. Then you can tell me all about it.'

She handed me an apron, pushed me to the sink to wash my hands and by the time I'd dried them, she'd switched on the espresso machine and put out several mounds of dough on a floured board. Quickly she showed me what she wanted me to do which thankfully was quite simple. Just roll them out into rectangles. Even I could manage that.

As I picked up the rolling pin, she held up a finger making me pause.

'And remember, do it with love. Think of the people who are most special to you. Who would you make this for?'

She waved the finger. 'And don't tell me. Just think of them.' When I levelled a polite but slightly disbelieving look her way, her eyes twinkled in merriment.

I rolled the first rectangle out, next to her, thinking of my dad, Brandon and John. God, they'd demolish a whole plate of Danish pastries faster than a horde of locusts. Connie would love them too.

The dough felt soft under my fingers and I took extra care, copying Eva's careful rhythm not pressing too hard and using the rolling pin in the way that I'd seen Sophie teaching Fiona. My rectangle was almost as perfect as hers. 'Look Eva! I did it.' I felt a ridiculous sense of achievement.

'Well done. Now for the next bit.' With her usual economic efficiency, she showed me how to spread the cinnamon mixture over the dough and then roll it into one fat sausage that she then sliced into the individual pastries. I copied her.

'OK, now we have several more batches to do.' She handed me a coffee. I took a sip, feeling a lot better as the hot strong coffee hit the spot.

'My company have sent someone out to ... keep an eye on me, I guess.'

'Oh.' Eva looked up, surprised.

With a scowl, I put down my cup, missing its heat and picked up my rolling pin. 'I feel a bit of a failure.'

'Careful,' she pointed to the pastry which had suddenly gone a bit wonky. I concentrated for a second and managed to get it straight again.

'Do you think you're a failure?' Eva waited as if she expected an answer.

I finished rolling the pastry before I lifted my head to look at her.

'You're doing it again, that white witch thing.'

She didn't deny it but instead prodded my dough. 'Gently.'

'You're worse than the Spanish Inquisition,' I said shaking my head, turning the dough, ready to spread the filling across the surface. I stopped because I was supposed to be thinking good thoughts. 'It's bad enough that they sent someone because they don't think I'm doing a very good job. Sending Josh Delaney, my ex and the man that was promoted rather than me has rubbed salt in the wounds.'

'Ah.'

'Ah indeed.' I could see nothing but the full story was going to satisfy Eva. I put down the spatula. 'Josh and I were together for a while but we kept it quiet because we worked together. I was too stupid to realise that he was keeping it quiet because we were both going for the same promotion. Which he never mentioned. And now he's here *to report back on my performance.*'

'Ouch.'

'Ouch indeed. Apparently, I've been too familiar with the journalists. Not keeping my distance enough.'

'But, why should you? I don't understand.'

'Because I'm working and I should have maintained a professional relationship and kept a business-like distance from them.'

'Says who?'

'Josh is my senior and he's reporting back to my bosses. For the next two days, I'm going to have to toe the line.'

'Why? Lars clearly thinks you can do this. And I've seen nothing that indicates otherwise.'

'That's very kind, Eva, but unfortunately Lars doesn't have any say in my promotional prospects.' I paused and picked up the spatula again. I might as well be honest with her; she had a habit of getting you to do that. The café had become quite the confessional over the last few days.

'The only reason I got this job was Lars came to the agency at the last minute. On the day that he came in, there was no one else to deal with him, so they let me do it because they knew I wouldn't say no. And,' I stopped trying to work out how to phrase it diplomatically, 'Lars had been quite ...' Although Eva's incredible English vocabulary might put some English people to shame, the word assiduous might test even her, 'careful, so they really didn't expect for him to choose us.'

Eva rested her hands loosely on the table, a knowing smile on her face. 'I know my son. He knows what he wants but he's not always very good at explaining it. He relies a lot on gut instinct.' The fierce maternal pride lit a tiny spike of envy. 'He's very like me, although he has his father's business drive.'

'My bosses were ... gobsmacked when Lars gave us the business. Me too. But then he insisted on us organising a press trip, which they didn't think was the right thing to do. It's challenging to get the press to commit to coming to something like this.'

'Do you think a press trip was the right thing to do?'

'I do now especially as Lars has arranged such a fantastic itinerary. Everyone has, well almost everyone, is having a great time. I think most of them will want to write about his new store and how it relates to the things they've seen on the trip. And I think it's left a lasting impact on their view of things. Some people will be making changes in their lives as a result, which,' I paused, 'is actually a rather lovely bonus.'

'But arranging for them to come on the trip? The difficult bit, that was left to you,' observed Eva, shrewd as ever.

I stretched my neck feeling the tension resting there. 'Yeah. That's pretty much it.'

'Lars is a very good judge of character. He talked to lots of people in London before he made his final decision.'

I sighed. 'I'm not posh like the other girls at work,' I blurted out. 'They all come from well-heeled families, they've got connections and know the right people. I've had to work my way up. I'm not really good enough.'

'Why would you think that? Of course, you are.'

'Oh Eva.' She was so kind but she didn't understand. 'I'm not.' I pushed my hair off my face with the back of my floury hand, wanting to be honest with her. 'I've been trying to get promoted for the last year and every time I think I'm getting close, they raise the bar.'

'Do you not think that says more about the people you work for? I've seen you in action. I see how much you want to do a good job for Lars' company. You're good with people, you look after them because you're a nice person. Not because it's your job. Look how you've looked after Conrad. And Avril. You've made Fiona feel good about herself with her photography. And I don't know what's going on with Ben,' her eyes twinkled wickedly, 'but he seems happier. David too. It's just Sophie, we still need to fix.'

'Sophie?' Sunny, happy Sophie. What needed fixing there?

'Yes, I worry about her. She puts on a great front, a bit like you, but there's something that isn't right. She's almost too happy. Too upbeat. Being positive to hide the truth. Like you've been hiding. You have choices Katie. You can choose to change things. Now finish this last batch and we're done.'

Just as I loaded the trays into her oven, movement beyond Eva caught my eye and I looked up over her shoulder towards the café door.

'Good morning Eva,' boomed Conrad pushing open the door. 'Ah, Kate fancy seeing you here.' He marched in, slipping off his leather gloves and slapping them down on the table as if he meant business. David and Avril filed in behind him looking decidedly furtive as they crowded around the table.

I peeled off my apron and went out to join them.

'Morning Eva,' said David quietly. 'Sophie and Fi are on their way. And I believe Ben is just finishing his call.'

The three of them brimmed with suppressed glee.

With a nod, Conrad indicated outside the window, where as usual Ben was pacing up and down talking on his phone. 'His sister, I believe.'

My pulse immediately picked up an unwelcome beat at the sight of him and the H&M bag under his arm. I'd returned the spare jeans to him yesterday before we'd gone out to the Tivoli Gardens.

'What are you all doing here? Not that I'm not pleased to see you guys, but ...?' Although I was particularly grateful that Ben had stayed outside.

'We fancied breakfast here for a change,' announced Avril, plonking herself down at the table and immediately arranging the table, moving the menus to one side and tidying up the napkin holder, assuming charge as if she were the queen at court.

'All of you?' I asked.

'Yes,' said Avril in a tone that brooked no argument.

Then Sophie and Fiona walked through the door and a second later Ben followed them.

I took a big slurp of coffee, examining the milk froth at the bottom of the cup for all I was worth.

'Morning all,' said Sophie coming to sit down next to me bringing with her the cold chill of the morning as she shrugged off her coat. I made a fuss of helping her pull it off and arranged it on the back of the seat for her as Fiona pulled up a chair from the next table squeezing it in next to David. Out of the corner of my eye I was aware of Ben sitting down next to Avril but I studiously avoided looking that way.

'Isn't this nice? Breakfast together,' said Sophie. 'Everyone together. Shame you couldn't get us all in a selfie, Fi,' she added picking up a menu.

'I can!'

Within seconds Fiona had set up a portable *War of the Worlds* looking tripod, screwed her camera to the top of it and placed it on the opposite table.

'Eva, you have to come in too,' I insisted.

Fiona set the timer and dashed over in time to hear the whine of the timer counting down.

'Whatever you do don't say sausages,' shouted Avril, 'because that makes me think of something completely different and not a look I want on camera.' Her theatrical shudder made us all laugh as the camera clicked.

Eva bustled off back to the kitchen as Fi showed us the picture. It was a one in a million shot, a perfect moment in time, capturing shared joy and one that made you smile just looking at it. Avril, eyes alight with naughty amusement, had her arm around Ben who had a secretive smile on his face, almost as if he were looking at me. Conrad between Fiona and Sophie was laughing uproariously while David next to me grinned, happiness shining from his face and Eva squished in the middle of all of us beamed proudly like mama hen with her chicks.

'Now what's everyone having?' Sophie had disappeared behind the menu again.

'Do you ever think of anything except food, Sophie?' asked Avril, leaning over the table and poking her.

Sophie laughed. 'Occasionally I think of ... Hi Eva. Ooh coffee and *kanelsnegle*. Yum.'

Everyone round the table burst out laughing as Eva brought over a tray of coffees with a plate piled with cinnamon rolls, which smelt delicious.

As plates and coffees were handed out I spoke to Fiona. 'Would you be able to email me that shot?'

'Sure.'

'When could you do it?' I'd had an idea but wasn't sure how feasible it would be in the brief timescale available.

'Right this minute.'

'Really?'

'Blue tooth to my phone. Email. Bish. Bosh. Bash.'

The picture appeared almost immediately in my email inbox.

I looked at my watch, the *kanelsnegle* had been demolished and an enthusiastic discussion had ensued about whether people wanted anything more to eat.

'And you didn't fancy breakfast in the hotel?' I asked.

Shit, Josh was going to have a cow. I had an image of him sitting alone at a table for eight waiting for everyone to rock up. It was hard to feel sorry for him though.

'That Josh guy was a tosser,' said David with a quick glance at the others as if he'd decided to be spokesperson. '*It's not been plain sailing*,' he mimicked. 'What does he know?'

I blinked a little at the unlikely words coming from him of all people.

'How dare they send someone out to check on you,' said Avril indignation quivering in her voice. She tossed her hair over her shoulder in true princess style. 'We heard what he said to you last night – we're not having it.' She, David and Conrad, the united front, straightened in unison as if preparing themselves to take on an army. 'No, we're not having it at all. We'll show him. He'll soon realise that he's not going to swan in and take charge of our little gang.'

'That's nice of you all but ...' Tears pricked at my eyes.

'But, nothing,' said Conrad. He put his elbows on the table and leaned towards me and pointed both his fingers at me, as if they were pistols. 'This is my fault. Isn't it? I'm a stupid old fool and now I've got you into trouble.'

'No Conrad—'

'Yes Kate,' he said. 'I behaved badly and you shouldn't be punished for it.'

'I think "punished" is a bit strong.'

'It's my fault too,' butted in Avril. 'If I hadn't sent that tweet no one would ever have known about Conrad. Not to mention my stupid bridge escapade.'

'You've looked after us really well, Kate,' added Sophie.

'Really well,' added Fiona.

'Quite well,' said Ben. At the sound of his voice I sneaked a quick look his way, which was a mistake because catching the tiny smile lifting his stern expression sent an ill-considered flutter in my stomach. My memory leapt into action, making me want to touch my lips at the remembered imprint of his mouth there last night. I stiffened. Not going to go there. It was a salutary reminder I needed to stay well away from him today.

'Very well, indeed,' pronounced Conrad, nudging Ben in the arm.

For a minute, I was too choked to speak, looking round at their earnest faces.

Perhaps I could have been a bit firmer with them all as it now seemed I had full-scale mutiny on my hands which wasn't going to do me any favours with Josh, even if it made me feel rather warm and lovely inside.

'Listen to them,' said Eva coming to stand behind me, putting her hands on my shoulders. For a second I wanted to lean back into her and I felt a warm glow in my chest at the sight of them all looking at me with such support.

'Sophie said you usually came here first thing, so last night when we were in the bar we decided we'd come here to see you instead of going to breakfast,' explained David.

'You're all so lovely. Thanks for the vote of confidence … it means a lot.'

'And so it should,' said Sophie linking her arm through mine. 'That jumped up little toad, isn't going to … I don't know. It's like in *Dirty Dancing*. No one puts Baby in the corner. Well no one tells our Kate that she's surplus to requirements. We love you. We love being on this trip with you. And you don't need reinforcements.'

'Thank you, I really appreciate your support but I ... well I don't think Josh is going to take much notice. They sent him because they think I've made a hash of things.'

'Well, today they're going to find out they're wrong.' Sophie squeezed my arm. 'Today we're going to be Team Kate.'

'So what can we do to help?' asked Fiona, picking up her camera and taking a shot of me and Sophie together.

I looked at my watch. 'OK, there is one thing you can do for me, I'd be so grateful if you could be on time to meet Mads at nine-thirty in the foyer.'

'Is that all?' asked Avril in disgust.

'That would be perfect.' I just wanted the rest of the trip to go as smoothly as possible.

'We're on it,' said David lifting a hand and turning to Avril who high-fived him and then like a Mexican wave, everyone joined in.

Chapter 21

At nine-thirty everyone was all present and correct in the foyer awaiting Josh. I could have kissed every last one of them. Even Ben.

When Josh emerged from the lift he looked a little put out at first but quickly rearranged his expression to hide his irritation.

'Ah, excellent. Everyone's here. I missed you all at breakfast.'

'Oh, sorry Joseph,' said Avril.

'Josh,' he corrected.

She waved a hand in a whatever gesture. 'I do like to take a quick walk in the morning, it helps me think of angles for the breakfast feature I'm thinking of running. You know, how the new department store, Hjem, brings the true flavour of Copenhagen to London. It's so helpful to do some extra research. You know, so that we do justice to the Danish concept of *hygge*. This trip has brought it home to me, what it's all about.'

'Yeah,' Fiona chipped in, 'and I like to get out and take lots of photos so that I when I do my blog posts, I can show my followers an insight into how the new store reflects Danish culture.'

Josh nodded looking quite bewildered, surprised by the well-drilled students in front of him. 'Right. Excellent. So is everyone ready for our trip to the Design Museum this morning? We have an excellent speaker who will be talking about the importance of Danish design to the national psyche.'

'Yes, so Kate's been telling us,' said Conrad with a lie so bare-faced I had visions of his nose growing a centimetre a second.

'Yes,' Ben piped up clearly not wanting to be outdone by the others, 'I'm thinking of running a feature on Danish happiness to coincide with the opening of the store. A lifestyle piece on how people can recreate the typical Danish cosiness and what they need to do. I think readers of the *Inquisitor* would be fascinated by the way that Danish culture is geared towards equality and togetherness.'

Ben's outrageous declaration had me turning away, there was no way I could keep a straight face at that one or tamp down the little warm glow his words elicited, even though he probably didn't mean them.

'Right,' said Josh nodding slightly wide-eyed. 'I need a quick word with Kate and then we'll be off.'

He drew me to one side. 'I think it would be a good idea if you brought up the rear, make sure no one wanders off or lags behind. I'll go up ahead with Mads. He seems nice enough but far too casual about things. We need to stay on schedule. I'm not sure he's left enough time to get to the museum this morning, so we'll need to walk quickly.'

'Copenhagen's very compact. I'm sure—'

'Kate,' his voice quivered with a definite repressed warning.

'I want you to make sure everyone keeps up. We've got exactly three hours at the Design Museum, quarter of an hour to get to the market and then half an hour there before we have lunch nearby. If we fall behind there'll be—'

'Josh,' I put up my hand, unable to keep quiet. He was clueless. 'Mads knows exactly what he's doing. Everyone is very laid back, that's the Danish *hygge* thing.'

'I'll be the judge of that if you don't mind. I think judgement might have been the issue.'

He clapped his hands to get everyone's attention. Conrad raised an elegant eyebrow and threw Josh a regal stare full of rebuke, Avril completely ignored him and carried on chatting to David and Ben while Fiona and Sophie were taking selfies and swapping phones.

Luckily Mads stepped in front of Josh. 'The Design Museum is one of my favourite places. Today, you're going to see a lot of chairs.' In his sing-song accent, seeing *a lod ov chess*, sounded rather charming and like well-behaved children, all six journalists fell silent, turning to face him and listening with studious attention.

Bloody hell, that was a first.

Conrad groaned and clutched his hands to his heart. 'Heaven, darling. Danish design. Chairs. Pure beauty. Strong, clean lines. Design classics.' He fell into step beside Mads and I could hear the names, *Arne Jacobsen, Hans Wegner, Alvar Aalto* being bandied about.

Josh acting like an overenthusiastic sheepdog constantly doubled back to round everyone up urging them to pick up their pace. It was like a route march across enemy territory.

I stomped along at the back, conscious of the growing irritation among the group. Even Sophie was muttering under her breath which was not a good sign.

'Illums Bolighus,' announced Conrad in theatrical tones, stopping dead outside the stylish looking department store on Støgnet that we'd passed umpteen times in the last couple of days. I knew for a fact he and Avril had visited before because they'd come back to the hotel with the store's distinctive carrier bags.

All of us had previously commented on the fabulous window display, a perfect outdoor garden picnic scene themed in tasteful lemon and grey. Forget wooden benches, Tupperware and plastic plates, this was garden furniture Danish style, a lemon canvas hammock full of grey pillows, ladder back shelves full of yellow and white pansies in silver conch shell pots, a glass table balanced on the top of six beech legs which curved out from the centre, lemon and grey chairs and a table setting with matching napkins and runners with chunky white pottery plates rimmed with grey lines.

'We have to go inside,' said Avril. 'Look how gorgeous it is.'

'Of course, we do,' agreed Sophie, the two of them exchanging a look I wasn't party to.

'We have a minute,' said Mads. 'It's not a problem.'

Josh glared at him. 'It will be if we stop every five minutes on the way.'

He stepped in front of the entrance which was a bit ridiculous as it was two double doors wide up a small flight of stairs and of course to Avril tantamount to throwing down the gauntlet.

'But Illums is famous throughout Scandinavia,' said Conrad, his moustache quivering. 'It would be criminal for us to pass and not take a peek. Fiona, get your camera ready.'

As Josh watched, they all skipped past, even Ben, who I'm pretty sure had absolutely no interest whatsoever.

'This is your fault,' hissed Josh hurrying after them.

'Mine?'

'Yes, you shouldn't have let them stop to look in the window.'

'Josh, there's plenty of time and don't forget what the trip is about. This place is a Danish institution.'

He rolled his eyes and tutted, trotting in after everyone.

I had to admit Illums Bolighus was one of the most beautiful shops I'd ever been inside. Not just the impressive atrium and balconies but also the merchandise and the way it was displayed. Scented candles, expensive scarves, unique and interesting jewellery, coloured ceramics. Designer names, Alessi, Lucie Kaas, Royal Copenhagen.

If Hjem was half as nice as this, it was going to be a roaring success. Suddenly as I looked up to the light slanting in from the third storey roof, across the planes of the wood clad walls into the muted halls of the store, I understood exactly what Eva had been talking about, the very first time I met her. It was somehow soothing to be surrounded by nice things. I didn't hanker after owning them all. I didn't want to buy many things (OK a few) but it was somehow balm to the soul to be surrounded by things of beauty, of style, of taste.

It was the Danish equivalent of stopping to smell the roses.

Even Josh who'd been in such a hurry all morning seemed to calm down and I saw him stroking the arm of a wooden chair on a display by the escalator, although not for long. Soon he was back in sheepdog mode chivvying everyone along. Just as we were about to leave I went back to a display of china that had caught my eye. It was my third circuit but I adored the quirky pattern on the mugs and plates.

'Aren't they gorgeous?' said Sophie over my shoulder.

'Yes and a gorgeous price. I don't need a mug that costs 160 Krone.'

'But that pattern is so cute.'

'I know.' I looked back at the china. 'Bugger it. I'm going to buy the egg cup. It's about the only thing in my price bracket.'

Clutching the tiny piece of pottery, I almost skipped to the till which was ridiculous. It was a thing. I didn't normally buy things. Not for myself, but I just had to own one little piece of the china.

'A little bit of *hygge*,' said Sophie.

'Exactly, I love the mugs but I can't justify them at that price but one little egg cup will remind me of this trip.'

Despite the side-trip to the shop, we arrived at the museum well before it opened.

'I'll just pop and get a coffee, if you don't mind,' said David almost apologetically indicating a coffee shop down the road, not quite out of sight.

'I'd rather you didn't,' Josh barked, almost jumping in his path.

I saw Fiona bristle on David's behalf. They'd all become rather protective of him since his shy confession of loneliness.

'Well, I'm not standing here for twenty minutes with nothing to do,' said Avril, pushing the handles of another new handbag further up her wrist. 'There was an interesting looking vintage boutique near the coffee place.'

'Yes,' piped up Sophie. 'I liked the look of that.'

Josh's face was a picture. They were all being very naughty, even on a bad day they'd never been quite this wilful.

'I tell you what,' I suggested quickly, giving Sophie a quick reproving glance to which she responded with a cheeky grin. 'We'll *all* walk to the coffee shop. The boutique won't be open yet anyway. We can get a coffee and by the time we walk back here the museum will be open.' Honestly, I sounded like a flipping kindergarten teacher refereeing over a fight about a toy.

The way they all immediately straightened and fell into line, with the promise of coffee, you'd never have thought they had been knocking back double Cappuccinos less than an hour before.

'Excellent idea, Kate,' said Ben, the slight twitch to the left of his mouth hinting at a secret smile. I gave him a brief business-like nod and ignored the pang when he shot me a confused look.

'You are such a brilliant host, Kate,' sighed Fiona.

That was it. They were up to something.

This time I led the way, Josh bringing up the rear, sporting a very disgruntled scowl.

I had a horrible feeling that today was going to be very interesting.

On first glance, the outside of the Design Museum didn't shout contemporary or uber cool. Don't get me wrong, it was a lovely building. Seventeenth-century rococo, according to Mads, and a former hospital which probably explained why it didn't look the least bit designer. Of course, I was in Denmark, inside didn't disappoint. The interior had been transformed into a series of beautiful rooms with interesting displays and Mads wasn't kidding, lots of chairs. Conrad was in his element.

I could hear him telling Fiona about the different designers, dates and the names of the designs and the elements of the chairs to look out for. Everyone knew Conrad by reputation but I didn't realise how much of an expert he was.

'You should do a coffee table book,' said David as Conrad stopped at one particular display his eyeballs almost rolling in ecstasy as he pointed out the design features.

'Or you could be a teacher,' said Sophie, 'you make it sound so interesting.'

'I know someone on the faculty at the University of the Arts in London, they have a furniture design course,' said Avril. 'That would solve your financial problems. You could teach and still freelance.'

I wandered off leaving them to an enthusiastic discussion about branching out Conrad's career, deliberately taking the opposite direction to Ben.

There was an interesting chair lined tunnel and I looked at each chair in turn. I don't think I've ever seen so many variations on a theme, simple, elegant bentwood designs with sinuous contours and flowing lines. Brandon would have been intrigued by the craftsmanship and the construction. I got out my phone and snapped a couple of shots which I sent him with a quick caption.

Wish you were here? Danish design.

'It's fascinating, isn't it?' At the sound of Ben's voice, my heartbeat kicked up a notch. 'A chair is such a practical thing and yet all these designs use the same basic precept.'

Damn, I'd been so absorbed, I'd let down my guard and now Ben had found me on my own.

I nodded suddenly tongue-tied, watching warily as he made his way along the brightly lit tunnel, stopping at each chair, to give each a quick appraisal. I should have moved. Walked away but my legs didn't seem to want to play. They were listening to my heart which was misbehaving, leaping about in my chest like a wayward gazelle.

I needed to play it cool, friendly and brush last night aside. Make him see it had been a mistake, for both of us. Post ride adrenaline and the romantic surroundings of Tivoli, which had been too generous with its fairy dust.

'Who knew chairs could be so interesting?'

Damn, his voice had lowered and as he got closer, prickles of awareness danced across the skin on my arms. I ought to move away. It suddenly felt rather intimate, like a secret tryst.

I drew in a ragged breath. 'Perhaps you could write a whole article on the joys of Danish chairs,' I suggested, trying to keep things light and flippant but not flirty. Definitely not flirty.

He smiled. 'I think I'll leave the chairs to Conrad. He's quite an expert. Although,' he nodded and looked into my eyes, 'I could persuade my editor to perhaps give Conrad some freelance work.' He'd taken a step closer and every nerve ending was suddenly conscious of his proximity.

Damn, why did he have to go and be so nice?

'Yes,' I said my voice stupidly breathy, 'he knows his stuff.'

'He also knows his wine.' Ben's gentle conspiratorial teasing made my heart lurch.

'Thanks for reminding me,' I said briskly. 'Not the best moment of this trip.'

'It's been an adventure that's for sure.' An amused smile hovered around his lips as he waited for me to agree, not picking up on my body language or words, both of which were screaming stay away.

'Yes, it has been rather eventful.' I screwed up my courage, sneaking one last look at his face. 'But with only one full day left, we need to be a lot more business-like. We are here on business.' I tried to sound firm, friendly and encouraging even though each word hurt to say especially when I saw the initial confusion in Ben's eyes sharpen into understanding as they narrowed and he processed the subtext behind my words.

He had stepped closer and I could see the tiny darker flecks of blue in his eyes. I bit my lip, my eyes pleading with his to understand. 'I mean ...'

'Ah, Kate.'

I whirled round startled by Josh's voice.

'And Ben.'

Somehow, he managed to convey disapproval in those few brief words as if he'd caught us in the middle of something.

I took a deliberate step back away from Ben as Josh strode

towards us, his nose twitching as if he were on the scent of something inappropriate. I immediately flushed feeling guilty.

'B-ben and I were discussing a p-possible feature on chairs.' I would be rubbish under interrogation. I hadn't even done anything and I was tripping over my words.

'We were?' Ben raised an eyebrow, narrowing his eyes.

'Yes,' I gave him a desperate look. 'We were. We need to talk about what angles you're looking at and the sort of follow up coverage we'll get in the *Inquisitor*. What sort of article do you think you'll write?'

Ben raised a disdainful eyebrow.

'Glad to hear you're making progress at last, Kate,' said Josh. He turned to Ben. 'We had a discussion about this last night. Kate filled me in on the press coverage that's been promised by everyone else in the group. She said she's been working on you.'

I flushed turning bright red. I'd said no such thing.

'Has she?' drawled Ben, a hard edge to his words.

'Yes,' Josh beamed oblivious to the undercurrent. 'Perhaps we can have a more detailed discussion over coffee later. I'd be interested to hear your ideas.'

Ben stiffened, and I heard him take a sharp indrawn breath.

He shot me a look of pure dislike. 'I'm not sure I've had enough of the right attention, yet?' Luckily, he had his back to Josh as he insolently looked at my lips.

'I think perhaps you need to do a bit more. Go a bit further.' I felt slightly sick at his intimation.

'Well if you need any ideas, I'm sure we can have a bit of

a brain storming session,' said Josh. 'Kate can be quite creative.'

'I'm sure she's extremely creative in the right circumstances,' drawled Ben. 'But I'm OK thanks, I don't need PRs to do my job for me. I'm quite capable of finding a *story* when there's one to tell.' He bit the clipped words out as if he were trying to keep his mouth closed and looking as if there was an extremely nasty smell under his nose that he couldn't wait to get away from.

'Excellent. Excellent,' said Josh ignoring the undercurrent of tension simmering between Ben and me.

Ben's eyes shuttered and his face reverted to the cool impassive expression I was more used to.

'We've only got one more day,' reminded Josh. 'The last chance for you to get anything more concrete to work on before we leave tomorrow.'

'Don't worry, I've had everything I need from Kate, thank you,' snapped Ben and walked off down the corridor to the next room. 'In fact, I don't think I'm going to need her personal services again.'

Ouch.

The weather had turned while we were inside and we emerged to solid rain and a grey gloom which felt as if the thick dark clouds pressed in on us. Suddenly the streets seemed deserted as if everyone had decided to stay indoors. We huddled in the entrance.

'How long will it take to walk to the market?' asked Josh looking up at the sky.

'Ten minutes,' said Mads studying the clouds with decided unconcern.

'I vote we go to Varme instead,' said Avril. 'If we go there we can dry out and it'll be cosy.'

'I'm afraid not,' said Josh. 'Torvallherne Market,' he'd been practising saying it, 'is part of the itinerary.'

'And we've already done it,' snapped Sophie, 'and it's miles away and in the opposite direction.'

'What do you mean?' asked Josh, suspiciously.

'We were ahead of schedule the other day,' I explained gently, 'and we were nearby so we popped in then. Fi got some fabulous shots and is going to do a whole feature on the amazing spread of stalls there.'

Fi nodded in agreement, which seemed to mollify Josh. He reluctantly agreed and this time decided he'd bring up the rear leaving me to guide the group to Eva's. After several days in the city, we were all getting our bearings and I walked along with Sophie, our heads ducked down against the horizontal rain carried by the wind.

It seeped in everywhere, fine drizzle that left everything damp and chilly, working its way into the seams of your clothes leaving a clammy touch on skin. It was difficult to see where you were going, so we hurried along following Mads who was hunched down into his quilted brown coat like a busy turtle.

'Where's David?' asked Conrad stopping suddenly and looking around ponderously as if he'd made the discovery of the century.

'David?' echoed Fiona, water running down her nose,

looking authentically wide-eyed. 'Oh, my goodness have we lost him?'

'Joseph dear, we need to stop,' said Avril catching Josh's arm, her face signalling alarm.

God, Conrad and Fi were dreadful actors, while Avril could win an Oscar hands down. What the hell were they playing at?

'Oh, for the love of God,' snorted Josh, his hair tufted into wet peaks. 'Where did he go?' He looked around, his face tight with worry.

I honestly started to feel a little sorry for Josh.

'Wait here everybody.' He hurried over to my side. 'Where do you think he is?'

I thought he was probably hiding around a corner quivering with amusement.

'Would you like me to go and look for him?' I asked. 'I'm sure he won't be far away.' In fact, I could guarantee it. 'You go on with the others to Varme and I'll find him.'

'Are you sure?' asked Josh, looking slightly less panicky. 'What if you don't find him?'

'Oh, I'll find him,' I said grimly, throwing a quelling look at Conrad and Avril who glowed with innocence like a pair of bright-eyed naughty pixies.

I'd bet my last pound they'd put David up to this. Happiest in the herd, he was absolutely the last person to wander off on his own. I waited in the street until the others were out of sight and then looked around. Sure enough less than an eighth of a second later, David emerged from a shop doorway.

I shook my head as I went over to him, to shelter in the doorway. 'Lost?'

'I ... er, saw something. In the shop.' He pointed over his shoulder towards the window behind him.

I raised a sceptical eyebrow and looked at the shop window. 'What – in Denmark's answer to Victoria's Secret?'

'What?' he whipped round.

'Ha! Got you.' The shop sold various kitchen items.

'I must have been distracted.'

'Yeah, right David. And Copenhagen doesn't have a cycle path to its name. What are you guys up to? All that dallying on the way to the museum. You going walkabout? It doesn't stack up at all.'

'Busted.' He grinned at me. 'We're just showing Josh how well you cope with whatever's thrown at you.'

'Please,' I sighed, feeling the rain running down my neck and shivering a little, 'tell me there are no more stunts planned.'

'Hmm,' he stroked his chin, his blue eyes twinkling with sheer mischief. 'You wouldn't want me to rat on the others, now would you?'

'David! What have you got planned?' I covered my wet face with my hands.

'Not me,' he said all innocence.

I stopped him before he could say anything else, shaking my head. 'Don't tell me. I don't want to know.'

I arrived to a chorus of *Kates* from everyone as if I'd returned triumphant from an epic voyage and completed some incredible challenge. Everyone except Ben who glowered at me before ducking his head down back to his mobile phone.

'You found him,' said Conrad, his voice full of wonderment.

'Funny that,' I said patting him on the shoulder with an extra nudge and giving them all a stern stare. At least here they couldn't get up to any more mischief.

'Kate, hot chocolate?' Eva, was already at my side with a steaming mug. 'With extra cream, just how you like it. And would you like some soup?'

I took the chocolate gratefully, my hands clasping the hot cup.

Everyone had ordered Eva's soup of the day, a fish chowder bursting with prawns and mussels in their shells in a pale yellow fragrant broth. It was exactly what was needed on a grey day.

I should have smelt a rat when Avril uncharacteristically ordered a tomato juice. The girl ran on coffee fumes. And also when she'd managed to inveigle her way into sitting next to Josh, a lot closer than even the cramped conditions necessitated.

Somehow to a great scream and lots of fuss the glass ended up in her lap, soaking her jeans.

'Oh, no.' She wailed flinging her arms in the air, jumping to her feet. 'What am I going to do?'

'Oh God, I'm sorry,' said Josh also jumping to his feet. Luckily only a few spatters of tomato juice had hit him.

'It was an accident,' said Avril, who'd clearly engineered the whole thing. And it was an Oscar worthy performance far outdoing Fiona or David's little turns.

The tomato juice had done its job as well as only tomato juice can, turning more orangey as it soaked into the pale denim. Part of me had to give her credit for sacrificing, what knowing her, were a pricey pair of jeans.

'Take them off and I'll soak them now before they can stain,' said Eva bustling over. I gave her a sharp look but she was intent on helping. No, the Machiavellian tricks had only one author; they had Avril written all over them. And just a little bit of me fell in love with her, not because I approved of what she was doing, but because she cared enough to try to help me. I'd done her a disservice, dismissing her as the spoilt princess.

'Oh God, I'll pay for them,' said Josh, still believing that he'd caused the spillage rather than being Avril's unknowing patsy. Avril pursed her mouth as if she were considering his offer.

It took me a second to realise that Avril had gaily stripped off the trousers, there and then in the café, revealing a pair of silk lavender micro-briefs. Mind you if I had tanned and toned thighs like hers and a bottom that pert and perfectly sculpted, I might have been tempted to do the same.

I put my hand over my mouth to hold in the giggles that were threatening to erupt. They were all mad but so lovely and sweet, going to these lengths to make me look good.

I thought Josh's eyes were going to fall out of his head, although David and Conrad did take a second look too. Even Ben cracked his face to let a grin break through.

Eva whisked them out of her hands and Avril stood there.

'How am I going to get back to the hotel?' She looked at me, her eyes pantomime wide.

'Gosh. What. A. Terrible. Disaster,' I said robotically, clamping my jaw tight so I wouldn't break into laughter. I saw her bite back a smile, swallowing hard as I added, 'I can't begin to imagine what on earth to do.'

Josh was frowning as if trying to come up with a solution. And I did feel sorry for him, he was absolutely clueless.

'I could walk back to the hotel and go to your room and get you a pair,' I suggested even as Avril was shaking her head vehemently. 'Or maybe Josh could.'

He looked suitably horrified. 'I don't think I'd be comfortable with that. It's going to have to be you.'

Avril was flashing messages at me with her eyes, raising her eyebrows.

'But I can't sit here in my knickers all that time,' she put her hand on her chest in mock horror.

Suddenly she was feeling modest?

The atmosphere held all the tension of a tennis match with everyone anxiously waiting for the next volley. They all looked at me and then Avril, and then back again and Sophie was kicking me under the table.

Ben rolled his eyes and I heard his impatient sigh. 'You wouldn't happen to still have those jeans that ... were bought for you, when you ruined yours. The ones you were going to take back to H&M today.'

The carefully placed words and avoidance of *that I bought for you* stung. No, they hurt. A lot. Buying the jeans had been a gesture full of innate kindness but also showed a thoughtfulness that I'd underestimated. Regret pinched at the loss of that brief bright connection between us.

I'd done the right thing putting him off but it didn't help. He was the sort of man you might be tempted to hang on to. Who might distract you from your purpose. I'd known the first time I'd met him that he might be more than I wanted. That gut instinct had been right.

'Silly me. I'd forgotten all about those.' I pulled the H&M bag out, which had magically worked its way to a spot under my chair and pulled out the three pairs of jeans with a hey presto flourish. 'Kate saves the day.'

'That's amazing,' said Avril grinning all over her face.

Josh looked utterly bewildered. 'You had those with you?'

'Just call me Mary Poppins,' I said gamely, after they'd been to all this trouble, I might as well capitalise on their ploys. 'It's always handy to carry a spare pair of jeans. You never know what might happen.'

'What else have you got with you?' asked Josh, looking genuinely impressed.

'Plasters, painkillers, tweezers, Swiss army knife, spare pair of tights, matches, torch and emergency chocolate bars,' I lied smoothly focusing on Josh, so I wouldn't start giggling at Sophie hiding behind her napkin trying to hold in her laughter.

Avril took all three pairs of jeans and disappeared with Eva to try them on.

'Well done, Kate,' said Josh. 'Well done, indeed.'

I sneaked a look over at Ben; he was stony faced looking at a point below my chin.

Chapter 22

'I need a large beer,' said Josh as he fell into step next to me as we walked back to the hotel. 'I take it all back. They are a nightmare group but well done for handling them.'

No, they were six lovely people, who had rallied round and I loved them for it.

'It's a shame we have to go back out again tonight in this miserable weather. And why do we have to spend the last night at that bloody café? I'd have thought Lars would want to push the boat out as a final hurrah! That waitress seems a bit too familiar with everyone. And who put her in charge tonight? She was muttering about a surprise. The itinerary is all over the place. It's not how I would have managed a press trip. This Lars bloke has some funny ideas.'

I held my tongue.

'And I'm not sure we want any more surprises after today.' Josh looked gloomy.

'No harm done.'

'There could have been. I don't know what we'd have done without you.' He paused. 'I owe you an apology. I'm sorry that I ... that I ... I was a bit of a shit to you really.'

I shrugged. I was long over it.

'So, no hard feelings?'

I stopped and glared at him. He had to be kidding.

Ditching Josh was easy. As soon as we arrived in the hotel foyer, like everyone else he was keen to go up to his room and warm up and dry off.

'I need to speak to reception,' I said. 'See you all later. At seven in the foyer.'

Conrad brushed several drops of water from his moustache, looking longingly beyond me.

'Seven,' I repeated, knowing that between now and then he could do some serious damage. 'Go and warm up.'

'Seven it is then,' he said his moustache drooping around his mouth.

Avril hooked her arm through his. 'Come on Conrad, this way.'

They all crowded into the lift and I immediately felt a sense of relief. Bless them, their hearts had been in the right place today but I felt exhausted after trying to second guess them constantly.

I headed to reception and the girl behind the front desk was more helpful than I could have imagined and let me use the colour printer in her office. I had to pay for the privilege but I was delighted when I saw the colour photographs spilling out. And even though I didn't want to brave the rain again, I knew it would be worth it. I just needed some photo frames for the pictures which Fiona had taken this morning. They would make perfect gifts for everyone in the group.

Eva had been extremely busy. Once again, she'd rearranged the furniture and this time, created a small seating area containing some low-slung leather chairs arranged in a corner with a lamp creating a pool of light around them and next to them two wide grey sofas draped with pale throws and pastel cushions. On the shelves behind them, tea lights flickered in the coloured wine glasses, creating little kaleidoscopes of colour dancing on the walls.

Beyond this, the tables had been pushed together to make one big square table beautifully laid out with the by now familiar blue and white Royal Copenhagen china. Silver cutlery sparkled among the crystal wine glasses. Varme had been transformed and now it felt as if we'd stepped into someone's home. Eva's home. By now I recognised some of her signature touches. The little pots of fresh flowers in the centre of the table in coloured glass jugs. The mix of china, plain and patterned that didn't match but coordinated all tied in with the pretty floral napkins. A riot of colour and style that came together in one indisputable signature that was definitely Eva.

'Oh, isn't it gorgeous!' Sophie clapped her hands as we all came to a standstill just through the door, the damp drizzly night immediately forgotten.

We were greeted by Eva's part-time waitress, Agneta, who offered us one of the traditional short-stemmed glasses with a measure of schnapps, to warm us up.

'I vote a toast to Kate,' said Avril. 'Who has looked after us through thick and thin, with patience and good humour. I think if I were her I would have ditched us as soon as we got off the plane.'

'Speak for yourself, Avril. I'd have ditched you at passport control, lovie,' said Conrad raising his glass.

She lifted hers and chinked it against him. 'You're such a charmer, Conrad.'

'I know.'

'Eva, this is wonderful.' Fiona waved, her windmill arms brushing the top of David's head as Eva appeared from the kitchen, her face wreathed in smiles and her arm was linked with the arm of a tall man.

'Be still my beating heart. Who's the Viking stud muffin?' drawled Avril.

'Avril!' squeaked Fiona. 'Although I have to admit he is pretty tasty.'

'Objectification ladies,' said Ben.

Josh jumped up, his face slightly strained at the unexpected arrival.

'Lars.' He swung across the room, holding out his hand. 'Good to see you.'

Lars' eyes went over his shoulder to me, a question in them and somehow in a genius move of hidden diplomacy managed to side-line Josh's outstretched hand by unhooking his mother from his arm and crossing behind to come over to me.

'Kate, how are you? And how has the trip been?' Twinkling blue eyes surveyed the group.

'Lars, lovely to see you. Can I introduce you to everyone?'

'Let me guess, my mother's been telling me about you all.'

She'd done rather a good job as he guessed everyone's names correctly as he went around the table. And then he came to Josh who was hovering at his elbow.

'Josh Delaney, from the agency.'

Lars frowned. 'I remember you but I didn't realise that the agency was sending two people.'

'I just came out for the last couple of days to offer support to Kate.'

Eva laughed rather charmingly and patted Lars on the arm. 'Kate? Support? Darling, she's been absolutely *vidunderlig*. We've all had such a lovely time together.'

Avril latched onto Lars as only she could, charming him at the outset. Josh loitered and grabbed me by the arm, frowning.

'Why didn't you warn me?'

'Warn you? I didn't know he was coming. I had no idea.'

'I didn't mean that. Why didn't you tell me that she was his mother?'

'Who, Eva?' I thought back. It hadn't been a deliberate omission. 'I assumed you knew.'

'Well duh yeah. You've made me look a right fool. I thought she was just a waitress.'

A lump settled in my throat, I was going to miss Eva.

'I'd like to thank you all for coming to Copenhagen,' began Lars. 'And I hope that you have enjoyed a taste of *hygge* and that you have a feeling for what it's about.'

'Not just candles and cashmere socks,' jibed Avril.

He grinned at her. 'As you know very soon we will be opening Hjem, bringing *hygge* to London. I really wanted you all to understand what it's about. That it's as much an attitude to living as well as essential Danish style.'

He pointed to a large intricate model at the back of the room and invited everyone to take a look.

There were clear references to Illums Bolighus in the large atrium and the nooks and crannies of different areas in the store.

There was a furniture section with lots of Danish style chairs and Conrad immediately craned his head over them. 'The detail is phenomenal, Mr Wilder. And you'll be selling all of these designs? My goodness this will become a destination for every furniture faculty in the country. I'd love to do a feature on this.'

Fiona had whipped her camera out. 'Can I use these pictures? On my blog?'

'Yes,' said Lars. 'I've also included floor plans in the press packs, so that you can see all the details.'

'We need to discuss embargoes,' I chipped in, looking at Lars.

'And what will go here?' asked Avril pointing to an odd shaped empty room tucked away to the side of the building.

'I'm talking to a florist about perhaps taking over the space,' explained Lars. 'But it's proving difficult to source the sort of native flowers she wants to stock, so she may pull out.'

Ben had wandered around the back of the model peering in the windows as if absorbing every detail. 'Who did the model for you? Was it the architects?'

'No, I had to find someone to build it for me. That was one of the hardest jobs. Finding a model builder.' Ben's grey-blue eyes sharpened, in a way that I now recognised they did when he was thinking through an idea. 'I'd like to talk to you more about that sometime.'

'It was important that the design comes alive and becomes a design statement in its own right.'

'It is stunning,' said David wandering around it like Ben.

'And which architects designed the building?' asked Ben up and running with his train of thought, 'I'd be interested in talking to you about financing the project and what your plans are for the future. Can we fix up an interview when we get back to London?'

There he was, the business journalist. It was the most animated I'd seen him in work mode. He was taking photos with his mobile and making quick scribbles in a slim notebook.

He and Lars put their heads and mobiles together and a date was arranged for the next week. Ben had finally come good and it had nothing to do with me.

Dinner was almost at an end and there was a definite party atmosphere. Lars opened another bottle of wine and no one seemed to be worried about the next morning's early start.

Avril and Sophie jumped up. 'We'd like to say a few words.' Sophie prodded Conrad in the ribs and he stood up too.

For a minute, they nudged each other whispering. Clearly this wasn't rehearsed.

Avril cleared her throat and looked round. 'This has been ... oh gosh I'm getting a bit teary and I don't do sentimental. I wanted to thank Eva, who has been amazing, looking after us, making us feel so welcome. I think we all agree Varme has become our little home from home while we've been here. And tonight it looks incredible. Thank you.'

There was a rustle from under the table and Sophie pulled out a large bouquet of flowers which she handed to Conrad who trotted around the table to where she sat.

'On behalf of us all, Eva, thank you. You have made this trip an absolute delight and I think all of us have gained so much from being here and knowing you.'

He kissed her on both cheeks and presented her with the bound bunch of roses in soft pale pink which magically matched her cashmere sweater. She beamed, burying her nose in them.

'It's been a delight for me, getting to know you all. And you will always be most welcome to come back. I shall look forward to seeing you in London at the opening.'

Everyone clapped.

'And Mads. Well you have been fantastic. So easy going. I've been on some press trips where it's … well it's not much fun. This has not only been fun but also very rewarding and I think you have typified what makes the Danes happy. I think we've all learned a lot while we've been here.' I could see why Avril was so good at her job.

'We've got a little gift for you. A reminder.'

They pulled out a little gift for him and when he opened it, everyone roared with laughter.

'For someone who must have seen the Little Mermaid a thousand times and still managed to make it come alive for us,' said Avril presenting him with one of the tourist plastic replicas of the little statue and then she turned to look at me.

Oh God no, I ducked my head.

'And Kate,' said Sophie. 'Stand up, Kate.'

'Do I have to?' I pleaded.

'Yes. I think we all want to say thank you to you for making this such a great trip. You've been endlessly patient with us.'

I had?

'Kind,' said Avril, her eyes softening as she looked at me.

'Good natured.' Sophie saying that was quite something. 'Whenever there's been a problem ...'

'And there have been a few,' chipped in Conrad dryly with a self-deprecating roll of his eyes.

'You've got on and fixed it. No fuss, no bother. You've been enthusiastic. Helpful. And not the least bit pushy.'

Did I imagine the quick glance at Josh?

There was another rustle from under the table and Sophie pulled out an Illums Bolighus bag and gave me a big smile.

My eyes prickled and I blinked hard, a fierce lump lodging in my throat that had me swallowing.

She brought the bag around the table and gave me a hug, we held on to each other for a second. 'Thanks Kate. You've been fab.'

'I-I don't know what to say. You shouldn't have.'

'Yes, we should,' said Avril.

Conscious of all eyes upon me I fought my way into a big bundle of tissue paper, worried about dropping it in front of them all. To be on the safe side, I put it on the table and peeled away the layers, like petals on a flower, to reveal the contents at the centre.

'Oh,' I looked at Sophie and bit my lip. 'You shouldn't have.'

Inside sat not one but two of the gorgeous and ridiculously expensive china mugs, I'd lusted after because they were things of beauty. Now they also signified so much more and the wave of emotion almost mowed me down.

'T-thanks guys. That's so ... so sweet of you.' I took in a gulp of air. I was supposed to be professional and cool, but they'd reduced me to tears. 'Like Conrad said, it's been interesting at times. But brilliant too. You've all been lovely.' I rallied feeling a bit of a fool but they were all nodding and smiling. 'I love them and of course, they'll go beautifully with my egg cup.'

Eva whispered something to her son and he winked at me and lifted his glass in silent toast.

'I have something for you too,' I dug under the table and like Santa with his sack, I moved around the table distributing slim wrapped parcels to all the journalists, Eva and Mads. 'Although Fiona gets most of the credit. Thanks Fi, for letting me have these.'

The photo frames I'd bought a few hours earlier weren't much but they framed the picture taken that morning in the café, capturing the sense of camaraderie perfectly.

As they all unwrapped their parcels there were cries of approval followed by lots of hugs and kisses. No one but me noticed that Ben didn't move from his seat, although I think I saw a brief smile touch his lips but I might have imagined it.

Chapter 23

'What do you mean, the flight is fully booked?' Josh folded his arms, planting his legs in front of the check-in desk. The mulish stance suggesting he wasn't moving until he got the answer he wanted.

I stood beside him, glad that this morning he'd decided to take charge. Since we'd assembled in the foyer of the hotel to get the mini-bus to the airport, there'd been a definite air of officious one-upmanship in his manner as if he had to prove that he was top-dog today. As we were homeward bound I'd left him to it, quite happy to take a back seat.

The lady at the check-in desk smiled serenely in text book customer service fashion. She'd seen it all before and one irate customer wasn't going to come close to denting her professional, I'm-the-one-holding-all-the-cards-here demeanour.

'I'm very sorry, sir,' she managed to inject exactly the right note of empathy in her gracious it's-out-of-my-hands tone, 'but due to poor visibility throughout the day, many of the flights were cancelled yesterday.'

'But we're checked in.' His indignation rang out carrying

to the back of the queue, causing a flutter of interest. 'We've got our seat numbers.'

'Unfortunately, the plane you were due to fly on was re-routed and the plane available today has fewer seats. I'm afraid I'm unable to offer all of you seats on this flight.'

'This is totally unacceptable.'

'I'm sorry sir but I can ...'

Josh pushed his shoulders back. 'Yes, you can. You can get us onto this flight. You do realise that I have six members of the press with me.'

I winced in time honoured British fashion.

Her plastic smile stayed glued in place.

'I'm sure you wouldn't want the publicity.' Josh threw down the words and leaned on the desk with both elbows.

Ouch.

The smile slipped.

'I understand that sir, but the flight is full.' She looked at her screen and Josh leaned over the counter, craning his neck trying to see it.

'Six journalists on leading national newspapers in the UK. Writing travel features. It's not going to look very good for your airline, is it?'

Her lips firmed and she shot him a distinct back-off-buster disdainful stare.

He tipped his head to one side.

With a quick toss of her head, she tapped at her keyboard, her mouth moving in time with her fingers signalling her veiled anger.

'I could ...' She picked up her phone and spoke rapid

Danish, giving Josh a steely look. The conversation was short and to the point and she put the phone down with a mouth as pursed as a prune.

'We can offer some seats but not all eight. However, if any of your party would like to forgo their seat, they can take a later flight.'

'When's the next flight?'

Now she did look troubled. 'I'm afraid the earliest available seats because of the problems with flight control and the weather ...' she paused and I felt quite sorry for her. 'Tomorrow. However, we will provide accommodation and expenses.'

'Tomorrow. I have to be back in London today.' Josh looked around at the group of us, huddling miserably in an embarrassed group.

Avril looked worried; I knew she was desperate to see her husband.

'It's my cousin's hen do,' said Fiona uncertainly, 'although I suppose it would be a good excuse to get out of it. I won't know anyone there.' The quick accompanying shudder was probably what made my mind up. She huffed out a reluctant sigh. 'It's just I said I'd take pictures for the bride's photo album.'

'And I've got tickets to the theatre tonight,' said Conrad. 'Although they are freebies.'

'I suppose I could stay,' Sophie offered chewing at her fingernail.

'No,' I wagged a finger, 'you told me you have a hot date with your man tonight and that James is never around on Fridays or at the weekends.'

Her awkward shuffle spoke louder than any words. James sounded a bit of a tosspot to me, there's being good to your mother but shouldn't Sophie come first occasionally.

'Kate.' Josh rounded on me as if he'd had the most brilliant idea. 'Do you need to be back today? I can explain in the office.' He lowered his voice. 'For the greater good and all that.' I looked at his sudden winning, weaselly smile. I had shocking taste in men. 'I'll let Megan know you gave up your seat.'

'I'll stay because it *helps* everyone else and I don't have any major plans this weekend.' I said pointedly. Trust him to think of it as a hot ticket to promotion. At this very moment in time the biggest bonus was that it was two hours less spent in his company. The girl looked at me with gratitude as Josh weighed it up.

'But you can't stay on your own,' said Sophie, twisting her hands together.

'Soph, I'll be fine. I'm a big girl,' I gave her a cheery smile.

'I'll feel awful leaving you.' Her eyebrows scrunched and I could see her wavering.

'No,' I said firmly. 'It'll be a little adventure.' The latter was said with more enthusiasm than it warranted, my idea of adventure lay between the pages of an Enid Blyton book and the Famous Five. 'And ... I'll go see Eva.'

Yes. Eva. She'd look after me. And feed me lashings of coffee and plenty of *kanelsnegle*s.

'I'll stay.'

Ben's deep voice cut through. 'My sister's still at my flat with her kids. It'll be my only chance of any peace and quiet. I've got some writing to do.'

'Oh, that would be brilliant. Just think you can have another day here. And Kate won't be on her own,' gushed Sophie before I could say a word which was probably as well because I couldn't think of a single thing to say, well not out loud.

Ben was absorbed in his phone for most of the short train ride back to the city, which suited me fine. I had no idea what to say to him. Yesterday he'd made it clear I was persona non-grata, so I was still reeling from the shock that I was the lesser evil compared to his family and that he'd volunteered to stay.

A couple of times I looked up during the journey to find his thoughtful gaze directed my way and regret pinched at me when he immediately went back to his phone rather than catch my eye. I wanted to apologise but there didn't seem much point, we were back to where we'd been at the start of the trip. Perhaps where we should have stayed.

As we pulled into Kopvahn Station, I was fully expecting him to ditch me and go off on his own. When I said, 'I'm going to head to Varme for a cup of coffee. Tell Eva what happened and see if we can get our rooms back at the hotel. They might not have cleaned them yet,' I was amazed when he responded, 'That sounds like a plan,' and fell into step beside me.

Thankfully it was virtually impossible to walk side by side and manoeuvre our cases through the street, which meant there was no need for awkward conversation. It was a relief to see the welcoming sign of Varme down the street.

Just as I was about to turn into the café, Ben laid a hand on my arm.

'Kate, I ... there are things I want to say. I was wrong about you, I want to ...' He stopped. 'That's odd. The lights aren't on.'

Although the door was slightly ajar the place was in darkness. I checked my watch again.

'Hello. Eva,' I called uncertainly, sudden fear eclipsing the jump of my heart at Ben's unexpected words.

It was nearly eleven o'clock but it felt closed. None of the little pots of flowers had been put out, there was no welcoming smell and not a customer in sight.

'Eva!' I walked into the middle of the room, calling more loudly this time.

'Over here. Is that you Kate?' Her voice echoed with disbelief, but then a tea towel flapped from behind the kitchen counter. 'Can you help?'

I dumped my case, hearing it clatter to the floor and strode towards the counter to lean right over, hitching myself on and sliding over, my bottom up in the air.

'Eva! What have you done?'

She was half on the floor, twisting awkwardly trying to drag herself up on to a chair which was the wrong height for her to gain any purchase.

I slid straight across the counter through into the kitchen, while Ben with more sense, chose to enter via the door.

Quickly realising that she was favouring one leg, Ben with calm efficiency went straight behind her and lifted her up into the chair.

'What happened?'

Her pain-pinched lips sent a stab of fear right into my

chest, especially when she didn't give an immediate dismissive everything's fine response. The lines of her face, folded tight in a sharp wince.

'I slipped. Went over. My ankle.' She looked beyond me. 'The *spandauer* ... can you get them out of the oven?'

I looked at her and the oven, my hands flapping a bit uselessly. 'What?'

'They'll burn.'

Ben took pity on my indecision.

'You do that first while I take a look. Let's see the damage, Eva.'

As I tended to the pastries, just in time to remove them as they were already glistening with golden glaze, I kept glancing over my shoulder at Ben as he gently lifted Eva's ankle onto another chair. I paid for not paying full attention when I caught my hand on the oven shelf and jumped at the neat slice of pain that slashed across my finger.

'Can you put them on the wire tray, Katie?'

'Eva, you worry about yourself.'

She wasn't having any of it. 'It's there.' She pointed to the cooling rack on the side. I rolled my eyes at her and slid the pastries from the cooking tray.

'Could you put the next batch in?' She winced as Ben gently unzipped her ankle boot. 'They're in the fridge over there.'

'Eva!' I remonstrated and ditched the oven gloves to come and stand over her. 'That can wait.'

'It's just a silly ankle sprain.'

'Hmm not sure about that,' said Ben as the three of us looked at the rapidly swelling ankle joint. 'Have you got an ice pack?'

'Kan jeg fa en kaffe?' interrupted a voice from the other side of the counter.

'Lige et øjeblik,' called Eva to the man who'd walked in. 'In the fridge over there. Katie, would you make coffee?'

'What?'

'Make coffee.' She made to move and I waved a stern hand at her.

'Stay there, I'll do it.'

Turning to the man, I asked, 'Do you speak English?'

He nodded. 'Can I have an Americano?'

'OK.' Having made coffee the other day I was reasonably confident, although dealing with someone else's customers in front of them made me feel like I had stepped on stage and wasn't sure of my lines.

Eva caught my eye. 'Take your time. Look after him, he's a good customer.'

Which meant he was one of her people and needed looking after.

He loitered for a moment looking wearily at the menu on the board propped up on the long counter.

'Would you like anything else?' I asked, with a smile. 'The *spandauer* have just come out of the oven. They're very good.'

'OK. Thank you,' his expression immediately brightened, making me glad I'd suggested the pastry. 'I'll take one.'

'Why don't you take a seat and I'll bring it over?'

He nodded, his attention now on his phone as he went off and sat down.

'Excellent, Katie,' said Eva, with an approving nod even as she winced.

Taking it slowly I selected a nice mug, pulled out a plate, put one of Eva's pretty floral napkins on it and then selected the biggest *spandauer*; the man looked as if he could do with cheering up, and placed it on the plate, grateful that Eva's immediate attention was on Ben who had found the ice pack, wrapped it in a tea-towel and placed it over her ankle.

'And what are you doing here?'

As I made the coffee over the hiss of the steam, I explained about the flights.

'Over there.' Eva pointed them out before I even knew I needed a milk jug.

I'd just served the first customer when two more people came through the door and took seats at the table in the window.

'Don't get up,' said Ben, as Eva tried to stand up on one leg.

'But ...' she protested. 'The customers. I should close the café. I'll call Agneta, my Saturday girl, see if she can come in this afternoon.' Ben gently pushed her back into her chair and turned towards me. 'Tell us what to do. Kate and I can do it. Can't we?' With his back to her, he pulled a wide-eyed, help-what-do-we-do-here face.

'Piece of cake,' I said for Eva's benefit, giving him an equally wide-eyed-oh-God-what-have-we-done grimace.

'OK, then.' He closed the small gap between us, and held up a hand in a determined, we mean business fashion. As I high-fived him back, our eyes met and we both nodded. A brief, silent accord. For the next however long, we were a team.

I took off my coat and grabbed one of the aprons hanging

on the back of the door, rolling up my sleeves and then passed him one before picking up one of the pads by the counter.

'Right. You can be washer upper and I'll be barista and waitress.'

'Washer upper.' Dismay echoed in his voice and he held up his hands, with a mock indignant pout. 'Do these look like hands that do dishes?'

They were extremely nice hands and I had a quick vision of them holding a champagne flute.

Eva let out a limp giggle.

'They do now,' I said firmly, turning away to hide the quick flush that stained my cheeks and sauntered out of the kitchen over to the table to take the two women's order.

When I came back Ben was closing the oven door. He winked at me, comrade-in-arms, as he followed Eva's instructions to set the timer and I busied myself making more coffee, ignoring the funny lopsided beat of my heart.

The kitchen wasn't the biggest and as I turned to grab the ground coffee from its canister, I cannoned into Ben. He placed steadying hands on my waist. Time stopped for a second as we stared into each other's eyes, our faces level. Then with a sudden click of mutual awareness, we realigned ourselves, squeezing past each other as he moved towards the sink. But after that it seemed impossible not to move, without brushing shoulders, catching hands, touching hips and coming face to face.

By the time, I'd served up the women's cappuccinos, he was ready with the chocolate shaker to dust off the coffees and had, following Eva's exacting orders, 'Make sure you cut them cleanly, and those plates not the other ones,' cut two slices of fruit torte and plopped them with the finesse of a fisherman dropping his catch off onto a plate.

As he picked up the tray, Eva held up a hand.

'Before you take anything out, you must look at it,' said Eva. 'Ask yourself is the plate right? Does the food sit prettily? Does it look good enough? Would you serve it to someone you care about?'

Ben's blue grey eyes sharpened with sudden intelligence and he put the tray down, giving the plate a careful examination. Crossing to the fridge he pulled out two large strawberries and he held them up, smiled at Eva and I and then carefully sliced them in half, arranging them like two perfect little love hearts at a right angle to the point of the tortes before dusting them with a fine coat of icing sugar. 'How's that? Would you eat it, Kate?'

My heart turned over in my chest, as he held out the plate.

I nodded, my eyes widening as my quick startled glance met his solemn expression. Without another word he picked up the tray and took it out to the two women.

Eva gave me a sharp assessing look and I turned away busying myself tidying up the old coffee grounds, wiping down surfaces and anything to avoid conversation.

'That wasn't so bad.' Ben strode back into the kitchen. 'I think we're going to cope just fine.' Eva and I exchanged a mutual smile and looked out at the near empty café. And then the door opened and a group of six people came in. While we served them, another two people came in and then four.

And suddenly there was no time to think about what we were doing. The milk frother hissed. The oven timer binged. Knives chinked on china as we sliced tortes, placed forks on plates and scooped up pastries. Orders came thick and fast and I darted around Ben, making coffees while he delivered the set up plates and trays. We moved into a seamless routine with him producing plates and cups before I needed to ask. He cleared tables and washed up as I took more orders and in between he bundled up cutlery in clean napkins, laid out trays and wiped up after me. He was quite a domestic god in the kitchen.

Things started to get more complicated as it neared lunch time and people began ordering open sandwiches. Eva insisted that we could manage these, after Ben raised her up on a couple of cushions and moved her to a side table. He ran around getting the ingredients from the fridge and then assembled them, under her watchful eye.

'Now put the rocket on the top. No. Do it again.'

'But it's just garnish. And we're busy now.'

Eva shot him a reproving glare.

'Remember the love,' I teased from the other side of the table.

Ben raised his eyebrows and then seeing Eva's stern look, rearranged the offending greenery more carefully and I caught the muttered, 'OK, so not just garnish.'

'That's better.' Eva nodded. 'There's no hurry. It's always worth taking the time ... you have to care enough. When customers see that, they don't mind waiting.'

More orders came in, and we got into a routine, me

producing coffees, banging the coffee out in the compost like a professional barista as if I'd never left my Costa days behind and laying out the trays as we took it in turns to whisk out into the café to deal with customers, clean tables and take yet more orders.

There were a few cock ups, like when Ben misread one of my scribbled orders and proudly took out three open sandwiches complete with crispy bacon garnish which he'd fried to perfection (after a second attempt) to be told that they were waiting for baked apple tarts but the Danes being Danish took all our mistakes in good part, especially when Ben explained that we were the B team. I suspect his English accent and winning smile also had a lot to do with it as many of the customers were women.

It was only when there was a lull, the number of customers slowing to a trickle and we caught up with ourselves managing to get rid of the huge pile of washing up that I realised how knackered I felt and how desperate I was for a coffee myself. Despite that a sense of satisfaction glowed in my heart. Empty plates all round. We'd done good. Seen happy customers come and go. Yeah, it felt good, even as I slipped one foot out of my shoe and rubbed my instep against my calf. My feet were killing me. With a grateful sigh, I watched the last customers depart, wondering if I dare nip out and turn the sign on the door to closed. It was nearly half past three.

'You OK?' asked Ben depositing the last plate and cup in the washing up bowl and cupping my elbow as I wobbled precariously for a second.

'Fine,' I said, not wanting to admit to my weariness but

giving in to the urge to lean slightly into him, my arm against his.

'I'm glad you are because I'm bloody exhausted.'

I let myself wilt then, glad to hear that he felt the same. 'I'm so glad Eva managed to get us back into the same hotel. I can't wait for a nice hot soak.' While we'd been busy she'd phoned the hotel and rebooked us a couple of rooms.

'No wonder you're so trim, Eva, this is hard work.' Ben slung the damp tea-towel over his shoulder. 'And I never want to see another dirty cup again.'

'Well Agneta will be here any minute, I'm sorry she couldn't come any earlier,' said Eva. In between directing operations she'd managed to use her phone to call in the cavalry. 'And my friend Marte is going to come and take me home. You've both been brilliant.' Her lip quivered as she looked at her ankle which was still very swollen. 'I don't know what I'd have done without you.'

'Neither do I,' said Ben dryly which made Eva and I burst out laughing. 'I've decided I'm not made for manual work.'

'You did well, for a man who professes not to like cooking. You cook a mean bit of bacon.'

'I noticed you stuck to making coffee.'

'I know what I'm doing there. I don't have time to cook … usually. I quite enjoyed today. It was quite relaxing.'

'Relaxing? How on earth do you figure that? I found it hellishly stressful.'

'Well you don't have time to think about what you're doing for a start. And I quite like dealing with the customers.' I'd forgotten how much I used to enjoy working in café a when I was a student. 'You see instant results. It's quite satisfying.'

'If you say so,' grumbled Ben stooping to rub his back.

'Well I'm very grateful to both of you. Now why don't you put the closed sign on—'

'Hallelujah.' Ben moved so quickly towards the door that both Eva and I burst out laughing.

We helped her hobble out to one of the tables and we all sat down. When it came to it neither Ben nor I could face a coffee or a pastry so we sat with large glasses of iced Coca-Cola, periodically resting the condensation bubbled glasses on our overheated faces.

'Actually,' said Ben thoughtfully, 'now that I'm sitting down and my feet are thinking about forgiving me, it was quite good fun. We make a good team.'

Eva beamed. 'You two work well together.'

'I think that's because we had a scary general,' I teased. 'She wasn't taking no for an answer.'

'Too right,' said Eva experimentally wriggling her leg with a wince of pain, 'Although, in a kitchen that size, it can be difficult. Not everyone can work that well together. I've lost staff who couldn't.'

I looked at the tiny kitchen and for a second marvelled that Ben and I hadn't stood on each other's toes both metaphorically and physically. Who'd have thought it? Ben and me? A good team. OK, he'd dusted my fingers a time or two at first with enthusiastic cinnamon shaking, but after that he'd been very good at anticipating what needed doing next without fussing or overcrowding me. He had a good sense of knowing when to help and when to stand back and let me get on with it. And likewise I'd known when he needed help and when he didn't.

It was a shame I couldn't have trained my family like that. I'd long since given up hoping they might help around the house, it was too irritating to watch their tepid pace, incompetence and apathetic disinterest. The only way to get a job done properly was to do it myself. A depressing vision of me in my fifties filled my head, still going home and sorting them out even down to a worn grey cardigan and baggy jeans. That wasn't what Mum would have wanted for me ... or any of us.

'I'd say a pound's worth of thoughts have just crossed your face,' said Ben thankfully chasing the unwelcome image away.

'They're definitely not worth that,' I said with a downward turn of my mouth.

'Agneta.' Eva waved enthusiastically to a small blonde woman coming through the door.

'Thank goodness,' said Ben, 'I'm not sure I've got the stamina for another round.'

'What are you? A man or a mouse?'

'Eek, eek.'

Chapter 24

The lift doors opened and as soon as we stepped inside, I slumped with weariness against the wall.

'I am so going to soak in a very hot bath,' I said, rubbing my back up and down against the mirrored wall. 'And pray that the restaurant isn't too far to walk.' Eva had recommended a restaurant for dinner and very kindly booked us a table.

'She said it's only ten minutes. Think you can manage that? Shall I see you in the lobby at six?'

I nodded, conscious of it being just the two of us again and the awareness of unfinished business suddenly burning between us. 'Of course, you don't have to have dinner with me. Don't feel obliged.'

He took a pace towards me as the lift slowed and lifted my chin with his hand. 'Kate Sinclair, sometimes you talk too much.' The doors opened and he dropped a quick kiss on my lips that left me staring after him as they closed and I was smoothly carried up another floor, the aftermath of that light touch dancing through me like delicate fireflies flaring and fading.

It's very difficult trying to keep yourself busy in a hotel

room. I ran a bath. Unpacked again. Had a long soak. Lay down. Tried to switch my brain off. Tried harder to switch my brain off which of course was totally counter-productive. Tried to think of work, which was until Monday away. Two days away, one of which it seemed likely would be spent with Ben.

And there it was, full circle. Ben and all those butterfly feelings humming with anticipation and latent excitement. And the lingering, hug to myself, memory of today, along with those tantalising words, *I was wrong about you, I want to …* What did he want? And those delicious brief touches and brush bys in the café and the warmth and satisfaction of that unexpected sense of teamwork. Who'd have thought?

'Did he just say porridge?' I whispered as the waiter disappeared.

Ben nodded.

'I'm not sure about that,' I said a tad alarmed. Having been brought up on a fairly bland diet – pasta with anything but Bolognese sauce was exotic in our house – since I'd left home, I'd forced myself to keep trying new things. Every now and then though, my brain shorted out and said no thank you. And today porridge was not winning the battle of mind over matter. It really didn't appeal.

'Me neither,' said Ben to my relief, 'but Eva insisted that the food here was fabulous.'

The restaurant was so popular the only reservation we could get was for six-thirty, but despite that it had none of the pomp and reserve of a London restaurant. No one was particularly dressed up and the waiting staff were friendly and informal. The walls were filled with shelves full of small pots of plants and over the stairs was a full-sized greenhouse teeming with hanging baskets brimming with greenery, as if the outdoors had been brought inside.

'Shall we go for broke and have the wine tasting menu,' asked Ben looking at the menu.

'Hello, yes. I have a company credit card and I'm not afraid to use it. Especially not after Josh weaselled me into staying.'

'Ah, she's back. PR girl. I missed her.'

'We aim to please,' I quipped.

'But I got you wrong. Today at the check-in desk. You gave up your seat, not to get ahead and score brownie points. You could've joined in with Josh kicking up a stink, playing his game. And you know if you'd pushed hard enough and created a big enough scene, the airline would have bumped someone else. Josh and his bad publicity was pretty much an ace in the hole.'

I shrugged uncomfortably, not sure I deserved his praise. 'Only because I didn't want to cause a scene and embarrass everyone.'

'Yeah right, not because you knew it was important to the others to get home.'

I lifted my shoulders again. 'Forgoing a weekend in Hemel isn't exactly a hardship.'

'You're a really nice person Kate Sinclair.' He smiled into my eyes which turned my legs into jelly and, yes, my heart to complete mush.

'You're not so bad yourself Ben Johnson.' Heat rushed along my veins.

'And I owe you an apology. Of course, you had to act professional in front of someone from work. I overreacted yesterday. I realised last night at dinner. You're not like that. Everyone else could see how genuine you were. And seeing you hand out all the gifts, the photographs, that was thoughtful. You even gave one to me after I'd been a complete bastard.'

'You almost didn't get one.'

'Yeah, but you wouldn't have done that, because you're a nice person.'

'Even though you were a moody sod.'

'Yeah and you're the only one with the balls to tell me.'

I shifted uneasily in my seat at that one. 'That was because I didn't like you very much. Not to start with. Not until I figured out that under that mad fox exterior,' I examined his chin as if it was of great interest, my pulse tripping a little faster, 'there beats a kindly heart. Possibly.' He'd shown it in so many ways.

'Nicely put. But last night I felt such a dick. Making a fuss at the Design Museum. Letting that prat Josh, who by the way is a bigger dick, make me believe you were just interested in column inches.'

'I'm not sure you should use that terminology.' Teasing him diffused things and avoided facing the compliment head on because I didn't know what to do with it. I wanted to keep things light but he seemed intent on pressing ahead.

'Five people, Kate. Six including Eva – all think you're great. Because you are.'

I fiddled with my cutlery. 'Yeah right, I'm pretty awesome.'

I let the *not* speak for itself and busied myself pleating my napkin.

'I think you are,' he said in the sort of voice that made it clear he was not about to be contradicted.

'Well you have been known to be wrong. Oh, look. Porridge.' The waiter was approaching our table with two bowls.

Ben's fingers slid up my wrist. The light touch on my skin had my nerve endings dancing in anticipation.

I looked at his face, a slight determined set to his mouth tinged with amusement at my avoidance tactics. I took a breath, maybe just maybe, I could afford to let go for once. I could just be. The thought was suddenly liberating. There was nothing to stop us seeing what happened. If it didn't work out it wouldn't matter; after this weekend I might not see Ben again. Our paths would never have to cross again if we didn't want them to. I had a choice.

'So any ideas about what we might do tomorrow?' Turning to the practical immediately made me relax.

'How about hiring a bike?' suggested Ben.

'Good plan.' I'd been rather envious of the young Danes we'd seen confidently cycling about one handed while they scanned their mobile phones. 'That way we could cover quite a bit of ground. The weather forecast is good. We could go to the Rosenberg Castle. And the botanical gardens.'

'You can be in charge then, it sounds as if you've given it some thought.' He looked slightly ashamed. 'Cutting my nose off to spite my face, I deliberately didn't read up before we came out here.' His honesty disarmed me.

'Eva suggested it. Apart from this evening, I haven't picked up the guide book since we got off the plane.' I smiled at him. 'We've got until four before we have to leave to get our flight, I reckon we can fit that in.' Our flight was at six thirty and the train only took twenty minutes out to the airport.

'Excellent idea, but what about this evening?'

Now that I'd got my bearings, having been here for a few days, Copenhagen was clearly more compact and easily navigable. One place had stuck in my mind.

'Tivoli, of course.' I glanced shyly at him. 'I'd quite like to go back there.'

His mouth twitched. 'What – a return trip on The Demon?'

A flush of heat burned my skin and I knew we were both remembering that brief kiss. 'I … the gardens were pretty at night and we didn't get much chance to explore them.'

Our eyes met. Oh shit, had I extended such a blatant invitation? Secluded walkways. Shadowy bowers. Romantic fairy lights.

'And then there's a bar I've read about,' I added quickly. 'Duck and Cover. A cocktail bar. Sounds very Danish. Looks lovely.'

With a smile, he wrinkled his nose. 'I'm not big on cocktails, but I'm sure they'll have a decent beer.'

We ate at a leisurely pace, easy with each other now that we'd navigated the plans for the rest of the evening. The veal which I hadn't been sure about, and the porridge, even less sure, were both absolutely gorgeous. The tasting menu of different wines matched to each dish were of course perfect and went down smoothly and before long we were savouring the last glass of sweet dessert wine as we finished the rhubarb mousse with pound cake which wasn't anywhere near as stodgy as it sounded.

It was still light outside as we shrugged into our coats, slightly embarrassed to find that Eva had already arranged payment. She knew the owner apparently.

'Good job we did go for the wine pairing menu,' joked Ben as we stepped out into the cool air, but somehow, I knew he didn't mean it. It wasn't his style to take advantage of Eva's generosity.

Now that the rain had passed, it had turned into a lovely evening, not the least bit cold. It was only quarter to eight and the streets held an air of calm and quiet as we walked arm in arm towards the gardens.

Somewhere along the way Ben reached for my hand and I smiled to myself, thrilled with the quiet confidence of the gesture and enjoying the feel of his warm skin against mine. I had no idea where this evening would lead to but I was going to enjoy every moment of it.

As we entered the gardens, the lilting strains of Vivaldi's *Four Seasons* filled the air with a siren call, I couldn't resist and I tugged at his hand to follow the direction of the music.

'Come on,' I said, pulling him down a path lit with strings of fairy lights, with a signpost to *The Lake*.

As we got closer, the music billowed out into the night air and I let out a little gasp of surprise and delight. In front of us lay an enchanted wonderland with an ethereal other-worldly atmosphere. Fountains rose and fell in the centre of the water, flowing and tumbling in perfect synchronization with the music. Underwater lights changed with the rise and fall of the music, sliding from purple, to blue to gold and the surface rippled gaily making the reflection of the pagoda opposite dance and shimmer.

As the music segued into the jubilant tune of *The Arrival of the Queen of Sheba*, violins joyfully serenading the horns while the woodwind section weaved in and out with lyrical rhythm, sending the notes dancing on the air, I stood and stared. Glorious. Beautiful. Magical. I was no expert and knew nothing but the popular classics. My heart swelled as my body swayed along with the lilts and accents of the music and under my breath I hummed along.

Ben put his arm across my shoulders and pulled me into him. I wanted to hold onto the moment, an instant of pure perfection and I leaned in, letting the melodies wash over me. Simple pleasure. Lights. Colour. Music. The pleasing flow and gush of water. And sharing it with someone else.

Handel gave way to the rousing introduction of Mozart's *Eine a Kleine Nachtmusic.*

'I feel we should be waltzing or something,' said Ben close to my ear. 'And you should be dressed in a great big frock.'

'I think you might be getting muddled up with Austria,' I said, my words coming out low and husky at the touch of his warm breath teasing my cheek.

'Are you quite musical?'

I turned to face him so that both his arms encircled me and sucked in a lungful of air trying to hide how his nearness affected me. 'Not really. I used to love singing and me and my mum used to listen to one of those CDs with a bit of every-thing on it. That's about the sum total of my knowledge. We always said one day we'd go to the Albert Hall to a concert. We knew we never would. Mum would have worried she wasn't posh enough.'

His arms tightened and he smiled into my eyes as if he knew exactly what my gabbling was about. 'That's a shame.'

'It's OK. She took me to a Take That concert.' I grinned at him. 'And that was pretty fabulous.'

'Oh dear.' He shook his head. 'I was starting to think there were hidden depths to you.'

'Nothing deep about me at all,' I said flippantly looking up into his face, shivering slightly. He pulled me closer assuming I was cold, which I wasn't at all. Inside I felt very warm and cosy, savouring the thrilling novelty of being with someone else for a change. Being one of two.

'Deep's overrated,' said Ben smiling down at me, making me feel I was in some special spotlight. 'I prefer straight forward and up front.' There was a rough timbre to his voice.

'I can do that,' I said, my words tailing off in a breathless whisper.

'I got that memo.' The teasing light in his eyes faded and the moment hung between us, as we stared at each other until he lowered his head and I lifted my face up to his.

Unlike our first kiss, spontaneous and of the moment, tonight there'd been a slow build up. Stolen glances. Unconscious gestures. Secret signals. Tension tightening and tightening. When the kiss finally came, it was like touch paper, setting light to a slow fuse that simmered and burned with gathering heat.

It was as if all the time we'd wasted since that night in

London was unravelling right now. Warm and slow, thorough and gentle, a steady build up as we explored each other's mouths. Where he led, I followed, like dance partners that had known each other for ever and were ready for every move.

And then when we'd established the easy, steady rhythm, his tongue touched mine, the kiss deepened and fireworks erupted. Toe curling. Sizzling. Sensation shot through me as his hold tightened on me, pulling me urgently towards him. The sounds receded to a pleasant background as I focused on the taste and touch of him, my heart racing. I wanted to hold onto this moment forever.

When at last, I pulled away to draw breath, I felt slightly drunk but it was pleasing to see that he looked equally glassy eyed. Still holding each other, I thought my system might just have been fried.

Bemused we stared at each other for a second.

'Kate,' he touched my face. 'That night in London.' The unspoken question burned in his eyes. I swallowed, my palms suddenly clammy, unable to say anything in case I'd got it wrong.

We stared at each other for a long moment. I didn't dare break first.

With a gentle smile, he stroked the side of my neck, his finger tracing gently down to my collarbone as I stood perfectly still as if standing on a cliff edge.

'That night ...' his sigh was heartfelt, wrung out of him as if he were about to dive off the highest diving board, uncertain as to how deep the below was. 'That night ...' The grey blue eyes were intent, piercing me with sudden memory of the shimmering magic of that evening.

'You were ... you stuck in my head. I thought you were something special, unique and ... I never ... say stuff like this ... I thought there was a connection.' His teeth gnawed at his lip.

Without thinking I squeezed his hand acknowledging the sudden vulnerability, my heart racing at the words because I knew exactly what he meant. It had scared the pants off me which was why I'd run. He was far braver than I'd ever be, saying this out loud, laying himself bare.

'You were on the same wavelength. And then when you turned out to be ... you,' chagrin stained his face, 'it was crushing. I'd made a mistake. And you weren't who I thought you might be that night. It made me react badly. I guess I wanted to punish you for shattering the illusion. I held onto that for as long as I could but I was wrong. Wrong about you.'

I winced, pressing my lips together, sadness and under-standing rolling through me. Then with some amazing wisdom that sprang from who knew where, I said, 'The great thing about mistakes is you can put them right.'

'Tell me, the first time we met ...'

I raised cautious eyes to his and something skittered between, like a ripple in the air. I wanted to ignore it. Pretend it wasn't there but Ben had the tenacity of a Mountie, hell bent on getting his man or rather in this case his woman. Except I wasn't his woman...

'I can almost see you denying it. And I don't have a romantic bone in my body. But tell me you didn't feel it. You said you were scared.'

Shit. Adrenaline charged honesty was a very bad thing.

'Scared of what?' His soft voice had me tied up in knots, the words twisting like a snake.

I couldn't tell him. I couldn't. It would open me up to too much. And I was still scared. Scared that I might feel too much for him. That I didn't have time to have feelings for anyone.

My career had to come first. I'd never questioned my role before. I had to stick at it. Having a proper job was important to me. I was the first in my family. Not like my mum. Not like my brothers. Not like Dad who hated his job and was stuck with it because he was the breadwinner.

And was Ben even looking for a relationship? Maybe he just wanted to take me up on the quick-fire heat that sizzled between us that night. After Josh, I doubted my ability to read men.

His eyes bored into me waiting for an answer.

'I was scared because ... I was worried it might mean too much.' *You might mean too much to me.*

'And now?'

I took a deep breath. 'I'm still scared, but I'm not going to run this time.'

'Maybe we take each day as it comes. Sometimes being scared is good. It makes you more careful.'

Across the park the screams of The Demon rent the air. He looked over towards the ride with a sudden smile, 'And sometimes you're supposed to be scared. The adrenaline rush.

That's why people let themselves feel. So why don't we do that, enjoy today?'

'OK,' I said in a small voice, remembering the rush of the ride and him holding my hand the whole time. The kiss this time was slow and sure, sealing the deal. Promise and hope simmering in the soft touch of his lips against mine.

When we pulled back, I sucked in a hefty lungful of air, trying to regain my equilibrium and looking over his shoulder at the neon lit track snaking across the sky behind him, said, somewhat shakily, 'That was a whole Demon ride worth of a kiss.' And just as heart racing.

'Is that a complaint or a compliment?' he asked pulling me close again and kissing the corner of my mouth, nibbling and teasing at my lips, almost tickling.

I ducked my head back, to escape the teasing torment, which was stirring my pulse again.

'If it was a complaint, I'm not sure I'd survive!'

His lips curved in a satisfied, thoroughly pleased with himself, alpha male smile. 'We aim to please.'

My eyes twinkled at him. 'Hmm, of course there's always room for improvement.'

'So, you are complaining?' He pretended to look stern but the playful arms on hips made me laugh at him.

'Let's just say ... perhaps it was a fluke.'

'A fluke!'

Quick as a striking snake he put both hands on my waist and yanked me to him, not that I put up much of a fight.

I can safely say the second kiss quite satisfactorily proved that its predecessor most definitely wasn't a fluke.

This fun, flirty interaction was a revelation. I felt an equal and that the attraction was totally mutual. Every other relationship I'd been in had seemed like I was the one waiting for permission to move forward or to take a particular step. This felt as if neither of us were in charge.

We wandered through the gardens, Ben's arm around my shoulders, keeping me close to his side, pointing to the sights, watching braver souls than I, high above us whizzing out into the night on the Star Flyer ride. We talked about the others, wondering how Avril's reunion with her husband had gone and whether she'd baked him a walnut and coffee cake, guessing when Conrad might move in with David and hoping that Sophie had enjoyed her Friday night date with James.

'Bet none of them are having as good a time as we are,' said Ben, his fingers squeezing the top of my shoulder.

I put my hand up and laced my fingers through his and squeezed back.

No words were needed.

'This is lovely,' I said looking around the bar. Duck and Cover wasn't at all what I was expecting. The dimly lit room was full of people but quiet and calm with none of the frenetic activity of the London night scene. Everyone seemed very relaxed and casual, sharing the low leather sofas in shadowy groupings around candle dotted tables and discreet lamps created pools of light around the room. With the wood clad walls, flax rugs and retro furniture there was a definite 70s vibe. We could have been in someone's lounge except we had our own personal, friendly and helpful waiters, patiently taking orders as if they had all the time in the world. People happily shared tables and it didn't feel as if everyone was watching everyone else to see who was the coolest or had the best spot.

I leaned back into the leather back, sipping a Sloe Gin Fizz. Like many of the places we'd been the cocktail menu was limited, which in itself was relaxing because there was none of the stress of choice.

'I have to admit I'm not a cocktail bar kind of person. I prefer a pub but this is great,' said Ben.

'I think everything about Copenhagen is great. Do you think Lars could persuade Eva to come to London and set up a café there? There's nothing like it. I'd love to be able to go to a place like that. And I'm going to miss her.'

'She's taken a bit of a shine to you,' teased Ben.

'Not just me!' I protested, secretly pleased at his comment.

'She was certainly very good at sussing out everyone.'

'Except you, maybe,' I said.

'Not much to suss.'

I raised an eyebrow.

'I'm sure she didn't want to know about my domestic traumas.'

'How is your sister?'

'Still complaining.'

'Are you close?'

He paused for a minute studying the picture over my head as if deciding how much to give away.

'Family. We love them even when they drive us demented.'

'Tell me about it.' I exhaled sharply.

'Do you see yours much?'

'I try to get back at weekends as much as possible.' I studied my drink. 'I probably shouldn't. My friend Connie says I should leave them to get on with it.' I took a sip before reluctantly putting it down. 'I guess I feel guilty.'

'Guilty?'

'Yeah. I've done so much better than them. My brothers are in dead end jobs. Brandon is so talented but I can't see him ever changing his job and John, well he changes every five minutes but that's because he's a lazy sod and thinks he deserves more. And my dad, well his get and go, got up and went after my mum died.'

'Let me guess, you go back and do everything for them.'

I winced. 'Not everything. I guess … I am a bit … interfering, but if I didn't the house would be even more of a pit and … Dad, well he relies on me to make sure the mortgage gets paid. And it's the least I can do; I do earn more than them all.'

'Not that much more surely.'

'Let's say earning more, would lighten the load. Me and my flatmate would like to upgrade but I can't see that happening for a while. God knows what Josh will report back about the trip. This was supposed to be my audition piece for promotion.'

'Perhaps if you said to your dad you couldn't help, if he had to, he might pull up his socks. Retrieve his get up and go. Instead of relying on you. Maybe you're letting him get away with it.'

His direct hit made me wriggle in my seat a little. 'Why are you letting your sister stay at yours?' I retaliated.

'Touché.' Ben let out a half-laugh. 'Because she's family. But maybe I should get tougher. It might make her sort things out with her husband once and for all, instead of leaving him the minute things get difficult. This is the third time she's left him.'

I tipped my head on one side. 'But you can't say no.'

'No. Dad did the classic run off with his secretary, although to be fair, he's still with her and she's great. I have a couple of step-brothers who are nice kids. She's very level headed. No dramas. Probably why Dad went off with her. They're very happy and I can't imagine him and Mum together now. She can be a bit of a nightmare. Her and Amy thrive on drama.'

'So, you're more like your dad?'

'Yeah, we get on well. Not that I let on to Mum and Amy. He's a bit he-who-must-not-be-mentioned.'

'Must be tricky.'

'Luckily Dad gets it. So, there's no tugging. None of that you spent Christmas with your mother last year crap. He's a good bloke.'

'Like his son,' I said softly.

Ben shrugged but a shy smile danced around his lips, which made me move my leg to rest against him.

He took my hand and laced his fingers through mine, where they rested on both our legs. 'Families eh? Fancy another drink?'

Chapter 25

Sleep proved elusive, my mind was far too busy reliving the delicious details of the day. Laughing in the kitchen at Varme. Kissing at Tivoli. Talking over several cocktails. The rather woozy walk back to the hotel. Ben holding my hand. The reluctant goodnight kiss outside the lift on my floor. Turning back to look down the corridor to see him watching me walk back to my room.

Me turning down his offer to walk me to the door because we both knew where that might end. One final clinging kiss as if to store it up to see us through the night.

I turned over again and plumped up the pillow.

On the bedside table, my phone beeped and the light of a message flashed like a lighthouse in the dark.

Thanks for a lovely evening. See you in the morning x

I touched the screen, a stupid dopy grin on my face.

For a brief regretful second I imagined his warm body next to mine, being wrapped in his arms and the delicious sensation of skin on skin. I pushed the sheets down as I suddenly felt overheated. It would have been easy to give into the spiralling longing and the latent lust that received one hell of a kick-start every time he kissed me. I turned and lay on my back, one hand behind my head. I'd done the right thing. There was something special about the build-up and anticipation at the start of something, the waiting, almost teasing and the unspoken promise of what might be. Courtship, I guessed you might call it. I smiled in the dark and turned over again, snuggled into the bed. Who knew what tomorrow would bring? And after that?

I think I still had a silly smile on my face when I woke up and my first thought was of Ben.

There was another text from him.

Morning. Breakfast at 8.30? x

It was already quarter to eight, but I was itching to get up and get moving, which was most unusual for a Saturday morning.

'I hope I can still do this,' I said hauling the bicycle out of the rack in front of the hotel. I was particularly pleased by the sight of the super plump leather saddles on the hire bikes, because it had been a while.

'Don't worry it's like riding a bike,' quipped Ben, as he slung one leg over and then hopped about trying to jump into the saddle.

'Ha. Ha. Very funny,' I said watching him make a slow, ungainly circle to face the right direction.

291

We set off, both a little wobbly to start with, but the wide cycle paths gave me confidence and in a matter of minutes I sat up straighter instead of clutching the handle bars for grim death and started to enjoy myself. We'd decided to ride out to the castle but thought we'd pop in to see Eva, check if she was OK and say our goodbyes. I'd texted her the previous evening and she'd reported back that the doctor had said it was a bad sprain.

We cycled along the full length of Støget where everyone had inbuilt bicycle awareness fields and seemed to move out of the way in plenty of time, which was just as well as I wasn't sure my rubbish co-ordination could cope with sudden braking, it was taking all my effort to stay upright and steer.

Despite the well-padded seats which looked like cheeky buttocks themselves, I felt every cobble as we bumped our way along the side street to Varme. With more than a touch of relief I hopped off outside following Ben to one of the many cycle bays that were conveniently placed around the city. This really was a place where the bicycle had equal billing with pedestrians and cars.

'God morgen,' said Eva, half hopping up from her position on a chair with her ankle, all strapped up, resting on a chair. 'Lovely to see you *both*.' A naughty twinkle danced in her eyes. I glanced back at Ben with a smile. Of course Eva had spotted that things between us had changed.

'Stay there,' I said walking quickly to her side and bending down to kiss her cheek in greeting.

'How are you today?'

She winced and waggled her foot a little. 'Feeling old and stupid,' she said grumpily which was so not her.

'Oh dear. Are you in a lot of pain?'

'No, but my pride is very badly damaged. I'm so cross with myself for not waiting for help and thinking I could manage with the ladder on my own.'

'What were you doing?'

'Rearranging the top shelves in the kitchen.'

Her brief frown was quickly replaced with a resigned self-deprecating smile. 'At least I timed it well. Luckily, Agneta works on Saturdays and she was able to bring a friend with her to help.' Through the serving counter I could see two teenage girls bustling about in the kitchen.

'Good, because I'm not sure my feet would survive another tour of kitchen duty,' said Ben with feeling. 'We've had to resort to bikes today.'

'Ben, that's not true!' I nudged him in the ribs.

Eva laughed. 'You poor old soul.'

'He's fibbing,' I said. 'We thought we could go a little further afield as it's our last day.'

'That's a good idea. What time is your flight?'

'Not until this afternoon. We've left our cases in the left luggage room at the hotel and we'll go back and get them later. It won't take us long to get to the airport.'

'Excellent. So have you time for coffee?'

I gave Ben a quick hopeful glance and he smiled back as he slipped into the chair opposite Eva. 'We've got plenty of time.'

'Do you want me to make coffee?' I asked.

'No, no.' Eva called our order over to Agneta, who brought

293

the coffees over in record time. She was much better on the coffee machine than I was.

'So what are your plans for the day?' asked Eva.

'We're going to Rosenberg Castle, like you suggested.'

'Oh perfect. The grounds are beautiful. You should go to the Radhuspladsen on your way. City Hall. It's a beautiful building and the world clock is incredible. A work of art. It's free and on your way. It's very romantic. You really should go.' The knowing glint was back in Eva's eye.

'OK,' I said looking at Ben to secure his agreement.

He lifted his shoulders, in a why not gesture. 'We've skirted around it several times. Might as well pop in.'

'I think you'll enjoy it,' said Eva suddenly doing her wise-owl grave nod thing.

All too soon we'd finished our coffee and it was time to say goodbye to Eva, again. Last night had been much easier. Now it was just us.

She insisted on standing up, holding onto the table.

'Thanks so much for everything Eva,' I said fixing the smile to my face so that it wouldn't crumple.

'Come here, you.' She swept me into a fierce motherly hug. I smelt her perfume, Pink Molecule, a scent I'd forever associate with her. I hugged her back, blinking furiously.

'Thank you for everything,' I said looking everywhere but at her face. 'Y-you've been amazing. I don't know what I'd have done without you.'

She patted my back. 'You'd have been fine. But it has been lovely having everyone visit each day. On Monday morning, I'll be looking at that table, wondering where you are.'

I swallowed trying to dislodge the stupid pesky lump in my throat.

'But,' she said straightening up, her natural perkiness reasserting itself albeit with a discreet sniff, 'I *will* see you in London. Very soon. When Lars opens the store.' She put her hands on my shoulders. 'But, you. You have to come back. Come see me. Come stay.' Her eyes suddenly twinkled. 'Maybe both of you.'

I shot a side-long glance at Ben and he winked at Eva.

'It's a distinct possibility,' he said amusement dancing in his eyes.

I should have known. Eva didn't miss a thing.

'I knew you two would be good together.' She beamed at both of us and gave me another hug, whispering. 'He's very nice. Not like that Josh. Give him a chance.' In a louder voice she added, 'And don't forget about that spare room. You'll always be welcome.'

'That's really kind.'

'I mean it, Katie,' her eyes twinkled. 'And make sure you look after yourself. You need some *hygge* in your life.'

That would be nice, if I had time.

'Don't,' said Eva pointing an accusing finger at me, 'give me that look. Make some time.'

I put my hands up in a *how?* gesture.

'Now go,' she said pushing me towards Ben and the door. 'Before I start crying.'

One last hug. A few sniffs. A lot of blinking and then Ben took my hand and we left the café for the last time. When I looked back through the window, Eva waved and then shooed us away mouthing, 'Go', at us.

I got on my bike and wobbled slowly out of sight, my vision slightly blurred by tears.

The impressive Radhuspladsen with its huge tower, by now quite familiar to us because it could be seen from various parts of the city including the Tivoli Gardens, was a striking combination of austere and ornate. Built in sturdy red bricks, with rows of forbidding neat mullioned lead-paned windows on one floor which contrasted with the modern windows below, there were interesting architectural features like the two semi-circular bay windows topped with mini turrets and the elaborate crenelated affair on top of the roof, which brought to mind the palazzo in Siena.

It wasn't the prettiest building I'd ever seen but Eva had said we ought to go inside.

As we mounted the steps, I noticed a pretty, tiny Korean girl. Her delicate dress caught my eye with its full bouncy skirt decorated with tiny gossamer flowers, trembling like butterflies about to take flight at any second. Over the top she wore a down coat a shade darker than the pale rose of her dress.

The ensemble looked rather incongruous on the top of the rather windy steps as she linked arms with a man in a suit rubbing the neckline of his shirt as if it were too tight.

We followed them through the huge arched doorway and into a beautiful great hall, with balconies around the top. Directly opposite on the balcony to the right was a couple having their photos taken. As I looked around I realised there were small groups of people, varying in size, milling about around couples. Two guys in matching suits and ties. A forty-something lady in a gorgeous purpley-blue dress coat with printed iridescent flowers around the wide skirted hem.

At the bottom of a stairwell tucked into the wall below the balcony a tall and rather handsome young blonde man in a striped T-shirt, jeans and Converse high tops held a clipboard, directing people to the stairs. I suddenly realised he was the wedding co-ordinator!

I watched the forty-something lady who clutched a posy of white roses in her hand, while greeting nephews, nieces or some other relatives, with great big kisses. Around her assorted relatives exchanged hugs and shook hands. Everyone looked so happy it was infectious. Tourists snapped away taking pictures of the buildings, the wedding parties and the brides' dresses. The Korean girl had stripped off her sensible coat to reveal dainty straps and thin elegant shoulders. Her husband-to-be had stopped rubbing at his neck-line but that was probably because he'd been struck insensible by his bride. He simply gazed at her, tenderness welling up and his mouth crumpling as if any moment he might cry.

The sweet moment had me swallowing hard but I couldn't stop watching as an older couple, his parents, came up and gave them both huge hugs. His mother taking the girl by the shoulders and kissing her soundly on both cheeks. There was no sign of her parents or anyone on her side, so I decided that her family were all back in Korea and that her mum would be sad to miss the day but looking at her mother-in-law to be, she was going to be in safe hands and well looked after. This was *hygge* country after all. Family. Cosy time was important.

I felt positively misty-eyed but was completely finished off when I turned to find the two men in matching suits kissing each other passionately and all their assembled family clapping and cheering. Tears ran down my face. Seeing the love and joy all around us felt so uplifting, a wonderful reminder of the important things in life, love and family.

Ben lifted a finger, wiping at one of my tears and placed a quick kiss on my cheek before taking my hand without saying anything.

Had I got things wrong? Was having a career that important? Was I missing out on too much of life?

PART THREE

London

Chapter 26

'Josh tells me you did well in Copenhagen.' Megan sipped at her shop-bought coffee out of a cardboard cup. She had no idea how much better it would have tasted in a pretty blue earthenware mug. Or how well a *kanelsnegle* would have gone down with it.

I shifted in my seat, it was uncomfortable and that wasn't just a saddle hangover. Eva's chairs were comfortable. Everything in Copenhagen had been comfortable.

'Apparently, they were a tricky bunch.' She rolled her eyes. 'He said Avril Baines-Hamilton was a complete diva.'

My jaw tightened. Megan didn't even know Avril.

'But of course, the important thing, the real proof of the pud, will be the press coverage. That's what we're going to be judged on.'

I nodded more interested in the sunlight slanting in through the window above her head. Outside a patch of brilliant blue sky contrasted with the yellow folder on her desk. The colours of Nyhaven. Those tall buildings along the harbourside. What was the weather like there, this morning? If it was the same as here, it would be glorious. Lovely out on a boat. Bobbing on the water. Past the Opera House.

I looked longingly out the window behind Megan's head, wanting to throw it open and let in some fresh air.

'How do you feel the trip went?' Her pen tapped on the desk and she crossed her legs and then uncrossed them again. 'Honestly.'

Megan's patience with my daydreaming was nearing its expiration limit.

'The trip was great. The journalists all got along well. They enjoyed it.'

'Of course, they did. Being wined and dined at great expense. Which reminds me, make sure you hand in all the paperwork to accounts.' Her lips pursed. 'I've been debating the wine cellar business. At least we've got Conrad over a barrel ... no pun intended ... if he doesn't play ball we'll send him an invoice for the wine.'

'I don't think you need to worry about that. Did you know he's a renowned expert in furniture design? He got a huge amount out of the trip.' I smiled to myself. I must drop him an email to find out what he had done about the lecturing idea.

'Don't we know it. Several bottles of Chateau Neuf du Pape,' snapped Megan. 'And I'm not sure how him being an expert on obscure furniture is going to translate into measurable results.' She stared hard at me. 'Are you alright, Kate? You don't seem very on the ball this morning.'

'Sorry. Still a bit tired. It was a long week.'

She softened, infinitesimally. 'Well, you'll have a lot of catching up to do as well. We've got a meeting with Lars tomorrow; you can join us at ten to present the planned coverage report. You'd better make chasing up all the press your priority today.'

I rose wearily to my feet giving the blue sky outside one last longing look. Copenhagen was starting to feel like a very long time ago.

Being back at my desk felt wrong. For the first time ever I didn't want to be here. I wanted to be back in Varme. I hadn't really been paying much attention to what Megan had been saying. That was a first too. I wanted to talk to Sophie. Or Avril. Or Conrad. Or ... or Ben.

Our parting at Heathrow had been shy and awkward as if neither of us wanted to make that first move. Now we were back in England, it was as if the real world had intruded and it was difficult to know whether what happened in Denmark stayed in Denmark.

We'd faced each other, our luggage a barrier between us as metaphysical as physical.

'Well, thanks for everything. Great trip,' said Ben.

'Ditto. Thanks for coming.' My shoulders had felt very tense. 'Even though it wasn't your choice.'

'Wouldn't change it now though,' Ben's voice had lowered and the meaningful look in his eye gave my heart a quick jolt.

'No. Right well. I'll be in touch. About ... stuff.'

'Right.'

Shit, remembering the stilted conversation, before we headed in opposite directions, him to West Ealing and me to Clapham North, I wanted to bang my head on my desk and I would have done but it would have attracted way too much attention from my colleagues. Why the hell hadn't I just kissed him? Why hadn't he kissed me?

The phone on my desk rang.

'I've got serious withdrawal symptoms this morning.'

'Sophie, how are you? How was your weekend?'

She huffed. 'Bloody James only went and cancelled on me. I could have stayed in Copenhagen with you and Ben. Although I think I might have been a tad green and hairy.'

The phone in my hand felt slippery under my sweaty palm.

'Kate, you still there?'

'Yes,' I found my voice. 'I'm trying to decide whether to say *how did you know* or *don't know what you mean*. Was it that obvious?'

'Don't worry. I caught Ben looking at you a couple of times.'

'Looking at me. That's it?'

'I know these things. Besides, Eva knew.'

'She knew everything.' I felt a prickle down my spine. What was it she'd said about Sophie? She worried about her the most.

'Anyway, it was pretty bloody obvious when he jumped at the chance to stay behind with you. So, what happened? Tell me. Tell me. Tell me.'

'Sophie, you're dreadful.'

'I know,' she said cheerfully. 'But I need something to cheer me up. Bloody bloody James. I know he's a good bloke, a really good bloke, I mean how many of them look after their mum like him, but seriously, her timing is … is rubbish. Although I did end up having a good weekend. I went to Avril's.'

'Really?' Disbelief echoed in my voice. I mean I had grown to like Avril over the week, and she was a lot nicer than I'd originally thought but even so she didn't strike me as one for a girly heart to heart.

'Yeah, she wanted me to help her make pastries to take into work this morning.'

'Avril did?' That didn't sound like her either.

'She's got a plan.'

'OK,' I said warily. That would make much more sense but Sophie didn't give any more away.

'I met her husband. He is super gorgeous ... and nuts about her. Honestly. She wasted no time. Judging by the strange places I kept finding walnuts – see, nuts about her – she did some baking for him on Friday or Saturday. Seriously, the way he looks at her makes your toes curl.' Sophie gave a lovelorn sigh and I could almost picture her face, dreamy and hopeful. 'It must be lovely to be the centre of someone's universe. The most important person to them.'

Ben's face popped into my head. Those intense blue-grey eyes fixed on me as he said, 'Sometimes being scared is good. It makes you more careful.' Would he be careful with me?

By eleven I'd pretty much cleared down my inbox. I'd spoken to Conrad, David and left a message for Avril, while Fiona, Lord love her, had already emailed me a detailed blog post plan for the next couple of weeks. Which just left Ben.

I picked up the phone. Put it back down. Picked it up again. Put it down. I went to the loo. Made myself a cup of tea.

I took a quick peek at Facebook. Twitter. Checked my emails.

It was now eleven thirty. I couldn't put off phoning Ben any longer.

'Ben Johnson, speaking.'

Hearing the sharp bark, I couldn't help myself. 'Ah Mad Fox is back, it's Kate. Kate Sinclair. How many seconds have I got?'

He laughed. 'That depends. Are we riding roller coasters? Kissing? Or is this a business call?'

I tightened my grip on my phone. Kissing would be good.

'It's a five seconder. I'm calling ... not for me, Kate, but ... this is awkward because I don't care one way or the other, for me, well I do but I'm calling because I have to ask ... it's my job, but you know that, but it's not coming from me, if you know what I mean.'

'To be perfectly honest, and,' he paused and I could almost hear the laughter in his voice, 'thousands wouldn't, that was the most inarticulate ramble I've ever heard. But strangely I do. I get it. I'm writing a feature on *hygge* and Lars as we speak.'

'You are?' I squeaked in surprise.

'Yes, Kate, I am.' He sounded a bit put out.

'Sorry, I didn't mean to offend you but ...'

'You don't really think that I'd go all that way, enjoy Lars' very generous hospitality and not write anything?'

I paused, thin fingers of guilt twisting my conscience. No I didn't. Ben was a good guy – that wasn't his style at all.

'Sorry, no I ...'

'I'm not sure when the feature will go in but I've nearly finished writing it. But I could do with a bit more information.'

'Oh, right, what do you need?' I asked.

I heard him make a kind of tutting noise. 'I'm not sure it can be done over the phone.'

I let the smile break out, 'Really?'

'Yes,' he sounded as if he'd given it a great deal of thought. 'We need to meet.'

An image of pretending to be stern and serious while his eyes teased filled my head, making me fidget in my chair, idly doodling on my notepad.

'Meet?' I wanted to draw out the playful flirtation.

'Definitely,' his voice lowered, 'And soon.'

Mexican jumping beans took up residence in my stomach doing a full-on samba and I knew I had a goofy grin on my face.

'Sounds as if it's a face to face, over a drink in a bar job,' I said suddenly feeling bold.

'When? I can't do today I've got a meeting but how about … tomorrow?' My heart lurched at the hopeful lift at the end of his sentence.

'Done.' It took us all of two further seconds to settle on a venue.

I spent the rest of the day with a silly smile on my face, unable to concentrate on much. At half past five on the dot, my desk was the tidiest it had ever been. I'd even cleaned off the coffee rings and emptied the pen tidy thing, and found one pound fifty-six in loose change. Officially it was the end of the working day, although apart from going to the dentist once, I couldn't remember finishing at this time. Ever. I'd done as much as I could on the report for tomorrow's meeting with Lars and was only waiting for Avril to get back to me. So far so good. I hoped he was going to be pleased with the promised results.

Chapter 27

'Kate!' There was a distinct combination of triumph and smugness in Avril's words. 'You. Are. Going. To. Love. Me.'

'I am?' I tucked the phone under my chin as I carried on typing. I was putting together a follow up report on the trip to Copenhagen and Lars was coming in this morning.

'I have sorted it. Breakfast broadcasts from Hjem. What do you think?'

'What?'

'You know, a show. From Hjem. Live broadcast. Munching on Danish pastries. Interviewing people. I've already asked Eva to come over and do a demo and tasting with Sophie. Conrad's going to do a session on furniture. My producer loves the idea. L. O. V. E. Loves it.'

'Bloody hell,' I almost dropped the phone. It was the last thing I was expecting. Megan would blow a blood vessel. 'That's ... well incredible. How did you swing that?'

'Well ... you know,' she said and then she let out a half-laugh of self-deprecation. 'The honest truth ... I'm baring all.'

'Sorry?' Avril was gorgeous but were viewers ready for that at breakfast time?

'Baring my soul, Kate, not my boobs. Although,' she added as if seriously considering the viewing population's reaction, 'I think the Scandinavians do have quite a healthy attitude to nudity, maybe we should take a leaf out of their book.' She sniggered. 'Not so sure Christopher would be too chuffed.'

'Baring all?' I prompted.

'About the importance of *hygge* ... and what I learned in Copenhagen. Looking after the little things. The importance of making the little things important, baking a cake for someone, taking time to be together, lighting candles and making an occasion. My producer almost bit my hand off when I said that I'd talk about my marriage.'

'Avril! You don't have to do that.'

'Kate, darling, I'm keen to help you, but this is my career too. Being completely single minded. Viewers want warmth. I can do warm, I've avoided it because I thought it looked weak, but do you know what, that's what the viewers really want. They love nothing more than a celeb showing a bit of vulnerability. It makes great TV.'

'And how does your husband feel about this?'

'He gets me. He understands this is what makes me tick. Don't forget he's a very successful business man. He loves me but he also recognises what it takes to make it ... and,' I could hear the gratitude ringing in her voice, 'he's happy to support that.'

'Wow, that is ... I'm not quite sure what to say.'

'You don't have to say anything. This is going to put me on the map.'

'That's fantastic.'

'Yup and for Sophie too. I have to give some of the credit, only a tad mind, to her.'

'I heard she came and cooked with you.'

'Yeah. She's a doll. Bribing the whole production team with Danish pastries this morning, certainly helped. And they thought having breakfast at Hjem every day—'

'Every day?'

'For a week, darling. A whole week.'

'What? You're going to broadcast from Hjem, every day for a whole week?'

'Yes!'

'A whole week?' My voice squeaked with incredulity. She couldn't be serious.

'Kate, I'm going to strangle you in a minute. Please don't tell me it's going to be a problem because getting an OB unit for less than a week is going to screw with my producer's budget.'

'No problem. Absolutely not a problem. In any way, shape or form. Definitely not.' I threw a quick glance around the room expecting people to be staring, this was monumental, huge, incredible, but everyone was oblivious.

'That's amazing. You're amazing. I can't believe it. You're amazing.'

'Yes, I am,' said Avril, laughing down the phone at me.

'I ... don't know what to say. How did you swing it?'

'I came back with so many ideas. I pitched them all. And all things Danish and *hygge* are very in. My boss said he'd never seen me so enthusiastic. He thinks the viewers are going to love it. Actually, he ... er ... said that I seemed a lot ... more in tune with viewers. Of course, I've no idea what he meant, but I'll take it.'

We both knew she knew exactly what he meant. Something had softened in her last week, maybe appreciating what she had at home, had made her realise that winning the battles at work wasn't as important as she'd always thought.

I looked around the busy office. Nope, still no one had any idea of what had just occurred or the massive coup I'd landed. Maybe I ought to take a leaf out of her book.

My report was all ready and with my pile of papers I knocked on Megan's door. Her office was empty.

'Do you know where Megan is?' I asked one of the girls who sat nearest her office.

'She's in a meeting.'

'Oh, we've got a meeting at ten.'

'No, she's in a meeting from nine. With the Danish guy.'

'Lars Wilder?'

'Yeah, that's the one.'

'Nine?'

'Yes,' there was an impatient sibilant hiss to her response.

I headed for the stairs, taking them two at a time. I couldn't muck about waiting for the lift. Yesterday's conversation. It clicked now. That's what you got for not paying attention. Daydreaming. *You can join us at ten.*

Breathless and fuming I burst into the room to find Lars sitting around the board room table with Megan and Josh.

'Ah, Kate,' said Josh. 'Take a seat, we're just finishing up with our launch proposals.'

I shot Megan a furious glare.

'Kate,' Lars rose to his feet and came around the table to greet me, taking both of my hands and shaking them before planting a kiss on my cheek with a big wink that no one else could see.

'Lars.'

'How was your flight back?'

'Good thanks.'

'Although, I'm very glad you were unable to get on the flight. My mother may have lain on a cold floor for several hours before anyone found her.' He turned to Josh. 'I owe Kate a debt of gratitude. She saved my mother.'

He was a terrible old ham and suddenly his English had taken a distinct turn for the worse. Helped would have worked just as well as saved.

Josh shifted in his seat and gave me and Megan the sort of look that said, *why didn't I know about this*. Megan jumped in quickly and said, 'She's a real credit to the company. A huge asset.'

'I can see that,' said Lars deadpan. 'And I'm sure you value her as one of your most important employees.'

'Of course.' Megan nodded.

'In Denmark, we believe in working together. So, this is good to see.'

'Now that Kate is here, perhaps we can get back to the guerrilla campaign,' said Megan with a conciliatory smile.

Guerrilla campaign? News to me.

'So, Lars, as we were saying,' interjected Josh. 'The plan would be, as part of a teaser campaign, in the run up to the official opening, to balloon bomb the capital.'

'Balloon bomb?' Lars' gaze moved around the table before coming to rest on me with a completely perplexed expression. I stared back wide eyed and clueless.

Josh interjected smoothly, taking over. 'This would be an extremely sophisticated operation. We have successfully undertaken these types of guerrilla marketing events to great acclaim, picking up several awards. In this instance, we plan to have ten thousand balloons printed with the Danish flag. They would be dispersed in targeted locations around the capital by our dedicated guerrilla teams in a fleet of Hjem branded four by fours ... we could do a cross promotion with our car client, to create a bit of theatre and a lot of stir. We'd bomb St Pancras, Kings Cross, Euston, Paddington, Waterloo ... all the key commuter entry points, as well as Trafalgar Square, Oxford Circus, Covent Garden ... all those sort of places. So that people start to ask, what's the significance of the balloons? Why the Danish flag?'

'Bomb?' asked Lars, suddenly losing his excellent command of English.

'Not bomb, bomb,' said Josh smiling winsomely. 'It's a term. Like photo bombing.'

Lars continued to frown.

'These balloons. I don't think that this is very friendly to the environment.'

'They'd be biodegradable of course,' butted in Josh. 'It would grab lots of attention.'

'But what does the Danish flag say about Hjem? The vision is about showing people a taste of *hygge*. This doesn't sound very *hyggelich*.'

Megan who could see they were losing his interest, frowned saying, 'Kate, I believe you have some news. Some post press trip updates. Perhaps you could tell Lars what coverage we're expecting.'

With a deep breath, I launched in. 'The response from all six members of the trip has been fantastic. They thoroughly enjoyed the trip and all of them have promised features, articles and follow ups.' I caught a glimpse of Josh's face, one of those, yeah-yeah-where's-the-evidence types of sceptical sneers.

'Great coverage, Kate,' said Megan. 'I'm sure you can provide Lars with a full report, I'm sorry but unless you've got anything else, I'm conscious that time is ticking on and we ought to get back to the teaser campaign to build interest in the opening.'

I could see Josh openly yawning.

'Excuse me,' I interrupted, 'I haven't finished.'

Lars' mouth twitched but he leaned back in his chair as if totally unconcerned by the political byplay and undertones going on in the room.

'In addition, Sophie will also be demonstrating how to make perfect Danish pastries.'

'I'm sure this could be covered in your report.'

'Demonstrating how to make perfect Danish pastries on breakfast television on the day of the opening. Avril has agreed to run a week-long series of broadcasts from Hjem.'

I let the news settle in, taking in Megan's widening eyes and slow nod of satisfaction as well as Josh's sick as a dog expression. 'Avril is sending over an outline schedule for the week.'

I sat back in my chair my hands clasped together on the table.

'That is excellent.'

'It's bloody fantastic,' said Megan, shooting me a look of admiration. Josh still looked as sick as a dog.

The bar Ben had suggested was a short walk from the office, via Covent Garden and I arrived bang on time, grateful to find he was already there at a table ensconced in a crossword, a half-drunk bottle of Corona in one hand. I stood in the doorway watching him chew his pen as he studied the clues and then absently picking up his beer to take a long swallow. Was it entirely crazy that watching him swallow caused a quick skip of excitement to trip along my pulse? Who knew that throats were sexy or that it brought back the memory of his scent and skin, up close and personal at Tivoli. I sucked in a hasty breath and started across the floor. He looked up and my heart did a little flip at the delighted smile that immediately lit up his face.

Nerves fluttered as I arrived at his table, awkward with the dilemma of how to greet him but he took any decisions away by drawing me into his arms and brushing my lips with a gentle kiss that left them tingling. I think I must have looked a bit dumb or dazed because his face crinkled into a knowing warm smile that left me in even more of a mess.

Oh dear God, I'd fallen, hook, line and sinker for Benedict Johnson. I'd kind of been kidding myself that it was all in my head, in Copenhagen. Not real life. And all those fun, flirty feelings would stay where they belonged back in Denmark but no ... this delicious sensation of fancying someone and them clearly fancying you back (and from the look in his eye I was reasonably confident that was the case) was just bloody lovely.

'Hi, long time no see.' There it was again that warm, toe curling twinkle in his eyes. 'Good day at the office?'

'Not bad.' I smiled back at him, a parallel unspoken conversation alongside our words. 'Not bad at all. Avril came up trumps.'

'Did she?'

'Oh yes. Did she ever!'

'Want a drink and then you can tell all? What do you want?'

'One of those would be lovely,' I nodded towards the bottle of beer in front of him. He'd chosen well; the bar wasn't too packed and had a calm vibe to it rather than the usual frenetic after-work London scene.

While he went to the bar, I cheekily swivelled the crossword to face me.

'You're not doing very well,' I teased when he returned.

He shrugged, with a secretive smile. 'I had other things on my mind.'

Fiddling with a beer mat on the table, I managed to flick it across the floor skimming like a stone under an adjacent table which Ben kindly ignored. I needed to get a grip; the excitement was getting a bit much.

'So what's Avril been up to? Did she mend the fences in her marriage?'

'From what Sophie told me, I'd say the answer to that is a

316

resounding yes and when I spoke to her this morning she was very jolly.'

I told him all about the live broadcast plans.

'It's all anyone at work could talk about. Honestly, you'd think I'd single-handedly rescued a clowder of cats, slain multiple headed monsters and made the tea for everyone.'

'Clowder?' Ben looked very impressed and shunted closer, leaning his head towards mine. The bar was filling up and the noise levels were rising.

'Collective noun for cats,' I said exuding smug. 'Great crossword word.'

'It is. I must remember that one. So, basically, aside from having a smartarse command of the English language,' he said with a teasing lift of his eyebrow making me laugh, 'you're heroine of the day.'

'Yes, for today at least. It'll all be forgotten tomorrow but hopefully it might stick with my bosses.'

'Any news on the promotion?'

I bit my lip and laced my fingers together on my lap.

'It's looking good ... they're still banging on about press coverage from the trip ...'

'I have good news. I'm in the middle of writing the article. In fact, the architecture was all so fascinating, I'm thinking about doing a second feature focusing on the buildings in the city and the contrasts between old and new. There's some amazing design and many, like the opera house, are commissioned and built in partnership with individuals and companies.'

'I loved that canal trip,' I said thinking of the striking

building sitting on the edge of the water and the gorgeous colours of the wharf buildings at Nyhaven. 'Apart from when Avril hit her head.'

'It was eventful, I'll give you that. I bet after the trip, you don't know what to do with yourself.'

'Actually, it's made me see things very differently. I joined Rock Choir,' I grinned at the memory of the previous evening, 'by accident and we've got a house road-trip to Ikea on Thursday night. A smash and grab raid, we've worked out exactly what we want to buy and we're going to hyggify our flat, me and Connie, my flatmate.'

'Is that a thing? Hyggify?'

'It is now. We've spent the last year moaning about the state of the place and planning to move, but it's in a great location. The rent is reasonable and the place is OK. The trip made me realise, we could do so much with it, if we just got our backsides into gear,' I was gabbling and worse still it was obvious that Ben was amused by it. 'You get used to things, like mould on the wall, and live with it. We're on a mission. Tonight, you've saved me from painting duty.'

'Well if that makes me a hero, I'll take it. He lifted his arms to flex his biceps. 'Although is that more about a make-over and not so much about *hygge*?' Scepticism touched his mouth.

'Are you in journalist verification mode? Double checking the facts?' I asked. 'The whole cosy thing and having nice furniture and accessories around you, lightening your mood, and making you value your time, really struck a chord with me. Made me think about my home in a completely different light.'

'Having my sister's children trash my place made me think about it in a completely different light. I'm changing the locks. So, tell me about Rock Choir and how you managed to join by accident. I'm intrigued.'

I laughed, despite being a tiny bit disappointed with his scepticism and his abrupt change of subject.

'It's one of those things I've always meant to do. I walk past the poster outside the church hall every week. Last night I left work early, so I popped in. To pick up a leaflet.' I stopped and laughed.

'What?'

'The ditzy woman, lovely but scatty assumed I was already in the choir, so she had me moving tables with her and before I knew it, I couldn't leave without embarrassing her, so I stayed and sang.'

'Just as well they weren't doing some weird martial art thing that night.'

'There's an idea, I've always fancied being a ninja!'

'Now you're scaring me. You can be quite fierce already.'

We were back to flirty banter again.

'I can?' I raised a challenging eyebrow.

'Oh, yes,' he paused for a beat before adding, 'but in a nice way. Protective. You go to bat for other people. And did you enjoy singing?'

I sighed with pleasure. 'I loved it. The people were all lovely and I'd forgotten what a buzz you can get from singing, especially with other people.' I knew I was gabbling again but with his arm casually sprawled along the back of the seat next to him, he seemed quite comfortable, with my sudden spew of information. 'I haven't done anything like that for years. When I first moved to London, it was all so over-whelming I didn't do anything. And it was so nice to be with people of all ages and backgrounds.'

Focusing on work and living within the narrow confines of that world had heightened that sense of not being quite good enough.

'That's what I enjoy about playing football. We've got plumbers, a baggage handler, an accountant, a landscape gardener, a film production manager and a podiatrist in our team. It's grounding when you get stressed at work about some stupid thing. And handy when your sister floods the bathroom.'

'How is she? Has she left yet?'

'Yes, thank Christ, although I'm still trying to get my flat back to normal and mend fences with my neighbours. They're not best chuffed at having bathwater come through their ceiling, although thankfully they're so relieved that noise levels have returned to pre-toddler occupation standards they might just forgive me.'

I winced. 'Ouch. That'll mess up your insurance premiums.'

'No, it won't. Her husband, Rick will be paying for the privilege of a domestic strife-free week. I'm thinking of moving and not telling her or my mother.'

'You don't mean that,' I teased.

He pulled a face, 'It's tempting. Honestly, I could bash Amy and Rick's heads together. What about your lot? Spoken to them yet?'

'No, I've been … putting it off. Too busy.'

'Are you busy this weekend?' The words snapped out, as if he'd been hanging on to them for a while and now that he'd made the decision to say them, they took immediate flight.

'Erm ... no.' Suddenly I didn't care if I looked like a sad loser with no social plans.

'Would you like to come to dinner, Saturday night? Do you like curry? Indian? There's a great restaurant near me.' Now he was gabbling and it was really kind of cute.

Our easy chat suddenly stalled as if we both realised that this was the next step. My breath got stuck in my throat as I looked at him, his face almost too blank, apart from the pulse tripping in his throat.

'Th-this Saturday?' Under the table I crossed my legs, hooking my ankle around my leg.

'Yes. This Saturday.' He leaned over the table and slid his hand along my forearm which sent little shivers dancing along my skin. 'Kate, would you like to come to dinner with me?'

All the air whooshed out of my lungs as I said a tiny bit breathily, 'Y-yes. That would be ... lovely.'

He turned my palm over and rested his fingers in the centre, sparking a more obvious tremor which elicited a dangerous smile from him. He knew exactly the effect he was having on me, although from the narrowing of his eyes I wasn't sure that he wasn't equally affected.

His phone beeped but he ignored it.

'I'll book a table. It's very popular.' He paused, holding my eyes with steady intent. 'It's down the road from my flat.'

There it was. Crunch point. A possibility.

'Great. Brilliant.' We smiled at each other, like a little island oblivious to everyone around us.

'It's a bit … quieter than this. I'll book a table. Eight OK?'

'Yes. That would be lovely …'

His phone beeped again.

'Oh bugger, I'm sorry. I need to read this and I know it's work and they'll want me back.' His face fell as he read his phone. 'Yup.'

He turned to me. 'Shit, this is crap. I didn't want to cancel on you … but running out is just as bad.'

'Hey, don't worry.'

'No, I wouldn't normally, I promise, but I'm trying to get back onto the business desk. There's a story breaking. I volunteered to help out. And bloody sod's law it's broken. I need to get back.'

He touched my hand, a brief featherlight touch which meant more than some heartfelt hand squeezing. 'Kate … It's not that work comes first … oh shit it kind of does … but this is different.'

I held up my hand, laughing at him stumbling over the words. 'I completely get it.' I stood up as he gathered up his newspaper and jacket. 'I'll see you on Saturday.'

Gratitude glinted in his eyes. 'Thanks for being so understanding.'

'You'd better pray there isn't a PR emergency on Saturday.' I grinned at him.

'Hmm, wallpaper has been declared out of vogue.' He tucked his hand under my elbow as we walked out of the bar. 'Curtains are a thing of the past. The sofa is dead.'

As we emerged onto the busy street, I turned to him and gave him a superior look.

'Very funny. Mock all you like. I love my job.' As I said it, I realised the words were habitual rather than heartfelt.

Several kisses later, punctuated by an increasing number of text alerts, he reluctantly pulled back, touching my lips with his thumb.

'Gotta go.'

Although Saturday seemed a very long time away, the wistful glance he gave me over his shoulder would last until then.

Chapter 28

'Crikey Mary, Pollyanna's alive and well,' said Connie clutching a black coffee as I bounced into the kitchen.

'Hangover?' There was a definite tinge of green to her cheeks and charcoal circles under her eyes.

'Queen-sized,' she moaned, slipping further down into the new kitchen chair. 'Remind me that margaritas should be drunk in moderation.'

'I've done that before and you always ignore me.'

'Well remind me harder. I should have stayed in with you last night and celebrated all things Ikea. But Friday nights are made for dancing.'

'If you say so,' I said, pointedly looking at her wan cheeks.

She lifted the new coffee mug, not one of mine, and glanced around at the open plan kitchen and lounge which had undergone a radical transformation. 'Looks great though, I don't know why we didn't do it before.'

Operation *Hygge* had been embraced with a vengeance. Connie put a forceful case to our landlord pointing out that getting new tenants was high risk compared to two very reliable ones currently in situ and lo and behold he came and sorted out the mould and boiler that very week. And just when she'd beaten him into submission, she added that the carpet might have fleas. Our landlord, being one of those ducking and diving types, managed to have a new mid-grey carpet (as specified by Connie) installed on Thursday.

With our pooled resources, investing some of the money we'd been saving for a deposit on a new flat, the trip to Ikea in Croydon, in Connie's ex-boyfriend's clapped out transit van, had been a roaring success.

'We did good.' Connie looked over at the new pale blue sofa, piled with cushions and a co-ordinating throw which contrasted beautifully with the pale blue-grey walls which had taken most of Wednesday night to paint. 'And the lamp makes all the difference,' she teased.

'I hope Megan never remembers how much it cost,' I said. The lamp I'd bought for the pitch had been stuffed in the stationery cupboard and had come home with me in a taxi on Friday and was worth every penny of the fare.

We'd transformed the flat with a bit of elbow grease and retail therapy. I'd bought some shelves and storage boxes which had tidied up my bedroom and made it so much more appealing. Not quite seductive boudoir but I could bring someone home for the night. Not that I planned to of course. Well not ... well possibly.

'You know, I feel like a proper grown up. Why didn't we do this before? It makes you feel so much better.'

'*Hygge.*'

'I wish you'd stop saying that.' Connie shuddered. 'I might chukka any minute. My stomach is on maximum spin at the moment.' She rose to her feet and switched on the kettle, leaning back against the kitchen units. 'I need coffee otherwise I'll end up going back to bed and today will be a write-off. What time are you off to meet lover boy? And are you planning to spend the whole day getting ready?'

I couldn't help beaming at her. 'His name's Ben, remember.' My stomach was full of silly, squiggly feelings. 'And I'm leaving at half six.' I checked my phone. 'In seven hours and twenty-six minutes.'

'Uh-oh, is our Kate in lurve?'

I closed my eyes, feeling the pink on my cheeks. 'I really, really like him.'

'What really like him or really, really, really like him?' Connie clasped her hands over her heart pretending to swoon.

'You're so childish,' I tried to be lofty but it was impossible.

'Aw, look at your smiley little face,' she teased coming over to me and poking at the corner of my mouth.

'Oh, just stop,' I said pushing her hand away.

'Soz, you'll have fun.' She gave me a swift hug. 'This Ben suits you, whereas Josh never did. He seemed to add to your stress levels.'

'He's lovely. He might just be ...' I'd told her about our original meeting which she'd thought utterly romantic.

'The one,' she finished for me.

'That'll probably jinx things now,' I said, crossing my fingers and holding them up.

'No.' Connie tipped her head on one side. 'You seem different ... I think there might be something to this *hygge* business.' We both surveyed the new improved home décor. 'Funny isn't it, how you put up with stuff. And then the minute you actually think about it ... and start doing stuff, your whole outlook changes,' she mused and shot me an assessing look.

'Are you psychoanalysing me?' I asked warily.

'You seem a bit different since you came back ... more ...' she cast about for the right word before coming up with, 'singy.'

'Singy? You make me sound like Maria Von Trap.'

With a giggle, she said, 'Go on give us a burst of *The Hills are alive ...*'

Even as I ignored her with a pointed roll of my eyes, I could instantly hear the notes and Julie Andrews' voice in my head. The song danced on the tip of my tongue.

'You know what I mean, you sing a lot.'

'And that's the big difference?' I was intrigued to hear what she had to say, but pretending to be indifferent.

'Yes,' she poked me on the shoulder, a gesture which on anyone else might seem aggressive, 'you're much more positive. Decisive. More upbeat. A lot less ground down ... and you've come home early from work, well, early for you, every night this week. And when you come home you're full of ideas, instead of looking knackered and anxious.'

'Maybe the Danish outlook rubbed off on me.' Singing aside, life did feel a bit lighter.

'Or maybe it's love?' The words hovered in the air, tantalising and terrifying, as she watched me carefully.

'Don't be daft,' I said, shooting them down, as if denial would remove all and any chance of them being anywhere near a possibility. 'It's a date, I like him ... but ...'

'But?' Connie was in one of her take-no-prisoners moods.

'We've both got stuff going on. Our careers. And he's too close to work. I'm not going to get burned like that again. Look what happened with Josh. And neither of us have time for anything serious.'

'You sound like you're trying to convince yourself. That's like, what seven excuses,' persisted Connie. 'If you like him, you can make it work.'

She made it sound so easy. I rubbed my hand across my mouth. *Was it? Could it be?* 'It's complicated.'

'Bollocks. Only because you choose to make it complicated. Girl meets boy. Girl likes boy. Girl dates boy. Girl and boy become a couple. Bam. Simples.' She held up a shushing finger. 'Don't give me all those excuses. If you want it you can have it.'

She saw the doubts hovering, 'Crikey Kate, you do it at work, make things happen for you. Why not in your personal life? You've put that place first far too bloody often. Think about you for a change.' Her face softened. 'Right, lecture over. What are you wearing tonight?'

'Not sure.'

Only because I couldn't decide what to do. Go out to impress or play it cool?

'And have you got new undies?'

'NO!'

'Right, we're going shopping.'

'Who said I was going to sleep with him?'

Connie was suddenly all innocence. 'No one. And it's not whether you do or don't, it's about feeling irresistible and knowing you can if you want to.'

'OK,' I jumped to my feet. 'You make a good point ...' And going shopping would fill the next few hours nicely.

It's amazing what a new bra and matching knickers does for your confidence, along with knowing that no stone has been left unturned during a two hour date preparation process overseen by Connie. Bullied would be too strong a word, encouraged was perhaps fairer. She insisted that I did everything to look my best. Eyebrows plucked, legs shaved, hair washed, dried and curled, make-up expertly applied with Connie's very expensive Clinique stay-put-mist stuff sprayed over the top and she'd generously let me use her Jo Malone body crème. If nothing else I smelled gorgeous ... everywhere.

Ben had insisted on meeting me at the tube station and as I rode up the escalator, I hung onto the rubber handrail trying to steady my slightly shaky legs, convinced I'd read far too much into this. Dinner. That was all. *Don't get ahead of yourself, Kate*. Unfortunately, my body had not got that memo. On the tube I was jumpy, my legs crossed tight, one foot jerking the shoe hanging from my toes up and down for most of the journey and I must have checked the contents of my clutch five times over. Phone. Keys. Money. Perfume.

In the end, I wore one of my favourite dresses, a little red number, with a rolled Bardot style neckline, emphasising my collarbone and shoulders, accessorized with blue shoes and the blue clutch. Figure hugging and sophisticated, it fitted in all the right places, demure but also hinting at more with the wide expanse of skin exposed by the stylish neckline, normally covered up with a sensible cashmere cardi.

My hair was up, a few strategic curls escaping skimming the top of my back whispering across my skin as I headed towards the entrance of the station. Ben waited leaning against the tiled wall and as soon as he spotted me I saw his eyes light up, a slow smile of approval filling his face as he gave me a long, unhurried once over. As his interested gaze roved second by second from my shoes, up, up and up to my chest, my neck, my face, excitement fizzed like a champagne bottle about to explode and when I reached him, without preamble, he pulled me to him and our mouths automatically fused in a short, desperate kiss as if we'd waited far too long.

Whew! Heady with hormones and lust, the kiss almost floored me and when our lips finally parted, I clung to him, trying to regain my equilibrium. It was gratifying to see that his eyes looked equally glazed and he held me firmly too.

'Hi,' he said, the huskiness in his voice rasping over me. How had I forgotten how bloody gorgeous he was? I reached up and touched a freshly shaven cheek, almost in a daze, as if trying to reacquaint myself.

'Hi, yourself.'

Together we smiled at each other, oblivious to the other people passing. We must have been in the way but I don't think either of us were thinking clearly at the time.

'You look …' His hand reached up to my hair, twisting one of the curls around his finger and I knew exactly why Connie had done it like this. 'I like the hair.' His finger skimmed the delicate skin on my neck, making me shiver. Nerve endings dancing all the way south, sending little tremors to places they had no place to be.

'Thank you,' I said, leaning in to touch his smooth jawline with my lips. 'I like ...' I dotted a series of kisses in a path along his face and down his neck. I inhaled the scent of him, musky tones, man and aftershave, intoxicating and suddenly very, very tempting.

My hormones were in danger of hijacking me, taking complete control. Actually, I lie, they had stormed command central and I'd all out surrendered to the hell-bent-on-getting-laid buggers or maybe it was just Ben. In a navy shirt with a tiny white ... pattern, flowers, things, I don't know ... to be honest – that shirt fitted, hell it really fitted ... broad shoulders, white buttons for the undoing, chest ... my mouth had gone so dry and I wanted to cross my legs, to stop the fierce need that had taken up residence. *What the hell was wrong with me?*

My fingers wanted to walk right down that shirt and peel open every last button. Push back the printed cotton from his shoulders.

Ben's indrawn sharp breath and husky, 'Kate,' drew me up quickly.

Thankfully the sultry, glazed look in his eyes and the fingers rhythmically stroking my upper arms, suggested he was as wound up and enthralled as I was, except he had a tiny bit of sense left. 'Kate.'

I nodded. Restaurant. Dinner. Reluctantly I pulled away, with one last nuzzle of his neck, my tongue tracing his skin ... yes OK, that was deliberate, making a point.

We pulled apart, eyeing each other with rueful smiles, our eyes meeting in knowing suggestion before Ben laced his fingers through mine and squeezed my hand. 'This way,' he said with a naughty, unrepentant grin, 'We should go to the restaurant ... before ... before.'

'Yes. Yes, we should.'

The short walk to the restaurant calmed things down and my pulse had just about returned to normal as the waiter pulled out a high backed, velvet cushioned chair, second cousin once removed from a throne and I sat down, glad that I put on a smart dress.

Ben ordered a bottle of red wine and the waiter left us with the menus.

'This is gorgeous,' I said, fascinated by the deep purple walls and the gold leaf elephants trooping trunk to tail around the top edges. Embroidery and sequins edged the table cloths, coloured glass votives glowing jewel bright with tea lights giving a touch of Bollywood verve and colour.

'Wait until you try the food,' he said. 'I've only been here once before, for my sister's birthday.' He paused, 'I was waiting for a good excuse to come back.'

'I'm an excuse?' I lifted an imperious eyebrow, propping my chin on my hands.

He reached forward with a smile and took one of my hands, his fingers sliding along the inside of my wrist, butterfly soft. 'A reason.'

I smiled back and turned my hand so that it rested in his, loose and relaxed.

The waiter returned and we sat in silence as he carefully opened the bottle, let Ben try the wine and then poured us both a glass.

'Cheers.' We tapped our glasses.

'Thank you, for bringing me here. It looks lovely.' I looked around the restaurant, every table was full. At the nearest table to us, with two older couples, a waiter unloaded a trolley, placing a candle lit food warmer in the centre of the table before placing silver dishes of golden rice, a dark red curry, and a creamy amber chicken dish as well as a pile of puffed, charred naans.

'Wow,' I gave a low moan of greed, 'it smells amazing.'

'Mmm, doesn't it just. It's Kashmiri food. Lots of yoghurt, cardamom, cinnamon and cloves. They use a lot of saffron and ghee. It's very rich.'

'Tour guide Ben morphs into food expert?' I said, impressed but determined to tease him.

He grinned and held up the menu, 'I've read it before.'

'And we all know you love your facts,' I said remembering his knowledge of the Grosvenor Hotel and his avid interest in the Opera House.

He nodded, slightly sheepish, 'It's the journalist in me. I like facts. Checking them.'

'Is that why you became a journalist?' My lips twitched, 'Permission to be ... curious?'

His fingers tightened on my hand, 'Were you about to say nosy, then?'

'Who me?' I feigned innocence.

'Do you think I'm a bit nerdy?' he asked, laughter dancing in his eyes.

'It crossed my mind. A pair of glasses and you could rock the Clark Kent look.'

He burst out laughing. 'I love that you never give me an inch. Half the women I know would have said no, and fluttered their eyelashes at me. Or at least inferred I was Superman.'

'Why? Because you're just,' I lapsed into a breathy sweet voice, '*so gorgeous*,' ignoring the compliment and the rush of warmth it gave me.

'Remind me why I like you so much?' His mouth quirked at one side as he tugged at my hand, his fingers linking through mine, his words filling me with warmth.

'Because I keep you on your toes and don't take any of that five seconds crap,' my warm husky tone was at odds with my words. I couldn't get the "like you so much" out of my head or the rush of feelings doing a happy dance.

Thankfully the waiter appeared, shook out our napkins and placed them on our laps because I for one was getting very hot and bothered.

'Sorry, can you come back?' I hastily picked up one of the leather-bound menus.

With a polite nod, clearly used to customers who had other things on their minds than food, he backed away.

'What do you recommend?' I asked.

'I had the Rogan Josh last time and it was amazing. I might have it again.'

'No, you can't,' I said. 'You have to have something different, as Sophie would say, it's ...'

'Good for your food education,' he chorused.

'Exactly, I'm glad she encouraged us ...'

'Encouraged? You mean bullied.' Ben lifted his wine in silent toast. 'To Miss Whiplash.'

'Encouraged,' I reprimanded him. 'And you can't possibly call her that.'

'True.'

'She's Little Miss Sunshine,' I paused, although she'd been not quite so sunny last time I'd spoken to her, but that was between us, I didn't need to share it with Ben. 'She was great about getting us to try new things, although I have to admit I never thought I'd like herring.'

'Me neither.' He laughed. 'But I wonder if they're like Retsina in Greece. Tastes great when you're there but don't travel well.'

'Don't say that, I was all set to borrow a bike some time.'

'Really?' Ben inclined his head in one of those searching sceptical gestures.

'Well, I was certainly thinking about it,' I admitted.

He gave me an approving grin. 'Fancy a trip out sometime?'

'I'm game if you are.' I met his look head on.

'The forecast is good next weekend.' His steady gaze set off the bubbles in my stomach sensation again.

'Well that's a relief. Kagoules and weatherproof trousers are in short supply in my wardrobe.' And not a dress code I fancied. Hardly attractive, although without being big headed, from the heated looks we'd been exchanging, I don't think the lifeboat rescue look would have fazed him.

The poor waiter had to come back three times before we were finally ready to order and then it was a bit of a rush because we still hadn't looked. In the end, we opted for Lamb Rogan Josh, Dum Aloo, a potato in creamy yoghurt sauce, pilau rice and a curry called Nadroo Yakhni, because it was made with lotus stem and Sophie's training had rubbed off.

'We might never get to try it again,' I reasoned as the waiter disappeared taking our order.

'I'm pretty sure, we could come back here.' His lazy observation made my stomach tighten in quick anticipation. 'But, if it's awful, I'll blame you.' His eyes darkened, the incipient threat of some punishment dancing on the air between us.

'Where's your sense of adventure?' I said, lifting my neck and chin to advantage, brushing back one of the loose curls, giving him a direct look of challenge.

'I'm saving it for later.' His naughty smile stopped me dead and I think I might have gulped. He was good at this. Suddenly I regretted the challenge, because he'd taken it up. More than taken it up, he'd declared all out war and my body was all for surrendering immediately.

And he pushed his advantage when the food arrived, pulling every dirty trick in the book.

Insisting that I try things from his fork and he try food from mine.

When he moaned at the taste of Nadroo, his eyes calculatingly held mine. When I missed a bit of rice, his finger scooped it up and lifted it into my mouth, his fingers grazing my lips with deliberate intent.

It was every cliché you could think of and then some, each of us trying to outdo the other.

By the time Ben fed me the last piece of Naan, his fingers lingering on my lips, my whole body was on a low simmer. As his forefinger skimmed my bottom lip, acting on pure instinct and lust, I quickly sucked in the tip delighting at his shocked gasp, clenching my thighs together. This was as much torture for me as him.

'Can I get you the dessert menu?' asked the waiter.

'No,' we said together, our eyes now meeting, all pretence at subtlety gone.

Ben paid for dinner, despite my demurs; I didn't put up much of a fight. I'd get the next one. I just wanted to get out of there and quick.

'Shall we go? Before ...' asked Ben rising to his feet, suddenly swallowing and I smiled at his uncharacteristic diffidence, the dip of his Adam's apple making me feel naughty, wanton and impetuous. Lots of things that I'd never felt ... ever. This sense of being empowered. Equal. Nothing to lose.

'Before what?' I asked, my voice lowering, thrilling to the power of being uncharacteristically suggestive.

He drew in a ragged breath, skirting the table and grabbing my hand, sending the nerve endings at the apex of my thighs, into an unladylike flutter and kerfuffle. Sudden warmth making me agitated and hurried. I wanted him with an urgency that left me breathless and fidgety.

'Before things get out of hand,' he muttered hoarsely into my ear.

I sucked in a breath and he smiled again. Not quite smug but sure and a touch satisfied, perhaps possessive. In that second, I vowed I'd wipe that look off his face ... later, much later, but in the meantime I was going to make him pay for it.

We hurried out of the restaurant into the street and three

strides out, we stopped and he hauled me into his arms, his back against a shop window, I think.

I stood on tip toe and kissed him again, my tongue touching the edge of his lips, feathering along his lower lip and then skimming the top lip. His low groan was worth every bit of the frustration I felt.

With a sudden, desperate jerk he pushed me away, his lips sliding to my ear.

'Kate,' his breathy words whispered, warm on my skin, 'Do you want to come back to my place?'

I turned my head, our eyes meeting. My heart pounded so fast and hard, as the moment weighed heavy between us, I was sure he could hear it or at least feel it in the air.

'Yes,' I whispered into his mouth, as his lips closed over my words in a soul sucking kiss that held strains of gratitude, relief and desperation, want, need and determination.

'This way.' He tugged at my hand, his fingers tightly woven between mine, pulling me through the crowds on the pavement in the early summer evening.

He missed the keyhole several times, but that was perhaps since we'd got in the lift we hadn't stopped kissing, and he had one hand pulling down the top of my zip and I was attacking the buttons on his shirt, which had been yanked out of his waist band. All the simmering feelings in the restaurant had exploded into completely mutual full on raging lust.

We burst through the door and he kicked it shut behind him, sliding a hand into the top of my dress and pulling it down in one fluid move. I toed off my shoes and stepped out of the dress as it pooled around my ankles, into his arms, sighing at the touch of his bare chest on my skin. His lips traced their way along my jaw and down my neck before working back up. Our mouths fused again and his hands were sliding down over my bottom, stroking and pulling me to him, where I could feel his erection taut against the fabric of his trousers, the cold of his belt on my stomach. I wound my hands around his neck, stroking the short hair at the back, my chest rubbing his.

His hands rode up, skimming my boobs, before sliding to the back and in one neat practised move undid the clasp.

'You've done this before,' I breathed into his mouth and then gasped as a firm warm hand smoothed over my breast, fingertips zeroing in on the nipple. I moaned at the sudden mix of heat, want, frustration and desire burning between my legs, pushing harder against him.

'Christ, Katie.' His mouth slid down my chin, his lips replacing his fingers.

My knees almost buckled at the touch of his warm tongue, swirling its way around my tight nipple. Oh! Tighter and tighter, so tight it might explode any second. I whimpered, the feeling just too much. Everything was going so fast but it felt ... ummm. He took the nipple right into his mouth ... aaargh, sucking, hot and fast. Words spilled. More, ahh, pleeease, yessss.

Head back, mindless, all I could feel was the heat of his mouth, sucking and licking, on one side clever fingers teasing and torturing, rolling and touching my other nipple sending tiny darts of pleasure so intense they were almost painful. I squirmed under his touch, breathless with want.

The explosive need thrilled and shocked me, making me wanton, craving more. My hands raced over his warm, taut skin, my fingers tracing the soft hair arrowing down below his belt. I stroked the waistline, my fingers dipping below, stroking the fabric over his erection, spurred on by his heartfelt groan.

His mouth moved back to mine, his body pushing me against the wall, his lips roving, his tongue sliding into my mouth with an electric touch.

The kisses got deeper and dirtier, and then something flicked the detonator switch and we passed into desperate.

My hands made short work of his belt, pushing down his trousers, while he pushed my pants aside, his fingers sliding straight between my legs, I grasped his erection. Gasps and groans filled the air as we slid down the wall to the floor. He kicked off his trousers and pulled away my pants and suddenly we were naked on the cool wooden floor of the hallway, kissing, trying to get closer still.

'Katie,' gasped Ben hoarsely, his hands holding my hips. I could feel his fingers firm, gripping the bones.

'Mmm,' I groaned, relishing the feel of skin on skin. Every bit of me felt on fire and I wanted to be consumed by the flames.

'I need to get ...'

'Pill. I'm on the pill.'

With his hand, he nudged my legs open, his fingers feeling their way.

I moaned loud and long, pushing my pelvis up to meet that clever, questing touch.

'Oh God. Katie?'

'Yes, please, now.'

He settled between my legs, the tip of his penis pushing at me and I widened my legs, tilting my hips, welcoming the sensation of him nudging and filling.

'Mmmm,' I panted, as he inched inwards, the sensation sweet and addictive. I wanted more and I tilted. He took the invitation sliding home and then retreating. Heaven and hell, thrust and retreat, I clutched his back trying to pull him deeper, wanting to hold him, feeling him solid and strong inside me.

I pulsed around him as he pumped furiously and I relished every slam home, sucking in a heartfelt breath as I tried to grip, hold him and then he pushed one last time, with a loud guttural groan before holding still and I felt my muscles tighten, the sensation of reaching the end, finishing that impossible race, rushing over me, as the climax burst, rippling in shades of pleasure, over and over.

We lay there, stuck together with a slight sheen of sweat, him still inside me, his weight heavy on me, his head buried in my neck. I felt utterly limp and supine, despite the cold floor beneath my back and bottom.

Ben groaned, nuzzling my neck. 'Bloody hell, woman. I think you might just have killed me.' He started to shift, sending a starburst of sensation.

'Don't move. Not yet.'

He settled, a lazy hand skimming my breast as his head lifted and two dazed eyes stared down at me.

'You OK?' he asked.

'Mmmm,' I said sighing.

'Sure you don't want to move? I do have a bed and everything.'

I summoned up enough energy to giggle. 'What constitutes everything?'

'You know, pillows, duvet, mattress.'

'Why the hell didn't you say before?' I muttered, stretching a little as the hard floor began to bite.

He laughed and slid his body from mine, rising to his knees and pulling me up.

'You didn't give me a chance,' he complained.

'I didn't give you a chance?'

'No. Come on let me introduce you to comfort.' He tucked me into his body, his hands skimming down my back to cup my cold bottom and shuffled me backwards towards the door to our right.

I turned my head to see the pristine bed, with grey cotton duvet cover and started to laugh. 'You do have a bed and everything. So why ...?' I nodded back at the hallway.

'What's a bloke to do? I wasn't going to mess up the moment,' said Ben, leading me towards the bed and lifting the cover.

'Of course not,' I agreed, giving a little shiver.

'Come here.' Together we slid in, my leg slipping between his and my head resting on his shoulder. 'I thought we could come back here for coffee and dessert, seems like we jumped the gun, a bit.'

I nuzzled at his throat where tiny bristles were starting to break through. 'I'm always up for seconds.'

Ben's hand skimmed down, brushing my breast. 'Funny, I was hoping you might say that.'

The boy needed black out blinds. It was half seven in the morning and sunlight filled the room. He lay on his back, one arm thrown behind his head. I studied his face, the stubble breaking out on his squared off chin, the hollows in his cheekbones. As I studied him, my stomach flipped over realising again just how good looking he was. And that was even before you took in the body. I gave a slight shiver, remembering the feel of masculine legs against mine, the dip of his stomach, the smooth taut skin over his hip bones.

I sighed and burrowed into the pillows, smiling at the smell of clean sheets. I dozed for a while but couldn't get back to sleep. It was bloody Sunday. Ben looked so peaceful and tempting as it was to gently wake him, I couldn't bear to. Instead I slipped out of bed to explore the kitchen and make myself a cup of tea.

I drew a blank, no milk. Looking at my watch which I still wore, I decided to slip out and grab some milk and perhaps something for breakfast.

Grabbing my handbag which was still in the hall, the contents spewed across the floor where I'd dropped it last night, I scooped the contents back in place, including my mobile which had a load of message alerts on the screen. With a quick glance back through the door at Ben's sleeping form, the duvet tucked around his waist leaving an enticing view of gently muscled chest and dark hair, I sighed, tempted to crawl back in and wake him up.

But if I went out now, we could stay in bed later. With that happy thought, I left the door on the latch and skipped out into the morning. I left the lobby door on the latch too, hoping no diligent neighbours would close it while I was gone. Luckily, down the street I could see a parade of shops. There was bound to be a newsagent open, for milk.

As I crossed the road, I scanned my text messages.

WTF! Sunday Inquirer!

Megan's text stopped me dead not quite in the middle of the road but near enough.

I opened up my phone screen to read the message in full and almost tripped up the kerb.

WTF! Sunday Inquirer! Have you seen the article on hygge today? Call me when you've seen it. Megan.

I smiled to myself; Ben had said the article was done. He'd clearly done us proud. I headed into the newsagent, catching sight of a coffee shop. I dithered about whether to grab a pint of milk and decided against it. I'd grab two coffees and hopefully some reasonably fresh pastries. Picking up the paper, I paid for it and headed to the rather inappropriately named Pump and Grind, which made me grin.

They'd literally just opened and the surly young man had to push the hair out of his eyes to focus on me as I gave the order.

'Just switched on, will be a minute,' he muttered.

'I'll wait.' I sat down and began to rifle through the paper, a satisfied smile on my face. This was a good result. It took a lot to impress Megan; Ben had obviously come up trumps in his article. The press trip had delivered. Bloody Josh could stick that in his pipe and smoke it.

The article was in the middle of the paper. Ben had a by-line, next to the headline.

Hygge or Hype? – Happiness or Hokum.

With my heart beat picking up a pace, nerves suddenly alert, I read the article, scanning the words quicker and quicker, picking out the pertinent phrases.

A passing fad.
  Candles and cashmere.
  A cynical attempt by marketers to emulate a deep seated cultural psyche that simply doesn't translate to the British way of life. A cultural chasm that can't be bridged with cosy and convivial. A simplistic quick fix philosophy of happiness that won't wash in our country where deep seated divides and nationally shared values shape our outlook.

There was more, a whole double page spread of more but I'd read enough. Ben had slated the whole concept of *hygge*, mocking the idea of happiness and trashing the whole Hjem campaign.

Every word sliced into my heart.

I stood up, left a fiver on the counter and walked out, putting one foot in front of the other, my vision blurred.

I walked for a while ... much longer than a while, switching my mobile phone off to stop the rush of texts and calls, none of which I looked at. After walking along several unfamiliar streets, I came to a road and saw the landmark of Ealing Common. At this time of day, it was quiet, the quiet hum of the odd car, around its borders, only the detritus of empty wine bottles, discarded beer cans and charred trays of charcoal hinting how crowded it would be again in a matter of hours.

I sat on a bench irritated by the mess and dumping the rumpled newspaper and my bag on the seat, I began angrily scooping up nearby bottles and chucking them in the bin. I couldn't think straight with all this rubbish around me, I needed a clear space.

The physical activity as I stomped about, picking up other people's crap, somehow made me feel a lot better. I fizzed with a barrage of emotion, anger at other people's thoughtlessness, irritation at their laziness, impatient that they couldn't see it for themselves and annoyance that I had to step in and do it and exasperation that people would assume that someone else would do it for them ... my fingers stilled on the neck of a beer bottle and I sank back onto the bench.

I should have seen the signs with Ben. He'd always been sceptical. I should have known better. People only did those things if they were allowed to get away with them.

The revelation settled on me, little bits of jigsaw slotting into place, one by one and I almost didn't know where to start. Ben, I pushed to the bottom of the list. I couldn't deal with that much hurt at the moment.

I'd let my dad and brothers get away with being lazy and thoughtless. By bailing them out, helping with the mortgage, tidying up after them, I'd just reinforced their behaviour, making it OK. It wasn't OK at all, but I was as much to blame as them.

Mum wouldn't have been impressed at all. She wanted us all to do our best for ourselves. She'd wanted us to have choices, not be stuck in dead end jobs. Education for me had been the key to opening up my horizons. But I'd shut them down myself. If I was honest, my job had begun to define my life. It was restricting my choices.

Eva had hinted as much … *you have choices, Katie. You can choose to change things.*

She was right. Like the space I'd tidied up around me, I no longer had any excuses for not clearing up my own life. With sudden resolution, I jumped up from the bench. It was time I made those changes.

Chapter 29

If I'd been a bit more myself, I might have wondered at the unmistakable smell of roast chicken or the total absence of shoes in the hall. Instead I slipped through the front door, peeling off my soaking coat and letting it fall to the floor. I was still in last night's dress but it was doubtful my family would notice.

'Dad?' I yelled, taking my wet shoes off. My feet were killing me. I'd walked for a couple of hours this morning before finally stumbling on a tube station and then for some bizarre reason, deciding I had to come home.

My mobile thankfully had died, a merciful relief from the gazillion texts from Megan, Connie and Ben. Lots from Ben that were deleted without even being read.

I hadn't bothered letting my family know I was coming. Not that they'd have bothered to stir themselves to pick me up. Blind instinct had propelled me to Euston.

I still had no idea why I was here.

'Dad,' I called again, needing him to be there.

'Katie?' Dad's head popped through the lounge door, like a startled turtle and it looked as if he wanted to duck straight

348

back into his shell. 'I wasn't ... erm ... expecting you ... love.' He squeezed through the gap and pulled it not quite shut behind him.

'I can tell,' I said, snapping, hurt that I seemed an unwelcome intrusion.

Then I did a double take. The carpet on the stairs had that recently hoovered look to it. 'Can I smell Sunday dinner?'

'Erm ... no, not really, er yes.' Dad's eyes darted left and right to the gap between the door and the jamb.

'New jeans?' My voice had an accusing shrillness to it. Here was I having a crisis and he had new jeans.

'Might be.' With a lift of his chin, minus the usual grey whiskers, he tried to look casual, smoothing down the dark blue denim.

'Patrick, who are you talking to? Are you going to come and carve this chicken?'

The door was wrenched open and a sturdy woman stood there, glorious in an eye-catching flowery skirt, covered in brilliant turquoise petals and a perfectly co-ordinated matching T-shirt stretched over a magnificent bosom.

Dad's mouth opened and shut, he looked excruciatingly awkward, shifting from foot to foot like an errant stork as his face turned redder than an overripe tomato.

The woman bustled past him, put her hands on my elbows, giving him a resigned head shake. 'You must be Katie, love. I'm Eileen. Nice to meet you ... at last.'

'H-hello.' *Eileen.* I shot a look at Dad. Since when had there been an Eileen around?

She rolled her eyes. 'He hasn't told you has he? Men, bloody useless. Come on through love. Crikey, you're wet. Come on in and get yourself dry, although why I'm saying that to you I don't know, this is your house.'

I liked her immediately for saying that.

'Are you going to have a bite to eat? There's plenty.'

'That would be great, thank you.'

She nudged Dad. 'At least offer the poor girl a cup of tea. Have you walked here love from the station? You must be gasping. You should have rung. One of your brothers could have come and got you.'

I pulled a face at that.

'Sorry, love. Stupid. Of course. They don't think, do they.'

Brandon was in the kitchen … washing up!

''Lo Sis. Didn't know you were coming?'

'Spur of the moment thing,' I said fascinated by the suds on his hands.

He grinned.

'How's the Sith Infiltrator coming along?'

'Finished. And a bloke contacted me via my website. Wants to meet me.' His face lit up. 'I'm hoping he's an enthusiast and might buy it.'

'Brandon, make your poor sister a cuppa, while I get the gravy on the go.'

Somehow, I found myself in the kitchen with a cup of tea while Eileen handed over a fistful of cutlery and placemats to Dad and Brandon.

I stared at the empty counter tops, the shiny stainless steel drainer and the clean tea towels hanging up.

'Not me,' said Eileen following my gaze. 'I don't mind

coming round and cooking a roast for all the family, but I draw the line at the rest. And,' she winked at me, 'I'm not cooking in a filthy kitchen.' She lowered her voice. 'I bet it didn't look like this come last Thursday.'

We both laughed.

'So how do you ... know Dad?' I asked.

'We met when he came to give a quote to do my driveway. Of course, stupid sod took weeks by which time I'd had it done by someone else.'

That sounded like Dad. 'Only despite being efficient with their quoting process and making out they knew what they were doing, they made a right pig's arse of it. Your dad finally rolled up with his quote ... caught me short he did. I was having a little bit of a weep ... and I tell you, I'm not a crier, but I felt so flippin' stupid, being fleeced by them cowboys. Your dad, bless his heart, made me a cup of tea.' Her chubby cheeks crinkled revealing dimples and she winked. 'Yeah, I know ... he can do it.' We exchanged a quick understanding smile. 'And offered to put it right for me, no charge, if I paid for the materials. Well I could see he could do good work ... he needs someone to sort him out. Admin wise ... and well we got chatting ... and chatting and chatting.'

Dad wasn't one for words; I suspected Eileen had done most of the talking. 'And well, here we are. And it's lovely to meet you. He's dead proud of you.'

I winced thinking about what I'd come to say to him.

'And I know what you've been doing for him.'

'Are you some sort of mind reader? You remind me of someone else who does that to me.'

'You've got one of them faces lovie ... and it's a bit of instinct. Mother's instinct.' She laid a plump warm hand on mine. 'And I'm not looking to replace your ma, or take over here. Your dad's very special to me but I don't want to go upsetting the applecart. No family dramas, thank you. But ...' she lowered her voice, 'Your dad needed a good kick up the backside. And I hope you don't mind me saying, so do those boys. Not for me to say it, mind. I'll take your dad in hand, that's my privilege, but the boys they'll have to do it for themselves. I think John's new girlfriend, Stacey might bring him up to scratch and Brandon, what a sweet boy, but Lord he doesn't know what's under his nose does he? Connie's a lovely girl.'

I shot her a wide-eyed *what the* look.

'When did you meet Connie and why didn't she say anything?'

'She was home last week to see her dad, although she seemed to spend a fair amount of time helping Brandon out with his latest project. Said it was your dad's place to tell you about me.'

'Connie and Brandon?' I whispered, taking a quick peek towards the lounge, where Dad and Brandon were laying the table at this end of the room.

'Yeah, plain as pikestaff. Except I don't reckon either of them realise the other has the hots for them. So, what's on your mind, lovie?'

'I need to talk to Dad.' But now I didn't feel quite so worried about it. Eileen's influence had almost certainly paved the way.

While John and his girlfriend – the spray tan queen, Stacey who was quite a savvy business woman, having picked my brains about PR ideas throughout lunch – did the washing up, Dad and I were somehow encouraged to go into the garden. Eileen had a talent for managing things but without being too pushy or interfering.

I stopped to reattach one of Dad's peonies back onto its stake, stroking the petals of the florid pink head. 'She seems very nice.'

'Hope you don't mind.'

'Dad! Why would I mind?'

He shrugged bending to tug at a weed. 'Your mum.'

'It's been a long time, Dad. I don't want you to be alone. I guess one day, John will go, and I suppose Brandon.' I shot a quick look over the fence at Connie's house. Connie? Brandon? Never saw that.

'Eileen makes me happy.'

His words gave me a brief pang but I pushed away all thought of Ben. He didn't exist. I'd made a mistake. One I was going to forget with a capital F.

'I've been sort of sleepwalking since your mum went. Going through the motions. Relying far too much on you. She's organising me ... or I'm letting her organise me.' Dad smiled, the first proper smile, one that touched his eyes and ridged his skin in wrinkles, that I'd seen for a long time.

'That's great, Dad. I'm pleased for you.'

'And I owe you an apology and a ton of money.' He dug in his pocket and pulled out his old battered leather wallet, his thick fingers rifling through notes.

'No, Dad, seriously it's fine.' I waved his hand away.

'No, it's not love. Those two boys should have been pulling their weight. Paying rent. With Eileen's help I sorted out my finances. And this is what you should have. Here.'

He thrust a wodge of notes at me.

'Take them and don't argue. And there's more coming. All the money you've paid on the mortgage. You should have it, you will have it back.' His attempt at belligerence, standing there bow legged and determined lightened my heart. For so long he'd worn an air of defeat and weariness. I took the folded notes and put them in my back pocket.

'Thanks Dad. I appreciate it.'

'And I appreciate the sacrifices you've made. Working so hard. Bailing us out, when it's so expensive in London. I should have seen it before. Your mum would have been dead proud of you, you know, I know she went on about you making the most of your brains, but she would have been the first to say, do something that makes you happy. What she really wanted was for you to have choices. To choose what sort of job you wanted, not to be stuck in something because there was nowt else you could do. I'm not sure that job of yours makes you that happy. Money isn't everything you know.'

'Thanks Dad, but I do like my job.' But I didn't love it. Not the way I used to. I was dreading tomorrow. A strategy meeting. A raking over of the coals. A post mortem. My performance would once again be brought into question, except this time, I'd been questioning my own judgement.

Dad patted me on the shoulder. 'As long as you're happy.'

I gave him a wan smile. Happy. I'd spent a week chasing happiness in Denmark and look where that had landed me.

Ben had gone and shafted me, literally and metaphorically. I'd trusted him and he'd played me.

I couldn't believe I'd been so stupid. Or that I'd fallen for him.

Now I looked back there were plenty of clues, he'd never any intention of playing the game. But he didn't have to sleep with me ... with a wince, I'd offered it on a plate. He was a red-blooded man. I'd been guilty of being indiscriminate. There'd been attraction there and I'd acted on it. He was hardly going to turn it down.

I really did have bad taste in men. First Josh and now this. I was a complete fool.

Chapter 30

'Well this is a fucking dog's dinner, isn't it?' snarled the Managing Director as I walked on shaky legs into his office. Megan and Josh were huddled like generals in a war cabinet around his desk.

I had nothing to say. What could I say? Inside I was fuming. It was eleven-thirty and they'd kept me waiting for three hours, after issuing a summons as soon as I walked in the building that morning. I didn't think I was going to get the sack and I did anticipate a lengthy post-mortem, but not this level of anger.

Some instinct or maybe it was pure self-preservation made me press record on the camera on my phone and pop it into the top pocket of my blouse. It looked to everyone else in the room as if I were switching it off and putting it away.

'You clearly took your eyes off the ball on this one.' He sneered at me over the top of his coffee cup. 'You had a whole fucking week ... and this is what you achieved. Bloody marvellous.'

I stiffened and clenched my fists. I hadn't even been offered a seat. Megan and Josh looked uncomfortable, him toying with the keys on the laptop in front of him and Megan twisting one of her rings.

'Have you spoken to the little scumbag?'

'No,' I said thinking of the unanswered texts from Ben.

'I assumed as much and in the interests of damage control, we thought we'd cut out the middle man. Since you're incapable of handling him, I've had Josh draft an email to the editor asking for an explanation. Not that it's going to make a blind bit of sodding difference. The damage is done. Johnson must be pissing himself laughing. A week's hospitality with a bimbo of a PR girl on call, and then screw you. Surely you had a heads up on this.'

I shook my head, my lips clamped tightly together. Christ knows what he'd say if he knew I'd slept with Ben.

'Well you fucking well should have.' Megan and Josh flanked him, looking accusingly at me. He looked at them. 'Looks like we made the right decision. You need a lot more experience before we put you in charge of anything like this again. I can't believe you've been so incompetent, but we'll explain to Lars that you're quite junior, and that in future we'll have more senior personnel running the account. Luckily for us we've been distancing you from the account since you got back.' He and Josh exchanged a look. 'You've become too close to the client. Thinking of him rather than the company. I've not seen one decent idea from you about how we maximise more fees or income from this client.' He shot one final furious glare at me before turning to Josh and pointing to the screen on the open laptop. 'In fact, as of today you're back to being a Senior Account Manager.'

'Pardon? You can't do that.'

'I think I can. I'm your boss. I can do what the hell I like. Right, where were we?'

Josh, the weasel, gave me a sad insincere smile before saying, 'How about if I add in here ...' He started typing.

Suddenly as if my fury had raced up a hill, reached the top and plateaued I felt utterly calm, an almost out of body experience. I swung around remembering Fiona's Dalek impression. There was no laughter now. Conscious of the camera recording in my pocket, I deliberately asked the question.

'Did you just call me a bimbo?'

The MD paused and looked as if I'd hit him. Megan's mouth dropped open and Josh's fingers stopped dead hovering over the keyboard.

'A bimbo?' I pressed again on the issue.

'Yes, I bloody did.' A fat pulse beat in his neck and he shook Megan's warning hand from his wrist.

'Just checking,' I said, things popping into place in my head one by one.

My growing inner calm was quite surreal and in direct proportion to the rising tension among them. Inside me everything settled like dust motes dancing to rest.

He raised an imperious hand. 'You should have known this was coming. Did you speak to him this week?'

'Yes, but—'

'The fact that you had no idea is doubly incompetent.'

'And still a bimbo?' I asked again.

The MD rolled his eyes as if to say *so what.*

I maintained eye contact with him waiting for him to speak.

'OK, so I called you a bimbo. What of it. You screwed up.

You are a bimbo. But you did good with the breakfast thing. So keep going like that and maybe you'll get promoted back to where you were before.'

'I don't think so,' I said in a quiet calm voice, which belied my quivering legs. 'Actually, not I think, I *know* it's a no. I'd rather get a job cleaning the portaloos at Glastonbury. I quit.'

Sitting in the coffee bar, I felt quite proud of myself. Dignified if foolhardy. Before I vacated my desk, I'd pulled my phone out of my pocket and uploaded the video footage and emailed it to the head of HR. Bullying. Constructive dismissal. Sexism. I had no idea how many employment laws had been broken but she would be horrified and although I had no intention of letting the video go anywhere else, the company would worry it might go viral.

After that I grabbed my bag from my desk, a couple of files from the top of my in-tray and walked out of the building without saying a word to anyone. Shocked adrenaline carried me here but now nursing a large Cappuccino, I felt the pinch of a headache. What was I going to do now? Since coming back from Copenhagen, the thought of perhaps leaving and going to join a smaller agency had crossed my mind several times, but did I want to play this game anymore? I could go in-house. Work for someone directly instead of for an agency. I straightened and pulled out my notebook, starting to make a list of possible options.

After I'd filled a page of notes, I paused. Closing my eyes, I listened to the hiss of the espresso machine and immediately thought of cinnamon snails, blue earthenware plates, glass domed cake stands, coloured glass displays on the walls and Eva's perky ponytail bobbing as she whisked around tables. When I opened my eyes, I felt a terrible sense of dislocation. Chipped Formica tables. Dralon upholstery in shades of green and plum, the same in every branch. The glass display cabinet with expensive packaged cakes and biscuits. The serving unit of milk in stainless steel jugs and wooden sticks. Not even real spoons. The lighting was all wrong. Too bright. Too false. Too cold. It all looked so ugly and commonplace. Not one of the waiting staff caught my eye.

I longed for the warmth and colour of Varme with bitter-sweet heartache. I wanted to smell baking, talk to people and feel I mattered. I might as well be invisible in this place. Once you'd paid for your coffee, you were done.

I studied the mass produced black and white photos of European cities from the thirties. Despite the nod to heritage, there was nothing authentic or particularly inviting about this place. Convenience. Coffee on the go. As far away from *hygge* as humanly possible.

If this were mine, what would I do? What would Eva do? I looked down at my notes and straightened. At least I had the beginning of a plan.

The front of the department store was still covered in scaffolding and the sounds of hammers, drills and a radio came through the polythene sheets shielding the front doors. I pushed through them and stopped dead. Inside certainly didn't look like a construction site. The interior was coming along well and already looked stunning.

'Katie!' I looked up and hanging over the balcony to my right waving madly was Eva in a bright yellow hard hat. The first genuine smile in days lit my face at the sight of her as she came rushing down the stationary escalator.

'Hello.' We hugged each other. 'You came.'

She beamed at me. 'Of course, I came. Lars says you have a meeting, but after that we can go to lunch and you can talk to me. I'm very intrigued. And you can bring me up to date with all the latest news. How's Ben?'

I'd been really strong. Mad, furious, and determined to erase him from my mind. It was easy on the phone, social media, a quick swipe, delete, block and done. For the last two days, since I'd walked out the offices at the Machin Agency, I'd been busy, plotting and planning. Refusing to think about Ben.

The HR department couldn't respond quickly enough when they saw my video. I had a settlement letter agreeing to a more than satisfactory pay-off. That gave me a lot of breathing space.

Eva's gentle question brought Ben back to the forefront of my mind and immediately my eyes filled with tears.

'Not who I thought he was,' I said, swallowing hard. 'And I'd rather not talk about him ... at the moment. I have a meeting with Lars.'

Eva nodded immediately understanding that I needed to ground myself.

'And here he is,' she nodded over my shoulder.

Now that I was sitting here in front of Lars, my palms had suddenly become very sweaty and I had the urge to keep wiping them down the skirt of my dress, but I needed to look in control. I was banking on coming across as gutsy and direct.

'I'm guessing you've seen the coverage in Sunday's paper.'

Lars nodded but didn't look terribly perturbed.

'I'm sorry about that.'

He held up a hand. 'Wait. You are not responsible for what Mr Johnson chose to write.'

'Well ...'

'Are you? I wasn't worried by the article. You have managed to secure far more coverage than I would have expected and the key thing about the trip was that you came to understand the concept of *hygge*.' He smiled gently. 'And now you are here, we can start planning the opening without any talk of balloons, bombs or any other such nonsense.'

I gave a quick frown. 'You do know I don't work for the Machin Agency anymore.'

His mouth tightened. 'I found out last night, but as you'd arranged a meeting today, I assumed you'd explain.'

'I ... resigned. They felt I could have done more to influence B—Mr Johnson's article. They weren't very happy about its tone.'

'Their loss and my gain.'

He opened a desk drawer and pulled out an envelope, sliding it across the table towards me, his blue eyes dancing. 'I have a proposition for you. I'd like to offer you a job here. As Press Officer for Hjem. Working here for me. I think you would do a great job.'

A few days ago, I would have snatched that envelope up,

but now ... I took a deep breath. 'Thank you, Lars. That's a very kind offer.'

'You haven't even looked at it.' He tapped the envelope with his hand.

'I don't need to. I want to do something else.'

Confusion creased his face and for a moment I wondered if I was completely mad but since I'd first thought of it, the compulsion wouldn't go away. With the promise of a year's salary I could afford to take some time for me. My conversation with Dad had replayed in my head. It was time to make a choice and do something that made me happy, instead of chasing promotions and hoping that ambition would one day pay off with the elusive golden ticket of happiness.

'Did your florist ever find the flowers she wanted?'

'No.'

'So is that space still available?'

'It is.'

I smiled at him. 'Then, if your mother is willing, I'd like to make you a proposition.'

Chapter 31

I pulled the tray of golden cinnamon buns from the oven, feeling rather proud as the spiced scent filled the air. This morning's batch was all my own work. Behind me I heard a chorus of sniffs and I turned to grin at three people waiting in a queue.

'Not burned then, Katie?' teased the middle-aged man who ran the printing business around the corner and produced our menus.

Since Eva and I had delivered baskets of freshly baked Danish pastries to the neighbouring businesses and residents the week before we opened, we'd quickly built up a loyal clientele, some of whom popped in every morning.

'They're perfect, Clive,' I said reprovingly.

'I'll take three then. The girls in the office love them and a double espresso to go.'

As I put the three pastries into a paper bag, Eva had already stepped up to the shiny chrome Gaggia coffee machine, easily the most expensive bit of kit in the café and I listened to the familiar clatter, the quick burst of coffee aroma, the shh as the pressurized water shot through the grounds.

Funny how quickly the sounds of the café had become such an entrenched part of my daily routine. I skirted Eva, twisting sideways with my arms aloft carrying the pastries, as she slotted the white plastic lid on the cardboard coffee cup to ring up the items on the till. We were like a pair of dancers who knew all the steps as we whisked about the tiny serving area.

Taking Clive's cash, I closed the till with a satisfying click.

'Thanks, lovely ladies. See you again tomorrow.'

'Bye, Clive,' chorused Eva and I in unison and then we turned and grinned at each other. I got as much of a kick out of a satisfied customer as Eva these days.

From the moment, at lunch, when I suggested to Eva that we bring Varme to London, we hadn't stopped. Like unleashing a tornado, Eva had immediately started making lists.

And she was doing it now. 'Is that the shopping list for next week?' I asked.

'Yes, I think we need more beetroot. The beet, goat's cheese and walnut open sandwiches have been very popular this week.'

I'd never met anyone more partial to a list than I was; the two of us were unstoppable.

'That's because Lars eats two for lunch every day,' added Eva with a hint of pride. Without fail every day he came to collect his lunch. He was our biggest supporter and when I suggested that we create a café in the empty unit next door, he'd immediately transferred a group of his contractors; electricians, plumbers and decorators, our way to rejig the empty space to our specification.

For three frenetic weeks, the long thin room with its glass

panels down the centre of the roof, had been full of sawing, drilling and banging, with deliveries of wood, tiles and kitchen equipment and piles of discarded cardboard and polystyrene beads, as a team of men worked miracles to bring the café to life, while Eva and I existed in a whirlwind of decision making. Lights. Tables. Wall paint. Coffee suppliers. Recipes. Menus. Chairs.

'It is our most popular sandwich,' I said with my own hint of pride. Despite her experience Eva had listened to all my suggestions, including my recipe ideas. After the depressing monotony of the coffee bar I stumbled into on the day I left the agency I'd been determined to create a little haven of cosiness. It would have been easier to attempt to recreate Varme but Eva insisted that this was mine and it should be my interpretation of *hygge*.

I cast a smug glance up at the three horribly expensive vintage brass pendant lights, they were exactly right.

'Yes, they are perfect,' said Eva with a very slightly superior smile. 'Aren't you glad now?' She'd had to talk me into buying them even though they were ridiculously over budget.

'It's a good job I love you so much, otherwise I'd think you were doing the old *I told you so* routine.'

'Who me, darling Katie?' She looped her arm around my shoulder and together we leaned against the kitchen units. 'Never.'

'Furniture looks good though.'

'It does.' Eva's gentle shudder made me smile. 'Even if you did drag me into some gangland turf.'

'Sorry … it was a parent from Connie's school. And we did save a fortune.' The job lot of discontinued retro furniture wasn't in mint condition but the scuffed chestnut leather worked well next to the assorted beech coffee tables and I wasn't about to ask exactly where they'd come from. Old hotel stock was good enough for me. They were quite battered already; surely no one would have stolen them?

Anyway, I was so pleased with the little groups of furniture and the way that they were arranged to create the feeling of someone's lounge, if they had been nicked, I might have overlooked the matter.

'My favourite,' I said, casting a look towards the front door, 'is the bookshelf.' I wanted people to come in and immediately want to sit down and stay because it felt comfortable and inviting. I'd filled the shelves with magazines, books and a couple of board games.

'My favourite,' said Eva, joining in the game that still hadn't lost its novelty value in three weeks, 'is the box shelf of tea cups.' Eva and I had had enormous fun trawling Portobello Road and Old Spitalfields Market to find the three delicate, floral china tea cups, and haggled for half an hour to get them down to a reasonable price.

'Not the wine glasses?' I asked. We both gazed at the collection of coloured glasses in smoky greys, purples and blues on the far wall.

'They're a close second after the jugs,' said Eva tilting her head in the familiar gesture which showed she was still thinking about them. We'd ummed and ahhed about buying them and left them and come back three times before we finally decided to buy them.

'Morning.' Both Eva and I jumped, startled.

'Are you two still admiring your handiwork?'

'Of course, we are,' said Eva linking her arm through mine. 'Morning Sophie.'

'Hey Sophie, how are you doing?' I said leaning against Eva.

'Great. I thought I'd pop by and let you know I've booked the day off next week, so I can definitely help.'

'Oh, that's brilliant.' I rushed over and gave her a huge hug. 'Thank you so much.'

'Katie worries too much,' said Eva bustling up and giving Sophie a kiss on each cheek. 'How are you?'

'I'm not worried,' I insisted, 'just nervous. I've never catered for a hundred and fifty people before.'

'You're nervous?' said Sophie putting her hands on her hips. 'I'm going to be doing a cookery demonstration to millions of people on Avril's breakfast show.'

'Listen to you both. Katie, you've never run a café before and you're doing fine. And Sophie the demonstration will be fine ...' Mischief danced all over Eva's face. 'Because Avril will demand it is. And the three of us will get everything ready and then the waitresses can take over and we can enjoy the party.'

Lars had asked us, no insisted, that we do the catering for the official opening of Hjem, next week, and Eva had come up with a menu of mini savoury Danish pastries, that she, Sophie and I would prepare during the day.

After staying for a coffee, Sophie skipped off as the café got busier for the lunchtime rush. Even though Mondays were our quietest days, the tables were all full. A gorgeous young blonde girl and an older, beautifully dressed, elegant woman were discussing a book deal over their pastries, while a young couple perused a guidebook to London and a steady stream of people came in for lunch. As Eva wasn't going to be around for ever, we'd agreed that we'd keep our main menu small and simple with an offering of four different open sandwiches and a daily special of soup with rye bread rolls.

It was after two and I took advantage of the lull to sit down in the café, rest my feet and tuck into salmon, horseradish and cream cheese on rye bread, which had rapidly become my second favourite sandwich on our menu. When the door opened I automatically looked up to gauge if Eva might need my help in the kitchen.

My heart thudded hard and almost came to a stop as I met the cold blue grey eyes of Ben. I swallowed as my mouth dried out and I couldn't think of a single thing to say. The air felt charged with tension as I stared at him. There was the briefest register of surprise before his eyes narrowed and he shot me an icy glare. He glared at me! Like he had reason to be aggrieved.

For a minute, I thought he was going to ignore me.

'Kate.' He nodded and stalked past me to the counter.

I flushed hot as I caught a glimpse of faded jeans and a blue shirt with white buttons. A mental image popped into my head. Wrestling with the button on his jeans. The feel of his smooth skin under my palms. Heat raced across my chest and I froze, trying not to squirm in my seat. I didn't want to let him see the immediate effect he had on me.

'Eva!'

'Ben!'

Oh great, now I had to sit and listen to the two of them exclaiming how lovely it was to see each other. I hunched over my coffee keeping my back to Ben. What was he doing here?

My stupid dumb brain insisted on the walk back to his flat from the restaurant. Heated kisses. His hands on my body. Sliding into my clothes. The touch of fingers inside my bra. Shit! I could feel my nipples hardening. Bastard traitors.

'Take a seat and I'll bring you a *kanelsnegle* right out.' Eva's voice sounded overly bright and cheerful. I was bloody going to kill her. Now I bitterly regretted not being more honest with her. I'd told her that neither Ben nor I had wanted to keep in touch after Copenhagen.

I hunched deeper into my chair, which was a bit pointless because in an empty café, he was duty bound to come and sit at my table. My vision had gone a little blurry and I felt sick.

He sat down opposite me; I could almost feel the fury coming from him in waves.

The air around us felt charged with emotion. Well I wasn't going to rise to it. What right did he have to be angry with me?

'Mad Fox is back with a vengeance, then,' I blurted out, unable to stop myself, feeling my heart rate pick up.

'I beg your pardon,' he spat in a low voice with a quick glance at Eva who was busy in the kitchen.

'I don't know why you're so cross.' Bravely I met his furious glare as his eyes widened and his mouth pinched.

'No one likes being used.'

'Used?' I echoed, flinching at the sharp dislike in his words.

'Yeah, the minute you got your article, you threw a hissy fit because it wasn't what you wanted and dumped me.'

I opened my mouth. 'I ... I ...' He thought I'd used him!

Like a pair of prize fighters circling each other, our eyes held. Sharp pain encircled my heart, like a fist squeezing. It hurt to be this close and remember. Remember him touching my face. Teasing my curls with his fingers.

'Got the invitation to the opening night of Hjem. I see your mate Josh is in charge.'

I lifted my shoulders in a dispassionate shrug. I'd had absolutely no contact with anyone but HR since the day I'd walked out.

The door opened and a group of six people walked in followed by another couple. Hastily I stood up and grabbed my apron from the back of my chair, pulling it on before looking at Ben.

Confusion marred his face, the blue eyes sharpening as he worked it out.

As I turned to walk back to the kitchen, he grabbed my arm.

'You work here?' He glanced at the menu on the table and realisation bloomed on his face. 'Katie's Kanelsnegles.'

'Yes,' I snapped shaking his hand off, anxious to be free of his touch in case I did something I regretted. He thought I'd used him. Was he hurt by that? Had he cared? I couldn't get my head around the implications. It hadn't occurred to me that he would see things differently. In that headlong flight I'd only been thinking of myself but surely he must have known I'd feel betrayed by the article. Confusion warred against pride.

'Why?' He paled. 'You didn't ... you didn't lose your job because of the article?'

With a sneer, I turned towards him. 'You mean the article where you completely shafted me. The one where you knew it was coming out but you still slept with me the night before. The one that made me look like a complete idiot in front of my colleagues, my client and the people that had been on the trip with us. Is that the one you mean? The one that came out but *you still slept with me.*'

Ben rose and put his hands on the table glowering as he spat, 'Yeah! Because that's the sort of man I am.' The words dropped one by one like stones, the emotion of them striking right into my heart.

Too livid to give an inch and determined to salvage something, I said, 'Well you'll be pleased to hear that I quit. I suppose I ought to thank you for opening my eyes.' With that I tossed my head and lifted my chin staring hard at him. Eva stood in the doorway, quietly observing, sadness haunting her eyes.

With an angry expletive, he pushed himself from the table, backing away, his furious gaze holding mine until the last minute, when he turned and stormed out of the café, the door slamming with an earth-shattering bang behind him. Ignoring the wide-eyed interest of the customers now gathered around tables, Eva came to stand behind me, her hand resting on my shoulder and we both looked out of the window watching as he strode down the street.

Neither of us voiced the words but I knew we were thinking *what was all that about?*

Chapter 32

'This is a great spot,' said Dave, Avril's production manager, opening up a big black box on the middle tier balcony hanging over the main atrium of Hjem, one of a series of five on either side of the store. 'From here people can see us doing interviews and we can get bird's eye shots. It'll look great on camera ... not that this place could fail to do otherwise. Thanks for the coffee and Danish.'

'No problem,' I said. He'd been my last delivery of the morning and I needed to get back to help Eva. Tonight was the official opening of Hjem and there was still a lot to do. Sophie, Eva and I had started at six this morning and we'd made a good start.

Since Ben's visit seven days ago, I'd felt bruised by the encounter and I didn't seem to be able to shake off the overwhelming sense of sadness even though in the last few weeks I'd enjoyed myself more than I'd ever done in my working life. When I was busy I was OK but every night I lay wide-eyed, sleepless, staring into the dark replaying his words. *Because that's the sort of man I am.*

During the day I could take my mind off him focusing on

seeing Hjem taking shape as all sorts of gorgeous products filled the shelves. There was a light, bright atmosphere in the store echoed in the colourful polo shirts the staff all wore after Lars agreed that perhaps some things had to stay British. He'd compromised by outfitting them all in egalitarian Hjem branded polo shirts in lovely shades of blues, greens and purples from, cobalt, teal, kingfisher blues through to mint, sage, pea and lime greens and lilac, deep and pale purples. The effect was stylish and thoroughly Danish.

Tomorrow the first of Avril's broadcasts would take place and the place buzzed with the seemingly huge crew required to make it happen.

'Anything else you need?' I asked as Dave shook his head, already busy with grey gaffer tape and various bits of electrical kit.

I left him to it picking my way carefully back through the trail of electrical cables that snaked their way across the floor and wandered down through the store, past the home department, already full of lots of gorgeous things, pretty china, stylish kitchen accessories and even designer tea towels, as well as an area set up for cookery demonstrations in readiness for Sophie.

She'd been in several times to see Eva, practising and perfecting her pastry skills. Like an excited magpie, she'd run around the store cherry picking bowls, spoons, rolling pins and plates from the shelves to make her TV cookery set look beautiful.

Fiona had come in last week and she'd photographed every last inch of the place and I'd helped Lars use her pictures to run a teaser campaign on Twitter, Instagram, Pinterest and Facebook, which was creating a definite buzz across social media.

In fact, the campaign was going better than I could have imagined, yah boo sucks to Josh's guerrilla balloon idea, although he was officially in charge of tonight's event, but much of the publicity had been as a result of my work and Lars knew where the credit was due. David's piece was due out today announcing tomorrow's official opening and special gifts for the first hundred readers through the door.

'Kate,' Avril waved her hand in front of my face, when I came face to face with her at the bottom of the main escalator, 'anyone in there?'

'Sorry, miles away.'

'I was asking about the dress code this evening.'

'Smart. Don't worry; you'll still look more glamorous than anyone else here.'

'I'm not worried about me, I was worried about you. It's still your big night, even if that prat Joseph thinks it's his, I hope you're going to do yourself justice.'

'Won't this do,' I glanced down at the sleeveless shift dress.

'I think you should wear one of the Danish designers from the fourth floor,' she announced and I realised that she'd already started propelling me that way.

'I'm working,' I protested.

'No, your work will be done by then. Eva told me you've got a team of waitresses to serve and that the canapes will all be finished by six. So, it's only right you should wear something from the Hjem collection. I've cleared it with Lars and he agrees. You need to represent the place properly. Not some M&S number.'

'It's Reiss,' I said outraged and then realised I'd been had; Avril knew full well what the label in the back of my dress read.

'I've seen exactly the outfit for you,' said Avril with smug determination. 'It could have been made for you.'

Part of me wanted to look my best tonight. Megan and Josh would be there and of course, Ben. Not that I wanted to look good for him. I wanted to look indifferent and so over him. I'd worked out exactly how I'd greet him. This time I'd be prepared. Friendly, impersonal and a bit too busy to speak to him.

Hi Ben, good to see you. Sorry, excuse me, must go and sort something out.

I'd even rehearsed it several times in the mirror in the bathroom at home, just to make sure that the words tripped off my tongue, with minor variations. My favourites so far were the slightly surprised, *Hi Ben* fancy seeing you here approach, the *Hi Ben,* the totally who are you again tone and the *Hi Ben,* totally sycophantic, false, groupie dismissal.

Before I knew it, Avril had steered me into the empty changing rooms with a pile of clothes that I never would have chosen for myself in a million years.

'I thought you said you'd seen exactly the thing for me,' I protested as she shoved me into one of the cubicles hanging up numerous outfits on the handy pegs inside.

'I lied,' she said blithely. 'I knew you'd come up with a load of excuses.'

When I came out in the first thing, I found Eva sitting expectantly on a small chair she'd stolen from one of the displays. I raised a questioning eyebrow at her.

'It's fine. Sophie's got everything under control. I'm taking a break.'

She and Avril each had a coffee and were clearly waiting for a modelling session.

'No, not you at all,' said Avril.

'It's not that bad,' said Eva.

'Yes, the length's all wrong. Cuts her legs off and she's got good legs.'

'Ah, yes I see now. You're right,' agreed Eva before adding, 'And the colour, drains away her natural complexion.'

'I am here, you know.' I attempted a petulant pout but with both of them sitting there like a pair of biased grannies, beaming benevolently, it was difficult to be irritated, even when they kept whispering together. They only wanted the best for me.

Eva smiled. 'Go and put the next thing on. I brought you a coffee. It's been a while.' She winked.

I'd been running on coffee for the last few days and she kept nagging me to eat properly. Since Ben's visit it had been hard work choking down an open sandwich each day.

I tried on another two outfits, a black trouser suit which made me look like a pall bearer – a unanimous no – and a beige asymmetric dress, although Avril insisted it was dusky pink. Luckily it hung off me, I'd dropped a few pounds, but I was grateful because I didn't feel like me in it at all.

As soon as I slipped on the pale blue silky jump suit, I

knew it was the one, the palazzo pants floated gracefully around my legs making them look an extra few inches longer and the top had a v neck at the front and the back with a little silver necklet. Pretty and feminine, it fitted perfectly and I loved it.

'Yes. Yes. Yes,' said Avril jumping up and circling me. 'That is the one.'

'You look lovely.' Eva nodded, a gentle thoughtful smile on her face. 'You're going to be the belle of the ball.'

'I don't want to be the belle ... Hjem is the focus. Everyone should be looking at the shop.'

Avril raised a sceptical eyebrow. 'You do know Ben is coming tonight.'

I glared at her and slammed the cubicle door of the changing room shut.

After the lunch time rush we put a closed sign on the door and got down to serious work. I'd been allotted the task of cutting out rounds of dark moist sourdough rye bread with a pastry cutter, while Sophie spooned out a mixture of herring, red onion and dill onto them. Eva sliced smoked salmon and cut tiny wedges of lemon to arrange on onion bread and the smell of cooking wafted from the oven where tiny red peppers stuffed with Jarlsberg were being baked. Slices of pumpernickel bread were lined up on a tray awaiting a topping of ham and tart mustard and a dish of sliced cucumber had been pre-prepared for a topping of crab meat, mayonnaise, chives and lemon juice.

I was absorbed in the job when I heard imperious rapping

at the closed door. We all looked up. Ben was outside. Both Sophie and Eva looked at me.

'What?' I asked. Neither of them stopped what they were doing and both ducked their heads.

I huffed out a sigh and marched over to the door and yanked it open.

'This is the article I wrote and submitted to the paper.' The weary tone in his voice echoed the disappointment in his eyes as he shoved two pieces of paper towards me.

Before I could say a word, he marched off.

I slammed the door. Men. What the hell was he playing at now?

I glanced down at the paper.

Hygge or Hype? – Happiness or Hokum.
When I was invited on a press trip to Copenhagen to find out more about the Danish concept of hygge and what makes the country one of the happiest in the world, I freely admit that I was deeply sceptical. As far as I was concerned it was all about candles and cashmere blankets, and most likely a cynical attempt by marketers to emulate a deep seated cultural psyche that simply doesn't translate to the British way of life. A cultural chasm that can't be bridged with cosy and convivial.

Instead what I found was a way of life that embraces the cosy, a society where the concept of social homogeneity is culturally ingrained, making its citizens feel equal with everyone and for that reason happy to pay the higher taxes to support everyone in education and for their health.

I saw a society where people take simple enjoyment in coming together to share and not judge, with an unconscious focus on taking special time to celebrate simple things. I discovered hygge, where making a celebration of a rainy day, prioritising to be with your special people and emphasising on togetherness, all add up to a happier way of life.

And yes candles and cashmere blankets have their place, which is why the new Danish department store, Hjem, Danish for home, might just be something to celebrate …

My eyes blurred and I couldn't read any more. I looked down the street as my breath hitched in an involuntary half-sob but Ben was long gone. I closed my eyes, a tear seeping out as the bottom dropped out of my stomach. Nausea, disgust and shame rose up. I'd never even given him a chance to explain. No wonder he felt used. No wonder he was angry.

Slumping against the door, I slid down the glass to the floor and clasped my knees tight to myself as if I might contain the painful explosion of regret that overwhelmed me, raining down in waves of despair. When Eva put her arms around me I let the sobs break free, tears pouring down my face, inhaling her subtle floral perfume and collapsing into her soft hug.

Chapter 33

After Eva and Sophie mopped up my tears, plied me with slices of cucumber in an attempt to reduce the puffiness around my eyes, we got back to work. They kept shooting sidelong glances at me, even though I was at pains to tell them I was fine. Luckily we were far too busy for me to brood.

The day raced by and suddenly everything was done, the waiters and waitresses turned up and transported all the canapes next door and guests started arriving, being greeted by the Hjem staff in their brightly coloured shirts with glasses of Prosecco and red berries. For the more adventurous, Danish Schnapps in traditional short stemmed glasses was also on offer, although it was less popular than the fizz.

'Oh my, it's so nice being a grown up for a change,' said Connie, waving her glass at me and giving me a hug with her other hand. 'Free Prosecco on tap, I think I might have died and gone to heaven. Maybe I should a get job like this.'

'What and forgo learning journeys, glue sticks and glitter?' I teased squeezing her back. 'I'm so glad you could make it.'

'I wouldn't have missed this,' she lifted her glass up. 'This is amazing. I love it. Not that I could probably afford to shop here.'

'Staff discount.'

'And that's why I love you, right there.' Excitement glittered in her eyes. 'And I've got some amazing news. You'll never guess ... Brandon's been offered a job. Today. A proper job.'

'What do you mean? A proper job?' He could do the job at the breaker's yard standing on his head and juggling knives with his feet, but he got a pay packet from it, so that constituted a proper job in my book.

'Pinewood Studios!'

'What?'

'Pinewood Studios. They saw the newspaper piece yesterday. Remember that guy that Brandon thought might buy the Sith thingy. Well he didn't, he wanted to interview him for a piece in the paper. Went down and did the interview last Thursday. A bloke from Pinewood phoned Brandon yesterday. Invited him to go see them this morning. Offered him a job on the spot.'

I was having trouble keeping up. 'What newspaper piece?'

'You didn't see it?' Her face crumpled in confusion. 'But ... I thought you must have set it up. With your contacts? How else would anyone know about Brandon's models?'

'When was this?'

'Here,' she delved into her bag for her phone and brought up a webpage.

I scanned the page quickly. There was an interview with Brandon and then a whole piece about how important modelling was these days in the world of film with the increased use of CGI. The piece included a photo of Brandon with his *Sith thingy* and quite a few of his detailed drawings and plans for other items he'd made. I looked at the webpage address.

'Oh,' I said faintly, a buzzing in my ears. The chatter in the room around me faded. My heart did a funny little bunny hop in my chest. 'Did you see the guy that came to see Brandon?'

'Yes, he was …' she pulled what I'm sure she thought was a dramatic face, 'smokin'!'

'Connie, the Jim Carrey routine got old last century.' Impatience made me snippy with her.

'Bet you'd have thought so, if you'd seen him.'

I'd already scrolled through a few pictures on my phone and found one. Ben on his bike outside the hotel as we dropped them off.

'Recognise th—'

'That's him,' squealed Connie in a guinea pig shriek, which had quite a few heads turning our way. 'Who is he?' She drew in a short breath and turned to me wide-eyed. 'It's him! Isn't it? Mr Super Hottie.'

'Ben,' I said quietly, suddenly feeling adrift. Everything I thought I knew suddenly floated out of reach like a balloon inadvertently let go.

Ben had done this. Since he saw me last week. But before today. I felt like I was in the centre of a seesaw and one step either side would bring it crashing down. Good Ben. Bad Ben. Which one was real?

I frowned trying to make sense of the timelines. Ben had contacted Brandon after he'd seen me on Monday.

It didn't make sense unless Brandon was purely just a story to him.

Or had he been trying to help?

I looked around the room anxiously scanning the faces. Connie had been one of the first to arrive, the crowd was still thin.

'Is he coming tonight?' Suddenly she was full of avid interest, her head snapping this way and that. 'Is he here?'

'He's invited but I don't know if he'll come.' I spotted Fiona arriving and greeting Sophie. 'There's Sophie and I'll introduce you to some people. You'll love them. They came on the trip with me.'

'Oh goodie, I can find out more about super hottie.'

I sighed and linked my arm through hers to cross the floor. Of course, she knew Sophie already, but she hit it off straight away with Fiona, who seemed to have curbed some of her shyness. She was never going to be Miss Extrovert but she could now look someone in the eye. A sudden rush of people arriving, lots of whom were journalists, demanded my attention, so I abandoned Connie with the two of them knowing they'd look after her.

Having a launch party is always nerve-racking, when things are free, people sometimes don't turn up even when they say they will – they get a better offer, they're knackered after a day at work or the night's telly is more enticing. Wondering if and when Ben might turn up only added to my anxiety. I'd spent all day planning my avoidance tactics and now, suddenly I was desperate to see him.

I didn't need to worry about the success of the evening, if

it could be measured in crowd numbers, Hjem just hit capacity. The bottom floor was heaving and it was getting difficult to navigate your way through the crowd. I'd spotted David and Conrad arriving together and made my way over reaching them at the same time as Avril.

'You look gorgeous, Kate.' She tugged at the fabric of my outfit. 'Very nice.' Then she turned to David, with a calculating gleam in her eye. 'You must come and meet my cousin Reece.' She dragged him off leaving me to chat to Conrad who'd already attracted a number of other journalists. As we were making small talk I spotted Ben, no one else had that shade of burnished copper hair. My breath caught and I paused, my heart thumping as I tried to decide whether to go over to him or not. What would I say? Where would I start?

As I started to push my way through, a pudgy hand grabbed me.

'Kate. Long time no see. Darling, how are you?' Andrew Dawkins pulled me to him and placed a clammy kiss on either one of my cheeks.

I drew back as far as I could. 'Andrew.'

He gave me a coy smile. 'This is quite a set up. I'm impressed and I hear you left The Machin Agency.'

'Yes,' I said, my polite smile cool. 'I'm working with Lars and his mother.' Trust him to be up to date with the gossip. Why didn't that surprise me?

'I could do with an intro to young Lars; I'd like to do a deal with all his suppliers. The blanket people, the candle people, the glassware companies ... especially at Christmas. Nice advertorial shopping feature.'

I stepped back. Was he for real? 'Seriously? After the article the *Inquirer* ran. I'm not sure Lars would be interested. *Hygge* or Hype? Happiness or Hokum?'

Andrew's little piggy blue eyes gleamed with a touch of malice. 'Au contraire, Miss Sinclair. That was a deliberate editorial strategy. A contentious article is great news these days. That went viral on the web edition, even made the *Huff Po*. Over five thousand hits in the first hour. *Hygge*-bashing was good for our circulation figures, great for advertisers, bloody marvellous for shareholders.'

'*Hygge*-bashing?' I stared at him and he took my sheer bemusement as encouragement.

'Brilliant, eh? Everyone's suddenly, ooh yes we love everything Scandi, and then the *Inquirer* comes along and says it's a pile of crap ... and everyone rushes over to read the piece and disagree.' His oily grin almost split his horrible little face in two. 'It's all about readership and circulation. Not that you can explain that to the hacks. Johnson threw a right hissy fit.'

'He did?' My heart did a little bunny hop in my chest sending my pulse haywire.

'Oh yes. Because it wasn't *what he wrote*,' Dawkins mimicked in a whiny voice.

In that second, I could guess how it might feel being bucked from a rodeo horse and landing smack down on the sawdust, so hard you think your chest has been flattened. He really hadn't known before the article came out.

'Pardon.'

Dawkins, clearly thought I appreciated his comedy genius, because he reprised his earlier delivery. '*I didn't write this, how dare you sub it like this?* I told you, these journalists think they're all bloody Pulitzer prize contenders, they forget there's a whole team behind them. Advertising, sub-editors. It was subbed and he cried like a baby. Made a right old stink.' Dawkins laughed, an ugly sneering laugh that made him look even smaller and pudgier and meaner than before. 'I tell you the figures were berluddy fantastic. They're so damn precious about their words. At the end of the day they're reliant on us making enough ad revenue to keep the paper afloat and pay their salaries. They ...'

I'd like to have seen his face as I turned my back on him and walked away, trying to melt into the crowd. I wanted to go and hide. I wanted to cry, scream and kick something very hard. Damn I should have stayed put, Dawkins' shins would have done nicely.

There was no sign of Ben anymore and I wondered if I'd imagined seeing him. I circumnavigated the room, keeping my eyes peeled for any sign of him but he seemed to have vanished. I checked with the girl at the entrance and saw that he'd signed in, but she couldn't swear to it, he hadn't left.

Then out of the corner of my eye I spotted him, travelling up the escalator to the third floor. Disengaging myself quickly from a friend of Lars I half-walked and half-ran to the flight of escalators in the middle of the store but Ben had disappeared again.

As I reached the top of the second flight I spotted him looking down over the crowd from one of the balconies on the next floor. Taking the back stairs, I raced up, pausing at the top to take a deep breath, feeling like a tracker about to corner a bear. And I had no idea whether the bear would play nice or maul me. Now I'd tracked him down, I had no idea what to say.

The sound of the chatter drifted upwards and now, nerves jangling, I walked slowly through the quiet dimly lit displays winding my way round to the balcony.

He had his back to me. I studied the outline of his broad shoulders, remembering holding on to them at the Round Tower, their solidity next to me on the roller coaster and the smooth touch of them beneath my fingertips after he'd peeled my dress off leaving me clinging to him as he nuzzled my jawline and neck with soft kisses. The dull ache in my chest intensified. I gazed at him, hope and longing sitting heavy.

I'd fallen in love with him ... I couldn't name the moment, but I knew it now and I almost couldn't bear it.

It would almost be easier to walk away, so I'd never know. So I'd never have to face him. So I'd never have to tell him and hear him tell me he didn't feel the same.

Instead I swallowed and walked forward, my heart thudding so hard I wondered if he could hear it.

My shoes clicked on the floor and I saw him tense. His muscles bunching under his jacket but he didn't turn around.

I almost chickened out. This was almost as bad as being about to board a roller coaster.

'D-did you know?' I hesitated, nerves making my voice rusty and hoarse, 'there are over four thousand pieces of wood in the balconies, each one hand carved. A different species on each floor rosewood at the top, walnut, mountain ash, birch, plane and pine.'

Ben's head moved, tracing the different floors I'd mentioned. At least he was listening.

'Each stave took twenty seconds to snap into place.'

I took a breath. 'Twenty seconds.'

I saw his shoulders loosen and took a step forward, forcing myself to be brave. I had everything to lose here and everything to gain.

'That's long enough for a kiss.'

Ben still didn't turn around. My breath caught in my lungs, almost burning and my fingers bunched as I forced myself to take the last few steps to stand beside him. I could see his jawline as he looked out across the wide-open space. The faint smile on his face gave me a tiny bit of courage.

The silence between us weighed heavy and momentous. I stood rooted to the spot but he wasn't giving an inch; I could see the tension in his shoulders and his stillness.

'You have five seconds,' he finally growled.

'You get four minutes for a nuclear warning,' I said, a mixture of regret and panic tearing through me.

'Four seconds,' he snapped. And I realised in that one second just how much I'd hurt him. I'd not trusted him enough to give him a chance to explain. I'd jumped to conclusions and cast him in the worst possible light.

'Thank you for the article you did for my brother. That was ... kind.' And thoughtful and incredibly understanding. Despite everything, for both of us, family was still important. He'd written it for me and my family.

'I got a story out of it.' With a barely imperceptible shrug of his shoulders, he dismissed it.

'Brandon was offered a job because of it.'

'Great.' He leaned forward, resting his forearms on the wooden rail.

My heart turned over but I resisted grabbing him. I suddenly realised why he'd thought I'd abandoned him straight after we'd slept together. No wonder he thought I was only interested in what I could get out of him, a positive PR story. I should have known he would never have written the article in the way that it had been published and too quick to assume that career came first, for him and me. Since Copenhagen I'd learned so much more about myself, my family and my priorities.

'I was wrong not to talk to you. I should have known you wouldn't do something like that.'

'Yeah, you should.'

'I should have trusted you.'

'Yeah, you should.'

The long silence after his words made my heart crumble and I wanted nothing more than to run. I took a step back, ready to flee but just as I decided, no, this was worth fighting for, he straightened and turned to face me, a serious expression on his face.

'You made the mistake this time, Kate Sinclair.' His eyes held mine, guarded, shielding both hurt and hope.

'I did.' I took a step forward. 'I didn't give you the chance to explain. I reacted badly ...' I held his gaze hoping he'd remember our conversation at Tivoli. 'I assumed you weren't who I thought you might be. It made me react badly. I guess

I wanted to punish you for shattering the illusion.' I repeated his words back to him and he acknowledged them with a wry twist to his mouth before suddenly closing the gap between us, his fingers sinking into my shoulders.

'Kate, you talk too much.' He pulled me towards him and dropped his head, his mouth brushing mine in the softest of kisses that left my legs shaky.

'Only when I'm nervous,' I muttered against his lips.

'You damn well should be, I've been so furious with you.' His mouth moved against my cheek as he spoke sending butterfly tremors racing across my skin. 'I'd been so anti the whole *hygge* thing. And then in Denmark, it was like some crazy epiphany and I completely changed my mind, wrote that piece and I was proud of it. I had no idea it was coming out that weekend, or that they'd subbed it so heavily. They lost a story and needed an alternative quickly. If I'd had the chance, I would have made a case. Tried to stop it or at least warn you. I had no idea. When you refused to respond to any of my texts ... I was ...' His voice broke and the emotion swirling made my breath catch.

'I'm sorry.' I moved my mouth to touch his, the words too inadequate to express my shame. All I could do was pour everything that the words didn't say into the kiss. Moulding my lips to his in silent, determined intent.

A beat later, I felt him soften as he responded, deepening the kiss, his mouth questing as if searching for the right answer. My nerve endings danced, the hard touch sent a hot flash searing through my veins, as I pulled him closer, praying that it was enough to give him the answer. The kiss lasted at least a full minute and when we pulled away, his ragged breathing made my pulse skip.

His face softened as our eyes met.

'Do you know something?' He smiled and held both my hands. 'The thing about mistakes ... you can make them right. Although you're going to have to do a lot of making up for it.'

'I really am sorry.' I reached up and cupped his face, feeling the roughness threatening to break through the skin on his chin but knowing that he needed the reassurance of my touch.

'Do you know what hurt the most?' he asked in a low, strained voice.

Silently I shook my head, regret pinching at his piercing, heartfelt words.

'The fact that you didn't realise ...' He gazed down at me. 'And you never gave me the chance to tell you ...'

My breath stalled in my chest at the burning intensity in his eyes.

'... that I'd fallen in love with you.'

Epilogue

'Come on Kate, we're late.'

We ran up the stone steps, through the huge arched doorway. Well, Ben ran, I sort of limped along after him in a sort of Tony Curtis type mince in my ridiculous heels, the silk of my dress swishing with a satisfying rustle. We'd raced almost the entire length of Støgnet to get here on time.

'Ben, Kate. You made it,' said Eva grinning from ear to ear as she jumped off the wooden bench to greet us. 'I was starting to worry about you.' She looked at her watch. 'The ceremony is in ten minutes.'

'Only just,' muttered Ben casting a wicked grin over his shoulder. I gave him a reproving look, praying that he wasn't going to tell her exactly what had held us up in the hotel. We'd flown in late last night coming straight from work.

Things had been a bit chaotic of late as Lars was planning to open a new Hjem in the north of England and had asked me to help set up a café within the store and Ben and I had been decorating. After commuting between our respective flats, never being able to remember what we'd left where, we decided it would be far easier to move in together ... that and the fact that we hadn't spent more than two nights apart since the official launch night of Hjem.

'Ben, Kate.' Avril appeared and swept us both into an excited perfumed hug. 'It's like old times. All the gang together again. Except Sophie couldn't make it. Isn't it lovely in here?' She twirled round in her gorgeous dress looking around the Radhuspladsen. Of course she hadn't seen it last time we'd been in Copenhagen.

'Has anyone seen David yet?' I asked spotting Conrad and Fiona walking towards us.

'No, but Conrad promised that he'd be gentle with him last night, so hopefully he won't be too hungover,' said Eva.

Avril raised a delicate eyebrow and snorted, 'Which is why I sent Christopher out with them.' She giggled and hooked her arm through her husband's. He rolled his eyes and said with a shake of his head, 'Conrad's a liability.'

'Tell me about it,' I muttered with heartfelt agreement.

'It's OK,' said Avril airily, 'me and Fi met up with them, although of course I wasn't drinking,' she patted her bump complacently, '... so it wasn't really a stag do, but I think David had a lovely time ... talking of which, here is groom number one.'

We all turned to see David walking towards us, resplendent in a blue three-piece suit with a pink rose on the lapel. Taking it in turns we all kissed him.

'Oi, put him down. It's my turn.' A handsome stocky man dressed in an identical suit pushed Avril away.

'Reece!' she shrieked and threw her arms around him. 'Don't you look fabulous.'

'I bloody should, given you chose the suits.' He slipped his finger between his neck and shirt collar, before smiling as he looked at David. 'But he looks bloody gorgeous in his, so you did OK cuz.'

According to Avril, she wasn't the least bit surprised that her cousin Reece had hit it off with David after she'd introduced them and followed up with them after doing a feature on dating on her breakfast programme. Her career had taken off big time and she was now the main anchor on the breakfast show. She also fancied herself as a match-maker and was currently keeping a close eye on Conrad and one of her ex-bosses Sheila, who she declared were made for each other.

The wedding co-ordinator, the same handsome man in the same stripey T-shirt, called us together. Conrad checked he'd got the rings again, smiling proudly as best man. Since Reece had come on the scene, David had converted the top floor of his house into a self-contained flat which Conrad rented for a nominal sum. In return, Conrad had given the rest of David's house a complete design make-over, which had been featured in several magazines and consequently Conrad's services as an interior designer were so much in demand that he struggled to fit private commissions in with his teaching and freelance commitments.

We trooped towards the little staircase, leading up to the room where the ceremonies were held, Avril and I bringing up the rear. She paused at the bottom step and took my arm, giving me a quick once over. 'You look great, Kate. So much happier. Life with Ben agrees with you.'

'It does,' I sighed happily, unable to help the silly grin on my face.

'I can't believe it all started here in Copenhagen. I honestly thought me and Christopher were heading for divorce and now look at me. Pregnant, successful and happy.'

I leaned up and gave her a hug. 'It's been a good year.'

'I wish Sophie was here.' Avril's face sobered.

'Me too,' I linked my arm through hers. 'Hope she's OK.'

'Bloody men. She really loved him.'

'Well hopefully one day she'll find a good one.' I gave a sad smile. 'There are a few of them.'

'There are,' agreed Avril giving me a cheerful squeeze. 'Right, we've got a wedding to attend. And I'm bloody starving. I hope Eva's got plenty of *kanelsnegle* at the café for the reception. I think I've got a small hippopotamus in here, the amount I'm eating at the moment.'

Ben caught my eye and we smiled together, a private secret exchange that made my heart glow. At six months, Avril's bump was much in evidence whereas at six weeks mine was no more than a bean and a much-treasured secret between the two of us. He slipped his fingers between mine with a gentle squeeze.

'Now?' he asked.

I nodded. We'd checked earlier with David and Reece, anxious not to steal their limelight.

'Actually,' said Ben, 'we …' he held up our interlinked fingers, 'we'd like to invite you to a wedding as well.'

David winked at me.

'Oooh,' squealed Avril. 'When?'

Ben and I grinned at each other. 'We were thinking straight after this one.'

Keep reading for an exclusive look at book two, Sophie's story...
The Little Brooklyn Bakery

Chapter 1

'It's a great offer,' said Sophie, with only the slightest sense of regret that she had to turn it down. One day she would visit New York. 'But I just don't see how I could go at the moment.'

Sophie's editor-in-chief, Angela, screwed up her face. 'I understand, it's really short notice. I could kill Mel for breaking her leg.'

'I don't think she did it on purpose,' said Sophie.

'Well, it's bloody inconvenient and while I've got plenty of people queueing up to take her place in New York for six months, you're my best food writer. You would be brilliant.'

'That's kind of you, Angela—'

'Kind?' Angela raised one of her scarily plucked almost to the death eyebrows. 'I don't do kind. This is honest. You're a brilliant writer and I wish ...' she shook her head, 'and don't you dare repeat this, you would spread your wings.'

'And you're desperate,' teased Sophie.

'Well, there is that,' said Angela, laying down her pen, with a self-deprecating laugh. 'But at least think about it. It's a fabulous opportunity. Job swaps don't come up that often and if I didn't have the twins, I'd be off like a shot.'

'What about Ella? She'd love to go,' suggested Sophie.

Angela tipped her head to one side, 'That girl is twenty-nine going on twelve, she'd be an absolute disaster.'

'She might not be that bad.'

Angela raised one eyebrow, 'And I know how much you help her. I don't think she'd survive without you.'

Sophie gave her a cheeky grin, 'So you can't send me to New York then.'

With a bark of laughter, Angela flipped her notebook closed, 'We'd manage.' Her face sobered as Sophie rose to leave. 'Seriously, Sophie. Think about it.'

Sophie returned to the main office where everyone was still talking about the horrible crack of bone when Mel leapt off a table in the pub at the end of her 'I'm swanning off to New York for six months' leaving do. Across the way the limp helium balloon, bearing the words *We'll miss you* still bobbed above a chair. Someone really ought to take it down before the incoming, very American sounding, Brandi Baumgarten tipped up to take possession of Mel's desk.

Poor girl deserved more than the current palimpsest of sticky rings of Prosecco and crumbs of Monster Munch (Mel's favourite) littering its surface. Grabbing a pair of scissors, Sophie advanced on the balloon and with a satisfying snip cut it down. She'd done the right thing turning Angela's offer down. The thought of taking over Brandi's desk on the other side of the Atlantic was far too much of a terrifying prospect. And poor Brandi coming here. To a strange city. All on her own. Sophie almost shuddered. Maybe she should make her some cookies, big fat squidgy ones with lots of chunky chocolate to welcome her and make her feel at home. And coffee. Americans did coffee big time. Perhaps a little welcome to England pack. An *A-Z* of London. An umberella. A ...

'Earth to Soph. How do you spell *clafoutis*?'

'Sorry. What did you say?' She tugged the balloon down and punctured it with her scissors.

'Well done,' said Ella, the other cookery writer on *CityZen*. 'I meant to do that. Well I thought about it. And how do you spell *clafoutis*? I can never remember.'

Sophie reeled off the spelling and sat down at her desk opposite Ella.

'What did Angela want? You in trouble?'

Sophie shook her head still slightly bemused at the suggestion she went to work on *CityZen's* sister publication in Manhattan. If she told Ella she'd never hear the end of it.

'How was your weekend?' Ella screwed up her face. 'Oh for feck's sake, spell check's changed it to clawfoot. Can you spell it again for me? I went to that new French place in Stoke Newington. A bit of a trek but ... oh, how was *Le Gavroche* on Saturday? Oh ... no, he didn't.'

Sophie winced and summoned up a blithe smile. 'Unfortunately, we didn't get there. His mum was ill.'

'Oh, for crying out loud, the woman's always ill.'

'She can't help it,' Sophie protested, ignoring the inner bitch that agreed whole-heartedly. Was it wrong to wish Mrs Soames could time being unwell just a tad more conveniently? 'And it was an emergency this time. Blue lighted to hospital. Poor James spent all night in A&E waiting for news.'

With a scowl Ella said, 'You are too bloody nice. And far too damn forgiving. He doesn't deserve you.'

'I wouldn't love him if he wasn't so nice. How many men do you know that put their family first?'

Ella pursed her pale pink sparkly lips. It looked as if she'd been pillaging the beauty editor's cupboard again. 'True. Greg forgot Mother's Day, my birthday and our anniversary.'

Sophie wanted to roll her eyes but refrained. Greg barely remembered anything but his next five aside football fixture.

'You're such a brilliant cook,' said James putting down his knife and fork. Sophie nodded, rather pleased with the way her Massaman curry had turned out, sweet and spicy with just the right amount of heat and the potatoes not too soft and not too firm.

They were sitting in her spacious kitchen, with a candle burning between them. Mondays were her favourite night of the week when she would cook a special meal because she knew James had been running around after his mother all weekend. He lived with her three days of the week and stayed at Sophie's flat the other four. Sophie suspected Mrs Soames wasn't really that unwell but just liked having her son at home. And who could blame her.

'I should marry you one day.' He winked and picked up his wine glass, swirling the ruby red liquid and sniffing with appreciation. As well he might, it was a very nice Australian Merlot that she'd tracked down on the recommendation of the wine writer at work and had cost a small fortune.

'You should,' she replied, her heart bumping uncomfortably.

It wasn't the first time he'd said something like that. And she'd thought on Saturday, at *Le Gavroche*, the second anniversary of their first date ... well she'd hoped ...

'So how was work today?' That was the lovely thing about James, he was always interested.

'Remember I told you Mel left on Friday. She broke her leg. Can't go to New York now.' Sophie hesitated, and laughed. 'Angela offered me her place.'

'What – to go to New York?' James looked alarmed.

'Don't worry, I turned it down. I wouldn't leave you.'

James smiled and patted her hand, 'If you really wanted to go, I wouldn't have minded.' He paused and then pulled her hand to his lips. 'But I would have missed you dreadfully, darling. I'd hate it if you went away.'

Sophie got up and wrapped her arms around him, glad that she'd not given too much credence to Angela's flattery. She would love to go there one day. Maybe she and James could go together. A honeymoon perhaps.

James turned and nuzzled her neck. 'Early night? I'm knackered. Driving back from Cornwall is such a killer.'

'I just need to tidy up.' Sophie gave the utensil strewn kitchen a quick look, wishing she hadn't made quite so much mess and that James wasn't always so tired but she could hardly ask him to help when he'd just driven over two hundred miles.

And she really couldn't complain, how many people her age had a kitchen like this? Or lived in a palatial flat in Kensington? Dad had insisted. It would have been mean to say no, she loved him to bits but that didn't mean she was going to let him help her find a job (have a word with someone on the board), or send her to an expensive private school (she was already settled in the local comprehensive) and it just didn't feel right using the title.

By the time she'd wiped all the surfaces down, loaded the dishwasher and washed the wine glasses and went into the double bedroom, with its king-size bed, James was sound asleep and the room in darkness. He never remembered to leave a bedside light on for her. Quietly, she undressed and slipped into bed beside him, snuggling in but there was no response. Poor thing was exhausted. Dead to the world. She smiled and pushed his floppy fringe from his forehead. He was a good man. Looking after his mother without a complaint. Sophie closed her eyes. She was so lucky. Who needed New York?

Running late, see you there. And it's my day off but love that you're so loyal Kx

Sophie smiled at the text, her friend Kate was even worse than she was, always trying to cram too much in and she could bet her last pound that Kate had stayed overnight at her boyfriend Ben's last night, which was the real reason she was running late. They were still in that loved up, passion boiling over, can't bear not to touch each other all the time phase. Not that Sophie could quite recall anything like that with her and James. Theirs had been a much gentler, soft landing into love rather than a plunge off the cliff-edge fall. Sophie wasn't sure she'd know how to deal with that sort of fiery sexual chemistry. It wasn't her style at all and part of her wondered if it wasn't a tiny bit selfish. Shouldn't love be gentle, embracing and warm? Something that grew with nourishment and care. Although Kate's happiness and joie de vivre was heart-warming and when Ben suddenly narrowed his eyes while looking at Kate, she couldn't deny the intensity of his look gave her goose-bumps.

As she waited for her Cappuccino, listening to the industrial hiss of the espresso machine operated by one of the Saturday girls, she gave the Danish pastries a second look. She shouldn't but they looked so delicious. Nope, it was no good; she couldn't possibly resist the cinnamon rolls.

Balancing a plate in one hand, the cup in the other and trying to keep her shoulder straight so her bag didn't slip off and bash any of the tables she managed to weave her way through vacant chairs to her favourite spot in the corner, looking out onto the busy street.

Unfortunately, her usual table was taken by a tired looking woman with a young baby who was squeaking with indignation, her big blue eyes flashing outrage as she waved a plastic spoon at the pot of yoghurt her mother held just out of reach in one hand. Sophie could see why the pot was out of the danger zone, the little girl had already managed to smear most of it into her hair and her mother was trying to clean her up, with her spare hand. From where Sophie stood it looked more like octopus wrestling.

She sat down at the adjacent table watching their antics with a gentle smile and was about to turn away when the young woman looked up and shot her a vicious glare, her mouth pinched tight in sneering disgust.

Taking a far too hasty gulp of hot coffee, which burnt its way down into her stomach, Sophie looked away shocked by the fierce, direct hatred which made her feel almost as if she'd been physically assaulted. She took a couple of deep steadying breaths. The poor woman was probably just very stressed, it wasn't personal. Plastering a smile on her face, she took a more measured sip of coffee and looked over at the woman, hoping that a reassuring, friendly face might make the woman feel a bit better.

Whoa, she got that wrong. If anything, the spite on the woman's face intensified, wrinkles fanning out around her lips like an ancient walnut and she was dabbing angrily at the child's face, the wipes in her hand flying like sheets in the wind.

It was impossible not to feel the woman's distress. Sophie hesitated for a second, she couldn't ignore the poor woman, who was clearly very unhappy.

'Are you alright?' asked Sophie with a tentative smile, feeling as if she were attempting to reason with a lioness.

'Am I alright?' spat the woman, as the little girl began to wail and then her face crumpled, falling in on itself, the anger and spite replaced by pure misery. 'Oh Emma, baby.' She scooped the little girl up, sticky fingers and all, and hugged her to her body, rubbing her back. 'There. There. Mummy's sorry.'

Sophie felt the slight pang of envy and the very merest tightening in her womb. One day.

The little girl held on tight to her mother and stopped crying, lunging with sudden glee towards the yoghurt pot. Her mother smiled, resigned and shook her head. 'You pickle.' She pressed a soft kiss on the top of the child's candyfloss soft curls and put her on her lap moving the yoghurt in front of them, giving her the spoon.

With a calm measured look, although her eyes were still full of anger and dislike, the woman stared back at Sophie. 'You asked if I was alright?' Her eyes sparkled with unshed tears, her head tilted defiantly.

'Yes, did you want a hand? It looks like hard work.' Sophie smiled at the little girl who seemed a lot happier now. 'She's gorgeous. Although I don't envy you the mess. Do you want me to get you some more napkins or anything?'

'Gorgeous and mine,' said the woman looking alarmed, wrapping a protective arm across the little girl's chest.

'Yes,' said Sophie warily, surely this woman didn't think she was a child-snatcher or something.

'Although that doesn't bother you, does it, Sophie? Sharing things?' The woman's tone turned weary and her shoulders slumped, an expression of pain darting across her face.

Sophie's smile froze into place, something about the woman's tone suggested she should have some inkling of what was going on here. How did she know her name?

'I was just trying to help.' She regretted even making eye contact now.

'You? Help?' The woman let out a bitter laugh. 'I think you've helped enough. Helped yourself to my husband.'

'Sorry?' Sophie's hand stilled as she paused about to take

407

another sip of coffee. She'd had a lifetime of hearing similar accusations, from her half-sister about her own mother.

'Are you proud of yourself? Miss Rich Bitch with your flat in Kensington and Daddy's country estate in Sussex. I looked you up. Lady Sophie Benning.'

Sophie's mouth dropped open. This woman had done her homework. None of her colleagues at work had any idea. She kept her passport well out of sight from prying eyes. In fact, Kate was the only one that had seen it and at the time, she'd been professional enough not to say a word.

'I don't use—' she protested automatically because she always did, but the woman interrupted.

'Nice cushy life. No wonder James would rather spend half his life with you. No washing hanging everywhere. No babies crying in the night.'

'James?' Sophie stiffened. Even as she opened her mouth, she knew her words sounded like every last cliché in the book. 'What's he got to do with this?'

'James Soames. My husband. Lives in London four nights, Monday, Tuesday, Wednesday, Thursday. Comes home to his wife and daughter in Newbury Friday to Monday.'

'But he goes to Cornwall.' Sophie's legs felt leaden as if she were weighted into her seat. 'He's in Cornwall now.'

'No, he's not, you stupid cow. He's mowing the lawn at 47 Fantail Lane in Newbury and then he's going to build a swing for Emma.'

Coming Soon from Julie Caplin
Grab your passports and get ready to fall in love all over
again with...

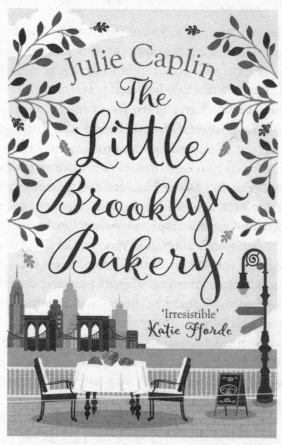

Acknowledgements

A humungous thank you to the flaxen haired, should-have-been-a-Viking-princess, Charlotte Ledger who first suggested Copenhagen as a destination. Her passion and enthusiasm for this project has been utterly heart-warming and she deserves a pile of cashmere blankets. Ever grateful thanks to brilliant Broo Doherty, for her wisdom, support and general all-round fabulousness (especially when I'm having one of those, I'm completely rubbish at this, sort of days).

A big thank you to Katie Young, Bristol based PR star, who very kindly shared all things Copenhagen and directed me to some of the city's finest haunts, as well as some amazing restaurants and bars.

Particular thanks to the lovely Katie Fforde for her ever-generous support, encouragement and cover quotes. If you ever have to spend three hours in a tiny BBC radio booth, Katie's definitely the person to do it with.

And last but not least the awesome pods at Heathrow that transport you Star Wars style from the car park to Terminal 5. Possibly the best start to a trip ever!